the baker's apprentice

ALSO BY JUDITH RYAN HENDRICKS

*Bread Alone*

*Isabel's Daughter*

# the baker's apprentice

## judith ryan hendricks

*WM*

W ILLIAM  M ORROW
*An Imprint of HarperCollinsPublishers*

FIRST EDITION

*Designed by Claire Vaccaro*

Printed on acid-free paper

Library of Congress Cataloging-in-Publication Data

Hendricks, Judith Ryan.
    The baker's apprentice: a novel / Judith Ryan Hendricks.—1st ed.
      p.   cm.
    Sequel to: Bread alone.
    ISBN 0-06-072617-2 (acid-free paper)
      1. Divorced women—Fiction.   2. Bakers and bakeries—Fiction.   3. Seattle (Wash.)—Fiction.   4. Baking—Fiction.   I. Title.

    PS3608.E53B35   2005
    813'.6-dc22                 2004050493

05 06 07 08 09 WBC/RRD 10 9 8 7 6 5 4 3 2 1

For Jo-Ann, best Bad Girl

Bread should be eaten
with the eyes closed and the heart open.

DANIEL WING AND ALAN SCOTT,
*The Bread Builders*

A bread baker's life isn't for everyone.

First of all, it's physically hard. These days the mixing and kneading are mostly done by machine. But at small artisan bakeries like ours, the loaves are still shaped by hand, and that takes a fair amount of muscle. Not to mention dragging fifty-pound sacks of flour, hefting the bowls of the big floor mixers, loading trays of wet dough into the oven, and unloading the finished bread.

The hours can be off-putting, unless you're a night owl to begin with. And even so, it's not much fun having to leave for work just when a party's getting cranked up or dragging yourself out of a nice, cozy bed occupied by a warm body that fits perfectly against your own.

Then, of course, there's the money. Or lack of it. Ingredients are cheap enough—flour, water, salt, yeast—but bread is labor intensive. And you can only charge so much for a loaf of bread, even if it does contain hazelnuts from Oregon or imported Kalamata olives. The bottom line is, you have to sell a lot of bread just to break even, and don't even think about turning a profit unless you're baking wholesale.

At the Queen Street Bakery, we think of it as a loss leader. That, and as a service to our loyal customers, who seem to like picking up a loaf of bread at the same place where they have their morning coffee and scone, or their afternoon pastry. I think it's that sweet little European fantasy of walking home from the neighborhood bakery clutching a still-warm loaf of bread.

part one

## · one ·

*Seattle, September 1989*

Linda LaGardia is about the most annoying human being I've ever met. Irascible, embittered, humorless, devoid of common courtesy—and that's on a good day. Fortunately, she's also totally lacking in imagination, one of those people who seems to go through life with her head down, watching her feet take each plodding step. Fortunately, because that means she's generally too self-absorbed to really get in anyone's way. Much as she can't stand me, most of the time she simply acts like I don't exist.

All through our shift tonight, she's been singing little tuneless songs under her breath, muttering to herself about her kids, Paige and Ed Jr., and her no-good scumbag of an ex-husband, Ed Sr., who's been dead now for over six months.

I'm standing, she's sitting at the worktable shaping loaves of cheese bread and dropping them into oiled pans. "Yeah, I went to the doctor yesterday," she says from out of the blue. Caught off guard, I can't suppress a chuckle. It's so totally out of character for her to start a conversation.

"Somethin' funny about that?"

"Not about going to the doctor. I just think it's funny that you want to talk to me about it. I've been working here for over a year now, and we've never had any kind of meaningful dialogue before. That I recall."

"That's because you're always runnin' your mouth or playin' that god-awful screechin' music."

I close my eyes. "Oh, right. Now I remember."

"Last time he said my blood pressure's too high."

"How high?"

She waves her hand dismissively. "A hundred and eighty."

"Over what?"

"What d'ya mean over what? A hundred-eighty's what he said."

"Blood pressure is usually two numbers, like one-eighty over one-ten or something like that."

"Ahh, who knows. He was throwin' all kinds of numbers around." A few minutes later she says, "He wants me to take some tests."

"What kind?" I keep my eyes on the bread in front of me.

"Stress test or somethin'." She detaches the dough hook from one of the Hobarts, carries it to the sink, then hesitates, lost in some internal debate. She turns on the water, then abruptly turns it off. "I don't guess you'd know what it is?"

The tone of voice is so unlike her that I turn around. "What *what* is?"

"Stress test," she mumbles. She scrubs the dough hook furiously.

"Didn't the doctor tell you?"

"'Course he didn't tell me. They never tell ya nothin' if they can help it."

"They just hook you up to these electrodes—"

"Electr—?" She makes a little sputter of alarm. "Does it shock ya?"

"No, no. It doesn't hurt. You just walk on this treadmill and they read your heart rate. It's not a big deal."

"I figured as much." She sniffs, embarrassed. "I gotta be there early. Guess you'll have to handle cleanup yourself. Too bad."

I reach over and turn up the boom box with my knuckles.

·  ·  ·

At five-thirty A.M. the sun is a faint pinkish glow filtered through fog. Linda's out front, loading banana-cinnamon-swirl bread onto the rack behind the register. The street is still quiet enough that I hear the engine before I see the headlights. The sound is unmistakable, as individual as a fingerprint. A truck. A 1971 Chevy El Camino in need of a tune-up. Mac.

My heart and my stomach decide to switch places.

I turn, just in time to see the Elky roll up in front of the bakery, unsavory looking as ever, its paint oxidized to a soft ivory that suggests that once upon a time it was white. Only the newly painted right-rear fender gleams like an anchorman's smile.

I thought he wouldn't be back till the end of the month. I thought . . . well, I thought a lot of things. Two weeks ago in the San Juan Islands, we wrecked a perfectly good friendship by making love for the first time. I sort of thought he'd call me, but he hasn't. Is he sorry it happened? Am I? What should I say? Should I run out and throw myself on him? Should I be cool? Let him know he can't take anything for granted? Act like it never happened?

I push my hair back and take a deep breath. Be casual. *Hi. How are you? I didn't think you'd be back so soon.* Then I remember that my hands are covered with wet dough. I wipe them on the towel that hangs from my apron strings and force myself to walk slowly around the end of the counter and out the door. He's on the curb, reaching inside the truck for something, and when he hears the door, he turns around. Before I have a chance to launch my carefully noncommittal greeting, he picks me up in his arms and crushes me against him till I can't breathe and don't particularly care to.

After we've tried kissing from a number of different angles, he sets me down on the sidewalk. I rearrange my apron and my bunched-up T-shirt, and he laughs as he extricates a few little globs of dough from my hair.

"I thought you weren't coming back till…later." I wish I didn't sound so breathless.

The look he turns on me makes my knees feel jointed at the back, like flamingo legs. "I couldn't wait that long," he says. "What time are you off?"

"Seven, but—"

"I'll be back then."

"Where are you going?"

"Kenny said I could stay with him for a few days till I find a place. I'm going to drop my stuff off there." He leans over to kiss me again. "And take a cold shower."

Gone again.

Linda rolls her eyes ceilingward when I come back inside, rubbing my bare arms from the chilly mist.

"Looks like one divorce didn't learn you nothin'."

"Teach," I say absently. "It didn't *teach* me anything."

I wander back to the work area, drawn by the warmth of the ovens, the perfume of roasting grains hanging in the air like incense. I pull open the heavy door to the top deck. One sheet pan with six loaves of lemon-poppy-seed tea bread is all that remains of our night's work. They're not quite done. I set the timer for five minutes and consider the possibility of truth in what I've just said.

It's not too late to bail. I could plead temporary insanity, say I've reconsidered, and that maybe taking our friendship to the next level wasn't such a great idea after all. But then I think about all the time we spent together last year. Listening to music and trolling for treasure in used-book stores, me dragging him to old movies. How he took me to the hospital in the middle of the April Fool's Day blizzard when I had appendicitis, read to me from *Gatsby* while I recuperated. I think about that night on the ferryboat, standing next to him at the rail while he pointed out the Big Dipper and Boötes, Polaris, and Arcturus, and how I felt when he said he was going up to Orcas for the summer.

Nope. It may be insanity, but I'm afraid it's not temporary.


Ellen shows up just before six and dives into her morning routine with frightening efficiency, turning on the espresso machine, unlocking the register and counting the cash into the till, wiping down the counters and cleaning the glass cases. She puts a saucer of milk out in the alley for whatever cats happen past, and a big bowl of water out front for customers' dogs. She takes a plastic baggie full of goldfish crackers out of her oversized purse and puts it next to the register in case the guy with the parrot comes by this morning.

By the time she's done, the espresso machine is blowing steam and she fills both brew baskets and punches the buttons for two long doubles. She taps her foot to make it brew faster as the aromatic dark liquid streams into the two majolica cups. When the machine clicks off, she hands me one, and takes a slow, breathy sip from the other—her first of about five for the day.

She sniffs the rising steam. "Have you thought of any questions for Maggie?"

I give her a blank stare. "Who?"

"Maggie Stanopolis. Our job applicant. She's coming in at eight. Did you forget?"

"Yes. Oh, damn. Ellen, could you... I mean, would you mind if—I sort of made plans for this morning..."

One dark eyebrow rises questioningly. "Plans?"

My face heats up. "Mac's in town. He's picking me up at seven."

"I don't suppose we should let something as frivolous as a job interview interfere with your love life."

I smile weakly.

"You'll have to talk to her at some point. I'm not going to hire her without you meeting her." She sweeps her wispy black bangs away from her eyes.

"Why not? You know a lot more about whether she's qualified than I do."

"Bakery policy. You're a partner now; you need to get a handle on the administrative side of things. Besides, it's not just her qualifications. We know she can do cakes or she wouldn't have lasted two years at Booker's. I think it's important to get a feel for someone."

"Exactly what I'm hoping to do."

"Not him." She tosses a wet towel at me. "I'll be interested to see what she can do. I've always thought of Booker's as sort of a factory."

"I don't know anything about them."

"They do a lot of kiddie cakes—template things like Mickey Mouse and Roger Rabbit and Smurfs. Shotgun cakes—"

"What?"

"Wedding cakes in a hurry." She sighs. "Oh, don't look so pitiful. I'll call her and tell her we have to push it back an hour—"

"One hour?"

"What were you planning—a marathon orgy? One hour. I'll talk to her first, at nine, then you can meet her at ten."


Mac insists on breakfast at Steve's Broiler, a Greek dive downtown with feta cheese omelets that would make your old Greek granny rise up from the grave.

"We can't just barge in on CM," he says, tucking me under his arm in our huge semicircular booth.

I lean my head on his shoulder, feeling his hair, still damp from the shower, cool against my cheek. "We're not barging. I called her and told her. Besides, I thought you couldn't wait."

"I couldn't wait two more weeks." He nibbles my ear. "I can wait an hour. As long as I get to sit next to you and look at you. And think about all the things I'm going to do to you in about"—he checks his watch—"fifty-eight minutes and thirteen seconds."

I sit back and study his face for a minute, the high cheekbones, the wide-set gray eyes that can look green in a certain light, the little amber flecks in the irises. It's a serious face, transformed by his unexpectedly sweet smile.

"You could have called," I say finally.

He considers this. "I just decided to come yesterday. I closed up the cottage, packed the truck, and left. Caught the last ferry out last night—"

"That's not what I meant."

"Okay." He looks innocent. "What did you mean?"

"I meant afterward. I didn't know what to think."

"About what?"

"*'About what?'*" I can't hide my annoyance. "What do you think? About us. About what happened—"

"I didn't have a phone—"

"They have pay phones in town, don't they? It's not exactly the Arctic Circle. I didn't know what to think. I didn't know how you felt..."

His expression softens and he looks straight into my eyes. "You didn't?"

I look through the service window into the kitchen where dark, hairy guys are flinging pans and flipping hotcakes and talking loudly in Greek.

He waits till I look back at him to say, "You really don't know how I feel?"

"Well..."

"I thought I was pretty transparent." He reaches over to smooth some hair off my face, and his hand lingers on my cheek. Just as he leans toward me, the waiter materializes, sets two thick, white plates down in front of us. The omelets are so big, they hang over the sides, brown and crisp around the edges, molten cheese oozing out.

He kisses me anyway. "I guess I should have called, but..." He picks up his fork. "It all felt so right. I guess I assumed you felt the same." He cuts into the omelet with the side of his fork. "Did I assume too much?"

How do men do this? They don't tell you a damned thing, and then they make you feel silly and guilty for questioning them.

"Of course not. But it's kind of a strange time for me."

He looks at me expectantly. "So the divorce hasn't gone through yet?"

I shake my head. "Soon. When I talked to my lawyer, she was expecting to get an agreement from David's lawyer any second." Just the thought of my ex-husband pending is like a wet towel in the face, so I change channels. "Have you heard from your agent?"

Mac laughs. "He's not my agent yet. He hasn't read the manuscript—in fact, he probably doesn't even have it. I just mailed it Tuesday. I figure I have to give it five working days—"

"Why didn't you FedEx it?"

"Because it weighs six pounds," he says patiently. "I needed gas money and a deposit for an apartment, and utilities and food—"

There are some days when I shouldn't go outside without duct tape over my mouth. Today is shaping up to be one of them.

"The good news is, Rick needs help at Norwegian Woods right now. And Kenny says Sean's not happy at Bailey's. Said he was talking about moving over to some new place on Capitol Hill. If he leaves, Harte might let me come back to Bailey's."

I set down my knife. "*Let* you? He should be begging you. Nobody goes there on Saturday nights anymore. Well, nobody except a few twenty-two-year-olds who don't know Bob Dylan from Matt Dillon. They play mostly elevator jazz during the week and top forty on Friday and Saturday. Kenny's too busy to deal with it and Sean seems to think his main job is hustling the single women."

"Maybe I should give Harte a call." He spreads a blob of ketchup over his hash browns, and I cringe.

"You're ruining those. They're going to get soggy."

He sighs. "Thank you, Detective Sergeant Morrison of the food police."

Somehow I manage to find the dead-bolt key and fit it into the lock, while Mac busies himself unfastening the big Navajo silver clip and burying his face in my hair. "God, you smell good." Through the forest of my hair, the tip of his tongue finds a vulnerable patch of skin. "Too good, in fact. It should probably be illegal."

His breath on my neck makes all the molecules in my body re-align, like iron filings to a magnet. I search frantically for the door-knob key.

"I believe it constitutes gross fraud and misrepresentation." When he slips his hands under my jacket, I nearly choke.

"Will you stop it and let me open the damn door?"

"Ms. Morrison, we have reason to suspect you of smuggling bread under your shirt. I'm afraid we're going to have to pat you down. Just to be sure."

I finally get the key in the knob and the door gives way and we lurch through. He catches it with one cowboy boot, kicking it shut behind us. The apartment is sunny and still and freezing cold, thanks to CM's polar-bear constitution, but I have reason to silently bless her. My ever-thoughtful best friend has left the futon open and made up.

My jacket falls to the floor and he tugs my flannel shirt out of my jeans. We fumble with each other's buttons. He's still muttering.

"No bread here, but I think the evidence warrants a full strip search." The flannel shirt follows the jacket to the floor and I pull him down onto the futon.

In that lingering afterglow that follows a fabulous meal or great sex, I burrow under the comforter, curled up against him, soaking up his heat like a lizard on a hot stone.

"I won't have to worry about finding a job," he says into my hair. "I'll be dead before the week's over. Not that I'm complaining, you understand. It's exactly the way I always hoped to die."

"No, McLeod, you won't be that lucky. I won't kill you off." I drag my fingernails lightly across his stomach. "I'm going to keep you alive and torture you."

Without looking, I can feel his smile. "Oh, please don't throw me in the brier patch."

The rhythm of his thumb stroking my shoulder is just about to lull me into REM state when I suddenly remember my ten o'clock appointment. Reluctantly I roll away and sit up.

"I have to go interview a job applicant." I look hopefully over my shoulder. "You can stay here and sleep. I won't be long."

He props himself up on one elbow. "Nah. I need to find an apartment. I don't think Kenny's wife was too thrilled to see me this morning. I'll come back about seven and take you to dinner. Ask CM to come, if you want."


Maggie Stanopolis says she's thirty-six, but she looks older. Maybe it's the industrial-strength foundation a shade or two darker than her natural coloring that cakes in the folds of her skin, giving her face the appearance of old linen that needs pressing. Her drapey blue shirt calls attention to her clear blue eyes. Thick blond hair erupts from dark roots into a startling fountain, secured by a clip on the top of her head.

"I know you work at night, so I really appreciate you meeting with me this morning." She smiles and pushes a three-ring binder at me. "My cake book."

"So why do you want to leave Booker's?" I ask.

"We had . . . I suppose you could call it artistic differences. That and they moved their operation up to Lake Forest Park because rent was cheaper. And I wanted to stay more central. Close to where we live.

And my husband's restaurant—maybe you've heard of it—Tony's?"

Her words come like ketchup out of a bottle—first slow and hesitant, then quickly in big, splashy globs. Her eyes are in constant motion, resting on mine for only a few seconds before finding another focus.

The golden puddle of sun pouring onto the table makes me drowsy. I keep seeing Mac, snuggled under the quilt on my futon, his slow smile, his pale hair against my skin.

"On Capitol Hill?" I stifle a yawn and she nods. I haven't been to Tony's, and I seem to recall that it's better known as a yuppie pickup joint than a temple of fine dining. "I've heard good things about it," I lie.

A smile hovers briefly without actually landing on her face.

"Did you go to school in Seattle?"

"Stadium High School, in Tacoma. Northwest Culinary Academy."

"When did you graduate?"

"I didn't ... finish. But I think my work speaks for itself," she adds hastily.

I scoot the notebook over until it's directly in front of me and turn back the cover. The first page is a picture of a cake with the words "Margaret Dailey Stanopolis, Cake Designer" done in frosting calligraphy.

I flip through page after plastic-sheeted page. Wedding cakes, engagement cakes, baby shower, birthday, anniversary, family reunion, graduation, Father's Day, Mother's Day, Groundhog Day—even a divorce cake, a clever image of a marriage certificate being cut in two with scissors. I'll have to keep that one in mind.

Some have real flowers, some are decked out with sculpted sugar. But the most impressive ones are like pictures painted with frosting—portraits, pictures of diplomas, even one of a Victorian house—looking as if they should be hung on a wall.

I look up into her expectant gaze. "They're beautiful. How long have you been doing this?"

"Thanks." She rubs her hands up and down her thighs, leaving tracks on the nap of her sand-washed silk pants. "Two years at Booker's, and before that about five on my own."

"How do you do the ones that look like paintings?"

"I do a sheet of rolled fondant on top, then paint it with artists' brushes and egg-yolk paints."

"What kind of cakes do you use?"

"Booker's was pretty much into basic chocolate and vanilla butter cake, lemon pound cake. Sometimes cheesecakes. But Ellen said you guys have your own recipes. I can do whatever you like." She looks at her watch, which annoys me.

"Are you in a time crunch?"

"I have another appointment at noon."

"Okay. Thanks for coming by. One of us, probably Ellen, w—"

"Do you have any idea when you'll make a decision? Because I really need to secure a position right away."

The bell over the door jangles as two women enter. Tyler, our blue-haired *barista,* strolls out of the kitchen to wait on them, wiping her hands on her apron, staring blatantly at our table.

I close the binder and slide it back to her. "I'm sure it'll be soon. Maybe tomorrow, but—"

"Are you talking to anyone else?"

"Not that I know of." That probably isn't the cool thing to say, but I'm too tired to lie.

"Well, then. I'll wait to hear from you. Thank you so much." She thrusts her hand under my nose and I shake it. Then she picks up the binder, holding it against her breasts like a much-loved child, and ducks out the door.


"Where's Ellen?" I ask Tyler after the women have left.

"Dentist. She lost a crown or something. In a sticky bun."

"Ouch."

"She said she'd see you later."

"Not till I get some sleep."

She smirks. "That's not what I heard you were getting."

"Tyler..."

She makes big eyes at me. "I saw him this morning. Not bad for an old dude. Nice ass, too—"

"He's not old."

She twists a blue spike. "Maybe there's a younger brother?"

"Older. Besides, I think he's a lawyer."

She pantomimes putting a finger down her throat.

"What happened to you and Teddy?"

"He's history. So maybe you could, like, will Mac to me? You know? When you kick?"

I smile smugly. "You won't want him by then. He'll be all used up."

I open my eyes in twilight to see a blurry, upside-down face. CM.

"What time is it?" I blink.

She raises a glass of red wine. "The sun's over the yardarm."

I push the hair off my face and sit up slowly, letting out a stale breath. "Ugh. Forgot to brush my teeth."

"Better do it quick before Cute Stuff shows up."

The desk lamp is on, casting soft shadows on the wall behind it. I look at my watch. I can't believe I slept till six. Good thing I showered this morning. I reach my arms toward the ceiling and yawn. "Can you have dinner with us?"

"Wish I could. I have to go back to the studio for a meeting. Besides, I don't think I could stand watching you two paw at each other."

Christine Mayle has been my best friend since third grade. And believe me, it's not easy being best friends with someone who looks like Celtic royalty—tall; slender; green eyes; long, auburn hair. She's one of those women who could put on a plastic garbage bag and start a new fashion trend. Once, in high school, she told me that she knew she was beautiful and that people were always going to notice her. Since then I've watched her accept admiration as her due, without fuss, the way a queen might accept homage from her devoted subjects. It's an attitude I've always admired for its honesty.

She sits on the edge of the tub, sipping her wine while I brush my teeth. "So . . . how did it go?"

I try to tell her around my toothbrush, but it comes out unintelligible.

"That good, huh?"

I rinse out my mouth, pull back my hair, and start washing my face with shaving cream. I know it sounds strange, but CM's always used it and her skin looks like an Estée Lauder ad, so I thought I'd give it a try.

"If you really want to know, somehow the whole thing feels weird."

"Weird?"

"I was sitting there at breakfast looking at him, and all of a sudden, it was like . . . vertigo. I mean, we used to be friends, and now we're . . . something else. Another horse of a different color, as my oma used to say. And two weeks"—I turn to look directly at her— "of silence makes me nervous."

"If he was calling you every day, that would make you nervous, too." She smiles indulgently. "Everything makes you nervous." She finishes her wine and sets the glass on the vanity. She kicks off her shoes. "Enjoy it, don't dissect it. Things will work themselves out."

She stands up and slips out of her jeans, hanging them on the hook behind the door. "And now, if you're through hogging the bathroom, I'm getting in the shower."


"What did you think of Maggie?" Ellen asks me between sips of espresso. Linda's in back washing up, and Tyler hasn't come in yet, so we have a few minutes of privacy.

"I don't know. I guess she's fine. We don't exactly have applicants lined up for a shot at it, do we?" I stretch my legs out in front of me and rotate my aching feet.

"Not really."

"She said two years at Booker's, five doing cakes freelance. That leaves almost ten years unaccounted for. Did she give you a resumé?"

Ellen laughs. "Nobody in this business has a resumé. She told me she was a starving artist till she met Mr. Wonderful. Taking art classes and trying to sell her paintings." She hesitates. "Did you notice her eye?"

"Her eye?"

"She had a black eye. It was pretty well camouflaged. Probably a few days old. And it looks like she's good with the concealer."

Now I feel really stupid. "I didn't even notice."

"You have to know what to look for. Before Food Bank started picking up the day-olds, I used to take them over to a battered-women's shelter. I saw quite a few women who knew how to use makeup. Maggie's was just barely a shadow."

"That's no reason not to hire her—"

Ellen shakes her head impatiently. "No. In fact, it may be a good reason *to* hire her. I just think you and I need to be aware of it. There's a potential for trouble."

"Like what?"

"You know—irate spouse, confrontations in the workplace."

"So what do you suggest?"

She shrugs. "I think we should give her a three-month trial. Her book looks good."

She sets down her cup and goes to unlock the door for Tyler, who's peering in at us, nose smushed against the glass. Ellen hands her a cleanup rag. "Take care of your grease spot on the door."

"Whoa. I'm the *barista* and the cake decorator, and now I'm the janitor, too."

"You won't have to worry about the cakes much beyond today," Ellen says. "We're hiring Maggie Stanopolis. She's from—"

"I know where she's from." Tyler gives us her drop-dead look. "Bet she does a great Smurf cake."

Ellen smiles. "Her style is a little different from yours, but I think she's very talented."

"Her face looks like it got left in the dryer too long. And that skuzzy blond hair. Looks like she's got a dead animal on her head."

It takes all my self-control not to laugh. "We're not hiring her to be our poster girl. Besides, I think having blue hair and a safety pin in your ear disqualifies you from commenting on anyone else's appearance."

Color flames in Tyler's paste-white cheeks. Her Doc Martens make dull clomping sounds on the rubber matting as she disappears into the work area and then we hear her slamming the cooler doors.

"Hey!" Ellen calls after her. "Knock it off unless you can afford to buy us a new Traulsen." She looks at me. "This could prove interesting."

"I'll say. Who needs an irate spouse when you have an irate cake decorator?"

## two

Mazurka Bars are, as Ellen likes to say, locally world famous—a killer combination of thin, flaky crust, then your choice of lemon, chocolate-espresso, apple-raisin, or raspberry filling, and on top the crumble layer with its habit-forming, sandy crunch. We sell them not only to our customers, but to cafés and delis and even some grocery stores around the city. Ellen invented them when she lived in New Hampshire, and she brought the recipe with her to Seattle, at first baking them in her apartment and selling them outside movie theaters and down at Seattle Center before Sonics games and every September at the Bumbershoot arts festival. A lot of our customers still remember her fondly as the Mazurka Bar Lady.

Production outgrew her tiny apartment a long time ago—one of the reasons she and her former partner Diane bought the bakery—and lately, demand has mushroomed to the point where we've had to hire three part-timers to do nothing but Mazurkas. Ellen supervises them closely, and still insists on making the huge batches of filling and topping herself, but Kristen, Susan, and Barb do the crust, the assembly and baking off, the cutting, wrapping, and labeling.

They work Monday, Wednesday, and Friday, usually coming in

around noon, so I rarely see them, but on this particular Monday, we've got a large special order for a convention event at the Sheraton, so the gang's all here when Maggie shows up at eight A.M. for her first day at work.

Linda left as usual on the stroke of seven, wary of turning into a pumpkin if she stays one minute over. But I'm still here, and Ellen, Tyler, Jen, and Misha, the morning crew, plus the Mazurka mavens. Maggie insists on shaking hands with everyone, no matter if they're talking to someone else at the moment or up to their elbows in dishwater or patting out scone dough with floury hands. She smiles directly into their faces, mentioning that her husband is Tony Stanopolis, owner of Tony's on Capitol Hill. As if that somehow places her in context for us. She seems oblivious to the surreptitiously exchanged glances and rolling of eyes.

Tyler has grudgingly agreed to help with the cakes for a couple of weeks, but her demeanor could be generously described as sullen. When Ellen takes Maggie back to show her how the storeroom's organized, Tyler gives me a fish-eyed stare.

"'Cake designer'? What a joke."

"She'll be fine. Help her out."

She folds her arms. "Sure. Front door okay?"

"Ha-ha, Tyler. Don't you remember what it was like to be the new kid?"

"Yeah, I remember." She looks at me sideways. "Nobody gave me any breaks."

"Oh, come on. You're starting to sound like Linda."

While Maggie fills out payroll forms, Ellen comes over to me. "You better get gone. You're about to fall asleep standing up. Where's Tyler?"

"I don't know. Probably sulking in the bathroom. What's with her, anyway?"

Ellen shakes her head. "Lots of things, I think. We're going to have to keep an eye on this." She lays a gentle hand on my arm. "But we can talk later. Go home. Go to bed." She grins wickedly. "I mean, go to sleep."

"Unfortunately, that's not an issue at the moment. Mac's trying to get a job lined up and find an apartment. I haven't seen him in two days."

Her expression is one of horror. "*Two days?* No sex for two days? Like, ohmigod!"


Mac and I didn't spend a lot of time at each other's residences last year when we were friends. We saw each other at Bailey's, where he worked as a bartender, or we went places together—cafés, movies, bookstores, coffeehouses. Weather permitting, we were usually outside. Walking in the Market or Pioneer Square, jogging in the parks, or—Mac's favorite—riding the Washington state ferries. In fact, the only time he was ever inside my house was when I was recovering from my appendectomy. And I never set foot in his place. The subject came up once, and he put me off by saying that it was "kind of like Motel Six."

His new apartment is on the fourth floor of one of Queen Anne's ugliest buildings. Six stories of prison-green cinder block on Myrick Street, a couple of blocks off Queen Anne Avenue. I show up Saturday about noon in the pouring rain with a bag from Thriftway containing one beautiful, fat filet, two russet potatoes, a head of romaine, fresh tarragon, olive oil, balsamic vinegar, butter, and a loaf of *pain de compagne* from the bakery.

"I'm not sure you're ready for this," he says when he opens the door.

Motel 6 was perhaps a touch optimistic. The living room is beige and very small. Fortunately, there isn't a lot of furniture, just an old wing-back chair, a desk, and a straight, wooden chair. A packing box next to the wing back serves as an occasional table, showcasing back issues of *Outside* magazine, legal pads, pens, and a collection of dirty glasses.

He follows my gaze. "Try to think of it as minimalist design. What's in the bag?"

"Dinner." He takes it from me and I follow him into the kitchen, a tiny galley with a two-burner stove, half refrigerator, and sink. The smell of bleach is overpowering.

"Sorry," he says, "but you should have smelled it before."

"Why don't you open the window?"

"It's painted shut. Also, in case you tunneled in, it's raining."

I wander back out through the living room and into the bed-room.

The bed consists of a box spring on the floor, a mattress on top. Boxes are stacked three deep at the head and along one side next to the wall. The only other furniture is an empty bookcase and a small chest of drawers covered with stacks of spiral bound notebooks.

I pick one up. "What are these?"

He takes it out of my hand and puts it back on the stack. "Just stuff."

"Why don't you let me read some of it?"

"Because it's really not that good."

"How about if I promise not to assign a letter grade?"

"I've heard old English teachers never die. Besides, you'd never be able to decipher my scribbling."

"You're talking to a woman who's deciphered hundreds of sopho-more essays."

"Wyn—" There's an impatience in his voice I've never heard be-fore. Then he softens. "Later, okay? I've got a few published articles, if you just can't live without reading some of my deathless prose."

"I can live."

He reaches for my hand, but I turn away.

"What's in the boxes?" I squeeze between two precariously bal-anced towers.

"Books."

I run my finger over one of the bookcase shelves. "We'd better

dust this first. We can put all the fiction together in alphabetical order by author. Then we can arrange the nonfiction by categories.
And the books could probably—"

"I don't need my books arranged. Has anyone ever suggested that
you might be just the tiniest bit anal?"

"It's not a matter of being anal; it's a matter of being able to find
things."

"I've been finding everything for quite a number of years now,
thanks. Besides..." He puts his hands on my shoulders, causing all
those little fluttery things to start doing tricks in my stomach, and
points south. Suddenly I forget that I'm annoyed. "I've got a much
better idea. The place hasn't even been christened yet."

"You mean you lured me over here with promises of unpacking
books and fixing dinner, when all you really wanted..."

He nuzzles my neck. "By God, Ms. Morrison. You're far too
clever for the likes of me."

As we're slithering out of our jeans, the change from his pockets
goes all over the floor, clanging and pinging and rolling away into
corners, but I barely notice it because all my hearing and seeing sen-
sors have been transformed, diverted to touch receptors and I seem
to be composed entirely of skin. I don't even hear myself saying his
name, but afterward, I remember that I did.

We spend the balance of the gray and quiet afternoon in his narrow bed. Making love, sleeping, listening to the soft staccato of rain
against the window. Books tomorrow.

Eventually hunger overcomes lust, and we reluctantly peel ourselves apart and out of the rumpled bed, then shower and dress. My
hair takes forever to dry because he doesn't have an industrial-
strength dryer like mine. When I emerge from the bathroom, all
damp and frizzy, he's already rattling around in the kitchen.

The toolbox has been excavated and the kitchen window pried
open a crack. The rain has tapered off to a slow, rhythmic dripping.
He even has a boom box, and when we stick the antenna against the

windowpane, we can pick up KBLU, his favorite local station—"all rhythm, all blues, honey, all the time," the DJ drawls.

"You do have a frying pan?" I pull the lettuce and butter out of the fridge.

He hands me an old, beautifully seasoned cast-iron skillet. "Direct from the gourmet department of the Salvation Army Thrift Shop." He rummages in the cupboard. "Ah. Day-Glo red. My finest bottle. Also my only bottle." He uncorks the wine and pours it into two coffee mugs and hands one to me. It's actually not bad.

"Remind me never to go camping with you. If this is how you live, I don't think I want to know your idea of roughing it."

He pushes up his sleeves and chops the potatoes while I put a pot of water on to boil and wash the lettuce.

On the radio a sandpaper voice backed by a twangy acoustic guitar asserts that "you can't never tell what a woman's got on her mind." Mac pauses in his search for plates to turn up the volume. "Listen to this. That's a real oldie. The twenties, I think. Maybe someone like—"

"Blind Lemon Jefferson, my man," the DJ interrupts. "By request for Franklin DuPree, who's at work tonight down at Pier One. Listen up, Franklin, to the Lemon's words of wisdom. Now go you and do likewise, my son."

I try to look suitably impressed by the music's authenticity, while I slice the filet in two horizontally, sprinkle salt in the skillet, and set it over a high flame. It's a small kitchen, but as I learned in France, size doesn't matter.

The summer after my sophomore year at UCLA, I did a work-study program at a bakery in Toulouse, and lived with the Guillaumes, the family who owned it. The first time I saw Madame Guillaume's kitchen, I was astounded by what wasn't in it. No food processor, no heavy-duty mixer, no electric coffee maker, no toaster, no microwave, no garbage disposal, no dishwasher. Just a big, black gas stove, some copper pots and pans, a few good knives, whisks and spoons, a rolling pin, huge ceramic mixing bowls, and not much more than that.

I used to love watching her work. She didn't own a cookbook; she cooked by tradition and instinct. The only recipes she had in written form were scratched in spidery penmanship on paper that was wrinkled and yellowed and as soft as cotton. They had been passed down from her grandmother to her mother and then to her, and she knew them by heart anyway. On Wednesday nights she always made steaks, and once I had them fixed this way, I never really liked charcoal-grilled meat again.

When the pan is nearly smoking, I throw the steaks in, searing a salty crust onto both sides. Then I put them on a plate and deglaze the pan with balsamic vinegar, reducing it to a syrup. Mac smashes the potatoes with a giant fork while I add butter and pepper and chopped tarragon to the pan to finish the sauce. In just under twenty minutes, we're sitting on the floor, using the packing box for a table.

"This is incredible. Where'd you learn to do this?"

"I got the idea in France. Except the sauce is my own shortcut. Madame Guillaume would just whip up real béarnaise."

He has this way of smiling with just his eyes. "It couldn't be any better than this."

"Is your mother a good cook?"

He's refilling our coffee mugs with wine, and he doesn't look up. "Not really. Suzanne was always domestically challenged."

"Nothing wrong with that. She's an artist, right?"

He just nods.

"What's she like?"

"I don't know."

"What do you mean, you don't know? She's your mother."

"We never got along." He breaks his bread into three smaller pieces. Then he puts it down and looks at me. "She's very ... attractive. Talented. And strange."

"Strange in what way?"

"She was never all there after—after my father died. I've never been close to her. Haven't even talked to her in years."

I push my last piece of steak around in the cold sauce. "My relationship with my mother wasn't so terrific either. For a long time. It's funny, though. When you think about it. Mothers sort of take the rap for everything, don't they? I mean, if they're attentive and loving, they're smothering. If they're independent or undemonstrative, they're cold."

"Sometimes both at once," he says quietly. "Depends on where you are in the family hierarchy."

"Being an only child, I was the hierarchy. Where were you?"

He lays his knife and fork carefully across the plate. "I wasn't speaking from personal experience. Just general observation." He gets up and carries our plates into the kitchen.

## · three ·

Shortly after I arrived in Toulouse, Jean-Marc Guillaume asked me why I had chosen a bakery for my work-study program. Nineteen years old and full of myself, I told him I was trying to decide if I wanted to be a bread baker.

A smile illuminated his coal-dark eyes, and he rubbed the back of one floury hand along his stubbled jawline. Then he said, "Wynter." Except he pronounced it *Weentaire*. "...you do not choose to bake bread, the bread chooses you."

Apparently the bread took a while to make up its mind about me. It kept quiet through my disappointing careers in real estate and teaching, and one disastrous marriage, but now, at last it has spoken. I can't imagine doing anything else.

That summer in France was a true awakening for me, but I didn't appreciate exactly what it meant or how much I learned because I was distracted by other things—like hanging out with Jean-Marc's sister, Sylvie, and her friends, plotting to lose my virginity, sleepwalking through the usual French language and culture classes that I was required to take at the university.

At the time, I saw Jean-Marc as a fusty, hard-nosed—although undeniably sexy—taskmaster, obsessed with details, too narrowly focused on the minutiae of his craft. Now I find myself doing the same things I laughed at him for—shredding bread in restaurants to examine the crumb, pulling croissants apart to inspect the layers. At the health food store, I've gotten odd looks from people who passed by the bulk-foods aisle and noticed me running my hands through the wheatberries, and I've caught myself standing sometimes in the predawn stillness at the bakery, just standing and listening to the bread hiss and sing and pop as the hot crust contracts in the cold morning air.

I've often thought that if I could go back now and do a real apprenticeship with Jean-Marc, how much more I could learn. Since that's not possible—at least not in the foreseeable future—I try to experiment with different recipes and techniques at work, something that's a hell of a lot easier since I bought out Diane's share and became Linda's boss instead of the other way around. I also read everything I can find on bread and baking, which is so much more than I ever imagined. Like *A Brief History of European Breads*, by Eleanor Heinz.

The book is mostly a history, kind of dry and scholarly, but tucked in between chapters on the evolution of flour mills and the rise of community ovens were a couple of recipes that intrigued me. One of them, *la fouace aux noix*, or hearth bread with walnuts, intrigued me sufficiently that I couldn't stop thinking about it, and so tonight, I arrive at work with the book tucked under my arm.

Linda reacts predictably with a disgusted snort and a rolling of eyes. "Here we go again."

I smile and say loudly in my cheesiest announcer voice, "That's right, Linda! It's time for another episode of Adventures in Baking. With your host, Wynter Morrison."

# La Fouace aux Noix

1 envelope yeast
⅓ cup lukewarm water
4 cups unbleached white flour
½ cup whole wheat flour
1 tablespoon salt
1 cup lukewarm milk
¾ cup coarsely chopped walnuts
½ cup (1 stick) unsalted butter, softened
Cornmeal, for dusting

*Dissolve the yeast in warm water. In a large bowl, mix the flours with the salt, make a well in the center, and add the yeast. Add the milk and stir well to make a spongy dough. Mix in the nuts and butter with a hard rubber spatula or your hands. The dough should be quite stiff. Cover with a damp towel and set in a draft-free area to rise for 2 hours. Punch down the dough and knead for 3 to 5 minutes, then form into a ball. Sprinkle a cookie sheet with cornmeal, place the loaf on it, and let rise 15 minutes, then turn the oven on to 425°F. When the oven is hot, slash a cross in the top of the loaf with a razor-blade or very sharp knife. Put a pan of hot water on the lowest shelf of the oven, and the bread on the middle shelf. Bake for 30 minutes, then remove the water and turn the oven down to 300°F and bake for 30 minutes more.*

Rabelais once wrote, "There is nothing better than warm *fouace* with grapes and a fresh rosé or mellow Vouvray."

While the dough rises in its crockery bowl and Linda grumbles her way through whole wheat walnut bread, I weigh out the *levain*, the natural starter that I pulled from the rye *chef* (one of the mother starters that we always have going in the fridge) last night and pour boiling water over the raisins for our pumpernickel-raisin bread.

"So what did the doctor say about your stress test?"

"What?" She turns off the big Hobart mixer.

"I said, what did the doctor say? When you had your stress test?"

"He put me on a diet." Her face grows suddenly puffy and pink, as if she might cry, and her voice takes on overtones of tragedy. "Said I couldn't have Cheez-Its anymore."

I can't meet her eyes because I know it's serious to her and I'm afraid I'll laugh.

"Bad enough that I had to quit smokin', and now this." She turns the motor back on without waiting for my reply.

God. Life without cigarettes and Cheez-Its. What's left?

Ellen comes in at five A.M. and throws her purse on one of the chairs, grabs the bottle of window cleaner, and attacks the display cases as if the food smears and fingerprints were left there as premeditated personal insults. Her face is a study in grim determination.

I turn on the espresso machine and reach for two cups. "Why are you here so early?"

She squats down to wipe the base of the counter, tucking her long, gauzy purple skirt under her butt. "Oh, it's this Maggie/Tyler thing. They're driving me crazy, and at this point it's a very short drive." She gives herself a boost back to standing and inclines her head toward the oven. "I thought we should talk about it. Is everything under control back there?"

I stick my head around the corner of the ovens.

"I need to talk to Ellen for a minute," I say. "Are you okay?"

Linda turns from loading bowls and utensils into a sinkful of hot water to give me a look that would fry an onion, as my oma used to say. "Used to do it all myself, just in case you forgot," she snaps. "A course I'm okay."

I grab the loaf of *fouace* from the cooling rack and beat a strategic retreat.

Ellen runs the espresso into latte cups and tops them off with coffee.

"Is it that bad?" I tear an end off the bread and hand it to her.

Her eyes brighten slightly. "What's this? Something new?"

"*La fouace aux noix.* Hearth bread with walnuts."

She takes a delicate bite. "Mmm. Good stuff." Then a not-so-delicate bite. Then she looks at me suspiciously. "How much butter is in this?"

"Not too much." I smile. "A quarter of a pound."

She shakes her head, but doesn't refuse a second piece.

We sit at one of the flea-market tables and eat in silence for a minute. She takes a long, slow sip of her depth charge. "Ooh, that's better." She sits up a little straighter in the chair.

"So what's happening on the day shift?" I lean back and prop my right foot up on my left knee.

"Tyler's decided she should've been hired as the 'cake designer.' She even came up with a slogan. 'On your special day, shouldn't your cake be cutting edge?'"

"What? She hated doing them. All she did was bitch and moan."

"That was before we brought in somebody else and started paying them more money. Also, Maggie has artistic pretensions, and so Tyler suddenly remembers that she's supposed to be the artist around here. Between her snide comments about Maggie's work, and Maggie's lecturing her about the difference between European fondant and rolled fondant, Swiss buttercream and Italian—close your eyes and imagine how that goes over. Also, I can't count the number of times we've now heard that at Booker's, the cake people *never* had to do cleanup, so she can't understand why she's expected to pick up trash in the café, bus tables, or any of that stuff . . ." Ellen gives me a pleading look. "It's all incredibly petty stuff, but it starts when Maggie comes in and it goes on all damn day, till Tyler leaves. I think I'll lose my mind. Or kill both of them, whichever comes first. The worst part is, it seems to be contagious. Now Jen's mad at Tyler because she feels sorry for Maggie, and Misha doesn't like Maggie because she thinks Tyler should have been offered the job, and on and on . . ."

She props her elbows on the table, rests her chin in her hands, looks through her fingers splayed out across her face like prison bars. She breathes in, then out. "And then yesterday afternoon, Maggie did this half sheet for a retirement party, with a picture of the guy on it—it was amazing. Looked like a painting—"

"I'd love to watch her do that sometime."

"Try to do it when Tyler's not around. So anyway, she puts this cake in the refrigerator, and when Tyler goes to get buttercream, she drops a container of sour cream off the top shelf—"

"Don't tell me."

"Right in the middle. Like target practice. Two hours before the woman was coming to pick it up."

"So what happened?"

"Maggie had to do another cake, but it wasn't what they ordered, so I didn't feel we could charge them for it. The woman was pretty understanding, considering the circumstances, but still, that's two cakes down the drain."

We look at each other.

"Do you think she did it deliberately?"

She shrugs. "If I knew that she did, I'd have to fire her. Which I really don't want to do. She made a pretty good show of apologizing, but . . . This has never happened before in all my years at the bakery. We've had people who weren't crazy about each other, but nothing so intense that they couldn't work together. I don't know what to do."

"Well, I know one thing you should do. Take a long weekend off. You look like shit."

She laughs ruefully. "Why, thank you, my dear. I sort of *feel* like shit. But I can't take a long weekend."

"Why not?"

"Because I'm afraid those two might kill each other if there's no-body standing between them."

"I'll stand between them."

She pats my hand. "Thanks, but I can't ask you to do that. Not af-ter working all night."

"I won't work all night. Linda would be the first to tell you she can do the bread by herself. And it's just Friday night. I'll come in Friday morning, and Maggie's off Saturday. They're both off Sunday. Tyler's off Monday and you're back on Tuesday."

"Are you sure?" She looks hopeful and doubtful at the same time.

"Of course. Piece of cake." No reaction. "Cake, get it?"

"Yeah, yeah. Okay, I'm going. It's too late to change your mind. Oh, and don't forget to take the bank deposit Friday afternoon."


Thank God I don't work days.

You can't even hear the music over the register ringing, the espresso maker blowing steam, people talking, cups and dishes rat-tling. Not to mention the blender. Whoever invented those damned blended drinks should be stood up against the wall and shot.

Maggie strolls in at seven A.M. Friday, two hours before her shift, carrying two giant shopping bags that she proceeds to unload in the back. She gives me an ingratiating smile.

"I hope you don't mind if I'm here early. I won't start till nine, but I wanted to bring in these display items."

From the bag she produces four beautiful willow baskets, a metal bowl and small platter painted in the tole style with fruit and flowers, and a gorgeous burl-wood box. It's an antique tea caddy, she says. By this time everyone in back has gathered around. Tyler is out front, doggedly pulling espresso for a couple of early birds. The sight of her trying not to look the slightest bit inter-ested tugs at me.

"We just redesigned Tony's—my husband's—restaurant," she

adds, just in case anybody's been vacationing on Pluto for the last three weeks. "I did the whole thing in a Moroccan-Gothic-Spanish pastiche—lots of dark, carved wood, wrought iron, mosaic tiles— it's wonderful. Incredibly evocative. Anyway, he was going to pitch these things, but I said, oh no, Tony, let me take them to the bakery. They could use some display items." She looks at me again, a little more tentatively. "I hope you don't mind."

Much as I hate to admit it, she has a point. The place is pretty funky, but on the other hand, it's always been this way, and people on the hill seem to like it fine. "You do understand we can't pay you for—"

"Oh, no, I never meant—I just wanted to do it. I think it would perk up the place. The display of our product is such an important part of our marketing strategy—it's not that the bakery looks bad, of course. I just thought . . ."

"Well . . . Go ahead, and we'll have a look. Let's just get it done before it gets too busy."

Almost before I've finished the sentence, she's buzzing around arranging scones in two of the baskets, cinnamon rolls and morn- ing buns in the other two, muffins in the metal bowl and on the platter, biscotti in the tea caddy. She rearranges the flowers that Ellen brought in before she left, cutting the sunflower stems down really short and putting them in a fat little butter crock on the case.

When she's finished, I have to admit everything looks more . . . picturesque, I guess. In a Martha Stewart kind of way. Jen and Misha are suitably impressed, and even a few of the customers no- tice.

At a quarter till nine, Myra, who owns Myra's Beauty Boutique next door, appears with her giant coffee mug. For a few seconds she surveys the room, threading her manicured nails through her long, auburn hair. Of course it's not really auburn; but then I've never been sure what her natural color is. It changes with her moods, from sassy blond to exotic blue-black.

She makes the mistake of saying to Tyler, "Hey, you guys dressed the place up. It looks cozy."

For her trouble, she gets the evil eye and a terse, "Yeah, just like a Bellevue fern bar."

Since it's Friday, the Mazurka mavens arrive at noon, adding their two cents' worth to the mix. "So Darlene says, personally I think Henry is a little bit passive-aggressive, if you get my drift, and I just go, not that it's any of your business. And then she says..."

By one o'clock I have a splitting headache. Not to mention that I'm exhausted because I couldn't sleep last night. After I initial the time cards, hand out the paychecks, count the money, and fill out the deposit slips, I can't wait to get away. I feel only semi-guilty leaving before clean up—not bad enough to hang around, and I'm happy for the excuse of going to the bank. How does Ellen stand it?

Saturday morning I'm wide awake at five, so I get dressed and go in.

"Must be nice working daytimes like regular people," Linda sniffs.

"You know you'd hate having to work with all those people."

For once, she agrees with me. "Yeah. Like those Mazurka morons. You should've seen this place when I got here. Crumbs everywhere. Dirty whisks and knives put back with the clean ones. Sticky stuff all over the floor." She laughs her nasty little laugh. "Those silly twits wouldn't last five minutes with me around."

"And neither would our customers," I mutter.

"What?"

"I said, why don't you go ahead and leave. I'll take care of cleanup."

I'm standing at the deep sink with a few leftover pale gray suds float-ing on top of the dirty water when Tyler knocks at the door.

"Hey, Tyler, how's it going?"

"Just frigging wonderful." She pushes past me, pulls an apron off the stack, and slips it over her head. It falls almost to her ankles.

"I think that's one of those super-long ones," I say. "Why don't we find you a smaller one?"

"This is fine." She picks up a tray of muffins and carries it out to the front. I tag along with a pan of scones, and watch as she slides the tray into the open case.

"Why don't you put those in the metal bowl?"

She stands perfectly still for a minute. I can tell she's contemplat-ing telling me where to stick the muffins. Finally she pulls the tray out, tilts it over the bowl so the muffins slide in like a pile of rocks, sets it on top of the case, and turns a level gaze to me, daring me to say something. I think I should be pissed off, but she looks like one of those awful paintings on velvet, the little kids with the huge, sad eyes and a gleaming teardrop on their faces.

"We can't put them out like that," I say.

"Yeah. Well, too bad Miss Spanish-Morrocan-Gothic-Pastiche isn't here to fix all my fuckups."

"Tyler, I want you to put it on cruise control today. Maggie's not here, so just relax. Okay?"

She shrugs. "Whatever." Her eyes darken, and I think she's about to say something else, but there's a knock on the door and she goes to let Misha in.

Rose comes in next, our weekend-mornings reinforcement. She's a freshman at UW on full academic scholarship, living at home with her folks on Eighth Street, and she's a fresh-faced Alice-in-Wonderland look-alike. With two of her, we could probably dis-pense with everyone else. She smiles a lot, is a math whiz, and never forgets who ordered what or how much it costs. Normally she just takes orders and presides at the cash register, but in a pinch she's fully capable of making a latte, busing tables, refilling the sugars, half-and-half pitcher, cocoa and cinnamon shakers, even replenishing the trays and baskets of baked goods. The best part is, she doesn't have to be told what a pinch feels like.

By eight-thirty we're in full crunch mode. Mrs. Gunnerson, who I think must be the oldest living person on Queen Anne Hill, has already made her weekly appearance. She comes in every Saturday morning, always wearing the same black knit pants, blinding fuchsia blouse, and mustard-colored sweater under her green raincoat. Her thin white hair stands up on top of her head in a little topknot, so that she looks sort of like a very colorful candle.

She spends at least ten minutes looking at everything in the case, asking what's in it, and then she says, "Don't you have any doughnuts?"

Every Saturday Rose explains that no, we don't make doughnuts, but how about a nice blueberry muffin instead? Mrs. Gunnerson always says, "You girls really should learn how to make doughnuts," but she takes one of the muffins and a cup of hot water and goes to her table by the window—and God help any unsuspecting newcomer who might be seated at *her* table—and she opens her cavernous black purse and extracts a Constant Comment tea bag and enjoys her breakfast.

This morning Delia Rae Johnson, also a longtime regular, although not nearly as old as Mrs. Gunnerson, informs me in a stage whisper that the toilet's broken, so I have to leave the counter for a quick inspection. To my immense relief, the problem is simply a broken lift chain. Since moving into CM's old apartment with its persnickety antique toilet, I've become one of the country's foremost experts on futzing with toilet lift chains.

The problem with this one is, the break is one of the middle links, which means both pieces of the chain are too short to reach from flapper to trip lever. They have to be reconnected somehow. When I go back to the register to get a paper clip, a blond woman in a hot-pink sweatshirt and jeans is talking earnestly to Rose, and I notice the traffic jam of customers backing up out the door.

"I'm sorry, ma'am," Rose is saying, "I don't have anything under that name. Could it be under a different name?"

The woman crosses her arms. "Now why would I put it under anyone's name but my own?"

When Rose sees me, she gives me a nervous smile. "Wyn, could you maybe help me for a second?"

"Sure. What's the problem?"

Before Rose can say anything, the woman blurts out, "The problem is, you've lost my son's birthday cake. Seven-year-olds don't understand that sort of thing very well."

I want to say, *Neither do twenty-seven-year-olds*, but instead I give her what I hope is a reassuring smile. "I'm sure it's in the back. It was probably moved to a different cooler—"

"Wyn." It's Delia Rae again. "Honey, I know you're busy, but my mother-in-law is about to go right through her Depends. Is the toilet fixed yet?"

"Give me two minutes, Delia. I'm just getting a paper clip—"

"A paper clip?" She shakes her hennaed hair. "Honey, this is more urgent than your paperwork. She needs to use the facilities."

"The paper clip is to fix the toilet chain, Delia—"

"My son's party is at eleven-thirty," the blond woman says. "I have to pick up the balloons, and the bouncing-castle guy is coming at ten-thirty, and I need to get the cake—"

"I will fix the toilet!" I announce. My words reverberate in the hush because everyone in the bakery has stopped talking to try to hear what's happening at the register. I lower my voice. "And then I'll be right back to find your son's cake. What name is it under?"

"His name is Leigh Adams. That's L-e-i-g-h, not L-e-e. But my name is Ann Carpenter. I've remarried and—"

Rather than wait for the entire rehash of *All My Children*, I bolt for the bathroom.

Five minutes later Delia's mother-in-law is barricaded in our bathroom and Tyler and I are ransacking the coolers in back for any trace of a Power Rangers cake. To no avail.

Ann Carpenter is trying to look calm while shifting her weight from one foot to the other in front of the cash register.

"Mrs. Carpenter," I begin.

"*Ms.* Carpenter. When I divorced Charlie Adams, I took back my maiden name. Where is the cake?"

"I'm terribly sorry, but I can't find—"

Her eyes close. "Oh God, no. You can't do this. My husband wanted to get the cake at Thriftway, but I said, no, we'll get it at Queen Street. Theirs are the best, and they're *so dependable.* That's exactly what I said. 'So dependable.' What am I supposed to do now?"

"Ms. Carpenter, I know we have a time problem here, so here's what I suggest. If you want one of our regular cakes, I can have our cake dec—er—design person do some birthday decoration on it, no charge, of course. Or if you want to buy a ready-made cake at"— I swallow hard—"the grocery store or any other bakery, we'll be glad to reimbu—"

"But it won't be Power Rangers."

"Unfortunately."

"I can't believe this."

"I'm so sorry. I feel terrible."

"Not nearly as terrible as my son's going to feel when I tell him he can't have his Power Rangers cake. I mean, he's been talking about it for—"

"Mrs. Carpenter, if you want one of our cakes, I should get Tyler working on it right away. It should only take her about thirty minutes or so, max."

"I don't have time to be running back over here because you lost my order. I've got a herd of seven-year-olds showing up at my house in three hours."

"I will personally deliver the cake if you'll just leave me your address and phone number."

"I gave all that information to the woman who took my order."

"Yes, well, the problem is, we have no record of the order. Do you remember who you spoke to?"

"Her name was Maggie. She said she specialized in children's birthday cakes. We had a long discussion about which theme Leigh would like and she even suggested the Power Rangers."

"Okay. I'll be sure and talk to her about this. She's not here today—"

"Of course not."

"Do you remember what day you ordered the cake?"

"Not really. I mean, the last couple of weeks have been crazy."

"I'm sure. Well, if you'll just write your address and phone number on this piece of paper, I'll go get Tyler started on the cake."

By the time we close at three P.M. on Saturday, the night shift with Linda is starting to look like a pretty cushy berth.


Everyone, myself most especially, is happy when Ellen comes back from Whidbey looking as relaxed and contented as a honeymooner. That warm, fuzzy feeling lasts until I have to tell her about the case of the missing Power Rangers cake. She confronts Maggie, who flatly denies ever having talked to Ann Carpenter or anyone else about a Power Rangers cake. Ellen sifts through all the back orders on the weekly clipboard and she and I go through the files. Jen and Misha move the desk and crawl around looking for that stray cake-order form that surely fell on the floor and got scrunched against the wall.

Through it all, Tyler shows admirable restraint. No gloating or finger-pointing. No whispering that she told us Maggie would be a problem. She quietly and efficiently goes about her work.

On Friday morning when Ellen comes in, she makes our espressos wordlessly, then motions me to sit down with her. "I sent Tyler home yesterday. She's officially suspended for three days without pay."

"Why? What happened?"

"Ann Carpenter called yesterday. She actually called to say thanks for the way you handled the mix-up. But she happened to mention that she looked on her calendar and saw the note from the day she ordered the cake. It was the twenty-third. Which was a Saturday. Maggie doesn't work on Saturday..."

"But Tyler does."

She nods. "Yep."

"What did she say when you asked her about it?"

"She denied everything. You know, righteous indignation, persecution of the martyr, et cetera. I don't know what to do about her." She wipes her hands on her black knit pants.

"Well, at least we know now why certain species eat their young."

"I hate to let her go, but we can't be looking over her shoulder every minute."

"She's been here what—two years?"

"Almost. We got her through a friend of mine who's a guidance counselor at Queen Anne High. Her mother left the family—Tyler and her sister, Tate, and their dad. Decided she didn't want to do the domestic thing anymore. I think she went back to school or something. In Wyoming. Or was it Montana?"

She gets up and slits open a new bag of espresso beans and empties it into the grinder.

"Tyler and Tate—kind of interesting names to give your daughters."

"Anyway, Tyler was a cheerleader and honor student, but she quit all her activities, her grades were slipping, and she was hanging with a bad crowd. Fortunately, Sandra was able to get her into a work-study program and she graduated last June by the skin of her teeth. She's been full-time since then, and she's a good worker. I really like her, but she has all these issues."

"Where's her sister?"

"She's at the U. Still lives at home. I think she and Tyler are pretty close, but, you know, Tate has her own life."

"Isn't she taking art classes?"

"Tyler?" She shakes her head. "She dropped out last semester."

"So she's not doing anything except working here?"

Ellen laughs. "I suppose one could do worse."

"You know what I mean, just being a *barista's* got to be sort of boring for someone who used to be an overachiever."

"Yeah, I know. Maybe that's the problem. But she kept saying she hated doing the cakes. I had no idea she'd get so territorial about it."

I dunk my biscotti in the tiny cup and stir it around absently till the end dissolves into mushy crumbs. "You think she'll come back?"

She shrugs. "I hope so, but I really don't know where her head is right now."


The Adler house on Phinney Ridge is a nondescript, pale blue craftsman bungalow. The front yard is essence of Pacific Rim, an obvious labor of love for somebody. Mostly evergreens, including some meticulously pruned and shaped cypress, a few rhododendron, and in isolated spots some bronze chrysanthemums poke their heads out. The overall effect is contemplative, like a Japanese temple garden.

Whereas the music blasting out the open windows is anything but contemplative, the kind of heavy-metal stuff that Mac calls head-banging music. Not surprisingly no one answers when I ring the doorbell, so I follow a trail of gray stepping stones around to the backyard and peer through a knothole in the wooden gate. There's a flagstone patio, a wooden chaise lounge with bright yellow cushions, a small, bathing-suited form stretched over it, rigid, like a sausage on a grill. Tyler.

I can see even from here that, instead of relaxing in the warm autumn sun, her whole body is tensed, not so much getting a tan as daring the sun to burn her. At the sound of the gate, she sits up abruptly. When she sees me she lies back down.

"What do you want?"

"I just thought I'd come see how you were doing."

"Well, now that you've seen, you can leave the same way you got in."

I slide into a folding wooden patio chair. "George Kennedy, *Riders of the Rio Grande?*"

She pushes up the giant black sunglasses that make her look like a blue-haired fly, and glares at me. "What?"

"That line. It came from some cowboy movie."

"So what?"

"Tyler, I want to ask you something."

"Let's see. Would it have anything to do with Power Rangers?"

"Well, you—"

"I love the way everyone just assumes that it was me that talked to her."

"Was it?"

"Why bother asking? You guys already made up your minds. Had to be me. My butt's outta there."

"It's only a suspension. Ellen didn't fire you."

"Might as well have. She will next time."

"Is there going to be a next time?"

She crosses her arms over her flat little chest.

"Ellen and I both really want you to stay at the bakery—"

"Then get rid of *her.*"

"You know we can't do that. We need a cake de—person."

"So what am I? Dog meat?"

"No, and you do great cakes, but you kept saying you didn't want—"

"Well, I've changed my mind. So get rid of her and I'll do the cakes."

"We can't fire her."

"Why not?"

"First of all, she's doing a good job." I scoot to the edge of the chair. "Can't you just verbalize what it is about her that upsets you?"

"*Verbalize?* That is like *so* L.A."

I sigh. "You know what I mean. Tell me. You have to have a reason."

"She's a bitch."

"I need you to be a little more specific. If there's an actual problem, we can work on it."

She sits up, crossing her legs Indian style, and turns to me. "Okay, fine. Here it is. She just walked in and took over, started bossing everybody around. Redecorating the place. She's got this attitude. Like she's too good to bus tables or do prep stuff. Miss Hot Shit Artiste cake designer, making more money than anyone—"

"How do you know how much she makes? Did she tell you?"

"No, but she said it was 'substantial.' A big, fat increase from Booker's. I've been here for two years and I'm still slinging espresso. How come nobody offered me that job? I could've—"

"Unless I'm hallucinating, I remember at least three occasions when Ellen asked you to do cakes, and you didn't want—"

"Well, *duh*. Not like that. Not when I was only getting paid to work the counter."

"You didn't even ask. You knew we were interviewing. Why didn't you say something?"

"It wouldn't have done any good. You guys all think I'm an idiot just because I have blue hair and I'm not some little yuppie princess."

I shake my head and clamp my teeth firmly on my tongue. "You know that's not true."

"No I don't."

"Look, can't you see how insecure Maggie is? She needs to make herself feel important—"

"Am I supposed to care about her psycho poop?"

I watch the sun glint on the iridescent green head of a hummingbird delving into a pink trumpet-vine blossom. "Have you talked to anyone about this?"

"Like who?"

"I don't know. Maybe Tate?"

She looks straight ahead, then, "She's in Montana."

"With your mom?"

She barely nods.

I nibble on a jagged cuticle. "When do you think she'll be coming home?"

"No idea."

I stand up. "Well, Tyler . . . I don't know what else to say. Are you planning to come back?"

A shrug.

"Let me know, okay?"

## · four ·

Spring in the Northwest is practically indistinguishable from winter except that there are more flowers. Summer is moody and coy and not entirely certain if she wants to stay or go. Not to mention that all the tourists hit town en route to the islands or to Alaska on a big, white cruise ship. Winter is . . . well, winter.

Fall is definitely the best season—golden days and blue skies, warm afternoons and cool nights and the smell of wood smoke. And fall in Seattle with Mac—it doesn't get any closer to perfection, at least not in this lifetime. Before I even notice it, I forget all the weirdness and my misgivings and I'm walking around in that haze of stunned gratitude and self-absorption that envelops you when you're absolutely crackers over someone.

We do all the same things we did last year, but the world seems to be playing in Technicolor instead of black and white. When he touches my arm to point out a golden eagle at Discovery Park, I shudder lightly with desire. Long walks along the waterfront—yes, it rains and we get soaked, but so what? We go home and warm up in bed. Bargain movie matinees, cheapie concerts and films at the University of Washington, cruising used-book bookstores.

We hit every ice-cream place in town, conducting our own taste tests. We jog along the waterfront. We ride the ferries to Bainbridge, Vashon, Bremerton. The destination never matters; the object is simply to be on the water.

Sometimes we take long drives while I give him shit about emissions standards for trucks. In spite of pollution guilt, I secretly love riding in the Elky. No matter where we go, somebody wants to strike up a conversation about it, what year it is, whether it's a 454 or Turbo Jet 400. Mac isn't really a gearhead, though. His feelings about vehicles are limited to a certain loyalty to the Elky, almost the way he might feel about an old, favorite horse.

At Snoqualmie Falls early one Sunday morning, we stand silent on the observation deck watching the water plunge over the cliff and thunder into the gorge below. We splurge on overpriced pancakes in the rustic-chic Salish Lodge, and sit there for an hour after we're through, arguing about the Mariners and the Dodgers. We hike the trails on the flanks of Mount Rainier to stare at the changing leaves, wander mutely through the green cathedrals of rain forest on the Olympic Peninsula.

We eat hamburgers on the deck at Green Lake Jake's, watching the skaters and cyclists and families with kids and dogs congregate around Green Lake in the cool, sunny afternoons. Sometimes there's a steel-drum band playing over by the bathhouse and it feels like we're on vacation. We hold hands and stare at each other and drink beer and it's almost possible to forget that winter's early darkness is coming on.

Because the bakery doesn't sell bread on Sunday or Monday, I'm off on Saturday and Sunday nights. I go to Bailey's, hang out there reading books and drinking wine. Then, after closing, sometimes Kenny's wife, Roz, comes over, sometimes CM shows up, and we all go out for pizza or Thai food or Chinese noodles at one or the other of the late-night places.

Mac and Kenny know most of the other bartenders, so they always send us a bottle of wine or comp a round of drinks, and we eat great food and laugh and talk until they throw us out. Then I go home with Mac and we make love, or sometimes, if we're too tired, we just fall asleep spooned up together. When I open my eyes in the gray half-light, we're already a tangle of arms and legs and soft, faded blankets.

CM finally says, "Why don't you just give him a key?," so I do, and when she's out of town, he stays at our place, going to sleep after I leave for work at eleven. In the morning when I get home, he might be drinking coffee by the window or propped up in bed reading. Or he might be asleep, only waking up when I come in. I undress, slip under the comforter next to him, and the bed is warm from his heat and it smells of him, like the woods, and the very first touch of his skin on mine steals my breath away, like jumping into icy water.

He always holds me till I fall asleep, and he leaves so quietly that I never know. I just wake up at three and he's gone. I like that—not having to watch him leave.

When Linda announces her retirement, it's cause for ecstatic rejoicing at the Queen Street Bakery. However, even before the exclamations of glee fade into silence, Ellen and I look at each other and tacitly acknowledge that whatever personal feelings we may have about her, the fact is, she's a warm body. One who knows how to make bread. One who hasn't missed but about a half dozen shifts in the last twenty years. One who's going to have to be replaced.

"Are we going to have a retirement party?"

It's four P.M. and the bakery is officially closed, the shades on the front windows and doors pulled down. I'm sitting cross-legged on top of one of the café tables while Ellen tallies up the day's receipts.

"I don't see how we can get out of it," she says. "We have to at least offer. She's been here so long."

"Good luck getting anyone to come."

"We'll have it right after her shift, so the morning people will be here. It doesn't need to be elaborate, just some soft drinks, coffee, tea, a cake."

"I can't picture her retired. She won't have anybody to harass. What's she going to do?"

"She told me she was going to go stay with her sister for a while."

"She has a sister?"

"Somewhere in Idaho. Sandpoint or something."

"How nice. Maybe she'll meet an attractive bull moose and set up housekeeping."

Ellen guffaws in spite of herself. "Meanwhile..." She tips back the dregs of her last espresso. "I guess we need to get an ad ready for the Sunday classifieds. I think the deadline is Thursday morning at ten."

"When's her last day?"

"Two weeks from yesterday, whatever that is."

"Doesn't give us much time."

"You know..." She looks at me speculatively. "We don't have tons of cash right now. It would be really nice if we could save some of the money that would normally go to Linda's salary. How would you feel about taking on an apprentice? Can you teach somebody and make bread, too?"

"I guess. Worst-case scenario is if it doesn't work, we find some-body with experience."

"Good. I'll tell Tyler it's okay with you."

I do a double take. "What?"

Ellen looks embarrassed and pleading at the same time. "She

wants to try it. She actually came to me and asked if she could learn 'the bread thing.'"

I close my eyes.

"You don't have to agree." She sighs. "But it would be the perfect solution."

"I don't know, Ellen. Bread making is—"

"I mean, it gets her out of direct conflict with Maggie. She already works here, so she knows how we operate and where everything is . . ."

"I'm afraid she'll get bored."

"She's already bored. She needs something new to distract her."

"It's hard work, and doesn't she like to do the club scene at night?"

"I think she really looks up to you."

"That's because I'm eight inches taller than she is."

"No, really, she does. Can't you just give her a try? If we don't do something, I don't think she'll be with us much longer."


While the idea of an apprentice was one thing, the reality is something else. I've never actually had an assistant before. As for training, well, I did teach high school, but that was my job. I wasn't trying to do a job plus on the side teach somebody else how to do it. Now I have to take the time to explain things and answer questions for Tyler, who has no experience with bread and clearly has other things on her mind. Every time I look up, she's either staring off into space, probably spinning baroque revenge fantasies about Maggie, or she's gazing at me with this wide-eyed, what-do-we-do-now eagerness. It's hard to say which is more irritating. She's also decided it's cool to call me "boss" and nothing I say will dissuade her.

· · ·

One night in her second week on the job, she comes in right behind me and goes straight to the bathroom. At first I'm too busy getting dough out of the cooler to think about it, but after a few minutes I realize she's still in there. I go out and knock on the door.

"Tyler? You okay?"

"Be right there, Boss."

"Are you sick?"

"Nope."

Then my nose catches the distinctively cloying smell of marijuana. "Tyler, open the door, right now." I hear the toilet flush and then the faucet running.

She opens the door, but avoids looking at me.

"What the hell do you think you're doing?"

"I threw it away." Her voice is squeaky, like a cartoon mouse. "I didn't take any. Not even one little toke. Want to smell my breath?"

"Not particularly."

She mumbles a half-assed apology, runs a nervous hand through the blue spikes.

"I don't care what you do on your own time, but we're not paying you to get high and stare into the ozone. How do you expect to learn anything about making bread when you're stoned? Not to mention the fact that we're working with hot ovens and sharp knives. It's dangerous."

Her mouth draws into a thin, tight line. "I said I'm sorry. What else d'you want me to do—put a broom up my ass and sweep the floor?"

I chew on the inside of my cheek while I fantasize about swatting her skinny butt with the wooden bread peel. "I didn't ask for you, you know. I wanted to hire a professional. You're the one who said you wanted to learn to bake bread. Or was that a lie, too?"

She's staring down, seemingly fascinated by her black Doc Martens. A shiny round spot appears on one of the toes. Then one on the floor. It takes me a few seconds to realize that they're tears.

"Tyler..." I stop short of apologizing, but I feel like a monster. *God, why can't I just work alone?* "Tell me one thing, okay? What do you want?"

She swipes a hand across her eyes and chokes out, "What?"

"I want you to tell me what you'd like to do. Do you want to work at the bakery at all?"

"Yes."

"I know it's not easy being on the night shift, it sort of puts a crimp in your social life—"

She makes a funny little sputtering noise. "What social life?"

"Would you rather work days?" I know I'm a terrible person, but I'm hoping she says yes.

"No." She swallows a couple of times, and finally looks directly at me. "I want to make bread. Like you."

I let out a deep sigh. "Then we're going to have to come to an understanding of how things are going to be. I can't work with someone I have to baby-sit."

She slinks behind me, back to the work area.

"Here." I hand her the dough-encrusted hook from the floor mixer. "Clean that off—"

"I'm sick of cleaning shit off," she says. "I want to make bread. I'm not stupid. How would you like to make espresso and put muffins on plates for eight hours a day? Just give me a chance. Let me do something besides clean the frigging dough hook and measure the flour. A monkey could do that."

"You probably don't want to hear this, but when I was your age, I worked in a *boulangerie* one summer, and you know what they let me do? Wash the equipment. Weigh ingredients. Put the bread out on the shelves. And watch the bakers. Toward the end I got a bucket of dough to practice kneading and shaping, and then Jean-Marc would bake my loaves off and point out to me all the ways they were inferior. The whole summer I was there, I never laid a finger on any dough that was destined to be sold as bread."

For a minute she's quiet. "So you mean I can't do anything but watch you for three months?"

"I didn't say that. But you still have to do your part of the prep and cleanup. And you have to do what I ask you to do." I attempt a persuasive smile. "Me boss, you apprentice."

She looks at the ceiling. "Does that mean I have to laugh at your jokes?"

"Yes. Absolutely. Look, let's try this: Starting tomorrow night, your job also includes doing one bread a week on your own. I mean one loaf. I'll give you time to do it during the night. I want you to do it first by the direct method, with commercial yeast, then try making it with a sponge. Then a starter. I'll answer questions if you need me, but basically you're on your own. Tomorrow night I'll give you a recipe to use for a basic white country bread."

"Okay."

Her enthusiasm is underwhelming. I start to turn away, but she says, "Are you going to tell Ellen?"

I shake my head. "She doesn't care how we set it up."

Her face flushes. "I mean, about the dope."

"Oh." I'd almost forgotten. "Well . . . that depends." I dredge up my classroom-discipline voice. "If you promise me it won't happen again, we'll call it a temporary aberration and forget the whole thing."

"I promise."


I love Thanksgiving. It's the only American holiday dedicated solely to the preparation and consumption of food.

When I was a kid we always went to my oma's town house in San Francisco, along with the few old aunts who were still alive and creaking around, a distant cousin or two, and Mr. Lewis, the crotch-ety bachelor who used to work with my opa. Dinner was very formal, with starched white linens, crystal goblets, and all kinds of silverware that I never knew what to do with, and salt cellars and finger bowls and six courses. But I never minded.

The weather was unfailingly wet and cold, so it wasn't as if you could go out and play, and I loved spending all day Wednesday with my mother and my oma in the big, warm kitchen. Ironing and folding the napkins was my first chore, then setting the table with the gold-rimmed plates. I loved the juggling of things from oven to stove to oven to refrigerator, the stirring and the tasting, listening to the family gossip.

This Thanksgiving Day comes at the tail end of a solid month of rain. CM and I have invited a few people for dinner—Mac, Kenny, and Roz. In a sudden burst of expansive goodwill, I'd invited Tyler to come, but she said she was going to San Francisco.

It surprised me. "What are you going down there for?"

Her expression fell somewhere between boredom and annoyance. "My dad," she said. "He's getting married."

"That's kind of exciting. Is this somebody he's known for a while?"

She shrugs. "I just met her in September."

"So, are they going to live down there?"

A sigh. "She's moving in with us."

"What's she like?"

Tyler scooped toasted hazelnuts into the bowl of the small Hobart. "Betty Crocker." When she saw my puzzled look, she added, "A house bunny. You know—tuna casserole on the table every night at six o'clock."

My first thought was that Tyler's dad was probably primed and ready for a house bunny. My second thought was that Tyler obviously was not.

· · ·

I'm doing most of the cooking for Thanksgiving dinner. CM's good at chopping things and cleaning up, but other than that, she's pretty much a culinary washout. Mostly she keeps the fire going and hangs out in the kitchen as self-appointed cheerleader and supervisory staff. Mac shows up at noon with six bottles of wine and a couple of tapes. CM scans the bottles.

"Ooh, Côtes du Rhone. Mmm, Alsatian Riesling. Good job, Barman!"

I should be used to this by now, but I can't quite squelch a prickle of annoyance at the way he smiles and stands up a bit straighter, basking in the glow of her approval. They load the Riesling into the refrigerator.

"Hey, don't take up all the room," I grouse. "I need someplace for the salad and the mousse."

A few minutes later the buzzer squawks again, and our tiny foyer is suddenly full of noise and wet coats and dripping umbrellas.

Under the banner "Invite an Orphan Home for Thanksgiving," Roz and Kenny have asked if they can bring a friend of theirs. Or at least that's the official story. Steve Grimaldi is a tall, buffed-out bus driver with gorgeous dark eyes. I remember that he went with us to Hong Chow's Noodle Parlor one night after Bailey's closed, and I'm pretty sure he wangled this invitation so he could see CM again.

I nudge her with my elbow as we stand at the sink together. "Pretty cute, *n'est-ce pas?*"

"Well, at least we have an even number of boys and girls," she says with a neutral smile.

From the living room I hear the muted roar of a football crowd and the hyper tones of the pumped-up announcer. Roz appears with a casserole of scalloped potatoes. "It smells wonderful in here. Just the way Thanksgiving should smell." She looks radiant in her gray jumper and wine-colored turtleneck, her dark hair brushed and shining, little strands of it haloed around her face by static electricity. I don't recall ever seeing her with makeup on before. "Where do you want this casserole and what can I do?"

"You can just set it on the stove." CM smiles. "My personal chef has everything under control, so there's not much to do. What are the guys up to?"

Roz makes a face. "Football. In a few minutes they'll be sniffing each other and marking their territory."

"Guess we'll have to party without them." CM reaches in the fridge for a bottle of champagne while I grab three glasses.

"Just a teensy bit for me," Roz says, holding her thumb and forefinger about an inch apart.

We both look at her in surprise, and she blushes. "I guess I'm not supposed to say anything till we make the official announcement, but I'm pregnant."

"Like omigod!" CM and I sandwich her between us in a hug.

"That is so awesome! Congratulations. Oops." CM licks champagne off her fingers as it foams over the rim of the glass.

"We'll have to imbibe more, then. In your honor, of course."

"Please act surprised when Kenny makes the announcement. He's so excited."

We touch our glasses together, and whisper impatient questions. "How far along are you? Do you know the sex? Have you thought of any names?"

"I'm due in May," she says, "and I don't know . . . well, clinically, I don't know. They can't tell the sex until twenty weeks, but I just have a feeling it's a girl."

CM grins. "A toast—to the baby woman!"


Although cooking isn't her forte, CM sets a beautiful table, hauling out her grandmother's rose-patterned china, the crystal she bought in Vienna, and her mismatched silver, collected on her travels from antiques shops across the country. In place of flowers there's a basket filled with bright leaves, nuts, pinecones, mahogany-colored buckeyes, and dried sweet-gum balls.

While the rolls warm in the oven, Roz tosses the salad, I whip cream for the pumpkin mousse, and CM ransacks drawers for serving pieces and trivets for the hot dishes. We arrange the food buffet style on the desk, and pour the wine while the men sit glued to the television, popping up every few minutes to cast doubt on the lineage of the referees or high-five each other.

We pause in our labors to study them.

"And I thought all they did for fun was fart," CM deadpans.

Roz purses her lips thoughtfully. "No, my dear. As every married woman knows, that falls under the heading of foreplay."

When we're all at the table, plates heaped with turkey and dressing and my oma's giblet gravy, scalloped potatoes, romano beans with toasted almonds, spinach salad, and homemade yeast rolls, Kenny says, "I guess it's corny, but I'd like to say what I'm thankful for." He picks up his glass. "Great friends, great food." He turns to Roz, and I could swear his contacts are fogging up. "And my beautiful wife, Rosalind, who is about to make me a daddy."

While everyone is exclaiming and clapping and shaking Kenny's hand and jumping up to hug Roz in a pantomime of surprise, I watch that familiar neutral expression replace the surprise on Mac's face. Then he recovers.

"So you really can teach an old dog new tricks." Grinning, he slaps Kenny on the back, kisses Roz.

After seconds—in some cases, thirds—after pumpkin mousse and coffee, when we're sitting around in a sated stupor nursing our brandy and finger-painting in the melted whipping cream, Mac puts on one of his tapes, and we watch the afternoon sink into early-evening darkness, lights winking on down the hill.

Steve and Mac compare rock-climbing escapades. CM describes her latest dance project, based on the caryatids. Kenny, who grew up on a farm, grosses us out by describing how his father killed their Thanksgiving turkey every year, and when Roz gives him the *Oh, honey, not that story*, he asserts that if everyone had to kill their own food, there'd be more vegetarians.

Steve stirs everything up with his "I'm a recovering Catholic" comment—Roz is devout, Kenny is simply Irish. Steve touts the mellow vibes of Zen and Kenny scoffs at "religion lite." Mac shocks all of us with the revelation that he was an altar boy.

I mostly sit listening. Watching Mac. Noticing how different he is in a group. More . . . I don't know. Convivial? Exuberant? He does the just-one-of-the-guys thing very well. But it seems hollow to me.


The first Saturday in December Mac is up on Orcas Island helping Rick Bensinger install a shower in his cottage. CM is out to dinner with Steve Grimaldi. I have a glass of wine at Bailey's around seven-thirty, but without Mac, the place could be any other bar on a Saturday night—crowded, overheated, too noisy to concentrate on my book. So I trudge back up the hill in the dark, pelted by rain, long scarf wrapped around my neck and drawn up over my nose.

All the shops and some of the houses are decorated for Christmas. Most of the windows in our building are outlined in lights, red and green for Christmas, blue and white for Hanukkuh. By eight-thirty I'm taking comfort in a blazing fire, hot chocolate, and hazelnut-cornmeal biscotti. I curl up on the couch, surrounded by pillows, ecstatic to find an Audrey Hepburn film festival on one of the movie channels.

Just at the point in *Two for the Road* where she comes back to Albert Finney after a night of illicit adventure, and all he says is, "Thank God," the front door opens and CM walks in.

I look at my watch. "What are you doing home?"

She hangs up her coat, kicks off her shoes, and inserts herself into my nest of pillows, tucking her legs under the blanket next to mine. She picks up my mug, and sniffs.

"Mmm. Hot chocolate. Is there any more?"

"On the stove. What happened? Was it ghastly?"

"No." She takes the last biscotti on the plate and gnaws on it. "Not ghastly. Just . . . I felt like I was sleep walking."

She gets up and goes into the kitchen, returning with her own mug of cocoa. She repositions herself on the couch and takes a sip. "He thought the caryatids were insects."

I laugh, but she doesn't.

"Don't you find that depressing?"

"Actually . . ." I hit the power button on the remote and the TV goes black. "I think it's hilarious."

"That's because you weren't trying to have a conversation with him." She stares thoughtfully into her hot chocolate. "I guess I've never really been very smart about men."

"Show me a female who has and I'll show you a black-widow spider."

She doesn't even smile. "I'm serious. What if my mother was right?"

"About what?"

"About everything. Love. Marriage and babies. My aunt Connie who fell down the basement stairs and laid there, for three days, till the yardman found her."

"What the hell are you talking about?"

"She was the family old maid."

"Stop it! You're not old and you're sure as hell not a maid."

Finally, a grudging little chuckle. She nestles into the pillows and pulls the blanket up to her chest. "The problem is, I want it all. I want to dance and travel and then I want to come home to somebody wonderful. But they won't let you."

"Who's 'they'?"

"Men. It's always an either/or thing with them. They want you to give up everything else to get that little bit of warmth. It's not worth it."

I turn myself around and sit cross-legged facing her. "But this was a first date. He wasn't getting into the dancing/traveling/coming home thing yet, was he?"

"No." She sighs. "But then, he wasn't wonderful, either." She picks up the remote and clicks the tube back on just in time for the end of the movie.

Albert Finney looks at Audrey Hepburn and says, "Bitch." She smiles her glorious smile and says, "Bastard."

## five

Unless you know someone who's short-listed for the Nobel Peace Prize or about to go into labor, a phone call at four A.M. can only be bad news. But I'm not thinking about that when I first hear Dorian the duck phone quacking obnoxiously. I'm cursing myself for forgetting to unplug him. I'm thinking that whoever is waking me up at this ungodly hour on my day off better have a damn good reason.

She does. "Wyn?"

"Mom?" I push myself into a sitting position, shivering in the cold darkness. The living room smells of the ashes from last night's fire. "What's wrong?"

"It's Richard." Her voice is small and sounds very far away. "He's had a heart attack. But he's all right," she adds quickly. "He's at Encino Medical Center. That's where I am. I'm sorry to wake you up."

Now I'm fully, wide-eyed, hair-raisingly awake. "Mom, for God's sake, don't worry about that. Tell me what happened. Are you okay? You want me to come?"

Even as I'm saying it, I know it's the wrong thing. I should have just said I'd be there on the first flight this morning.

"No, it's okay. I'm fine. And he's stable. I guess I should have waited till later to call you . . . I just wanted to hear your voice."

That about does it for me. All that's keeping me from bawling like a baby is the knowledge that the last thing she needs with her husband in the ICU is a hysterical daughter. "Tell me what happened."

"Well, after dinner Thursday night he wasn't feeling good. He said it was heartburn, so he took some Pepto and we went to bed. Then about midnight I woke up and his breathing sounded funny, you know—stressed or something. He was lying there with pains in his chest, trying to decide whether to wake me. I swear, men can be so—"

"Wait a minute. Are you telling me this happened two nights ago? Why the hell didn't you call me?"

"Oh, Wyn, I don't know. I can't even tell night from day right now. It's been a very strange forty-eight hours. I'm sorry I'm not making any sense. Anyway, as soon as he told me what was wrong, I called nine-one-one, and he kept insisting he could drive himself to the clinic. Can you imagine? It was a good thing I didn't listen to him because by the time the paramedics got here he was about to go into cardiac arrest."

I know she has to be wondering right now if maybe my father, who dropped dead of the same damned thing at the age of forty-five, had had symptoms, some kind of warning that he ignored or was too stubbornly macho or maybe too scared to tell her about.

"I'm sure I can get a flight this morning, and as soon as I—"

"No, honey, I'd really rather you didn't come."

"Why?"

"Because everything's under control, and I think it would upset Richard if everybody started hovering—"

" 'Hovering'?"

"He didn't even want me to call Gary. What I'd like you to do, if you can, is to come home for Christmas. Spend a few days with us. I think it would make Richard very happy. And me, too, of course."

Naturally she interprets the silent pause incorrectly.

"I know it's short notice, and I know you're probably busy at work—"

"No, it's not that. I'm just not totally awake yet, and I was—"

"Oh, the doctor's coming, honey. I've got to run. You see if you can work it out. Maybe you'd like to bring your . . . boyfriend? I'll call you tomorrow. Love you."

I close the door to CM's bedroom, and since there's no going back to sleep now, I tiptoe into the kitchen and put the teakettle on. I turn up the thermostat and pull on my sweats and sit at the table.

Memories are like those nested Shaker boxes, each one holding another half-forgotten surprise, some pleasant, some not so pleasant. Thinking of Richard reminds me of their wedding last year, how hurt and resentful I felt that she would marry this stranger—actually hold the ceremony in the house she and my father built—and then move him into it. I remember getting knee-walking drunk at the reception, but I don't remember much of what I did or said. This is probably a good thing.

What I mainly recall is meeting Richard's son, Gary, a perfectly nice guy with whom I ended up having a brief and mindless fling. CM charitably refers to him as my transition man. The worst part of the weekend—aside from the wedding itself—was David showing up on the doorstep the next day to announce that he'd decided we should get divorced so he could marry Advertising Barbie. Not that it came as a huge surprise; it was just the addition of insult to injury.

Each successive Kodachrome image in my mind makes me cringe a little more until the teakettle screeches, mercifully ending the reruns.

While I'm rummaging through the tin of tea bags, looking for an

Earl Grey, CM emerges from the bedroom in a green silk kimono with little Japanese dolls embroidered all over it.

"What's going on? Did I hear Dorian quacking?"

When I tell her the news, she groans. "Oh, God, how awful. Poor Johanna. They haven't even been married a year. Are you going home?"

"She didn't want me to come."

She pulls another mug out of the cupboard and pours boiling water in it. "Did she say why?"

"She said Richard would get upset if people started 'hovering.' She wants me to come home for Christmas. She says I should bring my 'boyfriend.' "

"Well, I guess it makes sense." She dunks a teabag absentmindedly in the cup.

"I'm glad it does to someone."


I slide onto my stool at the bar, and when Mac comes down to say hi, I tell him about Richard.

"How's he doing?"

"I guess okay. It actually happened Thursday night, and she didn't call me till four o'clock this morning."

He leans across the bar for a quick kiss. "How's she holding up?"

"Good. At least she sounds good. I mean, what do I know? I can't believe she didn't call me sooner."

"Maybe she wanted to know something definite to tell you. So you wouldn't worry."

"She told me not to come home. Don't you think that's weird?"

"Mac! We need another pitcher of Miller."

He goes off to take another pitcher of beer to a table of guys. When he comes back I say, "She wants me to come for Christmas."

He reaches for a tray of clean glasses and starts polishing them with a towel and putting them upside down on the plastic shelf liner.

"I was wondering if you might want to come. I know it wouldn't be terribly interesting, but I know she'd like to meet you, and there are a few fun things we could do in L.A...."

He doesn't look up. "I'd like to, but I don't think I can get off that long."

"We wouldn't have to stay more than a couple of days. I can't take off too much time either, but maybe..."

"I'll check with Harte and let you know." When he sticks the empty rack under the rinse sink without making eye contact, I realize it isn't going to happen.

"Forget it. I can tell you don't want to go."

"It's not that I don't want to. It's just that the holidays are usually busy, and since I just started back again, Kenny's got first choice. Besides that, it's a lot of money just to go for a couple of days—"

"It's okay."

"It's not okay. It obviously bothers you that I can't go."

"No. It bothers me that you don't want to go and you can't just tell me."

He slaps his damp towel on the bar. "Okay. I don't want to go to L.A. Is that what you want me to say?"

"I want you to say what you mean, not a bunch of bullshit excuses."

"Fine." He walks over to wait on someone.

I twirl my wineglass around and watch him talking to a couple of guys at the bar. Laughing as if we haven't just had our first real disagreement. How do men compartmentalize everything so neatly? They file you away in that relationship box and nothing in there affects any other part of their lives.

Why the hell didn't we just stay friends? That felt reasonably good. We had fun. I could tell him anything. Of course, he never told me very much about himself, but it didn't matter as much then. Now look at us. Throw some sex into the mix and it's like putting too much yeast in bread. It's all very fizzy and light and wonderful, but then it rises too high and can't support its own weight and the whole thing falls flat.


"Why did you do this?" Mac stands in the front door, looking around the apartment. CM has gone with Glenna to see the Queen Anne High School production of *The Nutcracker,* and since I'm leaving for L.A. tomorrow morning right after work, I've invited him over to celebrate our Christmas tonight. Or maybe I neglected to mention the *C* word when I said I'd cook dinner.

I follow his gaze around the living room. Okay, so it looks like Winter Wonderland. CM and I splurged on a huge tree, since she's not going home. We hung stockings and draped the mantel with pine garland. There are candles flickering softly, Christmas music on the stereo, mulling spices permeating the air...and of course, presents piled everywhere. The presents are kind of misleading, because they include CM's for my mom and Richard, and mine for her parents and her sister Katie and Katie's two kids, Kyle and Kelsey.

"Why did I do what?"

"This." A nod of his head encompasses the whole room. "I thought we were just going to have dinner. We agreed—"

"Mac, this is what CM and I do at Christmas. You won't be forced to participate against your will. I just thought it would be fun to have a nice dinner and some Christmas cookies and—"

"Sorry." He shuts the door behind him and kisses me.

"Ooh, you're cold. Did you walk over?"

"Yeah." When he takes off his coat and hangs it on the back of a dining-room chair, I notice how thin and worn the wool is. "Elky's in the shop."

While he builds a fire, grumbling all the while about how a fireplace is a waste of wood because it's just for show and doesn't really heat a room, I fix two glasses of *gluhwein,* that sublime combination of warm red wine, sugar, citrus, and spices that my oma used to make in wintertime. The year I turned thirteen, just before Christmas, my father said that I was old enough to have one small glass. I remember how I hated the taste—it seemed sour after hot apple cider—but I loved the way it felt, the warmth radiating out from my stomach all the way into my fingers and toes.

We sit on the couch with our glasses, wrapping our hands around them to draw the heat, and he stares moodily at the flames.

"Mac, what's wrong? Why are you so grouchy?"

"Sorry. I just don't have a lot of warm, fuzzy feelings about Christmas, I guess."

A laugh bubbles up in my throat, and he turns his face to me. "I wouldn't say you have a lot of warm, fuzzy feelings about much of anything right now."

His quick smile is like an unexpected present, warming me to my center, just like that first glass of *gluhwein*. "Except you," he says. He puts down his glass and kisses me till all the little white lights on the tree seem to sparkle.

"Better stop that, or we'll never make it to dinner."

He kisses my throat, just under my chin. "Would that be so terrible?"

"Um, yes, because I made all this wonderful food."

"Well, okay." He nibbles my earlobe. "But you're dessert."

I drag myself away, into the kitchen, and he works the fire, stirring it into a roaring blaze. Then he takes the Christmas tape off and puts on the tape he made for me last year just before he went away. I smile as Dylan growls "Tangled Up in Blue." When I come back to the living room, he's standing in front of the bookshelves reading my birthday cards from my mom and Richard, CM, Tyler, Ellen, Misha, and Jen.

"Why didn't you tell me it was your birthday? I didn't even get you a card."

"It's not important."

He looks at the cards all lined up on the shelf, then back to me.

"I think if that were true, you wouldn't have them all on display. When was it?"

"The fifteenth, and CM's the one who put the cards up there, when she was cleaning out the mail basket."

Dinner, all modesty aside, is fabulous. The thinnest of veal scallops, sautéed in butter and white wine with mushrooms and prosciutto. Crusty roasted potatoes with rosemary, a salad of endive and arugula with walnuts and apple. Of course, *pain au levain*. To drink, a wonderful rosé champagne. And dessert is chocolate soufflés with chocolate-peppermint sauce and thin, crisp sugar cookies. We take our espresso into the living room, and Mac stretches out his long legs under the coffee table.

I wait patiently for him to make good on his promise that I'm dessert. CM's spending the night with Glenna, and I've been entertaining myself with fantasies about her empty queen-size bed all day. But he sits staring at the fire.

"I know I've been kind of a pain in the ass lately. I've just been preoccupied. I guess 'obsessed' is probably a better word choice. Thinking about the agent. I hadn't heard from him, so right after Thanksgiving I wrote him a letter and asked if he'd had a chance to read the manuscript."

"And . . . ?"

"I got a letter back right away. He apologized for taking so long, said he was still reading it, and that he'd get back to me. And I haven't heard another damn word."

"It hasn't been that long since Thanksgiving," I say gently. "And people are busy during the holidays."

"Almost four weeks." He draws a long breath and lets it out slowly. "It's just making me nuts." He looks over. "Sorry."

"Have you sent it to anyone else?"

"No."

"Don't you think you should?"

"That's what everyone says you should do. Blanket the earth with your manuscript." He shakes his head. "I just had a good feeling about this guy."

"I know it's hard, but you have to try not to think about it. I'd say if you still haven't heard from him by the end of January, call him." I slip off my shoes and curl my legs up under me. "I wish you were going to L.A. with me."

His eyes close and he rests his head on the back of the couch. "I don't know. I just feel so damn useless."

"Oh, come on. It's a bad time, that's all. The manuscript's in limbo. It's Christmas, which you're obviously not into . . ."

He puts his arm around me and draws me against him, but he just sits there staring at the fire, which by now is mostly a bed of coals. After about ten minutes of silent staring, I get up and clear the dishes off the table. I load the dishwasher, and set it, and when I turn around he's standing in the doorway with his coat on.

"I can't stay," he says. "I'm sorry."

I want to tell him he's being ridiculous, wasting our time, ruining the whole night, but what's the point?

"Wait a second."

From under the tree I grab the shopping bag that contains the Black Watch plaid flannel shirt I bought him, wrapped in silver foil and tied with a green ribbon.

"I told you not to do this."

"I wasn't listening. So just shut up and take it. It's not a carved ivory chess set or anything."

He takes the bag and kisses me. "I'll see you next week," he says, and makes his escape.

I zap what's left of my *gluhwein* in the micro and sit on the couch listening to Christmas carols and wishing CM was coming home.

## · six ·

In spite of the red-and-green intarsia sweater, or maybe because of it, Richard looks pale and angular, a prototype for one of his own buildings.

"Hello, Wyn. We're so glad you could come." When I hug him, he feels frail, just skin stretched over a set of bones. "We've got your old room fixed up for you."

I wonder briefly what that means. "I hope you didn't go to a lot of trouble."

My mother careens out of the kitchen holding a tray of glasses, door swinging in her wake. "Orange juice?" Her eyes glitter with forced brightness as her lips brush my cheek.

"How are you feeling?" I ask him.

"Pretty good." He smiles. "Especially considering the alternative. How's everything up north?"

"Oh, fine."

"I'm sorry your . . ." My mother hesitates. "Do they still call them boyfriends? Anyway, I'm sorry he couldn't come."

I laugh. "He's not a boy, and he's not my friend. You can call him Mac. He couldn't get enough days off."

"What does he do?" Richard asks.

"He's a bartender."

"That's an interesting job."

"You said he was a writer, too," my mother prompts me.

"Yes. He's just finished a novel."

"Does he have an agent?" Richard sips at his juice. Deep lines fan out around his eyes—lines I don't remember seeing before.

"Someone's looking at it right now, I think."

"It's tough breaking into publishing." Richard crosses his arms. "You have to have the hide of a rhinoceros. Never give up. Jack London had a stack of rejections as tall as he was before he sold his first story."

*Thanks for sharing.*

"But I'm sure Mac knows that," my mother says quickly.

"Is he a Seattle native?"

"Actually, he's from New York."

"Really? Where did he go to school?"

"NYU."

"I know some people there. Did he go through the creative writing program?"

"Actually, he dropped out after his sophomore year." That lays a big, silent egg.

"Does his family still live in New York?"

"His father's dead. His mother lives on Long Island, I believe. And his brother's a lawyer. I think."

I stare at the Christmas tree, a flocked one. Lots of the tiny white twinkle lights that are so trendy now. I don't see any of our old ornaments. All these are made of metal or glass. My father would have hated it. The presents piled underneath are all wrapped in silver or gold with professional-looking bows or clusters of metallic stars and pinecones.

I drain my orange juice glass and stand up. "I'm really kind of tired. If it's okay, I'd like to take a nap."

"Of course." My mother sounds relieved. "I'll get you up in plenty of time for dinner."

Richard stops halfway out of his chair, remembering that he can't carry my bag upstairs for me. "I'm sorry." He flushes deeply. "I'm pretty useless right now."

His echo of Mac's words is downright creepy.

I smile. "That's okay. I'm used to slinging fifty-pound sacks of flour."

When I drag my suitcase up the stairs and flip on the light in my room, my stomach contracts. It's all gone. Everything that was mine. The place looks like some anonymous hotel room. An upscale hotel, to be sure, but it certainly doesn't look like my room.

It's all done in gray and white. My bed has been replaced with one of those daybed things that can be used as a couch. It's made up with gray-and-white pin-striped sheets, a white knitted blanket, and a charcoal gray spread, turned back. The only color comes from a solid red, square decorator pillow. There's a brushed-steel-and-glass table next to it that my ex-husband would love. A Tizio lamp and a clear glass vase that looks like a goldfish bowl, filled with red and purple anemones. The walls are upholstered in gray flannel and all my pictures are gone, my bulletin board replaced with black-and-white architectural photographs in black frames.

"Isn't it snazzy?" My mother is standing next to me, obviously proud of the transformation.

"It's great." I don't look at her. "So where's all my stuff?"

"Most of it's in a couple of boxes in the closet. I thought you might—"

"Most?"

"Well, some of the newspaper clippings on the bulletin board just disintegrated when Richard took them down, so he had to throw them out."

I swallow.

"He tried to save everything." She lays her hand on my arm. "But some of it was so old..."

I turn to her. "It's okay. I didn't expect you to keep it like a shrine."

I settle my bag on the chrome-and-black luggage rack, unzip the top and fold it back, resting it against the soft gray wall. I'm only half-listening to her saying she'll wake me in an hour, telling me where to find the towels. She sits down on the edge of the bed, one leg tucked up under her long, black gabardine skirt. The evergreen cotton sweater accentuates the differences in her coloring and mine, makes her hair look even darker and her skin like porcelain.

"What's the status with your divorce? Seems like it should be coming to some kind of conclusion by now."

"Oh, it is," I say vaguely. "Elizabeth is out of the office. I think she's skiing in Austria or something. Of course that didn't stop her bills from going out on time. I'm going to give her a call right after the first."

She clasps her hands together around one knee. "You haven't told me much about Mac." I glance at her, trying to gauge exactly what kind of information she's looking for.

"He's ... very different from David—"

"Johanna?" Richard calls from the foot of the stairs.

"Be right down." She stands up and kisses me on the cheek. "Get some rest. We'll talk later."

I wake up at four-thirty feeling stale and groggy. I turn the shower on hot, filling the bathroom with steam, and stand under, letting water rain down on my back. By the time I've pulled on jeans and a sweater and brushed out my hair, it's nearly six. I decide to forego makeup.

Perfumed with good food smells, the whole downstairs is an echo chamber of memories. There's a fire burning in the fireplace, but no one's in the den, so I shoulder through the swinging door to the kitchen and come face-to-face with one of my grossest lapses in judgment.

Gary lounges against the counter, sipping something out of one of those retro martini glasses that are suddenly back in vogue. Why am I so surprised? After all, he's Richard's son.

"Wyn!" When he kisses my cheek, I catch the drift of his subtly expensive cologne and a hint of gin. "You look terrific. Smell nice, too."

"So do you." It is the truth. Domesticity agrees with him. His sandy brown hair keeps getting shorter, his eyes seem bluer, his teeth more perfect, except for that endearing little chipped incisor that gives him the look of the roguish but essentially solid intern on a doctor-drama TV show.

He looks at me over the rim of his glass. "You obviously didn't know I was coming."

"Um, no. I didn't, but I probably should have." I open the cupboard where my mother used to keep wineglasses and it's full of liquor bottles. Well, of course. Richard's rearranged everything else in the damn house. Why not the kitchen? "Do you know where the wineglasses might be?"

He moves unerringly to the cupboard next to the fridge. "Red or white?"

"Red, please."

He hands me an outsized bowl of a glass.

"Suppose I just want a drink, not a bath?"

He pulls the stopper from a crystal decanter and half-fills my glass with the garnet-colored wine.

"How are Erica and . . . the kids?" I'm embarrassed that I can't remember their names. The soccer star and the cheerleader princess.

"They're fine. Andrew and Katie are in a school pageant tonight." He pronounces their names slowly and clearly for me. "I just came down to check on Dad, then I'm taking the red-eye back after dinner."

I don't know whether I'm relieved or disappointed that I'll be having Christmas alone with my mother and Richard.

There's a lengthy silence while I try to do the wine-connoisseur thing, swirling the wine in the glass so enthusiastically that it just misses sloshing over the rim. "So where are the parental units?"

"In the wine cellar."

"Wine cellar?"

"Otherwise known as the garage." He smiles. "How's Mac?"

For a minute my brain stumbles. Then I recall their brief accidental meeting when I was post-op and confined to my house. But how did he know I was seeing Mac now?

"That's who you're with, isn't it? The guy I met at your house. The bartender."

Maybe I'm imagining the dismissive tone. "Don't forget, he delivers firewood, too."

He gives me a careful look. "I'm sorry. I didn't mean—"

"No, it's okay." I take a big gulp of wine. "I'm just crabby and tired. I had to work all night and then get on the plane and—"

"I remember." He stirs the impaled olive around in his drink. It reminds me of the first time he came to Seattle. Drinking vodka martinis in the bar at Canlis. "Are you happy?"

"Very." It's automatic and too bright. But what am I supposed to say—my boyfriend's acting weird, my lawyer's in Austria, and I can't afford a pot to pee in, but other than that, everything's dandy? "And you?"

He smiles. "Yeah. The kids are great. I like us being a family again."

At that moment the back door opens and my mother appears, carrying a bottle of champagne. Richard follows with a bottle of red and one of white.

"Hello, you two," he says heartily. As if we were a couple. My mother smiles, but doesn't meet my eyes.

"Let's go in by the fire," she says. "I'll bring the hors d'oeuvres. Does everyone have what they want to drink?"

I want to stay in the kitchen with her, but she shoos me out, and I trail into the den just in time to see Richard lower himself into my father's leather chair.

Okay, fifteen Christmases have come and gone since he died, and yes, other people have sat there in the interim. But watching Richard claim it now, not thinking—maybe not even knowing—sends a tiny jab under my ribs. I sit down on the opposite end of the couch from Gary.

My mother appears moments later with a silver tray of crostini. They're hot and crisp, rubbed with garlic, brushed with olive oil, and topped with a bare sprinkling of sea salt. This from the woman who once served pitted black olives and Smokehouse almonds before all but the most elaborate dinners.

"Merry Christmas, everyone." Richard lifts his fishbowl-sized goblet of red.

Gary tells us about the growing pains of his valet-parking company, Katie's grades—straight As, naturally—Andrew's swimming prowess and how he's decided he wants to be called Drew, and Erica's workload at law school, more than I ever wanted to know. Richard and my mother listen raptly. All I can think of is how much I don't want to be here.

I picture Mac, standing behind the bar at Bailey's, shirtsleeves rolled up, towel in his back pocket. The way he looks at me sometimes when he thinks I'm submerged in my book. Sort of a pensive look. As if he's wondering how all this happened with us and what I really want from him.

I used to watch the women flirt with him, before. I'm sure a lot of them still do when I'm not there. A couple of the more brazen ones don't care whether I'm there or not. I think about being in his bed, the way he smells like pine trees, the salt on his skin. Before I can stop the thought, I'm imagining someone else with him. Of course he'd be honest with her, tell her about me—he's big on people making informed choices. But would he tell me, so I could make an informed choice? He doesn't really tell me much of anything. Okay, we have conversations. I tell him what I think and how I feel, and he tells me about dark matter and pygmy owls and the geology of the Grand Canyon.

Lately I find myself reflecting him, telling him less about how I feel and what I think, more about things I've read or seen. So in the relationship—oops, can't use the *r* word, he doesn't like it. I asked him what we should call it then, and he said, *Why do we have to call it anything? Can't we just be?*—so in this *being* that we're doing here, he really hasn't changed, but I have. I've come full circle from being a stranger to being an intimate, and back to being a stranger. While he's always been a stranger. And why do I suspect him of seeing other women? He's never given me any reason to think that.

Ironic that David was practically wearing a sandwich board that said *I'm cheating!* and I never suspected, but Mac seems reasonably committed—oops, bad word number two—and I'm always expecting Laura, his old girlfriend, to pop up. Or somebody new. Somebody I don't know about yet.

For dinner there's baked chicken and acorn squash and my mother's homemade applesauce. Then salad with bread and cheese, and having the salad afterward reminds me of my mother's friend Georgia Graebel, who always gets such a charge out of "eating French."

"How are Georgia and Tim?" I ask my mother, and the look on her face is somewhere between amused and perplexed.

"Funny you should ask," she says. "Georgia called me last week to tell me they're splitting up."

I nearly inhale a piece of romaine. *"What?"*

Georgia's husband, Tim, who worked with my father, is an inveterate womanizer. In fact, he holds the distinction of being the only man to ever hit on both me and my mother. Georgia's known about his extracurricular activities for years, but she seemed to have perfected the art of turning a blind eye.

"So is he leaving her for some nineteen-year-old in a fishnet jumpsuit, or did she get fed up and kick him out?"

I can tell my mother wants to smile, but thinks she shouldn't. "Neither, actually. Georgia met a man—a retired English professor—at her literacy program. They fell in love and she's divorcing Tim and marrying Phillip."

I let out a very undignified whoop. "Wow, there *is* a god. And she's a woman."


"Why didn't you tell me Gary was coming?" I hiss at my mother as soon as the kitchen door closes behind us.

"I was afraid you wouldn't come," she says simply.

"Oh, Mom." I open the dishwasher. "How could you think that?"

She sets the dessert plates, still streaked with orange sauce, into the sink and turns on the water. "I know it's not a lot of fun for you coming back here. I know how much you still miss your dad. And I'm sure you'd rather be with Mac than sitting around listening to Gary drone on about valet parking..." She rolls her eyes and we both giggle.

She starts rinsing dishes and loading them into the dishwasher while I pour some more wine in my glass.

"Want some?" I hold up the bottle.

"No thanks—oh, what the hell. Hit me—or however they say it." She fills a bowl with soapy water and begins to wash the sterling flatware. I open a drawer. Slam it shut, open another.

"Damnit, I can't find anything around here anymore. Where are the towels?"

She laughs. "I know. Richard's terrible about rearranging things. If it's this bad now, I can imagine what it's going to be like when he retires."

When I pull open the bottom drawer and yank out a towel, something heavy clunks. My oma's rolling pin. I lift it out and run my hand down the satiny maple. Traces of flour from a long-ago piecrust linger in a hairline crack.

"I think my pie-baking days are over. Why don't you take it with you?" My mother smiles.

"Thanks. I will." I put my arm around her shoulders for a second.

She rinses each piece of silver in scalding-hot water, so hot I can barely hold it even with the towel. My oma used to do the same thing, to kill all the germs, she always said. I dry each piece, polishing it with the flour-sack dish towel, and laying it on the table to be returned to the flannel-lined box.

She rinses the last of the silver, then starts on the crystal water goblets. "I was going to tell you about Gary when I went up to wake you. I didn't mean for it to be a shock."

"It wasn't exactly a shock. It was just kind of weird. Like déjà vu."

She nods and moves things around in the drainer to make room for more crystal. "He looks good. I guess he and Erica are happy."

"Whatever."

"He sure seemed crazy about you for a while there." She gives me an analytical glance.

I shrug. "I think he was just lonely. He was mostly crazy about the nuclear-family lifestyle."

"It's not such a terrible fate, you know." She empties the soapy water, rinses the bowl, and sets it upside down in the drainer. Steam rises to fog the cold window. "Just leave that, honey." She pulls off her yellow dishwashing gloves, lays them over the faucet, and dusts her hands together in exaggerated Western style. "Well, Tonto, it looks like our work here is done."

I laugh and start for the door, but she picks up the decanter of red wine and refills both our glasses. Then she sits down at the kitchen table.

"Don't you want to go out there with—" I begin.

"They can entertain themselves." She flashes a mischievous smile. "I don't think I can take any more cheerleader stories tonight."

I sit down across from her and ease my feet out of my shoes.

"Now don't be mad at me, I have to ask." She touches my hand with her warm, smooth fingers. "Does Mac make you happy? Is he good to you? Because if he's not, I'm going to fly up there and punch him in the nose."

Sudden tears sting my eyes. I'm not sure if it's this vaguely unsettled feeling I have about Mac, or her earnest protectiveness.

*Is he good to me?* I've never even thought about him in those terms. He's not bad to me.

I take a slow sip of wine. "Do you think it's worth it?"

She doesn't question what I'm asking about. "Oh, honey. Worth is such a relative thing. Sometimes you want something so badly that whether it's worth it or not doesn't matter."

"Was it like that with Daddy?"

"I just remember thinking that I could be completely ruthless. That I'd do anything it took to hold on. Was it worth it? I think so, but you never know for sure."

"Mac is very . . . self-contained. We can have these great, long conversations about ideas and books and music, and afterward . . ." I hesitate. "I sometimes feel like I was doing most of the—I guess I feel like I'm showing myself to him, and he doesn't reciprocate."

She frowns. "Do you know anything about his childhood or his parents or—"

"His father's dead. He doesn't communicate with his mother or brother."

"At all?"

"As far as I can tell. He doesn't talk about that—his family. If I ask him a direct question, he'll answer it as briefly as possible, and then go right on to something else."

"Wyn, are you sure he's . . . okay? There's a lot of wackos out there."

I laugh. "He's not a wacko. I think you'd like him. He's got this stillness inside. The way he can watch the ocean. Or listen to a song. As if nothing else exists. He doesn't just look at things; he really sees them."

My voice trails off and she sits back in the chair and looks at me.

"It sounds like that self-contained quality is the good news and the bad news."

"Sometimes it bothers me that he never has any money, and that he doesn't seem to care. He doesn't do the things most women expect. Like take me out for my birthday or call me and say he's thinking about me. But on the other hand, he never wants me to be anything other than what I am. I never feel like I have to prove anything to him. I don't need to perform."

"Do you love him?"

I set down my glass. "I know it's too soon."

"These things don't always occur according to schedules."

"All I know is, when we're together, I just . . . feel good. So good it's scary."

My mother smiles at me, crinkling the corners of her pretty brown eyes. "Life is scary, Wyn," she says. "If it's not, you're not doing it right."


Christmas morning. The clock says 5:20 A.M. I wish I was home. In Seattle, sleeping late, having cardamom coffee cake with CM, opening presents. Knowing I'd see Mac later, even though we wouldn't do the Christmas thing.

I slide out of bed. The house feels cold, so I pull on my sweats, stuff my feet into the big, fuzzy slippers that somehow escaped Richard's purge, and move soundlessly out onto the landing and down the stairs. They don't have an espresso maker, or even a stove-top espresso pot, but I can make the coffee extra muscular and heat up some milk. Hopefully they have real milk or, even better, half-and-half.

As I'm shuffling past the den, I'm startled to see a light under the door. I push the door and peer around it as it swings halfway open.

The hundreds of white twinkle lights on the tree are the room's only illumination. Richard is sitting on the floor, taking things out of a large box. His back is to me, so he can't see me, and I can't see exactly what he's doing. It feels awkward, sneaking up on him like this, so I pull the door almost shut and continue on to the kitchen.

My mother's automatic coffeemaker never gets the water hot enough for a proper brew, so I search in every cupboard till I find the old Melitta drip coffeepot that my father always used. No filters, of course, because the automatic one has a permanent filter. A paper towel will work. I fill the teakettle and set it on the stove, switch the setting on the grinder, and locate the coffee beans. Decaf? How am I supposed to stay awake till dinner? In the fridge there's skim milk and whipping cream. I can mix the two . . .

My oma's rolling pin is still on the table where I left it last night. I pick it up, stroke the fine grain. With all due respect to Lord Byron, I've always believed that much depends on breakfast. I open the pantry for a quick survey.

Flour, sugar, baking powder, salt. A bag of hazelnuts from Trader Joe's.

## Cappuccino Hazelnut Scones

2 cups unbleached all-purpose flour

⅓ cup granulated sugar

1 tablespoon baking powder

½ teaspoon salt

¼ teaspoon cinnamon

3 ounces (6 tablespoons) butter, very cold, cut into small cubes

¾ cup toasted, coarsely chopped hazelnuts

2 tablespoons instant espresso powder

¾ cup heavy cream

1 large egg, lightly beaten

Cream and sugar for glaze

*Preheat the oven to 400°F and line a heavy baking sheet with parchment paper. In a large bowl, whisk together the first five ingredients. Cut in the butter with a pastry blender, two table knives, or your fingertips until the largest pieces are about the size of peas. Add the hazelnuts and toss to combine.*

*In a small bowl, stir the espresso powder into the cream until dissolved, add the egg just to blend. Add all at once to the flour mixture and stir with a large fork, until just barely combined. Finish by kneading gently with your hands until all the dry ingredients are absorbed and the dough can be gathered into a moist, shaggy ball. Do not overknead. Tenderness comes from minimal handling.*

*Set the ball in the center of the prepared baking sheet and pat gently into a round about 1 to 1½ inches thick and about 7 inches in diameter. With a sharp knife, cut into eight wedges, and gently separate slightly. Brush generously with cream and sprinkle with 1 to 2 teaspoons of granulated sugar.*

*Bake until the scones are deep golden and a toothpick inserted into the center comes out clean, about 18 to 22 minutes. Let cool 10 minutes before serving. (These can be frozen, unbaked, and baked without thawing; just allow 5 to 10 extra minutes of baking time.)*

I turn the oven on and pour some hazelnuts into a shallow pan. I take my mother's chef's knife out of the knife block and start cutting the cube of butter into small chunks. While I'm whisking the dry ingredients together, the swinging door snaps open. "Wyn, I didn't realize you were up, too. Merry Christmas."

Richard is wearing a plaid flannel bathrobe and leather slippers. His dark hair is perfectly groomed, but he's unshaven and looks tired. The thought freezes me. If my father were alive, he would be sixty-one now. He would look like this, not the way I remember him—forty-five, tall, tan, and pulsing with energy.

Richard takes in the Melitta, my cup, then the automatic. "Is there something wrong with the coffeemaker?"

I smile politely. "Only that it doesn't make good coffee."

"Oh. Sorry. You probably don't drink decaf, either. I think your mother got some regular for you—"

"This is fine, honestly. Would you like some?"

"That sounds great. What are you making?"

"Scones."

"I love scones. I'm not supposed to eat them right now, but I think one on Christmas morning probably won't hurt. What do you think?" He gives me a conspiratorial smile.

Swell. If I don't think he should eat one, I'll look mean and self-ish, and if I do think so, it'll look like I'm trying to kill him. "I think..." I fumble for words. "I think pretty much anything is okay in moderation."

"My sentiments exactly."

An awkward silence fills the kitchen. I have no idea what to say to this man who is now my stepfather. And he apparently doesn't know what to say to me, either.

He goes first.

"Johanna's told me how close you were to your dad."

"Yes. I was." I wish he'd just go back to whatever he was doing and leave me alone. He pours nonfat milk in his coffee cup and nukes it for a few seconds before pouring in the coffee.

"I hate putting cold milk in coffee," he says.

"Yeah, me, too." I push the butter off the knife into a small dish and put it in the freezer.

"What's the rationale behind freezing the butter?"

"It makes the scones flakier." Heat blasts out of the oven as I open the door to put the nuts in. In less than a minute, the warm smell of toasting hazelnuts fills the kitchen.

Richard takes little sips of his coffee. "Wynter, I know how hard it is to come back to a place you love and see it altered almost be-yond recognition."

I set the timer for the nuts and turn to him. "Howard, I appreciate your concern, but everything's fine. I don't live here anymore; you do. The bedroom is beautiful, and a lot more functional than it was with my junk all over the place."

He's giving me an odd look, and I suddenly understand that it's because I just called him Howard. My face flares.

"Howard?" he says.

"I'm really sorry."

"That's okay. I was just wondering why Howard?"

I turn on the hot water in the sink, wash and dry the knife. "If you really want to know...I..." I press my lips together. "Did you ever read *The Fountainhead*?"

He starts to laugh. "Howard Roark. That's great." He laughs again, and then I laugh, too.

When the timer dings, I pull the nuts out and turn the oven up to 400. Richard puts the kettle on for more coffee.

"My first wife died when Gary was ten."

"I'm sorry. I'm sure it was hard..."

"It was very sudden. A brain aneurysm. She was fine and then she was dead. She was..." He looks at me for a few seconds. "Just about the age you are now." He stops talking while I grind more beans. "I was thirty-five, and I was totally devastated. Also totally incompetent at raising my son. Well, pretty incompetent at doing much of anything for a very long time."

"What was her name?"

"Gabrielle. Of course, we called her Gabby." It still makes him smile.

He pours boiling water over the ground coffee and we stand side by side watching it slowly settle into the pot below.

"Much as I would have liked to remarry, for Gary to have a mother, I just never could bring myself to do it." He turns his head slowly toward me. "Until I met Johanna. She..." He pauses. "Is a very special woman."

"Then why did you have to change everything about her?" It

comes out spontaneously, and I almost regret it when I see the look of hurt surprise on his face.

"What do you mean?"

I'm treading on shaky ground here, but this has been on my mind for a long time. "Her hair, her clothes. The whole house."

"I had nothing to do with her change of hairstyle and clothes, Wynter." He leans one elbow on the kitchen counter. "I think maybe that was something she'd wanted to do for a while. Being with me might have been the catalyst, but the decisions were all hers." He smiles. "I think you underestimate your mother if you imagine that anyone could bulldoze her into doing anything she didn't want to do. In fact, that's one of the things I noticed about her immediately, the way she took charge of that office . . ."

All at once I feel silly. No, worse than that. I feel like a petulant six-year-old.

"Sorry. It was none of my business anyway."

"As for the house . . . maybe I did push for some changes there, but I think Johanna was happy with the new direction."

"Probably. It doesn't matter." I grab the sponge and start wiping up the miniscule spill of hot water on the counter.

The coffee grounds go in the compost bucket, and Richard refills both our cups. "When you get the scones in, why don't you come in the den," he says. "There are some things I wanted to show you."

Inside the large box are two smaller boxes, one of which I recognize immediately. Christmas tree ornaments. The ones I made in school, like the paper-plate Santa face. The buckram angel, wings glittery with glued-on sequins. The cotton-ball snowman and woman. The felt Raggedy Ann. The cut-out photographs of my mother and father, pasted on cardboard.

There, too, are the ornaments that belonged to my oma and opa—the delicate glass birds with tails made of real feathers; tiny silver bells, engraved with their initials; wax images of the holy family, brushed with gilt; dolls and animals woven from straw; and carved horses and soldiers. There are my mother's painted eggs and origami birds, the Tour Eiffel that my father brought back from a trip to Paris, the tin whistle from his childhood.

The other box, of course, holds Gary's handiwork. Richard and I laugh because it includes the same cotton-ball snowman and paper-plate Santa. His box includes a string of those old candle lights with the perpetual rising bubbles and a lot of doily snowflakes and painted tin cutouts from New Mexico. We unwrap them all and spread them out on the coffee table, telling each other the stories of each one, and when my mother wanders in sleepily an hour later, Richard and I are nibbling on our scones and hanging the relics on the flocked tree, on top of the pristine glass balls and shiny metal stars.

· seven ·

Lit up in the dark, L.A. looks like the vast motherboard of a very unwieldy computer. The chimes ring—I've never figured out what they're for—and I sip my wine, wondering what kind of germs I'm inhaling from all the recirculated air. I feel tired and inexplicably sad, suddenly vulnerable to unseen dangers, of which hostile microbes are only the least.

I should be happy. It was a pretty decent Christmas, the first in recent memory. There was a sort of wobbly rapprochement between Richard and me. My mother and I actually talked about our lives. And stuffed in my carry-on bag is the Christmas present of my dreams—in fact, beyond my dreams. I was nearly speechless when I ripped open the envelope and found a round-trip ticket to Paris, with a connection to Toulouse, purchased using frequent-flyer freebies— Richard's, I'm sure, because my mother hasn't traveled enough lately to earn a free ticket to Burbank.

"We thought you could use a real vacation this summer," she explained after I stammered my undying gratitude. The thrill lasted just long enough for me to realize that I'll be going alone, because there's no way Mac can afford to go.

A cold, dark current circulates around me, like the air-conditioning on this damn freezing plane. I pull my jacket closer, tuck my hands under my arms. I change the channel of "in-flight entertainment" from jazz to opera just in time to catch Victoria de Los Angeles singing "Habañera," from Carmen. *L'amour est un oiseau rebelle.* "Love is a rebellious bird that no one can tame. Love is a gypsy child." My favorite line is "If you don't love me, then I love you, but if I love you, then watch out!"

When I close my eyes, I see—not Mac—Gary. Leaning against the kitchen counter, looking like the boy next door. The thing I recall about him now—in stark contrast to Mac—is his openness. He was always so forthcoming with his feelings, his own story. It probably would have been fairly painless to settle into a life with him. At the time, I was sneering at painless, but it might not be such a bad deal—a man who loves you, a nice man, let's not forget. Attractive. No shortage of cash. You could learn to live with stepchildren and ex-wives. People do it all the time.

*God, what am I thinking? It would have been painless, all right. Like being under anesthesia.*

I finish the wine and lean my head back against the scratchy white pillow, and what seems like three minutes later we bump and skid onto the rain-slicked Sea-Tac runway.

The air in the terminal doesn't smell much better than that on the plane, but at least it's not freezing. I told CM not to bother coming in, to just pick me up outside baggage claim. I push forward out of the crush, hurrying to break away from the press of bodies.

"Hey, lady. Need a taxi?"

I wheel around, already smiling stupidly, and there he is. Wearing the Black Watch plaid flannel shirt and jeans and his old down vest. Holding the most exquisite rose I've ever seen. Its petals are a pale salmon color on the outside, a warm shade of parchment on the inside. He holds it out to me.

"It's gorgeous. I've never seen one like that." It has a light, spicy fragrance.

"It's called a Caramella," he says.

I look around. "Where's CM?"

"I gave her the night off." When he kisses me he smells like the rainy night. "How was everything down south?"

"It was good. Better than I expected." For once, I don't feel like talking. I just want to soak him up. While we wait for the bags to come down, he puts his arm around my shoulders, pulling me against his side, and I look up into his gaze.

"I should have gone with you," he says.

I shake my head. "You probably couldn't have gotten off."

"Maybe. But I didn't try. I'm sorry."

The look he gives me at that moment is more than just an apology. It's a look that promises something. I'm not even sure what, but it's enough.


Mac has to work on New Year's Eve, having traded with Kenny so he could pick me up at the airport. It's just as well. CM and I have a long-standing tradition of spending New Year's Eve listening to oldies, eating good food, and drinking champagne until we are able to recall and perform the lyrics and choreography to all of the Supremes' greatest hits.

By the time our soup is simmering, the rain's turned to sleet. We hear it making little splats on the windows. We're starting out slow, with a Dave Brubeck tape, and I've just put some phyllo pastries with mushrooms and feta cheese into the oven to fill the role of hors d'oeuvres. The buzzer rings.

"Who the hell . . ." CM goes to the squawk box. "Yes?"

"W-Wyn? It's me. Tyler. Can I come up?"

CM buzzes her in and I open the door. On the landing is a wet, shivering mass of sleet and tears, looking like a drowned blue rat. "Tyler?" I grab her and pull her in. "What the hell are you doing?" She's shaking too hard to discuss it.

We drag her to the bathroom, strip her down, and get her under a cool shower, gradually raising the water temperature till she warms up enough to stop shivering. CM goes to make a cup of tea while I rummage through my drawers looking for some clothing she won't get lost in. Then simultaneously I smell smoke and the smoke detector starts emitting its piercing squawk.

"Oh shit!" CM says.

"What?"

"Our hors d'oeuvres look like they've been napalmed. Phew." She's opening the windows, fanning frantically.

When I take Tyler my smallest sweatshirt and some tights, she looks stricken. "Did I screw up your dinner?"

"Oh, don't worry. It was just snacks. Here. Put these on and then come out by the fire."

She wanders out, waiflike in my oversized clothes. She sits on the floor by the fireplace, takes a sip of the hot tea, and makes a face.

"This tastes like baby piss."

"You're welcome, I'm sure," says CM. "For your information, it's green tea and it just might keep you from catching pneumonia."

Tyler buries her nose in the mug, chastened, and keeps sneaking looks at CM, whom she's never seen up close and personal.

Finally I say, "Not to be nosy or anything, but what were you doing strolling around in the sleet on New Year's Eve?"

She mumbles into the tea, something that sounds like, "... asshole threw me out."

"What? Your dad?"

She shakes her head. "My date. We were going to this party and we had a fight and he threw me out of the car."

"Who is this paragon of chivalry?" CM asks.

Tyler giggles. "She talks like you."

"She isn't royalty; she just looks like it. Feel free to address her directly."

She looks at CM. "Jason Harris. He's a friend of my friend DeeDee's boyfriend. It was sort of a blind date."

"What was the argument about?"

"I wanted to go to Barton's party. He wanted to go get high and fuck."

CM rolls her eyes. "Ah, the answer to a maiden's prayer."

"Where did you and he part company?" I ask.

"Over by Olympia Pizza."

"You walked over here from there? Why didn't you take the bus?" She looks sheepish. "I left my purse in his car."

The timer starts buzzing for the new batch of phyllo bites, and I go to retrieve them. "Tyler, you want some champagne?"

"Don't we have to wait till midnight?"

"Not in this house."

"Cool."


On January 5 I call Elizabeth Gooden, my attorney in Los Angeles. I ask politely about her vacation.

"It was lovely, thanks. You know, you're the only one of my clients who's even asked."

I consider telling her that the others probably don't want to know how she's spending their money, but I figure that would nullify all the points I just made with her.

"How are you?" she says.

"Well, if you disregard the fact that there's another payment coming due on the bakery as of February first, and I still haven't paid my mother back the fifteen grand she loaned me as the first payment, well, then you could say I'm fine. I guess what I'm wondering is what my ex-husband-pending and his scumbag lawyer are doing with the paperwork."

"I've had an indication that we can expect an agreement soon, so I'm trying my best to chase Ivan down, but he hasn't returned my phone calls. I'm sorry my news isn't any better, but I don't see any reason why it should take longer than a few more weeks."

"Weeks? God, what am I supposed to do for money in the meantime?"

"I don't know, Wynter. If you recall, last year at this time, you were telling me to stall. To drag it out as long as possible, so for quite a while, that's just what I did. Then you changed your mind, and I changed my approach, but I can't do anything about their response, as long as it's within acceptable parameters."

There's not much I can say to that, since every word is the gospel truth. I even remember her saying to me, *She who seeks revenge should dig two graves, Wynter—one for her victim and one for herself.*

"I know. I'm just in a tight situation here. Monetarily."

"Well, I'm going to continue to do everything I can to bring this case to a swift and satisfactory conclusion for you, Wynter. I'll let you know just as soon as I hear something." She pauses. "Oh, and happy New Year."

It's the kind of day that's rare in Seattle in January. Which is a good thing, because if they happened too often, the rest of the outside world might discover the city and come swarming up here.

The sky is an inverted bowl of blue tracked by white contrails, and there's a gentle westerly breeze. The sun is warm on my face and I know I'm going to have a whole new crop of freckles, but it feels so good I don't care.

The other reason I feel good is that my mother told me not to worry about the fifteen thousand dollars I owe her, and she didn't even blink when I swallowed my pride and asked for another fifteen. In fact, she just made that little clicking noise she learned from my oma, and said, "David Franklin just better hope I never see him standing in a crosswalk."

Mac's in a really good mood because he finally heard from Alan

Lear, the agent who's been reading his manuscript. He said that he liked the work, although he couldn't take on any new clients right now, but he was passing the manuscript on to his new partner, a guy named Steve Devine. So we're sort of celebrating today.

We've occupied a tiny table in front of Two Dagos from Texas, a funky Italian café down on First Avenue, where we're having lunch. Mac's immersed in *Bonfire of the Vanities* and I'm watching the parade of assorted odd birds that nest here in Belltown.

You've got your starving-artist loft dwellers, your merchant marine contingent, thrift-shop patrons, the usual homeless, a few punkers who frequent the music clubs and retro shops, and an occasional yuppie resident of the high-rise condo and apartment buildings that are just beginning to sprout around the district's fringes.

If you sit here long enough, you can see almost anything, so at first I don't pay any attention to the bedraggled-looking guy slouching down the sidewalk, hands jammed into his pockets.

Until he gets right in front of our table and stares hard. "McLeod?" he says. Then louder, "Mac McLeod?"

For a second they stare at each other. A slow grin breaks across Mac's face.

"Son of a bitch." He closes the book and stands up and then he and this guy who looks like he spent the night on a park bench in Pioneer Square are shaking hands and pounding each other on the back. And then they actually hug each other. All I can think of is that this must be somebody pretty special, because I can smell him from four feet away, and hugging him would not be an option for me.

He isn't as tall as Mac, but he's sturdy looking and deeply tanned. His hair is long, stringy, and dirty blond, his eyes a deep, strange gray. "Holy shit, pilgrim. I heard you might be in Seattle, but I can't believe I just stumbled over you like this. How the hell are you?"

"Good. What about you?" Then he remembers me. "Oh, sorry. Wyn, this is Nick Hatcher. Wyn Morrison."

A hand is thrust under my nose, and I have to shake it, but I make a mental note not to eat anything else till I can go to the john and scrub.

Mac grabs a vacant chair and pulls it over to our table. When Nick Hatcher scoots up so close that his knee is almost touching mine, I try to identify the smell—week-old roadkill? Suddenly the rest of my blue-cheese turkey burger seems a lot less appealing, so the hand-washing thing becomes less urgent.

I try to be subtle as I check out every detail of his appearance, from the run-over loafers on his dirty feet, to his grimy cords that are ripped in both knees, to the faded Grateful Dead world-tour T-shirt stretched over his well-developed biceps. His hands, besides being estranged from soap and water for some time, are scraped and bruised, and his ragged fingernails look as if he's been digging in road tar.

"What are you doing here?" Mac asks.

"Provisioning, man." He leans his elbows on the table. "I'm meeting Duncan and Meeker in Spokane and we're going up to do some ice in the North Cascades. Then, I don't know, maybe head up to B.C. this summer. What are you doing here?"

"I live here. Going on seven years."

Nick's eyes slide briefly over to me, but he doesn't ask. "Well, you're looking mighty prosperous. What's your gig?"

"Tending bar, mostly."

Mac doesn't ask what Nick's into. Instead, for the next twenty minutes they sit around reminiscing like fraternity brothers at a reunion. And it quickly becomes clear that the fraternity they belong to is the brotherhood of rock climbing. They talk about people they've known. Lots of them have funny names, like Pooper or Sodbuster. I don't think I want to know.

At least one is no longer among the living.

They relive tense moments at places called Wingate and Garden of the Gods and Lumpy Ridge, and the parties afterward. They laugh about somebody named Dude trying to talk a topless dancer into going rock climbing, and the time Charlie's stove blew up on the miniscule ledge where he was bivouacked.

The waiter comes out and asks if I'm through. I nod, but when he starts to pick up my plate, Nick eyes the uneaten half of my sandwich. "You mind?" he says rhetorically. He wolfs it down in three bites and sits contentedly picking turkey out of his teeth.

Nick talks about climbing at the "Gunks," whatever that is, and about a freak blizzard last June in the Wind River range. He says he's more into alpining these days, likes ice, is thinking seriously about Alaska. Then he looks at Mac.

"But what about you, pilgrim? You're right here in the middle of hard-rock heaven. Where do you go? Leavenworth? Washington Pass? I heard Frenchman Coulee was awesome."

Mac looks across the street, then back at Nick. "I haven't been on rock in a while. Not since I came here."

I can't tell if Nick is surprised. He hesitates for a second. "Well, shit, McLeod. You need to get your ass back on the granite. Why don't you take a few days this spring and hook up with us in the North Cascades? Wouldn't that be a gas!" For some reason he looks at me. "Just like the old days."

Mac smiles. "Hard to get enough days off to make it worthwhile. You know how it is."

Hatcher gives an overly hearty laugh. "Yeah, that's the trouble with real work. You gotta learn to say no to that shit. It'll ruin your life if you let it." He gets up abruptly and Mac does, too, and they shake hands again.

"Where you working? I'll stop by before I head out."

He scribbles down Mac's directions to Bailey's on a clean napkin, and then he shuffles off the way he was headed and I can breathe through my nose again.

Mac picks up the book, and reads the same page for about five minutes before he finally looks over at me.

"A blast from the past," he says.

"Way past. Like the cretaceous era," I say. "You think he's doing controlled substances?"

He laughs. "Hard-core climbers tend to forget about the niceties of grooming. There've been times when I probably looked and smelled exactly like that."

"Like when you delivered my firewood."

He smiles and looks back at the book. He drinks some of his Coke, which by now sports a layer of melted ice on top. Finally he shuts the book and lays it on the table.

"A bunch of us used to hang out together in Colorado. Seems like a long time ago. I guess it was. About ten years. We were all essentially ski bums in the winter, rock bums in the summer. We waited tables, did construction—whatever we had to do to eat, but mostly we just skied and climbed."

"So why haven't you been rock climbing since you came here?"

He slides the glass around in its puddle of condensation. "Because if I was still climbing, I'd probably look like Nick Hatcher. It's not something you can do one weekend a month. Not the kind of climbing I liked. It becomes your life and you can't do anything else. You've got to keep up the practice to stay sharp. And if you don't stay sharp, someday you end up doing a free solo rappel."

"What's that?"

"A grounder."

"Oh."


February passes as one big, gray, wet blur. Every day is either cloudy or foggy or misty or pouring rain or some combination of the above. It doesn't get light in the morning till eight or so and it's dark by five. The only good thing about the weather is that it gives everybody something to talk about. I lose count of all the stories I hear that begin, *You think this is bad, you should've been here in the winter of* ———. Fill in the blank with your year of choice.

On the cusp of the month, Elizabeth calls. When she says, "Wynter, I have some news for you," I know immediately that this isn't the call I was hoping for.

"David has apparently fired Ivan Hochnauer and hired a different attorney, a woman by the name of Adele King. I've spoken with her, and she will, of course, need some time to get up to speed with the case."

"How much is 'some time'?"

"I'd say we're probably looking at two months before we can expect a settlement."

I want to lie down and kick my heels on the floor and scream. Instead, I say, "He's doing this on purpose."

"Chances are good," she says.

"What can we do?"

"Nothing at the moment. We have to allow her time to prepare. I'll be in touch."

Poverty looms in my rearview mirror. And it's gaining on me.


By the end of March, the days are noticeably longer, and there are signs that spring might be circling for a landing. Crocuses and snowdrops push up through the dank black earth, yellow and purple and white. Pale green lanterns of hellebore glow in the deep shade. Airy yellow forsythia. The flowering cherry trees that line Queen Street shed their blossoms in drifts of white.

Tulip trees are in full bloom. Ellen calls them magnolias, and technically they are. My father never liked them because they don't look like much the rest of the year, but to me, they're more than worth it for that brief interlude in spring when the creamy white or pale pink or deep pink blooms cover the bare branches, looking like a huge bouquet of tulips.

One of the houses on Galer that I pass every morning has an arbor at the gate covered with early sweet peas in lilac and hot pink. I always slow down when I walk past, lingering in the heady scent.

But the night wind is still cold and sharp and wet.


Just a twinge. When I roll over it pulls me back toward consciousness, but not all the way. Must have been sleeping with my arm bent weird or something. At three-thirty in the afternoon I get up and shower, and while I'm brushing my teeth, it happens again. A tiny, darting pain in my right wrist, so quick and then gone. Maybe I imagined it.

But I start tiptoeing around it anyway. I move my arm, hand, fingers deliberately and carefully. No sudden twists. It seems okay.

I hear CM on the landing, fumbling with the keys, so I go to let her in, and when I turn the doorknob, my wrist buzzes me like an angry bee.

She pushes past me, setting a cardboard carton full of dance shoes on the floor by the couch, shrugging out of her trench coat, hanging it on the brass hook behind the door. "Brrr. It's getting cold out there. Shall I make a fire? What should we eat? Is Mac coming over?"

I'm frowning at my wrist, rotating it, bending it back and forth. "No, he's delivering wood and then going right to Bailey's. We have some vegetable soup and I brought home a loaf of garlic-parmesan bread."

"What's the matter with your hand?"

"Nothing. I must've slept with it curled under."

"Try this. Elbow at your waist." She shows me how to do a figure-eight rotation that makes the joint pop noisily. "There you go."

She builds a fire with scraps of newspaper and kindling, then goes to wash up while I turn the burner on under the soup pot and set the table. By the time the soup's hot, the fire is grazing on a large chunk of alder, and she's filling our wineglasses. I pull the ladle off its hook and pick up the soup pot. Pain slashes at my arm, inner wrist to elbow.

"Shit."

"What?" She looks up from the front page of the paper.

"I don't know. This hurts."

She brings our bowls over to the stove and holds my wrist, prodding it gently. "Does that hurt?"

"No. It's just when I pick up something heavy or twist it a certain way."

She takes the ladle from my left hand and fills both bowls. "What's it feel like?"

"Sharp. Shooting."

"Could be a touch of tendonitis." She sets our bowls on the cork mats and we sit down. "Welcome to the wonderful world of physical labor."

"What should I do?"

"Go to the drugstore and get yourself a wrist splint to wear at night. Beyond that, about the only things I know of are aspirin and rest."

"Rest? How am I going to make bread?"

She grates some parmigiana into her soup and passes it to me. "That, I believe, is what apprentices are for."

At first Tyler doesn't believe me.

"You mean I'm doing it all?"

"Every single, last loaf. I can help you with the mixing and scaling. Not too sure about loading and unloading, but I definitely won't be doing any shaping or heavy lifting."

"What if I—what if we don't get everything done?"

"I think we're going to assume that things have to slow down. Instead of making four kinds of bread a night, we'll make two, just more loaves."

She looks dazed. "You're not kidding, are you?"

"No."

For the next three weeks, I teach her the way Jean-Marc taught me. How to judge the dough's temperature, its plasticity, its wetness, its resistance. How to form the *boules* and *bâtards*, stretching the outside skin of the dough, creating the surface tension that forces it to rise up instead of just spreading out. How to make her touch firm but gentle, so as not to de-gas the loaf.

Sometimes when I'm trying to explain these things to her, the image of him crystallizes in my mind. I can see his hands, encrusted with dough, his olive skin, the wiry black hair on his arms dusted with flour. It's his voice that says, *Non, non. Pas comme ça. This is bread, Wynter, not clay. It is alive. It talks to you. Écoutez!*

The memory is so clear that my breath stops for a split second.

Tyler works at it with an intensity that surprises me, almost a fierceness. And she becomes very good very quickly.

## · eight ·

A bad marriage is like the psycho killer in a slasher flick. Just when you think it's dead, it suddenly looms up in front of you, looking for blood. In the movies, you know it's coming, and you keep thinking, *No, no, no, do NOT go into that dark basement alone, you idiot.* Unfortunately, in real life, somehow you lack this foresight.

I've been trying not to think about the whole divorce thing—and doing a pretty good job of it, too—taking each day as it comes, trying to enjoy work, much easier since Tyler's become proficient enough to be a real help. We've even sort of bonded, as bread bakers tend to do. The only nagging worry is money—or the lack of it. This is a new experience for me, this being adrift on a sea of debt— even if my main creditor is just my mother—having to watch every single penny. But whenever I complain, CM smiles and tells me it builds character.

The last Thursday in April I come home from the library feeling pretty righteous because I've gotten some new books to read without spending any money. When I lay them on the desk, I see the light blinking on the answering machine. I hold my breath and press the play button. It's Elizabeth. Her message is terse.

*Wynter, please call me at your earliest convenience.*

I tell myself it's not necessarily bad news. That's just the way she talks. I mean, the worst is over. Isn't it? How bad could it be? But my stomach feels awash with hydrochloric acid as I dial her number. Her secretary puts me through right away—another bad sign.

"Thanks for calling, Wynter. I wanted to advise you that your husband and his attorney have filed a motion to bifurcate, that is, to divide the marital-status issue from the other issues in contention, namely, the financial settlement. The hearing on the motion will be in two weeks."

This isn't good, I'm fairly certain, but I'm not clear on exactly what it means. "What's this about? Do I have to be there?"

"No, you don't have to be present. Briefly, it means that since the six-month waiting period for termination of marital status is up, the divorce decree can proceed. Without the financial settlement, from which it has been bifurcated."

"*What?*"

"Essentially, David will be free to remarry and settle the financial issues separately at a later date."

I can't think what to say because I'm trying to decide who to kill first.

"Are you there, Wynter?"

"Is there any chance the motion won't be . . . approved?"

"Hardly any. There would have to be some very strong reasons—"

"Doesn't the fact that he's an asshole and he's trying to screw me out of what's rightfully mine count for anything?"

"Um, probably not per se . . ."

"I'm . . . I can't believe it. Are you sure they can do this?"

"Yes, I'm afraid so."

"But, it's not *fair!*"

Elizabeth wisely opts not to discuss that point. Oddly, my next thought is, how could this Adele King person do that to a co-woman? I feel utterly betrayed.

"So ..." I swallow. "What do we do? I mean ... *God. What do we do?*" I feel like my legs have been shot off. I stop pacing and collapse on the couch.

"His attorney has informed me that they want a full trial in front of the court to divide the assets. They've requested a trial date, but it will probably take six to ten months before we get to court."

It doesn't seem worth repeating that this latest development is beyond belief.

"Wynter, I'm sorry. I know this is disturbing news for you. But in my opinion, this maneuver is simply an attempt to discourage you and destroy your morale."

"Well, shit. I think it's working."

"I know, but let's consider this. If we have to go to court, it's going to be very expensive for him, as well as for you. And depending upon who the judge is, he or she may not look favorably on some of the things David has done. I firmly believe your husband is aware of this, and I know Adele is. I don't think they really intend to go to trial. But if they can make you feel like you'd rather just wash your hands of the whole thing than go through a trial, then it puts him in the stronger negotiating position. Are you with me?"

"So what do we do?" I ask again. My lips feel numb.

"My suggestion would be that we prepare to go to trial, but continue to try to negotiate a settlement. We have plenty of time to work it out, and I can't see any reason to go to court. Does that sound reasonable to you?"

I nod, forgetting that she can't see me. "Okay."

"Good. Then try not to worry too much about this, and I'll be in touch."

I'm standing in the bay window with the duck phone still in my hand when Mac walks in.

"What's wrong?" he says as soon as he sees me.

He puts the phone back in its cradle, sits down on the couch, and tugs at my hand till I drop down beside him. I lean forward, elbows on knees, staring at the tops of my cross trainers.

"I just talked to my lawyer. David has filed what they call a 'motion to bifurcate.'"

"What's that?"

"It means they're going to separate the financial split from the divorce decree. It means no matter how long the financial agreement takes, he can go ahead and get divorced. He can go ahead and marry Kelley." I hate the way my voice shakes.

"Is that so bad? Do you care if he marries her?"

"You don't understand. The divorce was my leverage." I pinch the bridge of my nose. "Now he can marry her and it doesn't matter how long the goddamn settlement takes, he has what he wants."

He starts making lazy circles on my back with the heel of his hand. It feels so good I can't bear it.

"I can't believe this. I thought it was over."

"Is there any chance the motion won't be granted?"

"Not really."

"Do you think your lawyer's doing her job?"

"Who the hell knows with lawyers? Anyway, I'm not up to starting all over with another attorney."

"So what does she propose to do?"

"She says it's probably just a ploy. To make me want to give up. So he'd be in a stronger position to negotiate a settlement." One tear breaks the surface tension and rolls down my face. He brushes it away, then licks his thumb. "She says we should prepare for a trial, but keep trying to work out a settlement."

"Sounds reasonable." He props a cowboy boot up on his knee.

"I know, it's just . . . I thought it was over."

After another minute of silent back rubbing, he says, "I know what would make you feel better."

"So do I. A telegram saying that David Franklin has disappeared into a crevasse on the Mendenhall Glacier."

"I was thinking more along the lines of a couple of days on Orcas Island."

I look at him. "When?"

"We could leave Saturday morning, as soon as you're off, and come back Sunday afternoon. I know it's kind of a quick turnaround, but Rick's been wanting me to take a run up to Eastsound and check the cottage. I guess they've had a couple of hard rains and a good blow in the last two weeks. I thought if I went this weekend, you might keep me company. A return to the scene of the crime, so to speak."

Saturday morning I'm standing outside the bakery, CM's gray overnight bag at my feet, holding two white bakery sacks and two lidded cups, when the Elky pulls up at the curb, gleaming like white porcelain.

Mac gets out, kisses me, and throws my bag in the back. He takes one of the cups. "I don't think I've ever been to a bakery with curb service."

"What's with the Elky? It looks fabulous." I climb in, waving at Tyler and Ellen, watching us from the window.

"I decided it was time for a complete rehab. Before it got to the point of no return. New clutch, new brakes, shocks, and tires." He hands me three tapes. "Had the tape deck fixed, too."

"Did you rob a bank?"

"Nope. I've been saving everything I made at Norwegian Woods. Anyway, it's cheaper than buying a new truck."

I pop in one of the tapes and we head across the Aurora Bridge with the haunting sounds of the Allman Brothers' "Midnight Rider" trailing out the open window.

·　·　·

By nine-thirty we're sitting in a line of cars that stretches halfway back to the road from the Anacortes ferry landing, foraging in the white bakery bags for the last crumbs of Jen's short scones. When the Elky is wedged snugly into a lane on the car deck with all the Jeeps and station wagons and vans and four-by-fours, we climb the stairs to the second deck. The passenger cabin is a forest of Gore-Tex-covered tourists. Groups of teenagers laugh too loudly and knots of children chase each other through the aisles, screaming with pre-weekend glee. We head for the cafeteria.

The coffee looks like black water, so I decline. Mac pours artificial creamer in his till it turns a sick, gray color. I get a small plastic bottle of orange juice and we go outside to stand by the rail. It's quieter on deck; most people are keeping warm inside, and there's something about fog that always makes people whisper. The ocean is flat and glassy, and the ferry seems to sit motionless on a cold, gray mirror while the seascape rolls by like a movie. Islands appear suddenly out of the mist and then vanish. Gulls float beside us, like bird marionettes, till they tire of watching us and peel off into the fog.

Every once in a while we spot a house, tucked into a cove or perched on its own island, connected to the outside world maybe by a sandbar at low tide or by the owner's boat, tied nearby. Or in one case, by a spiffy yellow float plane parked at the dock.

I shiver through my sweatshirt and parka, and Mac puts his arm around me. Just then a woman in a short-sleeved T-shirt walks past us, carrying a baby wearing only a diaper and a little undershirt. They both seem oblivious to the damp cold.

"Must be aboriginals," he says.

"I think it's good to acclimatize early in life. In France they say that when a baby is born, his father should dip a finger in good red wine and put it in the baby's mouth so he'll know what the good stuff is supposed to taste like."

"What else do they do in France? Take the little boy babies and put them in the crib with the little girl babies so they'll know about that, too?"

"You're perverted and sick. And I like that in a man."

As we drive up Horseshoe Highway from the Orcas ferry landing, we submerge briefly in pools of dense fog collected in the hollows. At first I think it's raining, but it's just water dripping from the trees that line both sides of the road. When we reach Eastsound's collection of little shops and businesses perched on a cliff over the water, Mac guides the Elky into a parking place.

We get turkey burritos at a little walk-up window and eat them while we wander around the two or three streets that make up the village of Eastsound. By now it's nearly noon, and the fog has burned off, leaving the sky a thin, watery blue. We stand for a minute at the wooden guard rail watching the waves lap at the foot of the bluffs.

I unzip my jacket in the heat of the sun, feeling the wind in my hair. "This is so beautiful. I wish I had my camera."

"Personally, I'm glad you don't," he says.

"Why?" I shade my eyes with my hand to look at his face.

"When you're busy taking pictures, you forget what you're doing. You forget to live in the moment. And you end up with some dumb souvenir of a nonevent."

I stare at him. "Oh, bug off, McLeod. Sometimes you're such an elitist curmudgeon."

His laugh is contagious. "Look who's talking about elitists. The croissant police. Ms. No-Ketchup-on-your-hashbrowns."

After a quick pass through the organic grocery, we head for the cottage, skirting the Crescent Beach oyster beds, and turning left onto Terrill's Beach Road, then right on Buckhorn. In a few minutes tantalizing glimpses of water appear on our left.

Mac turns in at the sign announcing "Madrone Cottage," and we bump up the gravel driveway. The white clapboard bungalow is just as I remember it from that day—has it really been nine months since then? The only difference is the way its new white paint glows against the backdrop of wet, green conifers.

Mac unlocks the door and we go inside. It's like a half-remembered dream of a grandmother's house—the knotty-pine paneling, the well-worn maroon couch, two green chairs. The battered trunk that serves as a coffee table. Book shelves overflowing with paperbacks and board games.

We carry our bags through the tiny hall that seems to slope downhill and into the bedroom with its iron bed, piled high with quilts. My memory of that first visit overlays everything like a fine layer of dust. The first time we made love was in this room.

Mac, obviously untroubled by sentiment, drops his duffle on the floor by the unfinished pine chest and empties his pockets onto the scarred top. "I'm going to check out the shed."

I go into the kitchen and stand at the sink, looking out into the woods, wondering what happened to Minnie, the scruffy yellow mutt that hung around here with Mac.

While he repairs the damage to the shed roof, I pull out my bag of organic whole wheat flour. In Seattle I've always used a pinch of commercial dried yeast to get a *chef* started. Up here the air seems so pure, it's probably teeming with microorganisms, and I want to try making a completely natural starter. I don't think there are a lot of chemicals in the tap water, but just to be on the safe side, I picked up a bottle of spring water. The laid-back dude at the store assured me that this brand truly was from a spring and not just designer tap water. I stir a half cup of the water into three quarters of a cup of flour, cover the bowl loosely, and leave it on the counter.

Then out to the porch, curling up on the love seat with a Ruth Rendell paperback that I found on the bookshelves. I whip through the first chapter, but a gradual drowsiness comes over me and I stretch out on the love seat, dangling my feet over one end.

The stillness is mesmerizing. I hear the wind in the same instant that I feel it washing over my face. Grace notes of a few birds. Dust particles suspended in a shaft of sunlight. A bumblebee hovers somewhere outside my line of vision, and I don't even have the energy to turn my head. A doe walks calmly out of the forest to graze less than fifty feet from the house.

The sound of footsteps crunching on gravel wakes me up. My feet are numb and tingling; the sun is behind the trees. Mac comes up on the porch, laughing that slow laugh he has.

"Catching up on your beauty sleep?"

"All the better to keep you awake all night." My mouth is dry. "What time is it?"

"About five. I'm heading for the shower."

I yawn and drag myself up to a sitting position, try to rotate the kink out of my neck. "What shall we do for dinner?"

"There's a great little wine bar down on the bluff. I propose we have some wine and contemplate the options."

The sun is inching toward the sea when we walk up three wooden steps, past a planter exploding with blue petunias, red geraniums, and white lobelia. There's no sign, but Mac says it's the place. Inside it's quiet.

"Hi. Two for dinner?" The voice belongs to a tan blonde with metallic blue eyes.

"Actually we just wanted a glass of wine," Mac said. "I thought this was a wine bar."

The blonde smiles. "It used to be. Alex bought it about a month ago and it's a café now. We don't have our sign up yet. But you can still get a glass of wine. Have a seat at the bar and I'll call him."

When Jean-Marc's clone walks out of the kitchen, I almost fall off my stool. The initial resemblance is uncanny, but upon closer inspection, there are obvious differences. He's slightly taller than Jean-Marc and his face is more mobile, ready to smile or frown; his eyes are just as dark, but less guarded, more expressive. The body could have been made from the same mold, stocky, muscular. His black hair is pulled into a ponytail—something Jean-Marc would never dream of—and he's wearing a white chef's coat over his jeans.

He holds out his hand to Mac. "Alex Rafferty."

"Mac McLeod. This is Wyn Morrison."

"Shawn said you guys were looking for the Orcas Wine and Spirits Company. I bought them out a few months ago, but I kept the wine. I've also got a lot of imported and domestic bottles from my restaurant in Seattle. What's your pleasure?"

"A cabernet or merlot," I say, looking out the window. "What a fabulous view."

"Isn't it? Sometimes it's downright distracting." He turns to a row of bottles behind him and studies them for a minute. "Try this Hogue merlot. I think you might like it. If not, we'll open something else."

"You have a restaurant in Seattle?" Mac asks.

"Had." The little half smile is devastatingly familiar. "I sold it and moved up here lock, stock, and bottles."

He sets two glasses on the bar and pours the deep purple wine in both.

"How's business?" Mac swirls the wine in his glass, sniffs, and tastes it.

"So far so good," Alex says. "It's fairly quiet right now, but I wanted to have the bugs all worked out before the invasion of the tourists. I hope you'll come back for dinner sometime. You guys live here?"

"Just visiting." I look over at the hostess station. "Have you got a menu?"

"We don't have printed ones yet. There's one on the blackboard by the door." Mac gets up to go read it, and Alex turns to me, leaning on the bar. "Do I know you from someplace?"

I shake my head. "I didn't mean to stare at you like that. You just look incredibly like someone I used to work for. Where was your restaurant?"

"The Union Café. The north end of Lake Union, near Gasworks Park."

Mac comes back and parks himself beside me, resting his hand on my shoulder. "Since we're here, we might as well have dinner."

The café is charming—small, but with enough elbow room so that you're not involuntarily eavesdropping on the next table. The other walls are painted a dark terra-cotta, setting off the plain, crisp white table linens, and candles are everywhere, flickering off mirrors and glassware. A perfect example of maximum effect with minimum furnishings. Of course, it doesn't hurt that the whole back wall is windows overlooking East Sound.

The blonde returns to bring us a wine list and recite the menu, and tell us our waiter will be right over. Mac stares out the window at the sky, shot through with gold and pink. Then abruptly he says, "I think I could live here."

"You mean on Orcas Island?"

He nods. "It reminds me of—"

Our waiter suddenly appears, smiling toothily and asking us if we've chosen a wine.

"Probably red," I say. "We liked the Hogue merlot."

"If you liked that, there's another merlot I think you'd really like. It's a Canadian wine. Okanagan Valley, in British Columbia. It's called Burrowing Owl. It's a bit pricier, but in my opinion it's worth every cent."

I'm about to tell him that his opinion doesn't count, since he's not paying for it, but Mac smiles and says, "Okay, let's try it." He doesn't even ask how much.

When the guy goes to dig up the Burrowing Owl, I look at Mac. "Did your Great-uncle Sylvester kick off and leave you his entire estate?"

He looks sheepish. "I'm practicing to be rich and famous. Besides, I have a bright, shiny, new credit card. Just begging to be run through somebody's machine."

He looks out the window again while I sit there and fret about how much the wine's going to cost. Alex brings the bottle himself, and two red-wine goblets.

"Great choice," he says, twisting the corkscrew. That's restaurantspeak meaning, *Thanks for paying this month's rent.*

The wine is truly magnificent—round and rich and mouth filling. After one glass I'm so mellow I recall that thing Ben Franklin supposedly said about wine being constant proof that God loves us. I sit there, watching Mac, waiting for him to say more about what the island reminds him of, but he's apparently already past that. I want to reach over and touch his face. In the reflected light of the candles, his eyes remind me of a piece of rock I once found on a hike. My father said it was a silicate. I just knew that I loved the way the tiny gold facets emerged with geometrical precision from the dull gray rock.

He's got that little patch of perpetual sunburn on his nose, like lifeguards always have. His mouth . . . God, I love his mouth. Kissing it. The thought of where it's been on my body and how it feels makes me dizzy.

Our dinners are beautiful. Mac has medallions of New Zealand lamb with a Dijon crust, and sumptuously artery-clogging scalloped potatoes. I go with seafood, since we're on an island, even if it's not local. But it's so fresh it might as well be—a fat tuna steak, grilled with garlic and herbs just to medium rare. The salad of spring vegetables is local—tiny, perfect squashes, new potatoes the size of your thumb, sugar snap peas and haricots verts—everything fresh and sweet, tossed in a warm hazelnut vinaigrette. Even the bread for each dinner is different. He has buttery whole wheat dinner rolls and I have a chewy peasant bread, rubbed with garlic and bearing the marks of the grill.

Instead of dessert, we opt for a cheese plate to go with the rest of the expensive-but-worth-every-penny wine. With it comes a little bowl of partially frozen red grapes.

When the check comes, he barely looks at it, just pulls out his virginal MasterCard and tucks it inside the folder. I reach for my wallet.

"Wyn," he says, "don't do this, okay?" His eyes are a warning all by themselves. So I say, "I was just getting my lipstick."

As we're climbing into the truck, he looks at the sky.

"I want to show you a place I found when I was here last summer. It has an incredible view." He slams the door, cranks the truck, and we take off down Horseshoe Highway.

"Can we see it at night?"

He just smiles and turns left past a sign that says PRIVATE ROAD: LOCAL TRAFFIC ONLY. "Are we supposed to be here?"

"Will you relax? You're such a good girl."

"And you're an anarchist."

"Was your father very strict?"

I ponder the question. "He never laid a hand on me—I barely remember him even raising his voice. I just never wanted to disappoint him. He could say my name a certain way . . ."

The road changes from gravel to dirt and gets narrower.

"What was the worst thing you ever did? That he found out about." The truck hits a king-sized pothole and the top of my head smacks the roof. "Oops, sorry."

I grip the armrest with one hand, massage my head with the other. "Let's see. Once when I was about ten, CM's big sister, Katie, dared us to shoplift a lipstick from the drugstore. We did, but then my mother found it and wanted to know where we'd gotten it. Being pathologically honest, I told her. She told my father and he made us go back and confess to the store manager. One at a time, so we didn't have each other for moral support. I was absolutely petrified. I thought for sure we were going to jail."

All I can make out now is a black tangle of trees and headlights disappearing into the dark, but he drives fast. "McLeod, how the hell can you see where you're going?"

"I don't need to see. This road is in my unconscious memory." He grins. "So what happened?"

"The manager said he wouldn't call the police this time. He was probably laughing his butt off. Then I went out and CM went in and confessed. The poor guy was probably hoping there were no more gang members involved in the heist so he could get back to work."

When it seems as if there's nowhere to go except back the way we came, he turns onto another road that's hardly more than a trail, so narrow that an occasional tree branch slaps the window as we bounce along. Finally he pulls to a stop in a little clearing encircled by tall evergreens and we get out. He unrolls a piece of thick foam rubber in the bed of the pickup, unzips his sleeping bag, and spreads it on top of the foam.

"Always prepared."

"I've slept a lot of nights in this truck." He jumps up in back, holds out his hand.

We settle in with our backs against the cab. "I thought you said this place had a view."

"Look up," he says.

"Oh ... my God."

It's like looking through a big porthole at every star in the universe. You can actually see part of the Milky Way's river of light. We sit silent; my impulse is to hold my breath because even that seems loud enough to disrupt the moment. A shooting star gleams briefly and vanishes. Another trails it.

"What did you start to say at dinner? About what this place reminds you of?"

He lays his head against the back window. "It reminds me of going to summer camp in upstate New York when I was a kid. I think it's the light."

"What about it?"

"When you're surrounded by mountains like this, it gets light in the morning before you can see the sun, and then at night, the sun disappears but it's still daylight. I always felt like it was never going to be dark. Like Alaska in the summer."

I shiver, and he draws me close against his side. "Cold?"

"Not really. It's funny, how I used to hate the cold. It could never be warm enough for me. Now it makes me feel more awake. A lot of things seem different to me now. Like I never thought I'd live anywhere but southern California. I never seriously imagined owning a bakery."

When he turns my face to his, I can't help wondering if he really wants to kiss me or if he just wants me to stop talking. Either way, it has the same effect.

"And, of course," I say thoughtfully, "I never pictured myself making love in the back of a 'seventy-one El Camino."

He laughs. "You're shameless. I think that's my favorite thing about you."

The hollow drumming of rain on the roof wakes me early Sunday morning. So much for hiking up Mount Constitution. In the kitchen the linoleum is cool and ridged under my feet. I get some orange juice and stand at the sink looking out into the woods. Dripping leaves and needles glow iridescent green against the shiny black of wet bark, and the slate sky seems close enough to touch.

I rinse the glass and go back to the bedroom. Mac wakes up long enough to make room for me under the covers and I curl up next to him and drift back to sleep.

When I open my eyes again, he's not in bed. I smell coffee. I pull socks over my cold feet and pad into the kitchen. He's buttering toast, and I stand behind him, resting my face against his back.

"Mmm. My favorite morning smell."

"Coffee? Or toast?"

"You," I say. He turns and kisses me.

I pull my *chef* out for a progress check. It's doubled in volume, soupy and roiling with life. I remember Jean-Marc saying that the wetter the starter, the more sour the bread. I pinch off a piece and put it on my tongue, savoring the vinegary bite. Mac peers over my shoulder.

"What's in it?"

"Just flour and water."

"So why is it bubbling?"

"Because it's now home to a passel of potent microorganisms."

"How many microorganisms does it take to make a passel?"

"More than you'd care to count. Isn't it amazing? All they need is a little food and a place to have sex, and they just show up and start reproducing."

"That's not so amazing. I would do that." He puts his arms around my waist. "Watching all this unbridled sexual activity makes me horny."

"Well, I've never known anyone to actually become aroused while watching a sourdough starter." I turn and hop up into his arms, wrapping my legs around him. "But I suppose there's always that first time."

By the time we get around to breakfast, the toast is cold, so we heat it in the oven. We pull on sweatshirts and eat out on the porch, watching the rain on the meadow and slapping the occasional mosquito.

I put down my coffee cup and arrange myself at one end of the love seat, facing him. "We're going to do an experiment. We're each

going to tell one hitherto-unknown fact. About ourselves. No discussing the mating rituals of rainbow trout or anything like that.
Okay?"

He shifts position slightly. "And what is this experiment designed to prove?"

I keep my eyes tight on his. "That we can, and that the seas do
not open and swallow us up when we tell about ourselves. Okay?" I
don't wait for him to answer. "I'll go first. For a long time after my father died, I couldn't cry."

"What does that feel like?"

"It feels a lot like not being able to have an orgasm."

"That bad?"

"It's the same general principle. There's a buildup of tension and
instead of a quick release, it just dissipates, slowly and uncomfort-
ably."

"Sounds kind of unhealthy," he says.

I shrug. "Lots of men never cry. In fact, I have this theory. My
theory is that the reason a lot of men are so obsessed with sex is because they can't cry."

"What?"

"It's their only release."

"Well, my theory is that the reason a lot of men are so obsessed
with sex is that they're not getting any."

"I think my theory is much more interesting. Okay, now you have
to tell me something."

"I flunked senior English."

"Bullshit."

He laughs. "Okay, I got an incomplete. I had to go back after
graduation and make it up before they'd give me my diploma."

"Not a very interesting fact, McLeod."

"You didn't say it had to be interesting. You want to know why I
got an incomplete?"

"No." I take a sip of coffee. "I want to know about your brother."

"That's not a fact about me," he says evenly.

"Yeah, I think it is."

A shadow passes over his face, like the smallest ripple on a still pond. "What about him?"

"All about him. Name, age, occupation, where he lives...the usual stuff."

He sighs. "Kevin Douglas McLeod. Born January 12, 1956."

"What does he look like?"

"Nothing like me."

"You'll have to do better than that."

"He looks like a football player. Which he was. In high school." He lays his arm along the back of the love seat. "Remember the day we had breakfast at Steve's ... those two little boys fighting over the crayons?"

"Of course. I distinctly remember you taking on that vicious seven-year-old."

"That vicious seven-year-old was Kevin."

"So, what does he do? For a living, I mean, and is he married? Does he have kids? Where is he?"

"We haven't talked in a long time." He stands up. "You want some more coffee?"

"What I want is for you to tell me why you always get that deer in the headlights look whenever I ask about your brother. Why you don't have any pictures—not one single photograph of him. Or your father. Or Suzanne."

For a minute he doesn't say anything. He doesn't even look at me. Finally he sits back down.

"Kevin was handsome. Smart. He was a great football player. President of his class. He made it all look easy. Girls. They were always calling the house. Suzanne used to get so pissed."

"But, all this stuff is so...trivial. There's life after high school, you know. Maybe he's changed. Maybe if you just called him—you know, just to say hi or—"

"He's dead." His voice is quiet and flat and almost relieved. "Kevin's dead."

I swallow my coffee and wait for it to find its way down. "When?"

"1974."

"But you said——" I stop, realizing how stupid it would sound. *But you said he was a lawyer.* "He was only eighteen? What happened?"

He puts the coffee cup to his mouth, then realizes it's empty. When he sets it down, the table tilts toward its shortest leg. "It was on a Friday night, the last football game of the year. There was a party afterward. He was a senior; I was a junior. Everybody was drinking. On the way home... there was an accident. This guy in a van ran the red light. Kevin was killed instantly."

"Oh, Mac." I feel so stupid, but I can't think of anything else to say.

"She had all these big plans for him."

"Your mother?"

He nods. "I don't think she ever forgave me."

"For what?"

"For being the one who walked away with a broken arm."

"For God's sake, didn't the two of you ever talk about it?"

"Not much. By the time I graduated from high school, she was living in her bedroom with a bottle of vodka."

"I don't know what to say. I'm really... so sorry. But why didn't you just tell me? All those times when I asked about him? About her?"

"It's not something I talk about."

"Why?"

He shrugs slightly, not looking at me. "I don't know why. I guess I just never felt like explaining it. Going through the whole..." He waits for the right word, but it doesn't come. "It was easier to make up a story. Maybe after a while I started to halfway believe it myself. I honestly don't know."

"How terrible. You must have been——" My voice falters.

"I don't know." Now he looks in my direction, but his focus is somewhere beyond me. "The thing is, in my head I'm still having the same stupid arguments with him. That's the hardest part. There's no resolution. We can't just have it out."

"Things don't always get resolved even when everybody's present in the same room. You know that." When I reach for his hand, he stands up again.

"True." He walks to the porch rail and stands there watching the meadow grass nod under the soft rain. Then abruptly he turns back. "Much as I hate to say it, we better get packed up and get down to the ferry landing."

"Mac, come on. You can't just turn it off."

"Yes, I can. And I have to. I shouldn't have told you."

I look at him, stunned. "But I think you'd have to tell someone. You can't walk around with something like that stuffed down inside you."

He leans against the porch rail. "There's a common misconception that you can focus on one terrible thing and say, this is it. This is the problem. You speak its name and acknowledge it, and you set yourself free. But that's not how it works. What happens is, you let it out and it's . . . like opening Pandora's box."

He pushes off the rail. "And now we really need to go. I'm working tonight."

The drive back to Seattle is gray and depressing. He puts on a tape of really funky blues—the singers all sound like ninety-year-old black men with no teeth and I can't understand any of the lyrics—to discourage any further conversation, I'm sure. It works just fine.

Then, just as we cross the line into King County, I realize that I didn't bring the *chef.* My starter. I put it in the refrigerator to slow down the yeast, intending to pull it out at the last minute, but in our rush to get to the ferry, I forgot it.

## nine

The silence between us fills up the week.

Finally, on Friday, he calls. "I thought you'd like to know that Roz had the baby Tuesday. Seven pounds, three ounces and her name is Sarah."

"Oh. That's great. When will they be home?"

"Today, I think."

"Maybe we could go by and see her this weekend."

"Sure."

"I was thinking about coming down to Bailey's on Saturday night—about ten?"

"Sure."

I look into my mug of rapidly cooling tea. Half full, I remind myself, not half empty. Still warm, not almost cold. Mac pulls a chair out with his foot and sits down, setting two steaming mugs on the table.

It's Saturday night, actually Sunday morning. Bailey's is closed, Mac and Kenny have cleaned up, shut down, locked the money in the safe. Now Kenny has gone home to Roz and baby Sarah, the shutters are closed, and the room's only light comes from the fire and the one lamp hanging over the table where we're sitting.

"I put honey in yours." He looks at the fire.

I've been here since about ten-thirty, drinking wine, switching to tea when my head started to buzz. I pull the spoon out of my mug, still smoothly coated with thick, golden honey. I watch it drip off the end, then stir it again. I look up at him.

We've crossed the border now, Mac and I. We're in a different territory and there's no going back. It's like being on a jury when the judge tells you to disregard some piece of evidence that's been presented.

I wanted information and I got it. But I also got the emotional carry-on baggage. The genuine easiness of being with him has been replaced by a sort of forced lightness in which we both carefully avoid acknowledging that I now know what I know.

He reaches for my hand, but it's an automatic gesture. His mind is elsewhere.

"Are you okay?" I ask.

"Sure. Why?"

"Well, for one thing, everytime I ask you a question these days, you say, 'Sure.'"

"I'm just tired."

"Tired of what?"

He gives me a sharp look. "Not *of* anything. Just tired. I haven't slept much the last couple of nights. Don't make something out of nothing."

I want to ask why he's not sleeping, but it doesn't seem like a safe line of inquiry. Suddenly I can't think of anything that is safe to say to him, and the space yawns between us like the Grand Canyon.

"I guess I don't understand you sometimes."

He smiles. "It's just that we have different ways of dealing with the fact that the universe is sliding inexorably into chaos."

"Can you please just stop this?" I fold my arms on the table and rest my forehead on them. I just want to go home, go to bed, make love, fall asleep with his arms around me.

"Stop what?"

"This defense thing that you do. Don't you ever let your hands down?" My voice is muffled in my sweatshirt.

"Don't you ever get tired of trying to fix me?"

I sit up quickly. "I'm not trying to fix you. I'm trying to understand you."

"Why do you need to understand me?"

*Because I love you, stupid.*

No, I don't actually say it. Mrs. Morrison didn't raise no dummies. But when I look at him, I know he sees it, as clearly as if it were tattooed on my forehead.

The lamp hanging over the table seems to swing in a barely perceptible arc, picking up some minute tremor, an earthquake too small to feel.

He pulls me out of the chair and onto his lap. He unfastens my hair, loosens it with his fingers, and I rest my cheek against his forehead.

We sit like that for a long time. I don't know how long, but long enough for the fire to completely burn away into a bed of papery ash and a few red coals. He just holds me, breathing into my hair and not saying anything.

Sunday is a heartbreakingly beautiful spring day. Our first stop is the bakery to pick up a box of cream scones with currants, and triberry muffins, to take over to Roz and Kenny's house in Green Lake.

The baby smell hits you as soon as the door opens. Kenny looks like he's been up all night, which he probably has. Red eyed, unshaven, shoeless, shirttail out, burp rag on his shoulder.

"Welcome to Babyland." He smiles weakly, but perks up when Mac hands him the bakery box. "I'll go put some coffee on. The queen and the princess are in the living room."

Roz, looking tired but serene, is propped against a pillow, feet up, adrift in a sea of pastel blankets and stuffed toys. Curled up on her stomach is a small, pink-swathed bundle. All I can see of the baby is a face the size of a latte cup, tiny perfect nose, lashless eyelids, the miniature rosebud mouth puckered in sleep and sporting a delicate tracery of drool.

"Lady Madonna." Mac grins and kisses the top of her head. I kneel down for a better view of Sarah.

"Damn, girlfriend, you do good work." I run the back of my index finger over the impossibly soft cheek. "How are you feeling?"

"Oh, tired. Sore. Happy. Stupid."

"Why stupid?" Mac lays my jeans jacket over the back of a club chair and sits down.

"'Cause you don't find out what all you don't know about babies till you get one." Kenny comes in from the kitchen carrying a plate mounded with scones and muffins in one hand and four coffee mugs in the other. He pushes a stack of books by Dr. Spock and Barry Braselton to the end of the coffee table with his foot and sets the load down.

Mac laughs. "Nice trick. What else can you do?"

Kenny sighs. "I have the feeling I'm gonna find out."

"Oh, listen to you." Roz rolls her eyes. "I'm the one who has to get up for every feeding."

"Thank God I don't have the equipment."

Her laugh changes to a grimace. "Owie. My stitches still hurt. Honey, you don't have to wear the burp rag when you're not holding her."

"Hey, this is my medal of honor." He pats his shoulder. "It proves I've been through the baby wars. No way am I taking it off." He heads back to the kitchen and we hear the buzz of the coffee grinder.

Sarah's pale eyelids twitch minutely. "She does that a lot," Roz says. "I think she's dreaming. Like a puppy."

"Which was harder," I ask, "having the baby or training the husband?"

She grins. "Having the baby was a piece of cake." She twists a little against the pillow. "Honey, can you come take her so I can visit the comfort station?"

"Yup," Kenny hollers back. "Just let me get the coffee started."

"Give her to me." I surprise myself with the realization that I can't wait to hold her.

"Oh thanks, Wyn. Here, just lean back and I'll . . ."

Sleeping Sarah lies on my shoulder like a small, warm beanbag, smelling of baby powder and milk. Her fist is curled up next to her mouth, thumb slightly extended, as if she's practicing to hitch a ride.

Kenny arrives with the sugar and cream. He grins when he sees me. "Uh-oh. Looks like a natural to me." Mac doesn't laugh.

When Roz returns from the bathroom, I hand Sarah back. My shoulder feels empty and a little cold. Probably due to the tiny spot of drool on my shirt.

We pass a pleasant hour of scones and coffee and Sarah stories. Kenny shows us the nursery, all pink and white, painted with fairytale characters. Roz opens the present I brought, a yellow terry-cloth sleeper with a duck pocket and webbed feet. We talk about having brunch when the initial flurry of confusion and novelty settles down. Then Mac stands up.

"Well, we should get going."

"No need to rush off," Kenny says, but he yawns as he lets us out the door.

Mac takes my hand as we walk down the brick steps. "How about a ferryboat ride?"

"Okay." When I turn my head to look at him, I can still smell Sarah on my shoulder.


The mountain is out. That's what the locals say on days like today when Rainier looks close enough to touch. I love the way it appears to hover, unattached, over the water, white cap of snow shimmering in the sun like a mirage. Tourists run around with their point-and-shoot cameras, snapping it from every angle, while the natives exchange sly smiles. They know that on days like this you can shoot a whole roll from any angle, using any exposure, but if you don't have a polarizing filter, the tricks of light and haze will render the mountain as invisible as a vampire in a mirror.

He puts his arm across my shoulders and pulls me closer. We've hardly exchanged half a dozen sentences since we left Kenny and Roz. Actually, since we left Bailey's last night. Now I'm wondering what he's thinking, he's wondering what I'm thinking—or not.

He hangs over the rail, staring down at the water, while I lean my back against it, watching a group of teenage girls pretend they're not watching a group of teenage boys.

"Mac..."

"Hmm?"

"Did you send the manuscript to any other agents?"

The silence becomes even more silent. Then he says, "One."

"Have you heard from him?"

"Her."

"Whatever. Have you heard anything?"

"No." Pause. "I'm sort of hungry. How are we fixed for lunch money?"

Anger rises in my throat. I want to shake him, and I would if I thought it would make any difference. I push myself off the rail and start to walk away, but he takes my arm and pulls me back, holding me. "I'm sorry. Look, I know you're trying to help. But I just can't—"

One long and two short blasts of the ferry's horn signal our arrival and the end of the conversation. We merge with the crowd moving down the ramp to the terminal. At Winslow Way we turn left, passing the first small shops, the carts selling ice cream and espresso.

First stop, as always, is Eagle Harbor Books. We browse the new fiction shelves and Mac buys a softcover copy of *Shout!*, a history of the Beatles that he finds on a bargain table. I purposely left my credit card at home so I couldn't buy anything, but by fishing out dollar bills and foraging for quarters in the pockets of our jackets and jeans, we come up with enough to have lunch at the Streamliner Diner.

He leans back as the waitress sets down our food. His eyes go from the plate to me, then out the window, then back to the plate. He waits till I have a mouthful of grilled cheese, and then he says, "I'm going to Alaska on Wednesday." In the tone of voice you might use for mentioning that you have a dentist appointment or the car needs new shocks.

The melted cheese seems to congeal, gluing my mouth shut. A coldness floods my chest, and my heart sinks into it. I swallow.

"You mean Wednesday as in *next* Wednesday?"

Understanding comes in a rush. All the work he had done on the truck. The new tapes he's been making. The new credit card. And, yes, even the trip to Orcas. It wasn't about making me feel better. It was about making him feel less guilty.

My eyes are approaching dangerously high levels of saltwater. I look off to the side so it won't be obvious, but I feel my chin tremble. I swallow very big and realize he's still talking.

"I was going to tell you when we went to Orcas, but then you wanted to know all about Kevin..."

Right. So it's my fault that I'm just finding out three days before blastoff. In the middle of the Streamliner Diner. I grope for my purse like a blind person, still not looking at him, and when I feel the worn leather strap in my palm, I stand up. I can't breathe. If I don't get outside right now, I might implode.

"Wyn, wait a minute..."

His voice submerges in the noise of other conversations, silverware clanking against plates, plastic glasses tapping against worn Formica, the scrape of chairs and the squeak of waitresses' rubber-soled shoes.

Halfway to the door I remember that I have the money for lunch. I dig in the purse for my wallet, turn, and throw it at him. I hear the thwack as it hits something—maybe his hand—and the coin compartment opens, sending change rolling and bouncing all over the linoleum floor. There's a momentary lull in the noise of the room, and I remember the first night at his apartment, how the change from his pockets went rolling all over the floor.

The door bangs shut behind me. I turn right, walking briskly down the street that runs along the side of the diner to a little park on the water. I'm sucking in air as if I were drowning. The lump is gone from my throat; now it's resting under my breastbone, painful and dense. I sit down on a vacant picnic table with my feet on the bench. There are people all around   kids with their jeans rolled up, shrieking in the icy chill of the shallow water, couples drinking coffee out of Starbucks cups, a white-haired woman dozing over an open book. But they're all background, like television with the sound turned off.

A Sunfish tacks across the cove, trying to sail into the wind—I think it's called a close haul. She's beating back and forth across the water, not making much headway. I know just how that feels.

He sits down next to me and puts a paper bag on the table. "It's not you. It's me." He hands me my wallet.

"Do they have seminars for this? Breaking up 101? Is that where you guys learn all these great lines?"

"Don't get dramatic. We're not breaking up. This is just something I need to do."

"Right. The old Babe-I-gotta-leave-you-the-highway's-calling-bullshit-blues." When I look at him, I can hardly see him, the sun is in my eyes. "Would you please go away now?"

"Wyn..." He puts his hand on my shoulder, but I shrug it off.

"I want you to get away from me. Please. Now."

He sighs. "I'll call you later." He turns and walks back up to the street, boots crunching in the sand and gravel. I sit there for a long time, watching the sailboat.

When I get back to the apartment, CM's sprawled on the couch with a pile of *Dance!* magazines on her stomach. She looks up when I shut the door.

"What's up?"

I take off my jacket and drape it over the back of a dining-room chair. "Mac's going to Alaska."

She licks her thumb and flips a few pages, frowning. "When?"

"Wednesday."

All in one graceful motion she sits up, letting the magazines slide onto the couch, pivots her perfect buns, and puts her feet on the floor. "You mean like . . . this Wednesday?"

I sit down next to her and slouch back against the cushions. "Does it ever seem to you like it's just one big, revolving door? And if someone's trajectory happens to coincide with yours, you get to go around a few times together before they go spinning off one way and you go hurtling off somewhere else?"

"Yeah, sometimes it does." She pats my knee. "But, honestly? I don't think this is one of those times."

"I don't know. It kinda looks like the ride into the sunset to me." I stare out the window. "I wish I was more like you."

She laughs. "No kidding. From my perspective, any guy who can do intelligent conversation, not bore me with his life story, make incredible love to me till I yodel, and then disappear for a few months would be just about perfect."

"I think I knew it was coming, and I kept acting like it wasn't."

"Would you really have done anything differently?"

"I don't know. Probably not. I'm such a masochist."

"Take a deep breath and relax."

I take a deep breath, but I can't relax.

When she stretches her arms up to the ceiling, she looks like a Modigliani woman, tall and lithe. "I'm going to go get the car washed and buy some groceries. Want to come with?"

I get up and move over to the window seat, letting my eyes find the blue water. "Thanks, but I think I'll just stay here and sulk."

I watch the sun drop behind the jagged purple ridge of the Olympics, ferryboat lights twinkling in the rosy dusk. I keep hoping I'll be seized by the urge to get up off my butt and fix some dinner or scrub the bathroom, or maybe just turn on a lamp. But so far, nothing's happening.

When I hear the door open, I think it's CM, but when I look up, there he is.

"Can we talk?" he says.

"Apparently not. Seems like every time we do lately, something bad happens."

He takes a few steps closer, but I turn back to the window. "Wyn, I know I should have told you sooner. There just never seemed to be a good time, and I didn't want to upset you."

I laugh. It's a loose sound, kind of crazed. "You didn't give a rat's ass if I got upset, as long as you didn't have to hang around and deal with it."

"I'm sorry." He's got that look on his face. The one men always get when you need to talk about feelings and the future and your relationship. They look like they'd rather be having bamboo splinters jammed under their toenails.

He sits down facing me and holds both my hands. I make myself look at him.

"Is this about Kevin?"

"No. Not at all—"

"Because I'm sorry it made you so sad talking about it. I just felt like something was wrong with that whole—"

"You were right. Something is wrong. But it's always been wrong and it always will be wrong, and there's nothing I can do about that except try not to let it make me crazy. Look, Wyn..." He lets go of my hands and leans back against the wall, turning his face to me. "This isn't easy to explain, but I'll try. All my life, whenever things get... strange like this, when I need to think, to decide what to do... then I have to get away somewhere. It's just the way I'm wired. It's not about you—"

"You made it about me. By shutting me out. Ignoring my feelings. You don't tell me what's going on with you. You just announce that you're leaving. In three days. How did you think I'd take it?"

"I knew you'd be upset. I was going to tell you last weekend, but then we got off on the Kevin thing—"

"So we're only allowed one difficult topic per weekend?"

"I'm just not good at... this."

"At what?" I hug my knees in closer.

"At being with anyone. I'm too used to being on my own." He closes his eyes. "This sounds bad, doesn't it?"

"Worse than bad."

"I'm sorry. This whole thing with the manuscript is just—"

"Why the hell don't you just call the guy? He's had more than enough time to get back to you. And if he—"

"Wyn." He looks sort of sad, sort of embarrassed. "He got back to me."

"When?"

"About a month ago."

"A month—why didn't you tell me?"

He leans forward, elbows resting on his knees. "I couldn't tell you. I couldn't even think about it."

"For God's sake, tell me what he said!"

"He wanted me to make all these changes. Not just little line ed-its. Major structural changes. He wanted me to rewrite it in first person, he wanted—"

"So what did you say to him?" This is like extracting wisdom teeth.

"Nothing."

"You can't say nothing. You have to talk to him."

"There's nothing to talk about. I'm not changing it. Not like that."

Suddenly I understand. This is something he was not prepared for. "He probably doesn't expect you to cop to every single thing. Why don't you let me read it? We could go over it together, make some notes—"

"Don't. Please don't. I know you want to help, but you can't."

"I can't believe you didn't even tell me."

"He obviously thought it was crap—"

"Oh, stop it! If he'd thought it was crap, he would've sent you back a form letter that said, 'Dear Author, Thanks for your submis-sion. We are sorry that it does not suit our needs at the present time.' He would have put it through his paper shredder or used it to light his barbecue grill or to line his parakeet's cage. He wouldn't have taken the time to read it, write back, give you suggestions if he didn't think there was something there."

When I finally stop talking, the silence is so absolute that it's as if I've gone deaf. A few excruciating minutes pass while we look at each other, and I think that any second now we'll start speaking the same language. The street lights blink on abruptly, glowing a pale yellow-green in the dusk.

I clear my throat. "Maybe you should just try some of his ideas."

"Not now." He shakes his head. "I can't write anything now. I've been staring at blank pages every night this week." He gets up, jam-ming his hands into the pockets of his jeans. "For the last five years, it's like I've had blinders on. All I could see was finishing. Now it's finished. So..." He tries to laugh. "Maybe I'll just be the world's greatest bartender."

"There's nothing wrong with that. If that's what you want."

"That's just it. I don't know. I thought I knew what I was working for, but obviously..."

He exhales. "I just need some time."

"But why Alaska? Can't you just go up to Orcas? I mean, it's not like I'm going to show up and distract you." I hate myself for this. It sounds like begging.

"I don't know how to explain it any better. I'm sorry. I should have told you before."

"Well." I stand up, too, and when I inhale there's an awful leaden dullness in my chest. "I guess this is it, then."

"Can I see you before I go?"

"Why?"

"Because I want to. Don't you?"

"It's too hard."

How can you love someone and want to tap-dance on his face at the same time?

"I'll be back by Labor Day," he says.

"A lot can happen," I manage around the knot in my throat. "Don't expect to find me standing on the veranda waving my lace hankie."

I try not to kiss him back when he kisses me, but I can't help it. In fact, what I really want to do is get him in a headlock and wrestle him to the floor and sit on his chest till he explains everything to my satisfaction or I talk him out of going, whichever comes first. I've always been a physical kind of girl.

My second choice would be enough anger to carry me till he's gone. I could throw things, slam doors, break glass. Instead, after he leaves the key on the coffee table and walks out the door, I sit down on the couch and hug the cushion and cry.

I still can't believe he didn't tell me about the manuscript.

# part two

· ten ·

# Mac

Crosby, Stills and Nash are getting to the point where they're no fun anymore. Probably because he's listened to the tape three times in a row. He turns it off and sits drumming his fingers on the steering wheel and listening to the hiss and swipe of the windshield wipers.

There's a long line waiting to cross into Canada, bored-looking men in businesslike sedans, and station wagons full of unsmiling families whose vacation plans are washing away in this late-spring storm. There are some pickup trucks, sure. Mostly the big, muscled trucks, wet fenders gleaming like the flanks of Clydesdales, huge, bristling tires and trailer hitches that look like they could pull half of Washington state across the border. But none like the Elky. A few heads turn as he inches closer to the row of booths with the green arrows and flashing red lights.

The border agent is prim mouthed, her black hair pulled severely back, like a caricature of a librarian. He hands over his passport.

"How long will you be in Canada?"

"Just long enough to get to Alaska."

"Is this a business or pleasure trip?"

"Pleasure." It sounds odd when he says it. Like something from a Victorian erotic novel.

"Any firearms or agricultural products?"

"No."

She looks at the bed of the Elky. "What's in back? Under the tarpaulin?"

"Clothes. Books. Camping gear."

"Moving to Alaska?"

"No."

She hands him back the passport with a sheet of white paper tucked inside. "Park over there, please, sir." She nods at a yellow-striped corridor of blacktop off to the right. "And take these forms to customs. That building just to your left."

In the overheated room that smells of wet wool, a tall, gaunt man with thinning brown hair takes the forms. His badge says "Geoffrey MacComber." "What are you carrying?"

"Clothes. Books. Camping gear."

"Not good weather for camping." He runs his thumb and forefinger across his upper lip as if he's recalling a mustache that used to be there.

"Hopefully, that will change."

His smile is more like a grimace. "Oh, it will. Eventually. Is the gear new?"

"Actually, it's very old."

"I'm going to need a listing of everything in the truck." He pushes a pen across the worn counter and stands, shifting his weight and drinking oily-looking coffee while Mac writes on the personal-effects form everything he can remember packing. Then the customs man sighs, as if he'd rather be anywhere else, doing anything else, shrugs into his drab green rain slicker. "Well, let's go have a look." The door rattles shut behind them.

His face brightens when he sees the Elky. "Ah. Nice truck, 1973, eh?"

"Seventy-one."

The inspection is cursory, lasting just long enough to ensure that everything under the tarp gets wet. Then it's back inside, finish the paper shuffling, signing, stamping, stapling. He hands over a copy.

"Drive safely, Mr. McLeod."

In Tsawwassen he stops for coffee, and debates taking a ferry to Salt Spring or one of the other Gulf Islands. To Victoria, and then messing around on Vancouver Island for a few days. But the rain doesn't show any sign of stopping, and he decides to head east, into the mountains. It'll be colder, but probably dry, and he can sleep stretched out in the tent instead of sitting up in the Elky's cab. When he tosses the empty cup into the conveniently located garbage receptacle, he swears he can hear her voice.

*Styrofoam can't be recycled, McLeod.*

For a few seconds he eyes the pay phone next to the coffee bar and actually considers calling her, but she's probably asleep, with the phone unplugged. And if she was awake, and she did answer, what the hell would he say?


British Columbia resembles nothing so much as one of those folding strings of postcards, twisting and winding and snagging the traveler in its gorgeous panoramas. But he drives almost without seeing, up Highway 99 through the spectacular alpine scenery of Garibaldi Provincial Park, past the blue, glacial lakes, the shores crowded with fir and spruce, the meadows still patched with snow.

He thinks about stopping in Whistler for lunch, but it reminds him too much of Vail, with its fake-Swiss-village architecture and expensive shops. The road is good, and the sun's still shining at eight-thirty P.M. when he pulls into a campground just outside of Lillooet. In the cluttered office, he pays for a tent site.

"Right on the river," the jovial host tells him. "Place is pretty much yours tonight. By the way, the pool's heated, if you're so inclined."

He sets up the tent and wanders around the campground, which is all but deserted this early in the season. "Campground" seems somewhat of a misnomer—at least, it's not his idea of camping. RV hookups with barbecue grills, hot showers, and a laundromat. Heated swimming pool and golf course, complete with electric carts.

Dinner is vegetable-barley soup—surprisingly good—in a tiny café near the campground.

The waitress doesn't have a name tag. She's sullen and tired looking and she doesn't do that *Hi, my name is Molly and I'll be your server tonight* thing. It's not that kind of place. She's a waitress, not a server. She'd probably be suspicious of any stranger who wandered in out of the rain showing an interest in her name. An interest in anything other than tonight's special, for that matter. But he hears one of the other waitresses call her Molly.

She stands beside his table, tapping the point of her pencil against the order pad, while he looks at the menu. Her mousy hair hangs in limp strings around her pale, tight face.

"How's the soup?" he asks.

"About the same as it was yesterday."

He tries not to laugh. "Okay. I'll have that."

When she sets the bowl down, he says, "Could I have some more water?"

The heel of her jogging shoe squeaks with her abrupt turn. She doesn't come back with the water pitcher and a basket of bread until he's about half finished. Her eyes are red.

He asks, "Are you okay?"

In answer, she rips the check off her pad and slaps it down next to his water glass. "You can pay up front." She disappears into the kitchen. He fishes the little notepad out of his jacket, takes a pen from his shirt pocket, and writes.

*Molly the waitress. Maybe her feet hurt. Or her shoulders. Or maybe it's not physical at all. Maybe her husband drinks or her kid's in trouble at school or her mother's sick. And when she gets home tonight she still has to deal with it—whatever it is. No matter how tired she is or how sad, she still has to make dinner for somebody, clean up the house, do a load of laundry.*

He orders coffee from the other waitress, who has vampire-black hair and a red slash for a mouth. Her fingernails are like talons; he can't imagine how she can work. When he hands her the check so she can add the coffee, her smile shows lipstick caked on her front teeth.

"Don't worry, I remember." She laughs. "Not like I got any other customers to worry about." She looks at the table. "You want me to clear this stuff?"

"Not yet." They both know he'll be wrapping the bread in a napkin and taking it with him. It cost more than he anticipated to get the Elky road ready and then there was the weekend on Orcas. In hindsight, he probably shouldn't have spent so much on dinner and wine, all of which Wyn correctly suspected was at least partly a crumb tossed to silence his noisy conscience.

He stuffs the bread in his jacket pocket and walks out.

By Friday morning the front has caught up with him. It's a light drizzle while he's collapsing the tent and loading the truck, but it's coming down steadily by the time he pours out the coffee dregs, persuades the engine to turn over, and pulls out of the campground, heading north. He pops in another tape. The Doors. Jim Morrison singing "L.A. Woman." Not his favorite group, but he does like this one. It makes him think of the only L.A. Woman he knows, sound asleep by now in a misty Seattle morning.

Twenty minutes later the rain is more like a solid wall than a curtain and the wipers can't begin to keep up with it. He thinks about pulling over, waiting it out, but while he's thinking, he keeps driving, peering into the mist, gripping the cold blue steering wheel.

His mind blanks out, and the memory just shows up, uninvited, like the black-sheep cousin at a family reunion.

Eight years old. The weekly trip to the city for allergy shots. Going in on the train, the hot, stale-smelling cars that rocked to their own haphazard rhythm, the grimy seats, the crumpled wax-paper cups on the floor, their contents spilled and drying, sticking to the bottoms of his shoes. He sat riveted to the window, watching the trees and houses, bridges and roads flash past. He figured out how to slow them down and look at each thing individually or speed them up into a blur of green and gray fusing together, all depending on the angle of his gaze.

He hated being taken out of school early on Thursdays, hated missing ball games, hated the shots, but Thursday became the high point of the week, the only time Suzanne was his alone. Kevin had wreaked havoc in the waiting room so many times, the doctor had politely suggested he be left at home.

The needle always made a bruise on his arm. Sometimes there was a reaction. His bicep would swell up, hot and tender and itchy. On the train coming home, she'd touch the swelling with her always cold fingers to see if it had gone down or if he'd have to take an antihistamine. Kevin demonstrated an uncanny intuition for the location of the injection, and made it a point to aim a brotherly punch or two on that exact spot.

He'd learned quickly not to favor the sore arm.

Prince George is like the town in cowboy movies where the wagon train gets outfitted for the trek west. It's full of RVs and campers loading up with food, water, fuel, last-minute items like kindling axes, extra batteries, camp shovels, the latest insect repellent. A salesman at the sporting-goods store sells him a bear banger—looks like a fountain pen, sounds like a high-powered rifle, makes smoke, guaranteed to make a bear turn tail. He has the uneasy feeling that if it doesn't work, most users don't make it back to argue about the guarantee.

The same salesman sends him to a local hardware store to buy quarter-inch mesh rabbit wire to screen the radiator from the thousands of bugs that make their home in the north, and clear plastic to duct-tape over the headlights. It all seems vaguely surreal, but he doesn't doubt the necessity of these things.

The rest of British Columbia is a beautiful blur. He feels slightly foolish, driving past some of the most spectacular scenery in the world without stopping. Some vague sense of urgency keeps his foot on the gas pedal, not racing, but pushing on doggedly toward his destination—as if he knew what it was.

At Liard Hot Springs he crosses into the Yukon Territory and picks up the Alaska Highway, following it to Whitehorse, only marginally aware of the changing landscape. The sky opens out now; braided rivers wander through valleys that stretch between horizons, fenced off by distant blue mountains.

The highway is buckled and cracked from frost heave, and in places the pavement is completely washed or scraped clean, leaving only the gravel roadbed and sizable potholes filled with water.

It's fording one of these, about fifty kilometers north of Carmacks, under a sky heavy with clouds, that he hears the sickening crack as something hard and unforgiving strikes the underbelly of the El Camino. He's not inclined to stop till he clears the current obstacle course, and by then, he can feel that something is definitely wrong. The truck is straining and slowing. A glance in the rearview mirror shows a thin plume of black smoke trailing him.

He pulls over and turns off the engine. When he gets out, the first drops of rain spatter on his face and the windshield.

· · ·

Welcome to the Yukon Territory. He tries to think of everything he associates with the Yukon up to this point; it's a vague pastiche of snow, aurora borealis, Sergeant Preston, grizzled miners panning for gold, and dance-hall girls and poker games in smoky saloons.

The first glimpse of Beaverton doesn't bear much resemblance to that picture. It's just a collection of mostly gray and brown buildings, nestled in the bend of a big, muddy, green river, with a range of lavender-gray mountains in the distance. Lining the road into town are a couple of motels that look like relics of better days, a boat and canoe rental, and the corrugated metal and cement building where the tow truck turns off the highway. The sign says simply GARAGE.

The driver, Ian Johnstone, pulls a ragged pack of cigarettes from the pocket of his jumpsuit and sticks one in his mouth but doesn't light it. "Trying to quit," he explains. "I'll have a look at 'er and let you know."

"Should I call you?"

Ian shrugs. "I'll find you."

With a last backward glance at the Elky, Mac pulls his bag out of the back and walks across the road to the Gold Rush Motel.

The woman perched like a delicate bird on the stool next to him has to be at least eighty years old. The skin of her face is crazed, like a clay pot excavated from some archeological dig. Her hair is thick and white, tied back with a black ribbon. She's the only woman in the place not wearing jeans and flannel. The skirt of her blue wool dress drapes gracefully around her legs, to the ankles, and she holds her beer glass in white-gloved hands.

She smiles at him. "I'm Pearl May Austen." Her voice carries the remnants of a British accent.

He returns the smile. "Mac McLeod."

"Welcome to Beaverton, Mr. McLeod. We don't see many visitors this early in the season. May I ask the nature of your visit?"

He turns on his stool to face her, resting his elbow on the bar. Her eyes are a startling, deep blue, almost lavender, her nose straight and long, her mouth firm.

"I'm not sure about the nature of my visit, except that it's going to be longer than I planned. My truck seems to need a new transmission."

She inclines her head, an odd gesture of long-extinct graciousness. "How unfortunate. Is Ian looking after that for you?"

"Right."

"That, at least, is fortunate. He's one of the finest auto mechanics of my acquaintance."

He wonders just how many auto mechanics her acquaintance includes.

"Where were you heading? Dawson?"

"Alaska."

"Ah, the last, best place. And what were you planning to do there?"

"Actually, my plans are somewhat . . . fluid at the moment. Find a job, I guess."

"Not one of those dangerous jobs on the fishing boats, I hope."

"No, something more sedate, I think. Like tending bar."

She raises one sparse gray eyebrow, but doesn't comment.

"Are you English?" he asks.

Her laugh is a dry, pleasant sound that makes him think of leaves crunching underfoot, New York in the fall.

"Only by descent. I was born and reared right here in Beaverton. Of course, my mother was a terrible snob and insisted I go to London to school, but other than those ten dreadful years, I haven't moved around at all, and I plan to die right here in Beaverton, hopefully on this very bar stool. Where is your home, Mr. McLeod?"

"Seattle."

"My family has been in this area since 1896. A colorful bunch, but I won't bore you with details." The almost imperceptible movement of her hand brings the bartender, a tall, sandy-haired guy with an easy grin. "Chris, Mr. McLeod's glass is empty. Please bring him whatever he's drinking. My tab."

Mac's already reaching for his wallet. "Thanks, but I'm not in the habit of letting ladies buy my beer." He holds out a five to the bartender, but he shakes his head.

"Like to help you out, man, but she's my boss."

He laughs. "You own the Beaver Tail?"

"I do. As did my mother before me. So put your money away, Mr. McLeod."

"Mac. And thanks." The bartender sets a beer in front of him on a clean napkin. "How did your mother end up owning a saloon?"

"She was a seamstress by trade, but she won the Beaver Tail in a poker game and decided that being a saloon owner would be a more interesting occupation."

"I expect it was."

She nods. "Oh, yes indeed. I could tell you stories..." She takes a dainty sip of her beer. "What did Ian tell you about fixing your truck?"

"He said the closest place to get a transmission is Whitehorse. If they have what we need. If not there, he'll try Vancouver."

"Either way, it appears you'll be with us for a while. Have you given any thought to accommodations in Beaverton?"

He pictures the barren, drafty motel room across from Ian's garage. The flimsy gold chenille bedspread, the curtains that feel more like paper than cloth. "I'm at the Gold Rush."

"An utterly ghastly place."

"True, but it's cheap. And I've slept in much worse and lived to tell the tale."

"It would please me very much if you would come and stay in my guest house."

"That's kind of you, but—"

"I do hate that word. 'Kind.' It's rather simpering, milquetoastish, don't you think? Besides, kindness has nothing whatsoever to do with my offer. I've some things around the place that need doing, and if you insist on working for a living, you can take them on in exchange for a place to sleep till your truck is ready."

He hesitates.

"Guest house is really a euphemism, the place is no more than a bunkhouse, but it's got a wood stove, and you'll be warm and dry. Please do come. You can bring your things over in the morning."

"Miss Austen—"

"If I'm to call you Mac, you must call me Pearl. Especially if you're staying under my roof."

The bartender grins. "You might as well give up, man. There's no denying Pearl May once she makes up her mind to something."


Pearl May Austen's house is a large, plain, two-story white box at the end of Third Street. A white picket fence in need of repair and repainting is all that divides the gravel yard from the gravel road that leads to it. Up close he can see that the house could use painting as well. The two second-story windows are set off by black shutters hanging crookedly, and the front door is painted red, giving the house the look of a menacing clown face.

He sets his bag down on the wooden stoop, but before he can knock, the door opens and a little boy with matted brown hair and dark, round eyes gazes up at him watchfully. Five, maybe six years old. His green-and-yellow-striped T-shirt boasts a large, sticky-looking spot, and his brown corduroy pants have slipped down from his narrow waist, causing the cuffs to pile up on top of his sneakers. He stares at Mac and chews his index finger.

Mac makes a stab at communication. "Hi."

More staring and chewing.

"Is Pearl May home?"

From somewhere inside the house, a woman's voice. "Emm? Emmett? Where are you? You didn't finish your sandwich." Footsteps. "What are you doing? Your pants are falling—" As she takes his arm she notices Mac and the half smile on her face disappears. She straightens up, regarding him with the same dark eyes, free hand tugging at her white blouse.

"Yes?"

"I was looking for Pearl May."

"She's not home."

"I'm Mac McLeod. She offered to let me stay in the bunkhouse while my truck's—"

"Oh, Jesus." She looks at the sky, and then back at him, the glare hardening into place. "You'd think we were running a damn hotel."

"This looks like a bad time." He picks up his duffle bag. "I can come back later."

"Wait a second." She steps back inside and shuts the door in his face. When the door opens again, she hands him a stack of sheets and towels with a paper-wrapped bar of soap and a key on top. "Around back. Follow the path." She jerks her head to the left and shuts the door, leaving him to pick his way between a couple of bikes and a rusted metal wagon that reminds him of one he had when he was a kid. He winds through a backyard, rampant with wild grasses. A potting bench sags beside a small greenhouse with filthy windows.

The bunkhouse is a small log structure nearly hidden by scrub and tall grass, about fifty yards from the house, on a high bank overlooking a creek. The door's not locked. It's not even completely closed. He toes it open with his boot.

The dim interior is dominated by a huge black stove on an apron of bricks set into a rough plank floor that looks freshly mopped. The rest of the furnishings consist of two narrow beds piled with wool blankets and pillows, a small wooden table, two chairs, and a

rustic hutch full of dishes and cups. In the corner is a large sink with
a red-handled pump. The only light comes from two windows with
wavy glass panes. Cozy for one. He can't imagine sharing it.

He sets his bag on the bed, and is starting to unzip it when
there's a polite knock and the door swings open.

"It isn't Buckingham Palace, but I hope you find it satisfactory."
Pearl May hefts a large metal can with a spout onto the table.
"Kerosene," she says. "Lamps are in the bathroom."

"The bathroom," he repeats, looking around.

"Here." She walks over to a faded green curtain, and pulls it aside
dramatically to reveal a large, white soaking tub in a closet-size
niche. She smiles, crinkling her eyes even more than they were before. "The privy is about twenty yards east."

She shows him the wire basket on a rope to lower perishables
down into the chilly creek water. She demonstrates the firebox and
vents on the hulking black stove, how to empty the ash compartment, points him toward the woodshed.

"You'll probably not be cooking many gourmet meals while
you're here, but I think you'll find this old thing a joy to use. Once
you get used to it."

"I really appreciate this."

She waves a hand. "You're most welcome, Mac."

"I . . . think I upset the—"

"Was she horribly rude?" Pearl's eyes narrow.

"No, I just caught her at a bad time."

"She was rude, wasn't she? It seems any time is a bad time for
Bernie. Bernice. My granddaughter." She opens one of the cabinets
in the bottom of the hutch, talking softly to herself. "Frying pan,
saucepan. Hmm, no teakettle. I'll see to it."

"I can use the saucepan to boil water."

She looks horrified. "Absolutely not. Even the sourdoughs had
proper teakettles."

After she leaves he stands in the middle of the room holding his underwear. Obviously, previous occupants didn't have much in the way of wardrobe. He stacks all the clothes on the single shelf by the sink. The spiral-bound notebook and a fistful of pens go on the table, and now there's just one thing left in the deepest recesses of the duffle. The twisted wreckage of his book, cleverly disguised in a mailing envelope and held by crisscrossed rubber bands. He grips the bag as if testing its weight, then zips it shut and stashes it under the bed.

He sits at the table and takes out the stationery he liberated from the Gold Rush Motel. He pulls the cap off a pen with his teeth and chews on it as he writes.

*Dear Wyn*

## · eleven ·

### *Wyn*

With Mac gone, days assume an orderly progression.

Day One: Guilt. I'm a woman, therefore it must be my fault. He left because I was too a) pushy, b) controlling, c) emotional, d) all of the above.

Day Two: Outrage. He's self-absorbed. Shallow. A commitment-phobe. In short, a typical man.

Day Three: Resignation. Whatever.

Day Four: Invigoration. I've got things to do. Lists to make. I need to research some new breads, clean the apartment, get my finances under control, start jogging again.

Day Five: See Day One above.

As the sun climbs higher and the days engorge with light, the neighborhood comes out of hibernation. The last sweet peas are spent, brown and brittle; the Red Riding Hood tulips have finished blooming, and the Shasta daisies, poppies, geranium and lobelia start to take over the empty spaces, spilling their blooms over the edges of planters in excited profusion. Drifts of maroon and gold daylilies nod along the parking strips. Regular customers start showing up with new puppies or kittens. Painting and construction crews drop by in the mornings on their way to somebody's renovation project. They replace some of our regular guys, gone to work on the fishing boats in Alaska.

With the changing weather come thoughts of France. The airline ticket I stuffed in the bottom of my underwear drawer suddenly beckons. Actually, it does more than beckon. It hollers at me. It waves its arms wildly, like the show-off kid in the back row who always knows the answers. I deserve a break today. Or at least sometime this summer.

"I was thinking about taking some time off."

Ellen's down on her knees in the corner by the front door. She looks over her shoulder at me. "Good idea. When?"

"August? September?" I shrug. "What are you doing down there?"

"Putting out roach motels."

"Roach motels."

"Yeah. You know." She gives an evil laugh. "They can check out anytime they like, but they can never leave." She stands up, dusting her hands. "They're traps with poison bait."

"You mean you're not capturing them live and sending them to repatriation centers where they can be reunited with their next of kin?"

"No. My love of living creatures does not extend to roaches." She turns on the water in the sink and pumps liquid soap into her hands. "And they make such a mess when you squash them."

"Mmm." I look at the Garibaldi in my hand, the raisin filling oozing out of one corner. "Thanks for sharing."

"How long do you want to take off?"

"Well . . ."

She shakes the excess water off her hands and grabs a towel. "You have four weeks coming, but—"

"I just want three."

"That's kind of a long time for you to be gone." She opens a gallon of skim milk and pours some into the frothing jug. "Are you that comfortable with leaving Tyler alone?"

"She's making amazing progress. All she'd need is an extra pair of hands to help her shape the loaves and clean up. I was thinking we could get someone from the culinary academy to do a three-week apprenticeship."

"Yeah, can you actually see Tyler teaching someone?"

"You have a point." I pour myself a glass of orange juice to wash down the Garibaldi. "Maybe one of the Mazurka crew could help her?"

"Good luck getting one of them to work nights." She purses her lips. "Where are you planning to go?"

"My mother and Richard gave me a ticket to France for Christmas."

Her eyebrows lift. "Ask them if they'd like to adopt another daughter. I'm really no trouble at all."

"It's a frequent-flier freebie, so I have to use it by November. And it's not worth it if I just go for a week."

"How about two weeks?"

"I was thinking I'd take two weeks' vacation and then maybe head down to Toulouse and kind of putter around with Jean-Marc for a week. If he's up for it. I might learn something interesting."

"Well, let me sleep on it. Maybe a brilliant idea will present itself at three A.M."

When I get home CM is dawdling over her scrambled eggs. When I tell her my plans, she says, "The company's going to England in August. If you go after we finish our classes, I could meet you in Paris for a week."

"Ooh. That would be more fun than humans are supposed to have. But . . ." I frown. "You think Paris is ready for us?"

She puts her elbow on the table, resting her chin in her hand. "I'd go so far as to say it might usher in a whole new era in foreign relations. Where should we stay?"

"Left Bank, *bien sûr*. Seventh arrondissement."

"Of course, there's always the Île St-Louis." She jumps up and goes over to the bookshelves, returning with my well-worn copy of Frommer's guide to France. "I've always wanted to stay in one of those gorgeous old town-house hotels. Where did you and David stay?"

"The Ritz." The memory makes me sigh. "The best thirtieth birthday I ever had."

She laughs. "Was it worth being married to shithead?"

I smile dreamily. "Yeah, I think it was. Five hundred dollars a night. I can't imagine what it costs now. Dinner at Taillevent. I felt like a princess."

"We'll have at least as much fun, even if we can't stay at the Ritz."

"Yes, we will. And you won't try to recover the cost of the trip from me in court."

We smile at each other, and our smiles expand as we consider the possibilities.


One morning Mitsuko's vegetable market across the street fails to open at the usual time, and sits, shuttered, all day. The next day, Mitsuko and her husband, Fred, are there early, hauling cash registers, tables, boxes, notebooks, baskets, and bins of produce out to a U-Haul trailer.

He comes over with buckets of lemons, apples, onions, carrots, just as Tyler and I are cleaning up and the day shift is arriving. "Whatever you don't want, just put out for your customers," he says.

"But where are you going?" Ellen asks.

He takes off his baseball cap and scratches the pink scalp under his thinning hair. "We're moving to Lopez. Gonna do a little truck garden there, sell at the farmers' market. Take it easier."

"What's going in your space?"

"Dunno." He looks over his shoulder. "I think some artists are renting it. I'm not sure what they're going to do."

"Great," Ellen mutters. "There goes the neighborhood."

"Oh, I hope it's a wonderful gallery." Maggie claps her hands together like something out of a Doris Day movie. "Maybe all the local artists could contribute some work."

Tyler's chin juts out. "They probably don't want any Power Rangers birthday cakes."

I link my arm through hers. "Hey, girlfriend, it's after seven, and we're at liberty. Why don't we go get some breakfast?"

"I gotta meet Barton," she says. "We're trying to find an apartment to rent."

We take off our aprons and toss them in the hamper by the back door. "Are you guys . . . in a relationship or something?"

She laughs loud and long. "In case you didn't notice, he's totally gay. He's just my best friend. Since first grade. He was the only one of the kids I grew up with who still liked me after my mom left and I did my hair blue."

"So where are you looking for apartments?"

"On Capitol Hill. It's cheaper over there than Queen Anne." She shoulders her backpack. "Anyway, I gotta do something. Betty's driving me wackadoo."

"Betty?" I puzzle, stepping out the door behind her.

"The wicked stepmother. Betty Crocker."

"What's the problem?"

"The woman's got bad epazootics of the blowhole."

I burst out laughing. "And what might that be?"

"She never shuts up. I don't know how my dad can stand it."

"He's probably been lonely for someone to talk to."

"Well, it's not like he gets any talking done. Plus, she keeps 'tidy-ing up' my room when I'm not there."

"I'm sure she means well—"

"She's looking for my cocaine spoon."

My head turns sharply and I realize that she's joking.

She rolls her eyes at me. "You and Betty. What a pair."

I leave her at the bus stop and walk down the Ave in the bright, cool morning, thinking about where I can have breakfast reasonably in-expensively. I really can't afford to be eating out so much, but I dread going home in the mornings to that empty apartment. Wan-dering around trying to decide what to do—shower? Go to bed? Read?

I haven't slept well since Mac left. There's a whole different dy-namic in effect when the bed is all yours. Nobody to push up against. Cold sheets. Total silence. It takes some getting used to. Again.

So instead, I treat myself to red-flannel hash at the Five Spot. I sit at a table near the window, reading the paper in the sun, listening to the energetic chatter of people whose day is just beginning, and the sounds of traffic as Queen Anne Hill comes awake.

My eyes open at two o'clock in the afternoon and refuse to shut again. I get up and pace the apartment in my T-shirt and under-pants, study the books in the bookcase, stare listlessly into the re-frigerator, turn resolutely away from the TV. Finally I pull on my sweatpants and go down to pick up the mail. Before I've even begun to sort through the bills and catalogs and circulars advertising car-pet cleaning for $19.95 per room, my eyes lock on the envelope with the Canadian stamp. I walk up the stairs slowly, turning the letter over and over in my hands, almost reluctant to open it, half afraid of what he might say. It's cheap hotel stationery from the Gold Rush Motel in a place called Beaverton, Yukon Territory. The postmark is smeared, so I can't tell if that's where it was mailed.

Back in the apartment I throw all the other mail on the desk, get into bed, and tear the end off the envelope.

*Dear Wyn,*

*They shoot horses, don't they?*

*The Elky's pulled up lame. I hit a pretty big rock driving through what I thought was just a puddle, but was actually a washout on the road north of Carmacks.*

*I'm in a little town called Beaverton, Y.T. (Yukon Territory)— well, actually a big town by Yukon standards, big being anything over 350 pop. It sits in a bend of the Yukon River, and it consists of about four big streets intersecting with a few smaller ones—all of which are gravel/mud and the sidewalks are wooden planks. They don't pave anything here because of frost heave. There's a post office, a general store, a hardware store, two cafés, a barbershop, a church that doubles as a movie theater in summer (so I'm told), a school that goes from kindergarten to whatever the age of the oldest kid, a doctor who doubles as a dentist in emergencies, two motels, and, of course, a saloon.*

*And a gas station/auto repair, where the Elky is staying. The owner, Ian Johnstone, is originally from Toronto, and he's an auto mechanic in summer and a musher in the winter. He's trying to put a team of dogs together to race in the Iditarod next March. I found all this out when I was riding with him in the cab of his tow truck from Carmacks. He said the transmission pan got shoved up and crushed the valve body. I know. It didn't mean much to me either. Loosely translated it means that I need a whole new transmission. Finding one for a '71 Elky and getting it up here is going to take some doing.*

*Up to that point, the drive was easy, only a little rain. I was making good time considering all the roadwork they have to do here in the spring.*

*Anyway, Ian says he'll try to get a transmission from Whitehorse (doubtful). If they don't have one there, he'll try Vancouver. Then Seattle. And so on . . .*

*Looks like Beaverton is going to be home for a while.*

*Fortunately, I've found a place to stay where I can pay my way by doing maintenance work for an old lady named Pearl May Austen, who seems to own about half the town, including the Beaver Tail Saloon, which she inherited from her mother, who won it in a poker game. She also has a psychotic poodle named Egbert. He's pretty old, too. I think he used to be white, but now he's turned sort of yellow, like old book pages. He sits under her bar stool and attacks any feet that get too close to his mistress. The first time I went there, he sank his little fangs into my Raichles. Maybe he thought they were marauding armadillos.*

*For a while just after I crossed the border I was picking up a Vancouver radio station and the woman who did the traffic reports sounded so much like you. I could sort of fool myself into thinking you were somehow talking to me—even if all you told me was to avoid the Burrard Bridge during rush hour because of lane marking. I miss you.*

*Mac*

I fold the pages along the crease lines and stuff them back in the envelope. I lie back on my pillow and stare at the dappled sunlight on the ceiling. The letter is so Mac. All the intimacy of a story from the travel section of the newspaper.

Lead off with an intriguing premise, not too specific, just enough to make the reader want to know more. *They shoot horses, don't they?* Give the reader a bit of orientation. *Beaverton sits in a bend of the*

*Yukon River, population approximately 350.* Then an interesting tidbit. *They don't pave the streets or sidewalks here because of frost heave.* Next, a personal anecdote. *Ian Johnstone told me he's a mechanic in the summer and a musher in the winter as we rode up from Carmacks in his tow truck.* Throw in some local color about Pearl May and Egbert the psycho poodle.

His idea of getting personal is to tell me about the woman who did the traffic report on the Vancouver radio station. Oh, Mac.

He's working for some old lady doing odd jobs. Next thing, he'll be tending bar. Just like he did here. It's like those houses you see sometimes sitting up on blocks, jacked up off the foundation, the destination written in white chalk on the black insulation paper. He's perfectly capable of picking up his entire life and taking it somewhere else, and setting it down again, intact.

## · twelve ·

## *Mac*

I t's early. The sun is low, the trees casting long shadows, and a
pale ghost of a half-moon lurks in the southwest. Back in Seattle it's probably still dark. He pulls on jeans and a sweatshirt in
the cool air, and walks down the winding gravel drive toward the
river. Breathing. That's the thing about the air up here. You keep
wanting to breathe more deeply, hold it longer. Like you could inhale the sky.

He walks along the high-cut bank awash in grasses and dotted
with yellow cinquefoil. A bald eagle scowls from a dead tree on the
opposite shore, and a pure, singular birdsong he's never heard before
sends a chill down his back. The sound of an outboard motor draws
his gaze to the water. A small, red square-stern canoe plows upstream through the chop, bringing cliff swallows pouring out of
their nests in the bluff. At the tiller, wearing a bright yellow dress
and an Aussie bush hat—Pearl May Austen.

Ahead on his right is the abandoned school bus he saw yesterday,
except it's now obvious that it's not abandoned. A black metal chimney pokes up through the roof, puffs of smoke escaping into the
summer morning. He watches for any other signs of life, and when
he's almost directly opposite, a woman steps out the door and waves.

She pantomimes drinking coffee from an imaginary cup, then motions him to come closer. Now he sees the sign that faces the road. MADAME BLUE'S MOOSEBURGERS AND TAROT READINGS.

He turns up the well-worn path. When he gets within speaking range, a brown blur rounds the corner of the bus and stops between him and the woman.

"Hah," the woman says. He thinks it an odd thing to say until he realizes that she has a southern accent, and what she said was *Hi.* "Don't mind him." She nods at the animal guarding the path like some Manhattan nightclub bouncer.

The dog stands stiff legged, making a low rumbling noise at the back of his throat, mouth pulled back to display a menacing set of teeth.

"Jester, shame on you, dog. That's real inhospitable. Now sit." He sits, but his golden eyes follow Mac's careful approach.

"Interesting eyes."

"He's part wolf."

"The front part, I bet. Nice doggie."

"He really is nice," she says. "In fact, he's nothing but a big, fuzzy cream puff. He just doesn't know you." She turns to the dog. "I want you to apologize to this man. Sorry, I didn't get your name."

"Mac."

"I'm Rhiannon. This is Jester. Jester, tell Mac you're sorry."

The dog cocks his head to one side. His ears flop down lazily and he makes a little crying sound. "Perfect. Good boy. Good Jester."

"His name's Jester?"

"I named him after the fool card. In the tarot. Means the same thing, but if I went around this place hollering 'Fool!,' half the town would show up." She grabs Mac's hand and places it on the dog's head. "Give him a scratch behind the ears, then a rub under his chin."

He does as instructed, but cautiously. After two strokes under the chin, the wolf dog lies on the ground, head resting on Mac's feet.

Rhiannon grins happily. "See? Is that nice? Now just don't try to walk or he'll take your leg off—just kidding!"

"Ha, ha. Listen, I already had one dog sink his fangs into my boot."

"What dog was that?"

"Egbert. Pearl May's dog."

She snorts. "That's not a dog. It's a rat with a bad perm. We call him Eagle Bait." A broad wink. "Not in front of Pearl May, of course. Want some coffee? I hope you like chicory coffee, 'cause I got hooked on it years ago and it's all I drink. I order it up specially from New Orleans."

Without waiting for an answer, she opens the door. "Come on in."

The inside of the bus isn't what he expected. It's outfitted like a thoroughly modern RV, complete with two sinks, a sizable refrigerator, and a four-burner stove. From outside, he hears the muted hum of a generator.

"Nice setup."

"Leon was pretty damn handy. My boyfriend. Ex-boyfriend. This was his end of the place and that"—she nods toward the back end of the bus—"was mine."

The far end looks like a gypsy fortune-teller's tent, draped with an astonishing array of shawls, scarves, rugs, blankets, and beach towels. Which makes sense, because Rhiannon looks every inch the gypsy fortune-teller. Wearing a long, red-and-yellow flowered dress—or nightgown, he can't be sure—a vest embroidered with more flowers, and a shawl. Her hair is long and wild and wavy and streaked with gray.

"So you're from Seattle, huh?"

He stops, the cup halfway to his mouth.

"What's wrong? Oh, I bet you want cream and sugar. I'm sorry, I got sugar, but I don't keep cream around. I don't like it and it just goes bad." She stands on top of a chair to reach a pink china sugar bowl. He drops two cubes in the cup and she plops a spoon in.

"Actually, I was just wondering how you knew I'm from Seattle."

She waves her hand. "If I was dishonest and shameful, I'd let you think I de-vined that." She closes her eyes and puts a hand on her forehead. "I'm picking up vibrations from . . . Washington. Spokane? No. I see a great white city on the water. Seattle. Yes, that's it. Seattle." She laughs. "Not that I'm saying I don't do that once in a while. My powers are always a bit rusty right at the start of the season, but they're there, I promise you. But this time . . . well, let's just say they got a moccasin telegraph around here that never quits. And you're the only stranger in town at the moment, so we all know you're from Seattle and you got an El Camino pickup truck sitting over in Ian's garage that ain't goin' nowhere no time soon. So welcome to Beaverton."

"Well, thanks. I guess."

She closes her eyes again. "I'm picking up vibrations of ambivalence. Best cure for that is one of Madame Blue's famous mooseburgers. You want cheese or onions or both?"

"Actually, I haven't had breakfast yet—"

"Of course not. This is breakfast. It's great protein, very little fat. It'll keep your motor runnin' all day. It's three-fifty with chips and a soft drink or coffee, fifteen dollars gets you all that plus a reading. Or, if you'd rather, you can sit here and help me make up some patties for this week and your breakfast is free."

"In that case, I'll work off my tab." He looks at a large tub of ground meat thawing in the sink. "This looks like a lot of mooseburgers. You get that many customers out here?"

"You'd be surprised. I get a lot of campers and fishermen. The locals. Tourists'll be picking up pretty soon. Lot of people stop on the way between Dawson and Whitehorse. I got a pretty good following. And then about two years ago they started including me in the official *Yukon Guide Book*. I s'pose that means I been here long enough to be an official Yukon tourist attraction—the eccentric Madame Blue and her famous mooseburgers. And then there's the spiritual adviser thing. Lots of folks around here won't make a move till they come see me."

"How long have you been here?"

"Ooh, let's see. About eight years. Maybe a little more. I don't exactly remember 'cause we went through here twice. When the bus broke down, my so-called boyfriend headed back to Texas and I decided to stay. Wash your hands over there and I'll get the music cranked up."

He's rolling up his shirt sleeves when a noise blares out of the two tiny speakers on top of her refrigerator. It's a vocal, he knows, but he can't understand the words. The singer sounds not only drunk, but also like his adenoids are strung together with barbed wire.

"Hope you like Texas music," Rhiannon says.

"It doesn't sound like any country music I've heard," he says.

"That's because it's not country. It's Texas. The Austin sound. This is Jerry Jeff Walker. You'll love him once you get used to it."

"I'm sure I will. But maybe you could turn it down a little? The coffee hasn't kicked in yet."


It's close to ten A.M. when he leaves Rhiannon, having narrowly escaped a tarot reading, and walks back up the road toward the house. He's crossing the front yard when he hears someone shout: "Hey! You want this or not?"

He looks up to see Bernice standing on the front stoop holding a battered copper teakettle. Instead of walking out to meet him, she waits for him to come back to her.

Her expression hasn't changed since yesterday—he takes it for a combination of boredom, frustration, and general free-floating bad mood—but her straight black hair is tied back with a white ribbon, and she's wearing an iridescent pink lipstick that looks all wrong against her smooth, caramel-colored skin.

"You must be Bernice."

"Yeah, too bad about that." She looks up at him from under a thick fringe of hair that's too long to be called bangs. Her face is round, nose short, eyes shaped like almonds. She's not exactly pretty, but there's something that compels you to look at her—an almost palpable sexual thrum.

"Thanks for the kettle."

"You can thank Pearl. I had nothing to do with it."

There doesn't seem to be much chance of striking up a conversation, so he starts back up the path.

"You better be careful walking around like that."

He turns. "Like what?"

"With your head up your ass. There's bears around here, you know. You better pay attention."

"Thanks for the advice."


The days, which at first were too long and depressingly free form, take on a loose and comfortable structure. Every morning at first light he walks the riverbank through white bedstraw, blue spikes of wild delphinium, yellow arnica. Tender new leaves on aspen crowns quiver in the light. The river trundles past, greenish-gray under wisps of fog, and the sandbars are black with birds—ducks, sandpipers, and plovers. He lets his mind go still.

After a breakfast of bread and cheese and coffee, or sometimes a mooseburger at Madame Blue's, he works around the house. Olivia Myles, who owns the hardware store, lets him use her radial saw to cut new pickets for the fence. He replaces the broken, rotted ones in one long morning. Afternoons he tends bar at the Beaver Tail with Mitch Cason, a weathered retiree from Saskatchewan. Dinner he keeps simple, usually soup and bread, because he hasn't quite got the hang of cooking on the woodstove, and afterward he tries to write, rarely successfully, but failing that, he sits on his porch in the long twilight reading books from Pearl May's extensive collection.

The following week he sets about painting the fence, proceeding slowly, methodically. Dipping the brush, scraping the excess paint off on the rim of the can, taking pleasure in the contrast of the smooth, bright paint and rough, drab wood. The repetition of the task is oddly soothing, and his thoughts float disjointedly among rock-climbing memories, the book he's reading about a canoe trip on the Yukon River, and the story of Tom Sawyer whitewashing the fence.

At some point he becomes aware of a dark shape in his peripheral vision, and he turns to see Emmett, one shoe untied, shirttail half out of his jeans, clutching a toy red fire truck to his stomach and watching him with an almost hypnotic intensity.

"Hi, Emmett."

He keeps looking, but doesn't speak.

"What are you up to this morning?"

In answer, Emmett holds out his toy.

Mac runs a finger over one shiny fender. "Pretty cool truck."

Emmett sets it down and squats next to it, pushing it through the gravel toward Mac, picking it up, pushing it the other way.

"How old are you, Emmett?"

He considers the question, then holds up his right hand, fingers spread apart, and his left hand, with his index finger up and the rest bunched tightly in his palm.

"I can't count too well. Tell me how many that is."

"Six."

The quick response and the confidence of the soft voice are surprising.

"I go to school," he adds.

"You like it?"

Emmett nods. He lets himself fall backward into a cross-legged sit, running the truck back and forth as if he were alone. Mac goes back to painting, and the only sounds are the soft rasp of the paintbrush and the truck's plastic wheels in the gravel.

"Me?" he says suddenly and Mac looks around.

"You what?"

He points at the fence. "Me." This time it's not a question.

"Okay. Come over here. Take the brush."

Emmett dunks it in the paint halfway up the handle and pulls it out from under the rim of the can, splattering paint in a wide arc. Mac picks up a rag.

"Here, let me wipe that——" He reaches for the brush, but Emmett holds it back.

"Nooo." It's a drawn-out wail.

Mac takes the brush. "Let me show you something." He wipes the paint off the handle and gives it back to Emmett. "Stand right here." He puts his hand on the bony little shoulder and places the child between himself and the fence. Then with his hand over Emmett's, he dips the brush, scrapes off the excess, and brushes a white trail down a new picket.

The sudden, delighted grin on the boy's face produces an unfamiliar constriction in Mac's chest. "Again?"

Emmett nods.

The rhythm of their labor is broken by a voice. "Emmett, what are you doing? You're not supposed to be out here bothering him."

Bernice frowns into the morning sun.

"He's not bothering me."

She hesitates. "Well, you're not being paid to baby-sit." She twists the hem of her T-shirt.

"I'm not baby-sitting. He's helping me paint."

"I'm helping," Emmett says.

Bernice looks dubious. "With that much help, it'll take you twice as long."

"I don't think Pearl cares. Do you?"

At the mention of her grandmother's name, her face stiffens. "Probably not." She turns back to the house. "If he gets to be a pest, send him back."

"'Bye, Mommy."

She turns back, and in her eyes is the first softness he's seen there. " 'Bye, Emm." It's almost a smile.

"So, what do you think?" Chris eyes him curiously, adjusting the bow tie that Pearl insists the bartenders wear for high season.

"Ripped from the pages of *Esquire*."

Chris laughs. "Not about the tie, shithead. The Beaver Tail. Beaverton. The decline of western civilization. Whatever."

"The Beaver Tail is actually pretty similar to Bailey's, where I worked in Seattle. Maybe a touch more rustic, but a saloon's a saloon, for the most part. Beaverton—I like it. It's like this little wrinkle in time. If the Elky had to break down, I'm glad I landed here. The decline of western civilization—inevitable."

He stuffs the clip-on bow tie into his jacket pocket and smiles back.

"Talkative bastard, aren't you? Whyn't you come for dinner sometime? My old lady's Irish, and she's a great cook."

"Sounds good. When?"

"Dunno. Sunday night? It's my only night off."

That's how he finds himself knocking on the blue door of the neat clapboard house three blocks from the Beaver Tail on Sunday night, after his shift ends. Chris answers the door unshaven, wearing jeans and a long-sleeved Indiana Pacers T-shirt. The twin aromas of roasting meat and baking bread float out like an invitation.

"Come on in."

"I tried to find a decent bottle of red, but . . ." He holds out a six-pack of Heineken.

"This is great. We've got plenty of wine, and Norie and I mostly drink beer anyway." He shuts the door behind Mac, calling out, "Norie! Company's here."

Footsteps, then a woman appears from what he assumes is the kitchen. Her hand is already extended and her grip is strong. "Mac, hi. I'm Nora. Welcome to Beaverton. What can I get you to drink? Ooh, Heiney's. Thanks." She takes the six-pack from Chris.

She's short, but sturdy. Next to her husband she resembles a boulder leaned up against a mountain. Her pretty face is un-made up, freckled and flushed from the heat of cooking. Her dark hair is pulled back into a haphazard arrangement. But it's her eyes that command attention—a deep, clear green, full of intelligence and humor.

"It's going to take a wee bit longer cooking, so you lads have a seat in the living room and pop a couple of beers. And don't tell anything exciting till I get there." A soft lilt is all that remains of an Irish accent.

"So what brings you up north?" Chris takes a long swallow of beer. "It's a bit on the early side. Weather's still pretty iffy. It's not unheard of to have snow in June. You might've— "

"Now I hope you didn't tell too much. I do hate missing out on things." Nora flounces back in and flops down on the couch next to Chris. "I want to know what brought you up here so early in the year and what you plan to do and how long you'll be staying— "

Chris laughs, a rumbling chuckle. "We're just getting started on all that, my love."

"I was just passing through on my way to Alaska. I was coming up from Carmacks when I rolled over something hidden in a pothole and it took out my transmission."

"That's all fine, well, and good," she says, flashing a dimple. "You're on your way to Alaska, but why? And why now? It's an odd time of the year to be traveling up here, I'm sure. We're somewhat like the French foreign legion up here, Mac. Everybody has a story. They don't come *to* the Yukon so much as come away *from* else-where."

"And what's your story?"

She leans her head against Chris's arm and laughs. "Fair enough. Can I have a sip?" Without waiting for her husband to answer, she takes the bottle from his hand and drinks. "I wanted out of Ireland. It's a hard place for an independent woman. They give you lots of guff and expect you to take it and swallow it down and say thank you, sir. I came to Toronto for school, earned a degree in finance. Now in Ireland, a woman with a degree in finance has about the same status as a duck who can juggle. She's a great conversation piece, something you'd love to take round to the pub and show the lads, but as for a job..." She laughs good naturedly. "The only position they like a woman for is on her back, you see. And when they're done with you there, it's into the kitchen."

"What are you doing up here with that degree in finance?"

Her grin broadens. "The answer is not a lot. I help some of the shopkeepers with their taxes, keeping their books and such. But here, it's my choice, not somebody else's. Now Chris, he's got a whole different story, being a Yank like yourself, but I'll let him tell it." She hands the bottle back to Chris, half empty.

"So you're American?"

"Yep." Chris rests his arm along the top of the couch and his fingers stroke his wife's dark hair absently. "I crossed the border in seventy-one. I was nineteen years old and my number came up. I didn't want to go to 'Nam and I didn't want to go to jail, so my best friend and I came to Canada."

"Where are you from?"

"Indiana."

"How did you get all the way up here?"

"I didn't come here at first. I went to Toronto. That's where I met Nora. We started working our way west and then north."

"Chris Moody, you're leaving out all the good parts." She looks from him to Mac, exasperated. "Why is it that all you men ever want to tell is what and where and when. If you're really pushed, you might tell how. But you'll never, ever say why." She glances down at her watch. "Our food's gonna be finished cooking. Come help me with the plates, both of you, and we won't say another word till we're sitting at the table. Mac, what'll you drink with dinner?"

In ten minutes they're eating. Shallow bowls hold some kind of pot roast, tender and succulent, carrots and potatoes and sweet green peas and tiny onions. On the cutting board is a golden loaf of soda bread, fragrant and still warm. It's disconcerting how the mere sight of a loaf of bread, the smell of it, inundates him with thoughts of Wyn. He eats in silence, stopping only to tell Nora how good it all is.

"It's moose," she says. "Best meat in the world, if you know how to cook it."

"Which you obviously do."

"I like this one, Chris. He can stay." She pushes the platter at him, and he helps himself to more carrots and potatoes. "Have some more bread, too."

"Thanks, I will. How did you two hook up in the wilds of Toronto?"

Chris and Nora exchange one of those looks by which longtime lovers acknowledge their shared history.

"I went to a party," Nora says, smiling at Chris, then turning to Mac. "It was one of those things—you're probably a bit young to recall— but it seemed like in those days a party consisted of a bunch of people in the same room getting so wasted that they might as well have stayed home alone. The ones who were still somewhat coherent were doing their antiwar rant, which you couldn't hear anyway because the music was so loud, and there were strobe lights and marijuana smoke so thick you could hardly breathe—just a typical seventies get-together.

"Anyway, I was there under duress. This girlfriend had begged me to go, so she wouldn't have to go alone, then about fifteen minutes after we got there, she disappeared into the bedroom with the host and left me standing there talking to his wife. All I could think of was how I was going to get home, because the car was my friend's, and then all of a sudden, something happened to the stereo system. I can't recall if it broke, or if someone tripped over the cord, or what, but the music just stopped. Everybody was standing there, looking stupid, trying to get the spark plugs in their brains firing again, and then this guy, who I hadn't really noticed, who'd apparently been sitting by himself in a corner, stood up and sort of curled his lip into this sneer and started singing 'Now and Then There's a Fool Such as I.' "

She pauses for a delighted laugh. "And looking straight at me."

Chris tips back his bottle of beer. "She was the most gorgeous thing I'd seen in months. Maybe years."

"So you're an Elvis fan?"

Nora's eyes close. "Is the pope Catholic? He'll have to show you his museum." Chris looks ready to bolt from the table till she adds, "After dessert."

Dessert is a custardy, vanilla-scented rice pudding, studded with plump raisins, and a pot of strong tea. The instant he sets down his spoon, Chris pushes back from the table.

"To the parlor?" he says.

"Been there before," says Nora. "You two go ahead."

Chris leads the way to the rear parlor, a throwback to the days when there was a gathering place for the family separate from the room where visitors were received. The room is cold, dimly lit, and lined with homemade, mismatched shelving, ugly but functional, the kind of thing you'd see in somebody's garage.

At one end of the room is a bank of black stereo components— receiver, turntable, two tape decks, graphic equalizer—a fairly serious audiophile's setup. Four large speakers in the corners face a black recliner sitting center stage. On the shelves are record bins full of LPs and 45s, including various artists, but one entire bin is devoted to the recordings of Elvis. From 45s in their slip jackets, bearing the yellow Sun Records label, to the cheesy, bland LP sound tracks of forgettable movies, to the last live performance from Hawaii.

There are books about Elvis, books about his music, books of his music. There are posters—Elvis in black leather, gold lamé, jeans, Elvis as Aztec sun god. Notebooks full of publicity stills from his movies. There are stuffed tigers and teddy bears, lunch boxes and shot glasses, salt and pepper shakers, wristwatches and handkerchiefs and hats.

"Holy shit. When you said you were a fan, you weren't kidding."

Chris extends his hands, palms up, a gesture of modesty, almost embarrassment. "I know it's probably a little strange . . . I don't know why, but I've always . . . I don't know, is 'love' the right word? Admired? Or maybe I just wanted to be him."

He offers Mac the recliner, and he plugs in a small space heater, pulls up the desk chair. "I've put together my own tapes. You want to hear one?"

"Sure."

From the corner of his eye, he watches, amazed and amused, as Chris lip-synchs every song, shaking his sandy-blond hair, eyes drooping half closed. His timing, expressions, and gestures are flawless, from the bluesy shout of "Jailhouse Rock" to the unctuous sincerity of "Are You Lonesome Tonight?," complete with the spoken bridge.

When the tape begins its auto-reverse, Mac signals time-out.

"Sorry," Chris says sheepishly. "I get carried away. I forget that not everybody's as into the King as I am. I even went to Graceland on my honeymoon. My first honeymoon. 1970."

Mac laughs. "What do you mean, *you* went to Graceland? Where was the bride?"

Chris shakes his head. "She was only there physically. She didn't want to go. She wanted to go to Florida or someplace, lie on the beach all day and drink those rum drinks and screw like bunnies all night."

"Sounds like a fairly normal honeymoon. Why Graceland?"

The look on his face implies that the answer should be self-evident. "He was the King."

"Yeah, but he was still alive then. It wasn't like you could take a tour."

"Kind of weird, I know." He pushes up the sleeves of his Pacers shirt. "I had this fantasy, like she and I would be standing at those big old wrought-iron gates and he'd just kind of walk out. Not even that he'd invite us in or anything, but that he'd find out we were newlyweds and . . . I don't know. Bless us or something."

"Bless you?"

"Yeah, you know. Bless the marriage or something. Like the pope. Like that would make it right. I guess even then I knew the whole thing was a mistake. The marriage, I mean."

"So . . ." Mac takes a sip of the now warm beer. "What did your wife think?"

The grin is innocently loopy. "That I was a few sandwiches short of a picnic. She never got it. Never got me."

"Why did you guys get married?"

"We were seventeen. I was horny as hell. She was, too, but she wanted to get married, buy some land, make some babies. We went to Graceland, and then we were supposed to drive to Florida, but . . . we were like this close to Tupelo . . ." He holds up his thumb and forefinger. "I made a quick detour to see his birthplace. Little white clapboard house with a porch swing. Then I wanted to see his school . . . Geez, what a sick sonofabitch." He laughs.

"She sat in the car with her hands in her lap and didn't say a word till we got back to Indy. After the first night we never even had sex. Just drove around in the damn car." He gets up and takes the cassette out of the tape deck, replacing it in its plastic case, refiles it carefully. He turns to Mac with his hands stuck down in his pockets. "Feeling alone when you're by yourself isn't nearly as bad as feeling alone when you're with somebody."

"Particularly on a honeymoon, I'd guess. But you still stuck it out till you got drafted?"

"Yep. We did. Both of our families would've croaked if we'd just come straight back from the honeymoon and gotten divorced. Hers would've told everybody I was queer and mine would've said she turned out to be not a virgin." Chris produces a beat-up leather pouch and proceeds to roll a joint. He flips the top back on an old Zippo lighter and flicks the wheel.

Mac stares, inhaling the sharp twangy smell of lighter fluid. The flame jumps and a long-submerged image surfaces. His father sitting on the gunwale of a small sailboat tied to a dock. A pack of Lucky Strikes, the red-circle logo clearly visible through the white shirt pocket. Smoke rings drifting up into the calm air.

Chris takes a long toke and holds it. Then, "Now you know all about me. What have you been doing for the past twenty years?"

"Fourteen." Mac grins. "I didn't graduate from high school till seventy-six."

"A kid. So you missed out on all that Vietnam shit." He holds out the joint, but Mac shakes his head.

"Yeah, I was lucky."

"Yeah, you were." He knocks a piece of ash into a glass ashtray and stares for a few seconds at the glowing red tip. "Pretty much tore my family apart. My old man never forgave me. He died last year."

"Sorry."

Chris sighs. "I guess he'd've died happier if I'd gotten my ass blown off in 'Nam." Chris takes another drag. "But what about you?"

Mac turns the green bottle around in his hand. "Let's see. Went to NYU for two years. Then I hitchhiked out west. Did a lot of rock climbing and skiing for a while, then I hitchhiked through New Zealand and went to Europe. Came back and started working my way west again. Six years ago I ran out of money in Seattle, got a job bartending, and I've been there ever since."

"Rock climbing? That's pretty scary stuff."

Mac smiles. "That's what most people think. Actually, it's not climbing that's scary. It's climbers."

"Ever been married?"

"Nope."

"You want to talk about scary..." Chris kills the joint and lies down on the floor, hands behind his head. "Of course, with Nora, it's a whole different thing," he says quickly.

"She seems like a pretty cool lady."

"And then some." Chris closes his eyes. "And then some. I could—" He looks over at Mac. "You still haven't said what you're doing up here in God's country."

"I'm not really sure. I just needed to get away. Always wanted to go to Alaska..."

Chris laughs. "What did you need to get away from? Did you rob a bank? Seduce somebody's wife?"

"Nothing that exciting. I just like to get by myself sometimes. It helps me think."

"So what are you thinking about?"

Mac takes another swallow of beer. "Have you considered police work?"

Chris laughs. "No, but I'm a bartender. You know how it is. I'm used to people bending my ear all the time. Then you come along and won't tell me a damn thing. Makes me curious."

"Okay, here's the truth..." He hesitates and Chris rolls over on his side, expectant. "I'm a... writer. Sort of."

"What kind of stuff do you sort of write?"

"I'm working on a novel. And it wasn't going too well."

"So you just hauled ass outta town. And now you're up here, writing about all of us." He laughs. "Sort of like a vampire. But instead of blood, you suck people's stories. Their lives."

Mac shrugs. "You could say that."

"I guess you probably think people who aren't writers don't understand." Chris is still smiling, but slightly unfocused.

"Actually, yeah. But then I don't understand plumbers or auto mechanics either. It doesn't mean one is better or worse than the other."

The sun still hovers above the horizon just after ten P.M. and the air is thick and sweet with the smell of the river and of damp, green, growing things. His boots clomp on the wooden sidewalk in front of the Beaver Tail, which is noisy with tourists and fishermen and locals trying to make themselves heard over a Waylon Jennings song on the juke box. Two mongrel dogs lie next to the door, patiently waiting for someone. The yellow one lifts its nose for an inquisitive sniff as he hurries past.

He cuts through the little park across the street where tall blue spikes of delphinium and larkspur, and masses of white daisies, cover the ground, and red geraniums tumble crazily out of planters, everything drunk with the excess of daylight.

Crunching through Pearl May's gravel yard, he heads around back to the bunkhouse. He retrieves a beer from his wire basket, slowly lowers it back down to the creek. He goes straight to the table, opens his notebook, uncaps a pen, and writes, carried on a burst of sudden energy like the plants in the park. It's twenty minutes before he stops to open the sweating bottle.

*Dear Wyn,*

*Pearl May offered me a job tending bar just for the summer, and I've accepted. It's some extra money, since getting the Elky up and running again is apparently going to cost slightly more than the GNP of a third-world country. I don't even have to stay the whole summer. If I leave in August, I can still get to Alaska and back to Seattle by September. Maybe mid-September.*

*The tourists have arrived, along with the mosquitoes and black flies. I think most of them see the Yukon as something to be driven through as quickly as possible on their way to Alaska or at least to Dawson City—which Pearl May refers to as the Klondike Stampede Theme Park.*

*After B.C., which is like nature on steroids, the Yukon is almost austere. Where I am is a huge golden valley ringed by low hills, and farther away, purple mountain peaks. The Yukon River is green—cold, swift, and dangerous. The sky is blue and goes on forever. The hardest thing to describe is the vastness, the emptiness. It's the sort of place where you could disappear without so much as a ripple.*

*It happens all the time here. People get lost, drown, fall, freeze to death, starve, get struck by lightning, attacked by bears, eat the wrong plants. Whole planeloads of people fall out of the sky or smash into mountains in the fog. Sometimes it seems you could simply be swallowed whole by the emptiness.*

*My father is buried somewhere in the Canadian Rockies—probably. Under the frozen remains of the light plane that was taking him and a friend to hunt moose. Or was it elk? Or were they on the way back? My memory of the event is sketchy. My clearest recollection of that day is Suzanne, lying on the kitchen floor. Screaming.*

*It was an eerie sound, not even a noise you'd think a human could make. I was twelve years old and scared—not scared like when I got a cramp in the ocean or when Kevin and Ted Banks threatened to beat the shit out of me if I told about their looting the collection box at church. It was a kind of scared that made me feel completely out of control. I wanted to run away. To put as much distance as possible between me and that noise.*

*But I was talking about the Yukon. I guess it stands to reason that this country where you could so easily lose yourself attracts people who are trying to get lost. The locals say that no one comes to the Yukon, they've all come from something or someone or somewhere else. With the exception of Pearl May, who was born and raised here, I've found that to be mostly true.*

*Chris Moody, bartender at the Beaver Tail. Left Indiana in '71 because he didn't want to go to Vietnam. He ended up here with his wife, Nora, who, I suppose you could say, came to be with him, although she was definitely trying to escape Ireland when she met Chris.*

*Ian says he came here to be a serious musher, but the rumor is that he had two wives . . . at the same time. One in Ottawa and one in Toronto.*

*Rhiannon Blue of Madame Blue's Mooseburgers and Tarot Readings. Probably not her real name. Although stranger things have happened, I suppose. And she is from Texas, after all. Lives with her half wolf/half dog Jester in an old school bus that her former boyfriend converted into a gypsy caravan/RV. Whatever she was coming from, it must have been really bad if she didn't even want to keep her name.*

*Foster. No last name. Or maybe Foster's his last name and he has no first name. Every week he runs the same classified ad in the Beaver Tale (get it?). He's looking for an Acme5X24 series time-transducing capacitator with built-in temporal displacement and AMD dimensional warp generator module. Object: time travel.*

*And then there's yours truly, who came to Beaverton ostensibly by accident. According to Rhiannon, who claims to be in touch with a higher authority, there are no accidents. She hasn't read the cards for me yet, but she reads the cards for the world at large every day— sort of like those VLA listening devices aimed toward outer space to pick up any stray extraterrestrial communications. She says I'm here for a reason, although she can't be more specific right now. I wish I had her certainty.*

*The only thing I'm certain of is that I'm here. And you're in Seattle. And there are too many miles in between.*

*Mac*

## thirteen

*Wyn*

When I get to work, Tyler's dancing around outside like a manic jackrabbit.

"Glad you could make it," she scolds me.

I look at my watch. "It's just now eleven P.M. Why didn't you let yourself in?"

"I can't find my key."

I give her an exasperated look. "Why don't you put it on your key ring?"

She returns my look and ups the ante. "Because I usually don't need it. You're always here before me."

"I wish you'd put it on anyway. I don't like the idea of the bakery key floating around in outer space somewhere." I unlock the door and she follows me in, practically on my heels.

"It's not floating around anywhere. It's probably on my dresser or in the pocket of my other jeans."

She runs around turning on all the lights, then thrusts a bedraggled piece of paper under my nose. "Look. It's my mom's recipe for squaw bread. She always used to make it at Thanksgiving."

"Let me just take my jacket off. Why don't you start pulling the dough out of the cooler."

She throws her jacket on the desk and heads for the storeroom while I turn off the answering machine and put on highlights from *La Bohème*. The paper that she left on the worktable is handwritten in that kind of penmanship young girls sometimes affect, with lots of loops and scrolls and every *i* dotted with a tiny circle. Not exactly the way I picture Tyler's mother, but I guess we were all young once.

Tyler comes out of the storeroom with a bucket of dough in each hand. "I found it when I was packing up some kitchen stuff. Isn't it cool?"

"Why were you packing up kitchen stuff?"

She sets the buckets on the table. "Don't you remember? I told you I was looking for a place to rent. We're moving in July first— Barton and me and DeeDee and Felice."

"Oh, right. But I thought it was just you and Barton. Who are the other two?"

"DeeDee got kicked out of Queen Anne the year before I graduated. She works at Tower Records. Felice isn't from here. I met her down by Pike Place Market one night. At the movie theater. She works at one of those shops downstairs by the Hillclimb. They sell, like, South American imports. Ponchos and sandals and stuff. Me and Barton couldn't afford anyplace good by ourselves."

"Barton and I," I correct her.

"You're coming, too? The landlord says we can't have more than four."

"Very funny." I hand her back the recipe. "This sounds okay, except there's an awful lot of sugar and wheat bran in it."

"So?"

"It just seems like it might be hard to raise with that amount of yeast."

"Can't we just try it?"

"Of course. In fact, take this back to the storeroom and see if we have everything."

She finds some molasses left over from Ellen's gingerbread experiments, and happily busies herself making squaw bread in the small Hobart while I stir up a sponge for semolina bread and put together some whole wheat Irish soda bread. By the time I'm finished with those, the whole wheat–walnut dough is at room temperature, ready to be shaped, and Tyler's still futzing with the squaw bread.

"How's it coming?" I ask.

"Okay. It's just really sticky."

I look over at her and swallow a laugh. It looks as if she's trying to extricate herself from a pound of bubble gum.

"Sometimes those dark breads are. Try wetting your hands instead of flouring them. As soon as I get this whole wheat–walnut in the pans, I'll help you shape it."

Just then Mimi and Rodolfo are singing their final "*Addio senza rancor.*"

"You listen to the weirdest music," Tyler says. "That chick sounds like she's dying."

"That's because she is. Not only that, but she and her lover are breaking up."

"No wonder. Can we put on some U2?"

I have a bad feeling about the squaw bread. It feels leaden when you handle it. There's no life to it, no elasticity. "Did you knead it long enough?"

She glares at me. "Of course."

"Okay, we'll just have to bake it off and see what happens."

She puts it in the oven and sets the timer. Thirty minutes later we have four little brown hockey pucks of squaw bread sitting on the cooling rack. Tyler's face draws into a scowl.

"Well, it never turned out like that when my mom made it."

"I'm sure it was wonderful. Did you double-check all the ingredients?"

"I'm not a troglodyte. The yeast must've been bad."

"You don't have to be a troglodyte to make a mistake. And the yeast worked fine in the semolina sponge. The other possibility is, sometimes home bakers modify their recipes and they forget to write down what they changed."

"Shit!" She throws the towel on the floor, then picks it up.

"Forget it. That's why you do a trial batch before a full batch. We'll figure it out. In fact, it might be a useful exercise for you."

Her head bobs from side to side as she mimics me. "'It might be a useful exercise for you.'" She chortles like some demented hobbit. "When she calls me I'll ask her if she changed something."

"When is she supposed to call?"

"Monday. It's my birthday. She always calls on my birthday."

When the morning crew comes in, the first thing that happens is, Maggie catches sight of the hockey pucks.

"My word, what are these little bricks?"

"Keep your meathooks off my squaw bread," Tyler snarls.

"'*Squaw bread*'? You can't be serious. Don't you realize what a pejorative that is?"

Tyler stares at her, wildly pissed off, and not about to admit that she has no idea what a pejorative is.

"It's an insult," Maggie rattles on. "'Squaw' is the worst kind of slang. It's a very vile term for a part of a woman's anatomy. It's totally dehumaniz—"

"You are so full of shit."

Ellen comes charging in from the back room with the cash box. "Maggie, are you here early for a reason?"

"I have a cake being picked up at nine."

"Then I suggest you get busy on it and not worry about the female anatomy of squaw bread."

When Maggie slinks off to the work area, Tyler flips her a bird.

· · ·

Monday night Tyler's late. It's almost eleven-thirty when she finally shows up, and I'm all ready with my punctuality lecture. But something in the set look of her face makes me swallow it.

"Are you okay?"

"Yeah. I was just . . . doing some stuff."

"What stuff?" Her shrug is elaborately nonchalant, and I suddenly wish I hadn't asked.

"Just—you know—waiting."

"She might not know you work at night now. Or maybe she went out to dinner."

She hangs up her jacket and slips an apron over her head.

I try again. "She could be sick or something."

"Too sick to make a phone call? She'd have to be circling the drain." She studies the bake sheet on the clipboard. "She probably just forgot."

When I put my hand on her back, I feel her pointy shoulder blades like little demon wings. "You know, some people have trouble expressing things they feel intensely, and your birthday is—"

"Wyn, save the bullshit. She forgot." She looks away from me. "It's not a big deal. I just wanted to ask her about the squaw bread."

I hold out the present and card I brought her. "Well, anyway, happy birthday."

She takes it from me and looks at the wrapping for a minute, as if she could see through it with X-ray vision. Then she tosses it on the desk. "I'll check it out later." She picks up the big metal bowl for the floor mixer. "Birthdays suck anyway. Who cares if you're another year older."

We try the squaw bread again, decreasing the bran, cutting back on sweeteners and salt, increasing the yeast. More hockey pucks.

"We can't spend any more time on this right now." I tilt the sheet pan, dumping the small, dark loaves into the garbage.

"But my mom made it just this way and it was great."

I look at her, exasperated. "She obviously did not make it just this way or it would be great now. You can keep trying it at home if you want, but here, we have other fish to fry."

She snatches up the piece of paper, crumples it into a ball, and shoots it into the can on top of the bread.

"Who gives a shit?"

"You do, obviously." I reach into the garbage and retrieve the paper. I spread it out on the worktable, blot off a slime of egg white. "Why don't we just hang on to this for a while. Keep it in the notebook. Take it out another day—"

"Why doesn't it work?"

I'm not sure what I can say here without sounding horribly condescending. "Tyler, I think your mom was probably a really creative woman and she made changes as she went. She made the recipe her own. If you want it to work, that's what you need to do—stop trying to figure out what she did and just do whatever's going to make it work for you."

The scene at Tyler's duplex-warming party would fit nicely into a painting—something by Hieronymus Bosch, I think. Ellen and I find the house without any trouble; finding a parking place is another thing altogether. We end up walking about five blocks uphill. Before we're even close, we can hear the Clash singing "London Calling."

"I think I'm starting to be old," Ellen says.

The place is a big old house that's been rather clumsily cut in half, with a carport tacked onto each side as an afterthought. There are a lot of strange-looking people on the sidewalk and the sundecks and hanging out of various windows. We ignore their stares, which clearly indicate that two women who look like we do could not possibly be at the right party. A guy wearing overalls with nothing underneath but a large dragon tattoo curled around his upper body gives us a cursory glance on his way out. The door's open, but Ellen knocks on the screen door anyway. Not that anyone could hear with the music blaring and people yelling over it. Tyler comes running.

"Cool! You came." She pulls us through a nearly impenetrable wall of bodies. "I want to show you the place, but you need a drink first. Are you hungry?"

Now we're in the living room/dining room, which is not totally without charm. There's a nice brick fireplace with bookshelves on either side. Of course, there are no books, only videos. The bar is set up on a metal trunk—a box of red and a box of white wine, and a galvanized washtub full of ice and bottles of beer. A retro white Formica and chrome dinette table that's beat up enough to be authentic is loaded with food—mostly sandwich stuff—American cheese, bologna, salami. Even a jar of peanut butter. Bags of potato chips and Doritos lie on their sides, contents spilling onto the table. There's a fondue pot that looks like a cast-off from a seventies wedding shower, full of that dip that's made with canned tomatoes and Velveeta cheese. A platter of Rice Krispies squares glistens stickily, and off to one side is a tin of brownies.

"Just FYI, the brownies are loaded," Tyler says. Ellen's hand stops in midair. "What do you want to drink?"

We both say red wine and Tyler starts looking around for two clean glasses. Failing that, she picks up two used ones and heads for the kitchen. "I'll just wash these and I'll be right back."

"Hey, short stuff. That's my glass." A tall, thin guy with an infectious grin and bleached-blond hair has Tyler by the collar.

"You can find a new one. These are for my bosses. Wyn and Ellen." She nods in our direction and disappears into the kitchen.

"If I'd only known." He flutters his big brown eyes at us. "I'm Barton." He holds out his hand to Ellen, then looks at me. "Ooh, I'm not good at faces but I never forget a head of hair. You're Wyn. Fourth of July last year."

Tyler comes back and hands each of us a glass of wine. "This is the good stuff," she says. "Now get something to eat." Ellen and I hesitate in the face of the bounty on the dinette.

"It all looks so good," Ellen says. Tyler and Barton erupt into giggles.

Ellen takes two Oreos and I take a tortilla chip, which breaks in half when it bounces off the clotted cheese dip.

"Shit, the fire went out," Tyler says.

"That's okay, I'll have a cookie."

Tyler grabs an arm and pulls it closer. It's attached to a girl who looks very much like Tyler, except that she's a blonde and has a nose ring. This is Felice, roommate number two. She's wearing black tights and a black turtleneck and a brown-and-green poncho.

"I love your poncho," Ellen says.

"Thanks."

"Did you get it at the store where you work?" I ask.

"No."

Barton puts his arm around her. "The only problem with this girl is, we just can't shut her up." Felice looks embarrassed and mumbles that it was nice meeting us and drifts away.

"You hurt her feelings," Tyler says. She follows Felice out to the front porch.

"I need to use the facilities," Ellen says, looking around.

Barton points down a long hallway. "Second door on the left. Just be sure to keep it closed. Tigger likes to climb in the toilet." He turns back to me. "My cat."

Ellen's back suddenly, looking flustered. "There's a guy standing on the john getting a blow job."

Barton sighs. "That would be Dickie. For obvious reasons. He knows we only have one bathroom downstairs. I'll go tell them to hurry up."

Ellen restrains him with a hand on his arm. "That's okay. Some things shouldn't be rushed."

"Why don't you go upstairs? There's a bathroom off Dee's bed-room, the first door at the top of the stairs."

"Don't start sending everyone up to my bathroom." So this must be DeeDee.

"I'm not sending everyone. This is Tyler's boss, Ellen."

"Really, I can wait," Ellen says.

"I don't like strangers going through my room," DeeDee says. She's tall and painfully thin; her bones seem about to break through her pale skin. She has deep-set dark eyes and a petulant expression. Of course, if the guy standing next to her was my boyfriend, I wouldn't be happy either. He looks like a cross between Wayne Newton and the Grim Reaper—short and chunky, with a greasy flourish of dark hair hanging over his forehead like a dirty snow-drift.

"Hi," he says. "I'm Skipper." Since his right arm is draped around DeeDee's neck, he extends his left hand. He looks older than every-one else here—even Ellen and me—and he's wearing a clingy knit polo shirt that shows off his nipples, not an attractive sight. He eyes Barton with barely disguised contempt. "Dee's bedroom isn't a hall-way to the bathroom," he says.

Barton's smile is frozen on his face. "I think we've just about set-tled that, thanks so much, Flipper."

Down the hall the bathroom door opens and a couple emerges looking pleased.

"That's my cue," Ellen says, and bolts.

"Who might you be?" Skipper/Flipper asks, looking at me. At least I think he's looking at me. His eyes are nearly closed.

"I'm a friend of Tyler's," I say. "Wyn Mor—"

"I never remember last names." DeeDee hands him her beer and he takes a long swig.

Tyler reappears to rescue me and take me on a tour of the house. Her room is a closet-size affair at the end of the upstairs hall. It's on the wall that separates the two halves of the duplex, and she tells me she can hear everything that goes on next door.

"Well, don't forget, that means they can hear everything you do, too."

"Yeah. Except nothing's ever going on in my room." We sit on her twin bed and she tells me who's on all the posters on the wall, and I think about the summer that CM and I shared a tiny apartment in Laguna Beach. How independent we felt—like adults, but much cooler. And completely oblivious to reality.

Later, when Ellen and I are eating green onion and Swiss cheese omelets, at her kitchen table, she says, "That Skipper guy made my skin crawl."

"Isn't he creepy? Did you see him groping his girlfriend while we were standing there talking to them?"

"I hope Tyler's going to be all right in that fun house."

"Sometimes innocence is its own protection." I push a piece of egg onto my toast.

"Unfortunately, she's not entirely innocent, but she's awfully naïve. Sort of a dangerous combination." Ellen pours white wine in our glasses. "You have to admire her, though. She never stops trying. I guess it's stupid, but I wish she'd meet a nice guy. A nice, straight guy."

"That's no magic bullet," I say.

She gives me an odd look. "No, it's not. But love has a lot of power, Wyn. I hope you haven't written it off completely."

"I've just learned that if you don't expect anything, you're rarely disappointed."

## · fourteen ·

## *Mac*

He likes going to Rhiannon's in the morning when he's the only one there. Sometimes he has a mooseburger, sometimes just coffee. She plays her entire collection of Texas music for him, some of it good, some awful, some he figures is simply an acquired taste. His favorite is one tape she has by a guy named Shake Russell. The recording sounds like it was done in somebody's garage, maybe just because it's a tape made from an old LP. But the tunes are contagious, the lyrics poignant, and the guy's voice has just the right amount of gravel.

Occasionally he'll help her make the burgers, or he'll roll up the plastic knives in paper napkins, but mostly they just sit and talk. As he suspected, she knows everyone and everything that's gone on in Beaverton for the last eight years, and she loves an audience.

She stops frequently in midstory to wipe the onion tears from her face with the back of her hand and warn, "Now don't you *dare* repeat any of this . . ."

Finally, one morning he says, only half joking, "I should tell you I'm a writer."

"I know that. You told Chris Moody weeks ago. Everybody in town knows by now."

"Aren't you worried that I might use some of this stuff?"

She puts her hands on her hips, still holding the big wood-handled knife. "Of course you will, but you'll change it around so nobody knows." She brandishes the knife menacingly. "Or I swear I'll hunt you down and make breakfast sausage out of your privates."

One morning he brings her one of his favorite blues tapes. "Oh, I don't like that stuff," she says. But in a few minutes she's swaying back and forth while she mixes in her secret seasonings to B. B. King's "The Thrill Is Gone."

"I thought you didn't like the blues," he observes.

"I don't, I'm just being polite. And speaking of polite, how rude you are to come here all the time and never let me read the cards for you."

He sighs. "I just don't—"

"Don't what?" She grabs a handful of meat and slaps it flat. "Don't believe in that stuff? You don't want to say that around me."

"Sorry, but it just seems like a crutch."

Her dark eyes flare. "A crutch comes in mighty handy when you've got a broken leg."

"My leg isn't broken."

"Something is." She slaps another burger on her pile and stops to take a count.

"What do you mean?"

"I mean . . ." She looks at him steadily and her voice gets softer. "Everybody's got some kind of wound." She picks up her coffee mug and the handle slips a bit from the grease on her fingers. "You take Pearl May. Doesn't she just look like a little old ant sittin' on a sugar sack? She's had it sad, I'm here to tell you. Lost her husband in a logging accident when they were young. Tom, her son, was just a little thing—three or four, I think."

"Where's he now?"

"Dead. Tommy got himself killed in a barroom brawl in Fairbanks when he was only twenty-three. Daughter-in-law started drinking and froze to death one winter. Pearl May raised Bernice herself. Couldn't do enough for that kid, and she gets precious little thanks for it."

Mac reaches for the coffeepot. "Who's Emmett's father?"

"You keeping track of how many cups you're drinking? I'm not running a soup kitchen here."

"Yes, ma'am, I am. But I wish you'd get some milk. If I have to pay these ridiculous prices for coffee, I'd at least like to have some milk in it." He props his right foot up on his left knee.

"Ridiculous prices? My Aunt Fanny. This is real chicory coffee from New Orleans. Imported!" She takes a breath. "Emmett's father. Well, only God and Bernice know the answer to that."

For the first time since he's met Rhiannon, he has a sense that she's hedging.

"She's a piece of work, that girl. Prickly as a damn porcupine. Treats Pearl May like dirt. Only thing she cares about is Emmett. He's such a sweetie, too." She gives him a pointed look. "But Bernice. That girl is trouble comin' downhill on roller skates. Don't mess with her."

July nineteenth is Pearl May's eighty-fifth birthday party. Announcements appear suddenly all over town, placards in windows, bills posted on light poles and bulletin boards. A full-page ad runs in the *Beaver Tales*.

When Mac asks if he and Nora are going, Chris laughs. "Attendance is not optional," he says. "Everything in town shuts down that day anyway."

At three o'clock he closes his notebook and wanders down to the big meadow overlooking the river, where festivities have been under way since noon. Flagpoles fly the Canadian flag, the Yukon flag, and the

Beaverton flag, and what looks like the entire population of the valley is milling around eating, drinking, playing games, and listening to music.

He gets a beer from one of the bars set up at strategic intervals and works his way down the edge of the field past the tents of two caterers, brought in from Whitehorse, the tables where the townswomen proudly offer their breads and vegetables and cakes and preserves. Huge haunches of moose meat and several whole pigs roast slowly over a pit lined with glowing coals.

Down by the river kids are shrieking their way through three-legged races while parents cheer them on. The sun is surprisingly hot, and several of the men have divested themselves of their shirts, displaying shockingly pale torsos.

From a wooden stage draped with garlands and pennants, sounds of another band tuning up float over the crowd. He passes Rhiannon, resplendent in a long white dress, flowers in her hair, at a folding table reading the tarot for seekers who are lined up, waiting.

He fills a plate with food, and then spots Chris and Nora on a blanket over by a makeshift volleyball court where a few teenagers are batting a ball back and forth, and he makes his way over to them.

"This is pretty impressive," he says, sitting down.

"It's only the beginning," Chris says. His hair is newly trimmed for the occasion, revealing half circles of white skin behind his ears.

"Just wait." Nora laughs. "By about six P.M., everybody's pissed as a fart and then the fun begins."

"Like what?"

"She means they're all drunk," Chris translates.

"Oh . . . fights, dancing, singing. People sneaking off into the bushes."

Mac grins. "Pearl May knows how to throw a party. Where is she?"

"She won't show up till tonight," Nora says. "In time for cake and fireworks."

"Fireworks?"

They nod in unison. "Just wait."

He eats slowly, amazed by how good everything is—or maybe it's true that everything tastes better outdoors. Nora nibbles delicately on a piece of brown bread.

Foster trails past in a beaver costume. The wide tail floats behind him like a fallen wind sock, and he carries the head under his arm.

"Hi, Foster." Nora smiles at him.

He waves at her and wanders on, muttering to himself about harmonic convergence.

Chris mops up the last of the sauce with a piece of bread, pushes his plate aside, and lies back drowsily. His eyelids flutter.

"Hey, none of that." It's the guy from the post office—Dirk something—grinning his snaggletoothed grin. "Volleyball tournament's starting. Our team plays first."

Chris groans, rolling into a sit.

"Mac? We could use another tall guy at the net."

"Maybe later. I did something to my shoulder taking down the shutters on Pearl's house. I'll pass for now."

"Okay, but if we blow our winning streak, it's on your head." He grunts to his feet and lumbers off with Dirk.

Nora smiles. "God, that was so sensible."

"Ouch. That's the kiss of death."

"Being sensible? Hardly. I quite admire it." She lifts her hair off her neck. "Too many of these guys feel as if it's not just a volleyball game, it's a test of manhood. Chris included, of course." She looks at him. "On the other hand, maybe you're just too young for a midlife crisis."

The volleyball match begins in a welter of swaggering boasts on both sides, but it's soon apparent that Chris's team—the Graylings, Nora says—didn't really need anyone else at all. They could probably beat their opponents playing one-handed. The game turns into a romp, with the Graylings doing lots of silly tricks in between points.

Emmett wanders over to stand on the sidelines and cheer for both teams. Mac looks around for Bernice, but doesn't see her.

Chris dives for a spiked return and Nora winces. "I can't watch. He's bound to break his damned neck one of these times."

He misses the return, picks himself up, laughing, and tosses the ball gently to Emmett to give back to the server. There's a freeze-frame in the glare of the summer afternoon—the man and the boy, the turn of a head, the tenderness of a lopsided grin. Mac blinks and tries to hold the image, but it's already gone. He must be imagining things. Then he looks at Nora.

She faces straight ahead, but her eyes slide over to him, too brilliant. She pulls a few pieces of grass, tosses them away. "Hard to believe some people in this town still think I don't know. You'd have to be blind, wouldn't you?"

He swallows the beer in his mouth.

"It's not—" she begins, then falters.

"You don't have to tell me anything."

She bites her lip. "Sometimes it's good to talk to someone who's not one of us. You know what I mean? Someone who's not in my hip pocket all the time, and I'm not in theirs. Who doesn't already have an opinion, eh?"

"Right."

"It's not that I don't care, you know? It's not that it didn't just about kill me when he told me. It's just that it's been nearly seven years now. I mean, when he first told me, I thought I would leave him." She swallows hard. "But then, where would I go?" She puts her hands behind her and lowers herself till she's resting on her elbows. "I can see how it happened. I don't hate her. She's about as miserable as a person can get. I can't even really blame Chris. Much as I've tried. I've seen how it happens to men. There's so much ego shit going on with you lads that women don't—"

A tear rolls down her face and she jabs at it quickly. He gets to his feet. "Come on, let's walk off some of that food." He reaches down, lifting her gently from behind and they head for one of the bars. He opens a Coke for each of them, and they drift toward the river.

They stop on a high, mossy shelf crowded with violets and the looping canes of wild roses. It's cooler here. Across the water, an owl glides into the shadowed woods. The warm breeze dries the tears from her eyes, but the one that fell has left a nearly invisible, silvered track on her face.

"Who's your girl, Mac? I know there is one."

He smiles. "How do you know that?"

"I just do. Did you break up?"

"Her name's Wyn. Wynter."

"What a lovely name. She's in Seattle?"

He nods. "She's a bread baker."

"Why did you leave her?"

"I didn't leave her. I just left."

"I see."

"It's hard to explain. In some ways it was just that guy shit that all you women are so understandably sick of. She called it the Babe-I-gotta-leave-you-the-highway's-callin'-bullshit-blues."

Nora's laughter peals out across the river. She throws her head back, and her long, dark hair reaches nearly to her waist. "Oh, I like that woman."

He smiles. "You would. She'd like you, too."

"So in some ways it was the guy shit, and in other ways it was what?"

"Some things I was working on didn't pan out. A book. I felt so . . . useless, I guess. I just needed to get off by myself and think."

She laughs again. "Instead you end up in Beaverton, the biggest little town in the Yukon Territory, where everybody knows everybody's business. So much for the hermetic life."

"So why didn't you leave him?"

She looks up sharply. "I was a coward."

"Seems like it took a lot more guts to stay."

"Well, it was mostly because I love Chris Moody more than the whole goddamned world. I told you how we met. At that awful party. But the truth is, my life up to that point was at least as awful as that party. I left Ireland and got to Toronto when I was seventeen. I was already pregnant, but I didn't know it. The job I was supposed to have in Toronto fell through, and one thing led to another, and pretty soon I was living in a cold-water flat with a bunch of hippies, panhandlers, thieves—oh, it was straight out of *Oliver*, only not so cute.

"It was a brutal winter. I lost the baby, nearly died myself. There were days when I wished I had. Losing the child was a terrible thing, but it turned me right around. I got help. Got a job. Got into school and got my degree. Of course I fell in love with one of my professors. He went back to his wife. I was thinking I'd go home to Dublin, not that there was anything for me there, but I just didn't know what else to do. Then I met Chris."

She looks down at the river, wiping the little beads of sweat that stand up from the fair skin on her forehead. "He made me feel as if none of those other things mattered. As if all my bad times were no more than a frumpy dress that I could just take off and throw out." She hugs herself. "So when this happened, and I thought about leaving, I thought, fine, Nora, but where will you go? You've been running your whole life." She tilts her face up and catches his eye. "You think you've put things behind you, but the problem is, you've put nothing in front of you."

A sudden explosion of shouting and laughter signals the end of the volleyball game. Wordlessly they start back down to the meadow.

"Want your cards read?" he asks.

She shakes her head. "No, I've got my hands full dealing with the present. I don't care to know what's in the future."

"Okay. I'll catch up with you guys later."

She puts up a hand to shade her eyes. "Thanks, Mac."

"I didn't do anything."

"More than you think."

He watches her disappear into the crowd before he drifts down toward Rhiannon.

Several teenage girls cluster at a table piled with pelts of wolf and marten and lynx, but they seem more interested in the trapper, a tall, well-muscled guy with a luxuriant brown beard. Oblivious to the girls, he stands, arms folded across his broad chest, talking to the woman in the next booth. She's listening to him, and explaining the fine points of a cable-knit afghan to another woman, while her hands continue to knit as if directed by a separate intelligence.

Rhiannon's taking a break, and she waves him over. Jester, who's been lying as immobile as a fur rug at her feet, gets up and immediately starts sniffing his crotch.

He gently moves the dog's head away. "Lady, I think your dog's gay."

"Nah." She winks broadly. "He swings both ways. Sometimes it's a necessity around here."

"Oh, come on." Mac looks out at the crowd spread over the meadow. "There's got to be at least four men for every woman here."

Rhiannon crushes her empty drink can and flashes a smile. "Yeah, well, up here we say the odds are good, but the goods are decidedly odd." She slaps his arm. "Which reminds me, it's time for your reading. Don't even think about runnin' away now. Come on over here and sit down."

"I don't—"

"Just sit." It's the same tone of voice she uses on Jester, and they both obey.

He shifts himself on the rickety camp stool while she covers the table with a piece of blue velvet and hands him the well-worn deck.

"Do you have a specific question to ask?"

"Nope."

"Okeydokey, then —"

"I don't think fortune-tellers are supposed to say okeydokey."

She ignores him. "I want you to hold the cards in both hands, shuffle them, cut the deck, and then lay it facedown on the table."

When he's finished, she picks up the deck and lays out the first three cards in a triangle, and the next four in a square around them. She turns them over one at a time, beginning with the apex of the triangle.

"This one"—she points to the top of the triangle—"symbolizes your essence, who you are. Yours happens to be the magician. A very powerful card."

He looks up, and her serious expression surprises him.

"Its meaning is creativity, imagination. It's about strong will and self-reliance, self-control. But it also can indicate deception." She taps a purple fingernail on the card. "Including self-deception.

"These two cards symbolize your relationship with the outer world." She puts her index fingers on the other two points of the triangle. "This one on the left, the priestess. It can mean wisdom, objectivity. But it can also mean hidden emotion, avoidance of emotional entanglements. This one on the right is the hermit. He stands for knowledge and inner strength. But also secrecy and a denial of the truth."

He smiles. "So far, everything you've said can apply to me or just about anyone at this party."

"That's right, sweet cheeks. The tarot's not going to tell you things you don't know. Its original and true purpose is to help you face the truths you already know subconsciously and figure out how to deal with them."

"So what we're doing here is medieval therapy."

She gives him an irritated look. "You call it whatever you want. Now keep quiet and listen up. These two cards, above your essence, are in opposition to each other. This one, the six of cups, stands for the past, memories of things that have disappeared, regrets. Of which we all have some," she says, preempting his comment. "This one, the seven of wands, is a great card. It points to success, not just money, but you know, fulfillment of dreams, contentment. Now these down here . . ." A frown troubles her forehead.

"The five of wands means unresolved conflict. A struggle. It can be a struggle inside you, or a struggle between you and"—she looks at the last card—"the page of swords. A man. Young. Strong."

She looks up at him, hesitating. "Do you have a brother?"

The hair rises on his scalp. "No."

She looks at him for a long time. "Then maybe it's your father. But he seems to be young. There's some really bad stuff here, this unresolved shit. Until you take care of that, make peace with him"—her eyes narrow—"whoever he is . . . you won't be at peace with yourself."

He reaches for his wallet.

"Honest to God, would you cut it out? I'm not through."

"Okay. What now? I toss three coins over my shoulder?"

"Just back off, bubba. I don't make fun of your writing. Don't you make fun of my cards."

"Sorry."

"Okay, then. Now, not that you deserve it, but just because I like you, I'm going to give you a bonus card." She puts the deck in front of him. "Cut it."

After he cuts the cards, she takes the top one and flips it over at the bottom of the triangle. And she gasps. A grinning skeleton dances on a field of blue, holding a scythe made from a human spine. The landscape is strewn with human heads, hands, and feet, and a raven lurks in the background. The death card.

"And I didn't think you were the type to hold a grudge," he says.

"Hush. Mac, this is great! This is a wonderful card. It doesn't mean anybody's going to die. I mean, it can, of course, but it's really the card of complete transformation. It's the clearing away of the old to make room for the new, you throw off the old ways, the old things that have been holding you back and you undergo a radical change. Oh, my Lordy! This is one of the best readings I've ever done. I've got goose bumps."

"Thank you, Madame Blue."

She grins. "My friends call me Rhiannon."

He hands her a twenty, and she fishes in her change purse. "Don't worry about it," he says. "Just tell me one thing. What's your real name?"

She leans forward. "Betty Pattle. Ain't that a hell of a name for a tarot reader?"

He told Nora he'd come find them, but he doesn't feel much like talking at the moment, so he just starts walking, skirting the edge of the meadow till somehow he ends up back at the bunkhouse.

He drags the duffle out from under the bed, blows the dust balls off, takes out the heavy package in the bottom. He sets it on the desk, unwrapping it slowly, folding the envelope, twisting the rubber bands together, stacking it neatly, gathering pens, notebook. Finally there's nothing left to do but read the pages. He hasn't looked at it since the day it landed with a thud in front of his apartment door nearly five months ago.

Steve Devine's letter is sitting on top. Just a note, actually, in a long, angular hand, canted hard to the right, like a man walking into a strong head wind.

> *This has real potential, but there are several issues that need to be addressed. First of all, is this a novel or a memoir? If there's any indication, I missed it. Doesn't really matter, since the line between the two keeps getting fuzzier, but either way, I found your omniscient narrator too aloof and objective. He feels cold, possibly even dishonest. There's too much distance between him and the story, and consequently between the story and the reader. You might try rewrit-*

*ing in close third or even in first person. For a good discussion of POV, see Oakley Hall's* The Art & Craft of Novel Writing. *See a few additional questions/suggestions on ms. I recommend reading them, then reading your ms., then putting them both away for a month or two. When you come back to them, your perspective will be fresher. Give me a call if you need clarification or want to discuss any of the points I've made. Look forward to hearing from you.*

It's been somewhat longer than a month or two.

He sets the note aside and stares at the first page, letting it slip out of focus, seeing only the shapes of white space between the lines, words blurring into gathered bundles of black keystrokes. It comes back to him—the day last August when he finished the draft at the cottage on Orcas Island.

He rolled the last sheet out of the old Smith Corona portable in a rush of elation and relief spiked with exhaustion. It was 10:30 in the morning.

He spent the rest of the day wandering around in a fog, walking into a room and forgetting what he'd come for. He tried to finish building the shelving in the storage shed, but the nervous energy whirring through him made concentration impossible and half his measurements were off.

He took a walk in the woods with Minnie, the yellow mutt that hung out at the place all summer, and found himself striding faster and faster, finally breaking into a trot, then a full run, arms swinging, feet pounding, wanting to shout just for the sound of it.

And all at once, a wall of melancholy stopped him. A sense of loss. It was over. The book was finished.

Now he grimaces at his own naïveté.

He arranges the pens and pencils in a row according to height. Then rearranges them by color. Then he picks up the one on the end, moves it to the middle, disrupting the pattern. He hooks the rubber bands, one by one, over his thumb and forefinger and shoots them at the pump handle. He goes to retrieve them.

His eyes keep wandering to the window, the sun's long rays on the golden seed heads of the wild grasses. He thinks about Pearl May's birthday party, in full swing down in the meadow. About Foster. About Nora and Chris. Bernie and Emmett. He slouches in the chair, one arm draped over the back, chewing on the cap of the pen. Maybe the problem is that this book's not ready to see the light of day. Maybe the problem is, it never will be.

He exhales softly, stacks the pages neatly, Steve's note going on top. He winds the rubber bands around the pile, two horizontally, one vertically, slides it back into the envelope. He opens his note-book, takes the cap off the pen.

*At eighty-five she's still splitting kindling, driving her own boat, running a saloon, and masterminding her own birthday party—an intimate gathering of three hundred souls in a meadow overlooking the icy, green Yukon River . . .*

## · fifteen ·

### *Wyn*

Just when you thought it was safe . . .

Linda LaGardia walks into the bakery at seven-fifteen A.M., bristling with attitude. I haven't seen her since she no-showed at her own retirement party some six months ago, and it's a nasty surprise, even though I knew she was back from Idaho. Misha told me she's been in a few times to buy bread—or should I say, pick up bread. Ellen insists on giving her a loaf whenever she stops by.

"I can't begrudge her a loaf of bread every now and then," Ellen said. "It's not like she has a pension or anything. I feel bad for her."

"It's hard for me to feel bad for someone who thinks of the world as her litter box."

This morning, I'm the recipient of a condescending smirk, and then she turns her attention to Ellen. "I got your message," she says.

I shoot my partner an alarmed look. "What message?"

She ignores me. "So what do you think?" she asks Linda.

"Well, I might be interested. Depends on the pay."

I put my hand on Ellen's shoulder. "What's going on here?"

"Linda's going to fill in for you while you're on vacation," Ellen says brightly.

"What?"

Without speaking a word, Linda manages to clearly convey her contempt for any bread baker who needs a vacation after only two years. "I didn't say I'd do it. I said I might be interested if the pay's right."

Ellen smiles sweetly. "You'll be paid at the same rate you were earning when you left, of course."

"*Ellen*—" I begin, but she taps my foot with hers.

"How long you want me for?"

"Three weeks."

Her face screws up in concentration; with a corncob pipe, she'd be a dead ringer for Popeye. "Who's working with me?"

"Tyler."

Her trademark snort. "Since when does she make bread?"

Ellen smiles again. "I think you'll be pleasantly surprised by how much she's learned."

"Oh, all right. I suppose I'll do it."

"Thank you so much, Linda. It'll be great to have you back."

My gag reflex kicks in.

"You gonna call me about the dates?"

"Just as soon as Wyn gets her plane reservations booked."

"Where's Miss Designer Pants jettin' off to?" she asks Ellen—like I'm not even there.

I give her a teeth-gritted smile. "Cleveland."

She frowns. "What the hell for?"

"I'm going to France, Linda."

Another snort. "Figures." Then I'm dismissed. She turns to Ellen. "Got any cheese bread?"

When she exits, leaving the bell over the door jingling manically, Ellen bursts out laughing. "You two."

"Us two?"

"I think you must have been mother and daughter in a former life."

"Thanks."

"Hey, don't complain. You got your three weeks, didn't you?"

"Yes, and I appreciate it. I just hope Tyler doesn't quit."

She pats my arm. "Tyler's handled a lot of shit in her young life. Linda won't faze her."


Tuesday night when I let myself in the back door, the lights are on and the Ramones are blasting out of the boom box.

"Tyler?" I hang my denim jacket on a hook by the door. She must be in the storeroom. When I go over to turn down Joey Ramone singing his glue-sniffing song, I see the bread. A fat, dark round with a beautifully glistening slashed crust sits on the table. Squaw bread.

I call her again and then turn to find her standing practically in my shadow. "So . . . it looks good. In fact, it looks great. Have you tried it?"

"Not yet." She rakes a hand through her blue hair. "I wanted to try it with you."

I pick up the loaf. It has a lovely weight, and a thwack on the bottom produces just the right hollow sound. My nose picks up the caramel whiff of molasses and roasted grains. "You want to do the honors?" I hold it out to her and she takes it. She wraps her hands around the loaf and holds it for a second as if it were still warm, then she tears off a chunk and passes it to me.

I bite off a piece and chew it slowly. It has a good balance of sweet and salt, and a smooth, nutty flavor. The crust is slightly chewy and the crumb is tender, but not too soft.

"Tyler, this is great." I try not to sound too surprised. "I hope you wrote down the recipe."

She rolls her eyes in response and digs into her back pocket, holding out a piece of yellow legal pad with handwriting that's poignantly reminiscent of her mother's. I smile at the title, but I don't say anything.

# Tyler's Indian Maiden Bread

2 cups water

⅓ cup oil

¼ cup molasses

½ cup raisins

5 tablespoons brown sugar

2 packages dry yeast

½ cup warm water

2½ cups unbleached all-purpose flour

2½ cups whole wheat flour

1 cup rye flour

2½ teaspoons salt

½ cup cornmeal

½ cup oat flour

Cornmeal for dusting

*Combine the water, oil, molasses, raisins, and brown sugar in a blender and liquefy. Soften the yeast in the warm water. Sift together 1 cup unbleached all-purpose flour, 2 cups whole wheat flour, the 1 cup rye flour, and the salt in large bowl. Add the molasses and yeast mixtures. Beat at medium speed until smooth, 2 minutes. Gradually stir in enough of the remaining flours to make a soft dough that leaves the sides of the bowl. Remember, the moisture content of various flours can vary widely. You may not need all the flour called for. Turn the dough out onto a floured surface and knead until smooth and satiny, 10 to 12 minutes. Place the dough in a lightly oiled bowl and turn to oil entire surface. Cover and let rise until doubled, about 1½ hours. Punch down and let rest 10 minutes. Divide into 4 round loaves and place on cookie sheets covered with parchment paper sprinkled with cornmeal. Cover and let rise in a warm place until doubled, 1 hour. Bake at 375°F for 30 to 35 minutes.*

"This is interesting—the part about pureeing the raisins. I guess that's what makes it so moist without being squishy. I wouldn't have thought of that. Where'd you get the idea?"

She looks slightly abashed. "I read it in one of those baking books Ellen has. About cakes. I guess that's cheating."

I laugh. "That's not cheating. You learned something new and then you used the knowledge to solve a problem. That's called becoming a professional baker. I'm proud of you."

Her expression is equal parts wistful and wary, and when she says, "You are?" the voice doesn't even sound like her own.

The rest of my vacation plan seems to fall into place with astonishing swiftness. I call Sylvie Guillaume, although it's Sylvie Herschel now. She's married to an architect and has two kids, but she still lives in Toulouse, only a few blocks from her brother and mother. We've exchanged Christmas cards over the years, so she's not hard to track down, and seems genuinely delighted to hear from me. She's the go-between, since Jean-Marc's English has always been patchy and my French is pretty rusty. She calls me back a few days later to say that Jean-Marc will be pleased to welcome me back to the Boulangerie du Pont.

"He is married, you know."

"No! Finally? Your mother must be pleased."

"*Bien sûr.* They have a little boy—so serious, just like my brother—and Annette, his wife, she runs the shop. Wynter, where will you stay?"

"I'll find a pension near—"

"*Non, non, non. Absolutement pas!* You will stay with me. We have plenty of room, and it will be such great times, like before."

I laugh. "*Oui. Comme ça, mais plus ancienne.*"

"I cannot wait to see you."

I book the flights, a room at Hôtel de Lutèce, in deference to CM's wish to stay on the Île St.-Louis, and ten days later, the TGV to Toulouse and the return. It's going to be hideously expensive to stay in Paris for ten days, but this is something CM and I have talked about doing since we were in high school.

We drink champagne, read travel guides, and practice our French on each other, and then, the last week of August, she leaves for London. There's nothing left for me to do but pack. Which for me means beginning with everything I own, and then taking away a few pieces every day. It's agonizing. After all, it could still be warm, or they might get a sudden cold snap. And what if it rains?

Three days before D day, I'm still moving things from the closet to the bed, to the couch, and back to the closet. So far all I'm sure of is underwear. And it's while I'm playing musical clothes that thoughts of Mac come flooding into my mind, overwhelming me, obliterating my anticipation of this trip. It's utterly weird. Why now? I know he won't be back by Labor Day. I never really thought he would. I'm not even certain he'll be back at all. Maybe he's gone to Alaska by now. There's not much time left to do anything; maybe he'll stay through the winter. Maybe he'll decide he likes it so much he won't ever leave.

I can see him doing that. Like that night in the café on Orcas.

*I could live here.* That's exactly what he said. He could say it again.

Maybe he'll meet a woman. Somebody strong and brave and independent. Not demanding and emotional and bossy. I sit down on the futon, pushing a stack of sweaters out of the way, and take his last letter out of the mail basket. It was written over a month ago.

*Dear Wyn,*

*Foster has appointed (or anointed) himself the official town greeter. Every day he dresses up in a beaver costume and patrols the sidewalks, snaring unwary travelers and insisting that they take his picture.*

*When he's not out greeting his public, he's at the Beaver Tail, where he wanders around talking to the pictures on the walls, most of which are the founding fathers (and mothers) of the community.*

*More about Foster:*

*He's short, pale, and skinny, with a beak nose. He's got a lot of soft, fuzzy red hair and a beard that looks like he trims it with hedge clippers. I noticed the first time I saw him that he'd shaved about a two-inch-square patch on the top of his head.*

*Chris told me Foster showed up in town about five years ago. Nobody knows him by anything but Foster, and they have no idea where he came from. He has a little house about a mile from town, and money doesn't seem to be a problem.*

*If you ask about his ad in the paper, he'll tell you he needs this equipment in order to return to the Future, where he used to live, until a woman cult leader who feared he was becoming too powerful had him kidnapped and implanted a chip in his brain that would enable her to read his mind. During the surgery something went awry, and he was teletransported back to the twentieth century. He claims to have fought in Vietnam. Or maybe he just says that to needle Chris. But in case he finds the time-travel equipment, he keeps the patch shaved on his head in order to facilitate the chip removal.*

*People like Foster have always intrigued me because of the totality of their "otherness." He (obviously) does not inhabit the same world that you and I do. I think he's quite aware that most people consider him mad, and he simply doesn't care. Think what it must be like to be so certain of your own reality.*

*Occasionally I wonder if my father wasn't like that in his own way. He apparently did exactly what he wanted, when he wanted, regardless of anyone else's opinion. On the other hand, maybe he was just a self-absorbed bastard.*

*Another memory. One of the last. I was twelve, Kevin was fourteen. He was supposed to take us sailing on a Saturday, and Kevin got sick. Suzanne just assumed that if Kevin couldn't go, no one would go. When she saw us getting ready to leave, she pitched a fit, but we went anyway. It was a perfect day for sailing. Sunny, cool, with a good, stiff breeze. He'd borrowed a friend's little day sailer, and that thing just flew over the water—at least it seemed that way to me.*

*He showed me how to cast off, let me raise the sail, held my hand under his on the tiller so I could understand how to steer the boat, showed me how to duck down when we came about . . . and when we got back, and we were cleaning up the boat, he said, "I want you to remember this, Matt."*

*Being a pretty literal kid, I assumed he meant the boat-handling stuff, and always cleaning up the boat when you were through. Three months later he was dead. For years I wondered if he was trying to tell me something. Did he have a premonition? Was he planning to leave Suzanne? Or did he just want me to remember how to take care of a boat? I guess it doesn't matter. I've always remembered the day, just like he wanted.*

## Mac

Dorian comes suddenly to life, startling me. I don't know if I'll ever get used to having a phone that quacks. Some really stupid, needy part of me wants it to be Mac.

A man's voice says, "Is this Wynter Morrison?"

"Yes."

"Ms. Morrison, this is Sergeant LeFevre, Seattle police. I'm calling for a Ms. Tyler Adler."

My stomach turns over. Now what is she into? "She's not here. I mean, she doesn't live here." Then it dawns on me what he means. "What is it? Is something wrong?"

"Ms. Adler is here at the station. She gave us your name to call as her closest relative. I wonder if you might come down to the station and take her home."

"Is she all right? Why is she there?"

"Ms. Adler's roommate apparently died suddenly." *Apparently?* "She discovered his body, and it's been very upsetting—"

"His? Oh God. Barton?"

"Yes, ma'am. Mr. Barton Tullis. Ms. Adler doesn't want to go back to the house. Can you make arrangements to—"

"Yes, yes. I'm sorry. Where do I go?"

"It's the East Precinct, Twelfth and Pine, two blocks east of Broadway. Are you familiar with the area?"

"Yes. I'll be there as soon as I can." I hang up.

I see Barton's funny face, his infectious grin, his Hawaiian shirts. How can he be dead? I wipe my damp, shaky hand on my sweat-pants and dial the bakery. When Ellen answers I stammer through an explanation. "CM's car's in the shop. Can I use your car to go get her?"

"I'll come pick you up."

When I get in the car, she says, "I can't believe it."

We drive a few blocks in silence, both of us staring straight ahead. Then she asks, "How did he . . . ?"

"I don't know. The guy said he 'apparently died suddenly.' I was too blown away to even ask."

"Tyler must be starting to feel like she screwed up big time in a former life. First her mother bails. Then Tate takes off for Wyoming. Now Barton's dead."

She parks on the street and we run up the steps of the ugly fifties-style flattop that houses the precinct offices. The air inside is cold and stale, with a green-blue cast from the fluorescent lights.

Ellen's already talking to the desk sergeant, explaining who we are, asking where we should go. He picks up a phone and dials, speaks briefly, tells us to have a seat.

There's no place to sit. There's only one long bench against the opposite wall, and it's fully occupied. A fat, tired-looking woman with a sullen teenage boy. A dark-skinned, dark-eyed family—old man and woman, a young woman holding a baby. The blond guy in a suit talking to them in measured tones has to be a lawyer.

I stand on one foot, then the other. Ellen paces. Finally a gray-haired woman in pants and a long, red sweater comes down a hallway, and calls my name. She holds out her hand. "Janice Meeker. I'm a crisis counselor. Your friend Tyler's had a nasty shock."

"How did Barton die?" I ask.

"Heroin overdose. It's not a pretty sight. From what Tyler says, she and Mr. Tullis were very close."

"I think so, yes. I didn't know him that well."

"Are you a relative?" she asks.

"No. We're friends. Did you call her father?"

"She only gave us your name. She said she had no other family locally. She doesn't want to go back to the house where they lived. Is there someone she can stay with for a few days?"

"She can stay at my place as long as she needs to," Ellen says. Janice Meeker looks at her for the first time. "I'm Ellen Liederman. We're Tyler's employers."

"Come with me." Down the hall, third door on the left. Janice opens it for us, shuts it behind us. Tyler sits in a wooden chair turned sideways to a scarred wooden table. The room looks like the set for the good cop/bad cop interrogation scene in the movies. It's not large, but the emptiness dwarfs her. She's leaning forward, elbows resting on her knees, head down. At the sound of the door, her head jerks up. Tears and mascara make multiple tracks beneath her eyes, and her hair is a blue mat. She looks past Ellen, directly at me.

I walk over to the chair and stand there biting my lip. "Tyler, I'm so—"

"I knew you'd come," she blurts out before she buries her face in my sweatshirt.

At that moment things become very clear, the way I've always imagined it happens when you're drowning and you see your whole past flash before your eyes. Only it's the future I'm flashing on here. It's not that I've changed my mind about going to France. It's not as though I've made any kind of decision. The matter is out of my hands. All I do is recognize the truth of this fact: I'm not going to France or anywhere else—not any time soon.

When the three of us get into the car, Ellen says, "Tyler, you can stay with me as long as you need to. Till you decide whether to move back into the house or get a new place or—"

Tyler says stiffly, "I'm staying with Wyn." She looks out the window. "Until you—go to France. Or whatever."

Ellen gives me a weird little smile. "For tonight, why don't you both stay with me?"


We bed down early in the little glassed-in porch off Ellen's living room. At ten-fifteen I get up and tiptoe around in the dark, dressing in the bathroom. When I go into the kitchen, Ellen's sitting at the table reading, a cup of coffee in front of her.

"There's a mug for you over there." She nods toward the counter. "Milk's in the fridge."

"What are you doing up?"

"One of my insomnia attacks," she says.

I pull out a chair and sit down to tie my jogging shoes. When I look up she says, "She's imprinted on you."

"What do you mean?"

"It's that thing that ducklings do—as soon as they hatch, they follow the first moving object they see, thinking it's their mother."

"Right." I take a sip of coffee and sit for a minute, still trying to understand this thing that's just happened to my life. I take a breath and then let it out. "I guess you better call Linda and tell her that her services aren't needed."

"Tyler could stay here while you're gone, you know. You don't have to miss your trip."

I shake my head. "She has nobody else. Can you imagine going through that and then having to work alone all night?"

"Linda will be there." Ellen sets down her cup.

"Right. Like I said..." I take a breath and then let it out. "I don't understand it. I don't know why, but when she looked at me today in that room, it wasn't even in question. I just realized that I can't go off and leave her. It's the strangest thing..."

She smiles knowingly. "Yeah, it is strange. Being needed."


One of the worst things I've ever had to do is call CM in London and tell her I'm not coming. When they finally track her down at her "lodgings," she's all burbly. "Better bring your long undies," she says. "It's supposed to be cold next week. One of the students gave me the name of a really great Basque café. I was wondering if it's the same one you were telling me about—"

"CM, I can't come."

There's a pause, which is either one of those trans-Atlantic hiccups or my best friend crashing to the ground.

"What do you mean?" she says finally.

Being CM, after I tell her what's happened, all her concern is for Tyler. "Oh my God, that poor baby. What a terrible, terrible thing."

"I'm thinking about looking for an apartment for her and me. I mean, she could go home to her dad's, but apparently there's some kind of problem with the new stepmother, and I don't think there's anywhere else she can go... I'm sorry to be calling you with all this good news—"

"Oh, don't even think about it. I know how upset you must be, too. Take good care of her. I'll call you from Paris."

I have to smile. "You're going anyway?"

"Might as well. For a few days, anyway. I'll check out the hotel, and give *tout le monde* fair warning of what to expect when we come next year."

"CM..."

"What?"

"I love you."

Tyler moves into the apartment with me temporarily, and I begin to scour the rental ads. I call Daisy Wardwell, the agent who helped me find my first house, on Queen Anne. I talk to everyone I know and some people I don't know. I put up a notice at the bakery, and we spend every spare minute for the next week running down leads on apartments and houses, but everything is either too expensive or too small or too awful or too far away.

Tyler's functional, but not fully conscious. She just tags along behind me like a little silent puppy. Sometimes when I think she's asleep, I find her lying on the futon, just staring. I keep waiting for the numbness to wear off, like Novocain. That's when the ceaseless, drilling pain begins to bore right through you.

I do remember how that feels. After my father died, I was fine for about two weeks. Went to school, did my homework. I even went to a basketball game. Then one afternoon, I came flying into the house with something to show him, and the sight of his empty chair hit me at just the same time as the knowledge that I couldn't show him anything ever again, because he was gone.

On Monday morning, our day off, we walk over to the bakery for coffee, and afterward, we make another quick sweep. I feel as if we've cruised every street within a two-mile radius of the bakery. Rental signs, places we called about but didn't see, as well as those we looked at, are all starting to run together.

So when Tyler grabs my arm and points at a red do-it-yourself rental sign beckoning seductively from the other side of Cedar Street, I hesitate. *Have we already been here?* The other thing is, the sign's stuck in a strip of worn grass between two houses and it's hard to tell which one is for rent.

"Don't get excited," I tell her. "If it's the big one, there's no way. And there's a good chance the little one's too small." But I dutifully haul out my little notebook and walk across the street to write down the phone number. The location couldn't be more perfect. About the same distance from work as CM's place, but in the opposite direction, down the hill, toward Fremont and Wallingford.

"Hi there, ladies. Can I help you?"

An oversized, myopic teddy bear with a reddish-brown beard and metal-rimmed glasses ambles out the front door of the big house.

"We were just wondering which house is for rent." I give him what I hope is an ingratiating smile and wish I'd at least put on some blush and a little lip gloss.

He sizes us up. "Which one would you like it to be?"

Tyler looks at me sideways.

"I'm sure we can't afford that one." I nod at the big, well-proportioned craftsman bungalow.

The guy laughs. "Probably not. Anyway, it's not exactly ready for occupancy. You're looking for a two bedroom?"

I nod.

"Why don't you go on in there and have a look." He cuts his eyes to the small house.

"We should probably ask first what kind of rent we're looking at."

"Thousand a month," he says. "Pay your own utilities. I put all new appliances in there, even a stackable washer/drier."

I wince. "It's a little more than we're looking to spend."

"Might as well have a look." He shrugs. "Since you're here. It's un-locked." He lets us go in alone.

Set almost at the back of its long, narrow lot, the house is a non-descript white shotgun with green trim and a small porch in front. The inside's not fancy, but it's big enough for the two of us. There's a small living area with a Pullman kitchen and room for a table and chairs. Behind that, a long hall leads to two bedrooms, a bath, and a mudroom, which is where the washer/drier resides. When we come back out front, he's on the porch.

"I was thinking about living in the cottage myself while I'm work-ing on the place next door, but I could use the rent money," he says while we walk around inspecting the outside.

"Where are you living now?" I ask.

"In one of the bedrooms in the craftsman. It's pretty cozy for me and Turbo together. My basset hound." He strokes his beard thoughtfully. "One good thing, I'm here a lot of the time, working on the house. So if you need anything, I'm usually available to see to it. Where do you two work?"

"The Queen Street Bakery. Both of us."

"Oh." It's almost a sigh. "My wife used to love that place."

"Doesn't she love us anymore?"

"No, she doesn't love me anymore. We split up. Last year."

"I'm sorry."

"It happens, I guess." He sticks his hands in the pockets of his dirty blue jeans. "I got custody of Turbo and she took off for New York. Anyway, what do you think of the place?"

"It's really nice," I say. "The rent might be a bit of a problem for us. We should probably talk it over first. Make sure we're not getting in over—"

"I left myself some room to maneuver," he says quickly. "Tell the truth, I had a couple of guys looking at it yesterday, and I'd prefer to have female tenants. I know I'm not supposed to say that, but you won't turn me in, will you? Women just seem to take care of a place better. I don't need some hard-partying dudes trashing this place while I'm trying to fix up the other one. Would nine hundred a month help you any?"

He holds out his hand. "By the way, I'm Josh—"

"Keeler," I finish. "You're Joshua Keeler."

He gives me a questioning look. "Do I know you?"

"I'm Wyn Morrison. I was your tenant on Fourth Street. Behind the big Victorian."

"Well, I'll be." His placid face breaks into a grin. "Dang, you're the one who painted the walls that red and yellow. Pretty interesting stuff." He wags his finger at me. "This one stays white."

I smile. "Cross my heart."


The following Sunday is moving day and the bottom of a long, downhill slide for Tyler. The excitement of finding a house has worn off, and the reality of what's happened to Barton has sunk in with a solid thud. By three in the afternoon my furniture has been delivered, and everyone from the bakery comes by to lend a hand. I take a picture of the house. Ellen takes one of Tyler and me at the front door. Then Josh wanders by and takes the last one on the roll of the whole bakery gang draped around the porch. Ellen has Lloyd's pickup truck to go pick up Tyler's stuff, but as we're about to leave, Tyler sits down on my bed and starts to cry.

"I can't go back there. Just leave my stuff. I don't want it."

"You have personal things in your room that you're going to need," Ellen says. "Not to mention all your clothes."

"And you have to have your bed," I say.

Tyler shakes her head. "I can't go in there."

"Wyn and I can get it. You don't have to go in."

"Can't I just stay here?"

"No, you have to be present," I say. "I don't want DeeDee or her creepy boyfriend to have any excuse to have us busted for breaking and entering. Call Felice and tell her we're coming. And get your key."


That evening when the great furniture heist has been accomplished, and Ellen has gone home, Tyler and I have pizza delivered. I'm starving. I devour my half while it's so hot it burns my mouth. Tyler nibbles at hers and pushes it aside. I pour myself some more red wine.

"You want to talk?"

"No."

"It's been two weeks . . ."

"You think I should be over it?" she blazes at me.

"Of course not. I don't think you ever get over something like that. But if you don't talk about it to someone, you'll never get beyond it. It doesn't have to be me."

Tears are streaming from her eyes. "You should've seen him." She looks out the kitchen window. "He looked so gross. All this foamy shit all over his face. He never did heroin." She puts her head down on the table.

I stand behind her, rub her back, feel myself choke up. "I'm so sorry, Tyler. I don't know what to do to help you."

"You can't do anything," she manages between gasps of air. "Nobody can." She goes into her bedroom, shutting the door behind her while I stand there looking at the pizza. Finally I wrap it in foil and put it in the refrigerator.

When I was crazy with grief over my father, CM always seemed to know when to push me into talking and when to leave me alone. I don't have a clue how to handle this. I pull on my jeans jacket and take my wine outside, sit down on the steps under the amber porch light.

All the lights are on next door. I try to imagine how it might look when everything's finished, although I'm not good at envisioning the shape of things to come. There's plenty of room for a patio or a deck and gardens. I wonder if the teddy bear will see it all the way through or whether he'll get a great offer and sell out.

"How was moving day?" I look up to see our landlord strolling up the driveway, carrying a can of beer. Trotting beside him is a dog whose face resembles the Knight of the Woeful Countenance and whose body design would best be described as a low-rider Sherman tank.

I can't help laughing. "Moving day was pretty easy. We had lots of help. I'm sorry. I didn't mean to laugh. This must be Turbo."

"He has that effect on people. It's pretty interesting. He looks so sad that it makes 'em laugh." Turbo lumbers up on the porch and drapes himself facedown over the top step, long ears swinging free. I pet his short, sleek fur and he turns slightly to check me out.

"Where's your roommate?"

"She was tired. I think she's in bed."

"At seven o'clock?"

"We have to be at work at eleven. We don't do a lot of late nights."

His heavy brows lift. "Really? What do you do at the bakery?"

"We're the bread bakers."

"Wow. I guess I'll have to stop by sometime. I haven't been in there since Fran left."

Hearing his mother's name, Turbo raises his head, looks around, and then sets it down again, this time in my lap. "Well, aren't you sweet." I scratch behind his ears. "I usually don't have this effect on males."

Josh laughs, a nice, booming laugh. He finishes his beer. "Let me know if you gals need anything. Come on, big guy, we still got things to do before bedtime." He turns and walks back toward his house.

The dog doesn't move until Josh disappears from sight. Then he sighs and heaves himself off the porch, takes off running with a grace that truly is amazing.

"You want some breakfast?"

It's Tuesday morning and Tyler's sprawled on the couch. "No thanks."

"You need to eat something."

"I had a muffin at work."

"Woman does not live by bread alone. You're looking too skinny. How about some oatmeal?"

"I'm really not hungry."

"Why don't we go for a walk, then? Maybe you'll work up an appetite."

She gives me an impatient look. "Wyn, you don't have to be my mother."

"Funny, I thought that's what you wanted me for."

"I changed my mind."

"Fine. Now that I've given up going to France."

She gets up abruptly. "So go to fucking France. Just leave me alone." She goes in her room, slams the door. So this is motherhood. Ignoring all the unopened packing boxes stacked on the kitchen floor, I fix myself two pieces of Indian Maiden toast and a glass of orange juice and go sit on the front porch. Before I've swallowed the first bite, Turbo comes galumphing up and screeches to a halt at my feet. He's very cool. Doesn't beg. No pawing. He just sits and stares at me. Or at my toast. His long, pink tongue lolls out to one side.

"You're shameless," I tell him. "It's one of your most endearing qualities." As soon as I say it, I remember where it came from and I'm embarrassed, as if he knows I'm stealing lines. I buy his silence with a bite of toast. He scarfs it down and resumes staring.

"I should've known you'd be where somebody had food. Shame

on you." Josh jogs out the back door of the house. "You've got to harden your heart," he says, "or before you know what's happening, he'll have your whole breakfast."

"Normally, being hard-hearted isn't a problem for me, but I must be a sucker for big brown eyes." I hold out another piece of toast and the dog takes it delicately with his teeth, careful not to graze my fingers. "Nice table manners, too."

"You don't look so hard-hearted to me." He smiles. "Is that some of your bread?"

"Don't tell me you're going to beg now?"

He really does have a nice laugh. "No, I'll go buy some. What kind is that?"

"It's Tyler's Indian Maiden Bread."

"Tyler's what?"

"It's like squaw bread, only more politically correct. Would you like to try a piece?"

"Will I ever live it down?"

"Probably. Sit down, I'll be right back." I go inside and pop two more pieces in the toaster. I hear water running in the bathroom. When the toast is done, I put butter and honey on both pieces and take them outside, give one to Josh. He lounges against the porch rail, the dog slumped across his feet.

"This is great," he says after a bite. He eats the rest in silence, holding one hand up to shade his eyes from the sun.

I stretch luxuriously. "It's so nice this morning."

"Yeah, this has always been my favorite...." His voice dies, his gaze frozen on the doorway. I turn around. Tyler stands on the threshold, hands on hips, propping the door open with her foot, looking grim. She's totally bald.

Josh recovers first. "Hi, Tyler. Like your hair."

She gives him a cold stare. "I'm in deep mourning." She lets the door swing shut, sits down next to me. "Can I have a bite of toast?"

I find my voice. "You want me to make some more?"

"I just want a bite." I hand her my toast.

"I'm sorry to hear that," he says. I can tell he thinks it might be a joke, but he doesn't want to push his luck.

"The Santee Sioux cut their hair as a sign of mourning," she says. "The more they loved someone, the more hair they cut off." Turbo waddles over to check out the new food supply. She ignores him. "My best friend died." She finishes my toast, licks her fingers. Josh looks from her to me. "The moron OD'd on heroin."

"Oh. I'm sorry." He frowns.

"Wouldn't you think he'd have more sense than that?" The dog gazes up at her, considering her words. "Even Turbo's smarter than that, aren't you, Turb?" She rubs the top of his head. "Unless, of course, he did it on purpose, which is what I think."

I look at her sharply. "Why do you say that?"

Now her chin trembles and her eyes are darting everywhere, as if that might stop the tears. "One—he never did heroin. Just pot, and once in a while a quaalude. Two—he got tested." She licks her lips. "For HIV. I saw the envelope from the clinic. He never said a thing about it. I never asked him." Two drops fall on her arm and Turbo's long tongue slurps them off. She looks down at him. "I was his god-damn best friend. Wouldn't you tell your goddamn best friend?"

Her face crumples. The dog lays his head on her lap, heedless of the tears dripping on him and her clutching at him. I put my arm around her, but she's oblivious. She just holds Turbo, rocks back and forth, cries.

## · sixteen ·

## *Mac*

June is spring, July is summer, August is fall. The rest of the year is winter. That's how Chris explains the four seasons of the north. Now it's August.

Mac rests his elbows on the bar and looks through the front window and onto the quiet street. He's pretty sure Pearl May will have to lay him off by the end of the month. It was a busy summer, but there just aren't that many customers now. In fact, the only person on the sidewalk at the moment is Foster, looking forlorn in his ratty beaver costume, not a camera-toting visitor in sight.

Daylight still stretches out for thirteen hours, give or take. The sun still feels warm on his back when he walks to work. But the signs of change are unmistakable. In the surrounding hills, the leaves of aspens and birch flash like new pennies, spiked by the brilliant red of wild blueberry bushes. Ragged formations of ducks and geese cut across the pure blue sky, and the air is smoky from distant forest fires.

Options. The Elky will be good to go by the end of the week. Or he could take the money Ian offered him for it, buy a plane ticket to Seattle. It feels as if he's waiting, but he's not sure for what. The other option, the one he hasn't even admitted considering yet, is to stay the winter.

He eases down on the plastic bench that's supposed to look like wrought iron.

He's watched from the front window of the saloon as this park has gone from the tail end of winter, through spring, summer, and now fall over the last three months. Birch trees leafed out seemingly overnight, bulbs came up, and annuals sprouted from planters and pots. Sweet, green grass grew almost as he looked, just like in one of those films of time-lapse photography.

Families wandered the boardwalks, posing with Foster, peering in windows, women carrying shopping bags, men laden with camera equipment, children running and laughing, bear-shaped backpacks bouncing against their backs.

Suddenly it's all gone. The people, the flowers. Now the color comes from the golden leaves, the browning grass. The sun warms him to the point of drowsiness.

He pulls out his sandwich, but before he can unwrap it, a motion in his peripheral vision makes him look up. Bernie. Her hair is loose, falling around her face. She's wearing a man's windbreaker with sleeves so long that her hands are invisible, and dirty jeans, frayed at the cuffs. She sits down next to him, sighing loudly, looking straight ahead.

"Am I incredibly rude?"

"I wouldn't say incredibly. Just rude. Why?"

"Pearl says I am."

"Do you care what she says?" He offers her half of the tuna sandwich, and she takes it, but doesn't eat, just sits silently.

"Not really," she says at last, still staring at the sandwich.

He takes a bite, then a swallow of water. He offers her the bottle, but she shakes her head.

"If you're so miserable here, why don't you leave?"

She nibbles at the tuna, carefully avoiding the bread. She chews slowly, as if it's painful, swallows, and turns to him. Tears brim in her eyes, but don't fall, held by some invisible effort of will.

"Right." Her voice is a cracked whisper. "Where would I go?"

"Anywhere."

"Easy for you to say. You don't have a six-year-old—"

"I guess it is easy for me to say. It would be difficult. But people have done it. It just depends on how badly you want out."

Another long silence.

"My mother named me Seentahna," she says.

"What does it mean?"

She shrugs. "I don't remember any of the words. Her family was from the Koyukon River people."

"How old were you when she died?"

"She didn't die. Pearl killed her."

A large chunk of sandwich goes down unchewed. "What are you talking about?"

"She killed my mother. Not with a knife or a gun or anything. She just took away her reason to live."

"I thought she—"

"Pearl hated my mother because she wasn't white. She wasn't good enough for her son to marry. She didn't want the Austen family to have mixed blood." She takes a bigger bite of the sandwich, chewing slowly. She sets it down on her thigh. "When my father got killed, my mother started drinking. You can see why she would. Her husband dies, she's got this four-year-old kid, no way to make a living—"

"Couldn't she go back to her family?"

She gives him a withering look. "The village was a nightmare by then. Everybody drunk or old. Everyone dirt poor, all the young people gone. It was a slum. She wanted to stay here where there was at least a chance at a better life. For me." She picks up the sandwich again, shifting her fingers on the bread as if she were fingering piano keys.

"But she started drinking, and it got hold of her. That sickness. It gave Pearl an excuse to get rid of her. She told my mother that she would take care of me, educate me, give me everything. On one condition. That my mother would go away and never come back. Never see me again."

"So she went away?"

"She killed herself. The way the old people did when they knew they had to die. When they couldn't contribute anymore and the village couldn't support them. She walked out on the river ice during a storm, with the wind at her back. She walked till she was exhausted. Then she turned around and walked into the wind till she fell down."

"I'm sorry."

She shrugs and takes another bite of the sandwich, pushing it into the side of her mouth, talking around it. "Everybody thinks Pearl is so wonderful, how she raised me, sent me to school. She's just a selfish, evil old woman."

"Which brings us back to why you don't leave."

Her head whips around. "Because my son, my Emmett, is all she's got. He's going to get all her money someday. She'd like for me to do the same thing my mother did. Just go away and let her have the kid. Well, I'm not my mother, and I'm not going anywhere."

"Mac, when are you leaving us?" He looks up from the remains of his dinner to see Pearl standing in the open door. "May I come in? Oh, I didn't mean to interrupt your meal."

"I'm through. Would you like some tea?"

"Thank you, no. We've just finished supper, as well."

He gets up and holds out a chair for her. There's a barely discernible wince as she lowers herself into it, smoothing her long skirt. "These bones of mine are the best weather predictors in the Yukon Territory." She smiles. "I say we'll have rain by tomorrow afternoon."

"So I should take my umbrella to work?" He sits down across from her.

"Actually, work is what I've come about. The season has come and gone for another year, I'm afraid. And I won't be needing your services at the bar much past the end of the week."

He smiles. "You haven't really needed them this week, but thanks for letting me stay."

She flicks her hand, as if to swat a fly. "I like to keep things even. End of the month, you know. Makes accounting so much easier."

"Right."

"You're a good boy, Mac. I'm going to miss having you around."

"Does that mean you're booting me out of the bunkhouse, too?"

"Good heavens, no! I just assumed you'd be heading back. Or on to Alaska or whatever."

"Well . . . I think my timing's off for Alaska. And I'm not sure I'm ready to head back to Seattle. I haven't quite finished what I came to do."

She folds her hands sedately and looks up at him. "Does that mean you're thinking about overwintering?"

"I'm thinking about it."

Her lovely eyes twinkle. "It's an experience. Just think, you'll be a real sourdough."

"I will?"

"Oh, yes. The definition of a sourdough is someone who's seen the river ice up in the fall and break up in the spring. Also, in the old days they used to say you'd have to sleep with a squaw and shoot a bear—or vice versa. But we tend not to enforce those last provisions anymore."

He grins. "That's a relief. I guess what I was wanting to know is what you'd charge me to stay here in the bunkhouse."

"I really hadn't thought about it. Are you sure you want to stay here? Nobody's spent the winter here in years. I don't want you to be uncomfortable. And what will you do with yourself all day?"

"I've got plenty to do. I'm working on a book. I like this place be-cause it's quiet and private. As far as being comfortable, I think that stove could just about heat the whole town."

"She's a beauty, isn't she?" Her gaze rests fondly on the black hulk. She turns back to him. "Let's just say we'll work it out—"

"No, let's figure out a price, or you'll end up doing that brush-off thing that you do. I have the money I was going to spend in Alaska, so it's not like you're taking food out of my mouth."

"Very well, then. Shall we say fifty a week?" She holds out her small white hand. "And I'll bring you an eiderdown."

"I think that's more than fair." He can feel the tiny, brittle bones of her fingers, but her grip is strong.


Chris invites him over to get outfitted for winter, but it's Nora who opens the door.

"Mac! What a lovely surprise." She offers her cheek. "Unfortu-nately Chris isn't here. He's gone hunting with Dirk."

"He didn't mention the clothes, I guess."

"Clothes?"

"I told him I decided to stay for the winter, and he said I should come by and pick up an old parka—"

"Really? You're staying for the winter? Why?" She shakes her head. "Sorry, come in. I'll make us some tea."

He follows her out to the kitchen and sits at the big wooden table while she puts the kettle on the stove.

"Where will you stay?"

"At the bunkhouse."

Her dark eyebrows lift. "You'll freeze your bum off, you silly man. Do you have any idea how cold it gets here in the winter? Twenty below isn't uncommon."

"I'll be fine. I just thought Chris had a good point when he said the clothes I brought with me probably weren't designed for this kind of winter."

"One of his more astute observations, I'm sure. Well, at least he's about your size, and he's got plenty of jackets and gloves and such that aren't terribly attractive, but they're serviceable." She gives him a side-long glance. "What's Pearl May asking you to pay, if I may be so bold?"

He laughs. "You're a pisser, Nora Moody."

"What does that mean?"

"It's an East Coast expression. I don't know if it translates. But it's a compliment."

She gets their cups and pours the boiling water into the pot. "Come on, then. How much?"

"Fifty dollars a week."

"That's outrageous—"

"It's a steal."

"It is not. The place doesn't even have indoor plumbing. Just wait till you wake up in the middle of some minus-twenty night and have to use the privy."

"She wouldn't have charged me anything. I insisted."

She looks indignant. "You could stay here for free."

"Thanks for the offer, but I wouldn't inflict my company on you two for the whole winter. Besides, I need to be alone so I can get some work done."

"You Yanks really are crackers, you know that? Here's your tea."

He drops some sugar in the cup. "Pearl May said I'd be a real sourdough if I survive the winter."

"She does love her local mythology." Nora sniffs. "I suppose she told you her mother won the Beaver Tail in a poker game."

He looks up quickly and she laughs. "Look at your face. God, you're gullible. Just remember, a good story helps pass a winter's night. Up here we've got plenty of those, so everyone has a ready supply of stories. Less than half of which are true."

"What about Bernie's mother?" he asks quietly.

Nora's smile disappears. "What did she tell you—that her mother committed suicide?"

He nods.

She pushes a damp wisp of hair off her forehead. "Of course, all this happened before we came here, but that's her story. Most of the old-timers say Alice got so drunk at the Beaver Tail that she got lost on the way home. They found her two days later when it stopped snowing."

"The story had that sound—that sort of half-romance, half-excuse sound."

"Strange, eh? I remember seeing a movie once. *Rashomon*. Do you know it?"

Mac nods. "Everybody had a different story. And they all seemed perfectly plausible. I can't remember if you ever found out what the truth was."

"No," she says. "Just like real life." She drains her cup. "Very well, then, let's get you outfitted."


October.

All morning long the wind toys with the clouds, finally persuading them to release a torrent that muddies the creek behind the bunkhouse. In late afternoon the rain dissolves into fog. Wood smoke mingles with the metallic dampness and hangs in the air.

He stands on the porch for a long time, watching the mist rise from the creek and thread through the spruce and pine, listening to the rush of icy water and the breath of wind. Feeling the temperature drop.

Until today, he's been able to tell himself that he could still change his mind. He could go down to Ian's, gas up the Elky, and head south. But the bite of this wind means snow. Probably tonight, more likely tomorrow. He remembers driving Wyn to the hospital in the April Fool's Day snowstorm last year. He'd pushed the Elky to its limits, and it had proved surprisingly surefooted on the slick streets. But that was in a big city where there was help available if you got stuck in a drift or ran off the road. Up here, you'd be on your own. So it would appear that, as of now, he's committed to winter in Beaverton. To mark the occasion, he decides to try baking corn bread to go with the chili that's been simmering on the range all afternoon. He mixes it according to the directions on the sack of cornmeal and pours the batter into the misshapen metal baking pan. When he opens the door to the tiny oven, he realizes it's going to take more heat.

It was stupid not to check the firebox before mixing the batter, but there's nothing to do except throw in another chunk of aspen wood. He waits ten minutes, watching the baking powder puff up the batter in the pan. Then he slides it into the oven and sits down at the table.

*Dear Wyn,*

*You said a couple of times that you wished you could have known my family. So do I. What a collection we were. My dad was hardly ever there physically, and Suzanne was rarely on call emotionally. I don't know that any of us knew much about each other. I think the closest thing to a real relationship was between Suzanne and Kevin.*

*My earliest memory of my dad is him standing in the downstairs hall of our house with his beat-up Samsonite suitcase the color of split pea soup. He's wearing khaki pants and a short-sleeved plaid sportshirt, high-top tennis shoes, and what used to be called an Eisenhower jacket slung over one shoulder.*

*I can't recall if he was coming or going, but I do know that Suzanne was pissed. I knew it not just by the hangdog look on his face, but by the blue of St. Elmo's fire crackling in the air. Suzanne when* she was angry was an electrical storm about to happen. Although I also recall that there were sparks anytime they were together.

They were always, in Kevin's words, either fighting or fucking. Other kids' parents argued; ours went to war. Things got broken, doors slammed off their hinges. Once she went after him with the phone. One of those wall phones everyone used to have in the kitchen, just ripped it out of the wall. We had to have the phone company come out and fix it a couple of days later, and I overheard her telling the repairman that she'd been talking to someone when her son fell down the basement stairs and she was so upset that she ran to him, not even noticing that the phone was in her hand. I remember thinking that I didn't know Kevin had fallen down the stairs, and then later I realized she was lying. Why she would bother lying for the telephone company I had no idea.

Kevin and I could hear them making love, too, and it didn't sound a whole lot different from the fighting to a seven-year-old and a five-year-old. Maybe a little quieter. Kevin used to stand with his ear to their bedroom door trying to figure out if he was hurting her, while I ran to our bedroom at the other end of the hall, and put my pillow over my head. Eventually I discovered that music would drown out the sound, no matter what they were doing, and shortly thereafter I realized that it worked just as well for everything else I didn't want to hear.

My taste in music has gotten a lot more eclectic since I first took my head out from under the pillow and plopped some of those big headphones with the black squishy padding over my ears.

I was eight years old in 1966 when the Byrds' "Eight Miles High" became the first psychedelic rock hit. Later that year the Beatles released Revolver. I listened to the experimental studio stuff—the artificial double tracking, tape loops, saturation—and I was grossed out. I didn't know what all that stuff was, but I knew it sounded awful. They ruined my music.

At night after my homework was done and Kevin was ensconced on the couch with Suzanne watching Batman or Get Smart, I laid on the upstairs landing with my head next to the radio, twirling the dial slowly and endlessly, up and down the band, searching for the sounds I thought were lost. One night when I'd been there for so long that the loop pile of the carpet was imprinted on my face and I was nearly asleep, I heard something that caused me to sit straight up, banging my forehead on the phone table.

It was about the coolest song I'd ever heard and it had a really different beat. I listened, mesmerized, tapping out the rhythm on the floor till the song was over, waiting for the DJ to give the title and artist.

"Jeez, what a spaz." Kevin's voice effectively drowned out the information.

"Shut up," I snapped. "I'm trying to hear something."

"No you're not. You're twitchin' around like a spaz."

"Get lost, butthead."

"Hey, Mom. Matt called me a hmmmhole."

"Did not."

Now Suzanne was at the foot of the stairs. "Mattie, watch your language. Kev, come on back. The commercials are over."

"Be right there." He smiled down at me, which immediately made me wary. "Whatcha listening to, Mattie?" He was ten now, not much taller than me, but sturdier, fair haired and square jawed, with clear gray eyes. It was probably already apparent that he'd gotten whatever looks were to be had in our family. Suzanne was always saying that he was a dead ringer for her favorite brother, Lucas.

On his way back down, he poked at the radio with the toe of his sneaker, dislodging the station. I grabbed at his foot and he fell partway down the stairs. Then, sensing opportunity, he somersaulted the rest of the way down and started yelling.

Suzanne was back in an instant. "What are you two doing? Are you okay, Kev?"

He started limping around theatrically, yelling that I'd tripped him.

"I did not. He kicked the radio."

"Matt, why are you lying on the floor?"

I shrugged.

"Well, whatever you're doing, stop doing it. And go get ready for bed."

"But I was just—"

"No buts. Move it. Kevin, come here. I want to check that ankle."

I went to get ready for bed, but not before I'd slipped into Suzanne's bedroom and used the phone to call the radio station—WJJD in New Jersey—and found out that the song I'd been so taken with was "Not Fade Away" by Buddy Holly.

I don't remember the DJ's name—in those days the night jocks answered their own phones—but I remember him saying, "How old are you, kid?"

"Twelve." I tried to make my voice lower, but I'm sure he knew I was lying.

"Izzat so? Well, listen, if you dig that beat, you might want to go to the source, know what I mean?"

"Uh. Sure."

He laughed. "Try getting your hands on some Bo Diddley records."

So I did, and I was hooked on the "Bo Diddley beat," that strident African-sounding rhythm he played, not on drums, but on his guitar. Then a few years later some other DJ—I'd gotten to be a regular caller at some of the stations—told me that Bo Diddley was actually inspired by John Lee Hooker's "Boogie Chillen." The first time I heard that hard-rocking stomp with its chantlike melody, no chord changes, and heavily amped electric guitar, I realized there was a whole new world of old music out there just waiting for me.

Wyn, I know I said I was coming back in September, but obviously I didn't. And now I can't. You deserve an explanation, but at the moment, I don't have one. Even for myself. I think about you so

*many times during the day (and night), and I can see you so clearly.*
*Much more clearly than any of the past.*

Mac

He's flipping through the notebook in search of an envelope that he's certain is stuck between two pages when he suddenly realizes that something besides wood is burning in the stove. He grabs a towel and opens the oven door, releasing a cloud of black smoke into the room. Eyes tearing, he pulls out a pan of charred corn bread, and rushes it outside, smoke pluming behind him.

He sets the smoldering pan on the ground and props the door open to let in the cold, fresh air. Hopefully this doesn't foreshadow the tone of his rookie winter as a sourdough.

"So, you like it well done, huh?" Bernice is coming toward him out of the twilight, seemingly oblivious to the cold in only a long-sleeved T-shirt and gray sweatpants. Her laughter makes little clouds of steam in the air and transforms her face, filling her eyes with light.

He smiles. "I guess I'm not exactly the wood-stove gourmet. Yet."

"No shit." She looks down at the cooling black lump of char. "What was it?"

"Corn bread."

She folds her arms. "Here's the deal, tenderfoot. You gotta get the fire going, really hot, then when the fuel's almost gone, you put in your bread and let it cook while the temperature goes down. You try to cook it while the temperature's rising, this"—she pokes the pan with her toe—"is what you get."

"Sorry about the pan. I'll get a new one at the store."

She makes a soft puffing noise. "Nah. It was a piece of crap anyway. I'll bring you one in a little while. I'm just going to get some wood."

"You want some help?"

"Nope."

"You sure? I'm not—"

"What part of no don't you understand? I don't need any help." Her abrupt shift of expression surprises him.

"Sometimes you let people help because they want to, not because you need it," he says evenly.

"Why do you want to?"

"Why did you tell me how to bake in the stove?"

She smiles slightly in spite of an obvious effort not to. "Because you're pretty clueless. You'd probably starve. Then I'd have to get rid of your dead body. What a pain in the ass."

"Well, then, while I'm still among the living, why don't I make myself useful?"

She shrugs and looks away. "Up to you."

## · seventeen ·

# *Wyn*

CM's banging on the door. "Avon calling."

"You're supposed to ring the doorbell."

She comes in and throws her arms around me, then holds me at arm's length.

"This is a sweet place." She raises one eyebrow. "I like the land-lord, too. Much cuter than mine. Is he married?"

"Separated. Or divorced. I'm not sure how official it is. You're not into the lumberjack type anyway."

"I could rethink my preferences."

I shrug. "He's a really nice guy, but he's still carrying the torch for his ex. He's actually my landlord from Fourth Street. Got a great dog. A basset hound."

"Where's the poppet?"

"She went shopping, thank God. She's driving me nuts."

"Motherhood—it's not just a job, it's an adventure."

"You said it. By the way, she's shaved her head, so for God's sake, don't say anything when you see her."

"Shaved her head? Why?"

"She's in mourning."

"Poor baby. Can you imagine finding your best friend like that?"

"No. If I found you unconscious, with white stuff on your face, I'd think it was whipped cream."

"Wyn, that's terrible."

"I know. But I have to laugh or I'll slash my wrists."

She sits down on the couch, rubs her hands together. "Is it too early for wine?"

"Somewhere in the country it's five o'clock." I open a bottle of zinfandel, pour two glasses. "Tell me everything. How was France?"

She sighs a smile. "Divine. I was only going to stay a few days, then every day, I thought I might as well stay one more, and...I walked and shopped and ate my way through every arrondissement that I could manage. Of course, it would have been more divine with you. I took lots of pictures to show you. I got taken out to dinner a couple of times—"

"Anybody I should know about?"

"No. One American attorney. One French computer salesman. Nice, but no sparks."

"When did you get home?"

"Day before yesterday. But I stopped in New York to see Eva Schutz. My old teacher. It's been so much fun being off, I'm going to hate going to work tomorrow."

"What are you doing this week?" I ask her.

She eases off her shoes, and raises her feet to the coffee table, going through a little routine of pointing and flexing her toes. "Thinking about next year."

"What about it?"

"Well, my grant's up in April. I don't know what's going to happen after that. If they don't get some money, I'm out of a job. I'm going to put out some feelers when I go home for Christmas."

"Oh, sure. Get me up here, then abandon me and go back to L.A."

"I don't want to," CM says, "I'll just have to see. How's your mom? Is Richard doing okay?"

"They're great. In fact, they're cruising through the Panama Canal as we speak. They'll be home next week."

"Heard from Mac?"

"Another letter last week. He still hasn't said anything about coming back."

"Why don't you call him?"

"I don't have a phone number."

"How many saloons can there be in Beaverton?"

"I just don't know what to do. I don't know how I feel. And I sure as hell don't know how he feels."

"Then you're not as smart as you look."

"Don't start on me, Mayle. I'm not in the mood."

She sighs. "Okay, have it your way. I had a good feeling about him, though."

"Fine, you call him."

The door opens then, and Tyler makes her entrance, toting a bag from Nordstrom Rack. "Don't say it," she says to CM

"Say what?"

"You know what. About my hair."

"I didn't."

"I'm sick of everyone making a big deal out of it. I got shit for having it blue. Now it's gone and I'm getting even more shit."

"I didn't say a word. I just came by to see if you guys wanted to have dinner, but you're both so grouchy I'd be better off with my own company."

"Where should we go?" I ask.

"I was thinking the Two Bells Tavern."

"They have good burgers," Tyler says almost to herself. "On sourdough rolls." This is about the most enthusiasm she's shown for anything in weeks. She reaches into her shopping bag, pulls out a black bowler hat, and sets it on her head. She looks like Boy George, but I'm not about to say anything.

"I'm ready," she says.

. . .

When I hear the piano, I walk quietly around to the front of the big house, tiptoe up the steps to the bay window. The parlor is full of power tools, boxes. A few old doors and a stained-glass window lean against the wall. Josh sits at a baby grand piano, his back to me. A drop cloth lies in a heap on the floor and in the middle of it, Turbo has made himself a cozy nest. Josh's playing "Love Letters Straight from Your Heart," and it's so sweetly sad that after he finishes, I stand for a minute, half-forgetting why I came.

He turns around quickly when I knock, motions for me to come in. The room smells of fresh sawdust. "That was beautiful," I say. "Is this the same piano from the Victorian?"

"Yep." He nods, looking embarrassed. "What can I do for you?"

"I wanted to ask a favor. I was wondering if it might be possible for Tyler and me to plant a garden."

"Sure. Where and how big?"

"I was hoping you'd tell me. Herbs, maybe some flowers. I thought it might be good for her. Therapeutic."

"That's a nice idea." He gets up abruptly. "Sorry, I'm not used to visitors. Sit down."

"No, I'm fine, really. I didn't know what your plans were about the yard, and I—"

He laughs. "Neither do I. Haven't got that far yet." He leans forward, resting his arms on the instrument. "How about right in front of the house? That way you could see it from the window. And I could see it from my kitchen. How big?"

"I don't know. I wanted to be sure it was okay with you before I started making any plans."

"Just draw me a sketch of what you want. I can rototill it for you."

"That's really nice of you."

"In fact, since it's an improvement to the property, I'll spring for the plants."

"You don't need to do that." I bend down to stroke Turbo's long, silky ears.

"I don't mind. I'll be getting the labor for free." He hesitates. "How's Tyler doing?"

"Not good. She and Barton grew up together. He seemed like a really sweet guy."

"That's sad," he says. "She's lucky to have you looking out for her."

I stand up. "I guess. Well...thanks. I'll sketch a garden plan. Maybe this weather will hold and we can get it in before the monsoon."

"Yup. Maybe." By the time I get to the door, he's already turned back to the piano.

The following week, Ellen arranges for Tyler to start seeing Terry Dumont, a friend of hers who's a counselor at the Queen Anne Community Crisis Center. While she's at her first appointment, Josh and I stake out the garden. It's small and simple, just a border, really. Six feet by fifteen feet, bisected by the walkway leading to the house. My tentative plant list includes lots of lavender, some lamb's ears, lady's mantle, artemesia, fern leaf tansy, pennyroyal, hyssop, rose geranium, lovage, lemon verbena, and yarrow.

"Where are you going to get your herbs?" Josh asks.

"I thought Ellen might take me out to the Herbfarm. In Fall City."

"Fran used to go—" He stops himself. "Silly, isn't it?"

"No it's not. How long has she been gone?"

"One year and eight months, one week, three days."

"That's a long time."

"Yeah. And it seems even longer."

"Sometimes it takes a while to realize you miss—someone. Maybe she'll come back."

"Thinking stuff like that'll run you crazy in a hurry." He shakes his head, the way you do to fend off a buzzing insect. "It probably wasn't real smart for us to get married in the first place. She always had an itch to see the world and I always wanted to get some land and stay put." He shrugs. "Live and learn, I guess."

While we're tying string between the stakes, Tyler drags up to the house, barely looks at us, goes inside without saying a word. Somehow I was hoping for more of a reaction.

Josh smiles. "She'll come around. Give her a little time. She probably has no idea what it's supposed to be."

I beard the lioness in her den. Her door's closed, so I knock.

"Yeah?"

"Can I come in?"

"If you want." She's lying on the bed with her butt against the wall, legs sticking straight up.

"How was your session?"

"Okay."

"Do you like Terry?"

"She's okay."

I attempt a laugh. "I guess you were wondering what Josh and I were doing."

"Not really."

I sit down next to her. "I'll tell you anyway. We're laying out a garden."

"That's good."

"I thought maybe you and I could plant some herbs and flowers."

"What for? Josh owns the place. Let him plant stuff."

I want to slap her silly little face.

"I thought it might help you feel better. I remember when I first got divorced, I was really depressed. Doing physical things like gardening and making bread seemed to help me—"

Her legs slide down the wall and she scoots into an upright and locked position. Her eyes are throwing off sparks. "Well, I'm not like you, and this is totally different. All you did was lose some jerk you didn't even like. I love Barton. And he's dead. You know, stone-cold dead. So how could you think it's the same?"

I count backward from ten, just like my mother always said I should do when I'm about to lose my temper. "Tyler, I know it's not the same. I just thought watching the plants grow and working in the garden would make you feel better. Maybe we could make it a kind of memorial to Barton. We could get Josh to make a marker—"

"How too cute. And maybe we could get Turbo to come shit in it. Sort of add his two cents' worth."

I get up abruptly. "I don't know why you feel compelled to be such a bitch, but I'm getting sick of it. I'm trying to help you."

"Well, you can't!" She jumps off the bed, stands glaring at me. "He wasn't your friend! You just have to take over and run everything. I don't need you to make me feel better. Why don't you just go to fucking France and leave me alone."

"Tyler, it's not your fault, you know."

"What the hell are you talking about?" She swipes furiously at the tears that won't stop.

"I know you think he died because you didn't ask him about the HIV test—"

"Shut up! You don't know jack shit!" Her voice reminds me of squealing brakes. "Get the hell out of my room!"

She slams the door behind me.

I stand looking at the blank face of the door till I realize I'm holding my breath.

In the kitchen I take some leftover soup out of the refrigerator and pour it into a saucepan on the stove. When it's hot I put the pan on a trivet and sit at my little table, eating the soup and listening to her sobs on the other side of the door. For this I gave up going to Toulouse?

We hardly exchange two words the remainder of the week. At first I think I should probably just blow off the whole idea of having a garden. Seeing it in front of the house every day might piss her off even more. But it's only mid-October and there's no sign of a change in the beautiful weather, and I can't stop thinking about how good it feels to dig in the dirt. The plants will have the long, wet winter to develop their roots, and by spring, there won't be an herb garden this side of Fall City to compare with mine. Forget Tyler. I can do a garden without her help.

Josh and I leave Sunday morning while she's still asleep. We have omelets at Steve's Broiler and I carefully avoid thinking about the mornings Mac and I sat here. The time we were in the booth next to the woman and her two little boys. The morning when he first came back from Orcas. And all those other Sunday mornings.

After breakfast we hop back in the cab of his white Ford Ranger and take off down Boren to Interstate 90. Sunday-morning traffic is practically nonexistent and we fly across Lake Washington on the floating bridge to Mercer Island.

"What does Tyler think about the garden?" Josh asks me.

My eyes follow a sailboat with a red-and-blue spinnaker skimming across the whitecaps. "I have no idea. She's barely speaking to me. I'm doing the garden for myself."

"That poor little critter," he says, and I look at him sharply.

"What about this poor little critter?"

He laughs his funny laugh. "I'm not wasting any pity on you. You got the world by the tail, lady."

It's my turn to laugh. "Yeah, right." I fold my hands and unfold them a few times. "I really don't understand it—whatever's going on with her. I must have been insane to think I could help her. That she needed me."

He turns a serious look on me. "It's pretty plain to me that you can and she does."

"She acts like she's furious with me."

"I could be wrong, but here's what I think. Besides being about as sad as a person can be, she's scared. Know what I mean?" I look out the window and his voice gets even quieter than usual. "Sometimes when you love somebody—when you need that somebody—you get so scared of losing them that you just push them away. So you won't be the one who gets left behind. Know what I mean?"

I turn to look at him. He's looking straight out the windshield. In profile he's more Paul Bunyon than teddy bear. Except for the wire-rimmed specs.

"Yes," I say. "I know what you mean."

I kneel in the freshly tilled black dirt, surrounded by plastic pots of herbs. A handful of the stuff under my nose, smelling clean and damp, leafy and almost chocolatey, makes me happy, sort of like walking into a bakery. The piney scent of rosemary, a whiff of licorice from the tarragon, the astringency of lemon thyme, the soothing floral breath of lavender—I don't even notice when Josh disappears, but when I'm almost finished, I look up and he's gone. I remember guiltily that I didn't even thank him. As soon as I stick the last of the fuzzy gray lamb's ears in the ground, I follow the sound of the power sander.

"All through?" He pushes up his plastic goggles when I walk in and Turbo runs to meet me, covered with a fine layer of dust.

"Yes. Listen, Josh, I feel terrible. I didn't even say thanks for all your help."

"It's okay. Turbo was in the mood for a walk. But, I've got something for you. For the garden." He sets down the sander and retrieves a brown paper bag from under the piano. Inside is a small plaque attached to a stake. It's hand painted with flowers and a butterfly and it says "Barton's Garden."

"The woman who makes them has a table at the Market. I know it's kind of cutesy-poo," he says, grinning. "And it sounds like something from Monopoly, like Marvin Gardens. So if she doesn't like it, just pitch it. Won't hurt my feelings." *Au contraire,* I can see quite plainly that it will, and I decide that if Tyler says one nasty thing about this plaque, I'll use it to beat her senseless.

"It's really nice. Maybe I'll just wait awhile to show it to her."

For the first few days, she pretends not to notice that there's a garden in front of our house. I usually do the watering/weeding/routine maintenance every morning when we get home, so she can have breakfast by herself if she wants. Then by the time I'm ready to eat, she's in the tub or asleep or just holed up in her room with her Walkman on.

On Thursdays she goes to see Ellen's friend Terry. A couple of times—once when I'm spreading my sand-and-gravel mulch, and once when I'm watering—I look up to see her watching me from out of the window. Both times she turns away quickly.

She announces that she and Felice are going to a Halloween party. That suits me because I'm going over to CM's to hide out inside her walled fortress. I've always hated Halloween—at least since I got too old to sneak around egging cars and toilet-papering yards. I hate having my evening interrupted a thousand times by a bunch of overdressed little beggars extorting candy. And then there are the teenagers who think they're way too cool to wear costumes, but they expect you to fill up their king-size pillow cases with food anyway.

It's already dark when Tyler emerges from her room at six-thirty P.M. wearing black tights, a white turtleneck, and a black jacket with a white scarf. Her face is pale, made up with heavy eyeliner and lipstick that's so red it's nearly blue.

"Who are you supposed to be?" I ask.

The look she gives me is startlingly like one of Linda's—a combination of disdain and impatience. She reaches for her black bowler and sets it on her head. "Boy George, of course."

She disappears out the door.

I hike over to Galer Street and press the buzzer on the door. CM's best witch cackle comes over the intercom.

"Bubble, bubble, toil and trouble, fire burn and—"

"Whatever's bubbling, I hope it's cold and from France."

She buzzes me in. "It's cold, but it's from Sonoma," she says, opening the door. I hand her the pumpkin bread I carted away from the bakery and some brownies cut out in the shape of pumpkins and glazed with chocolate.

She's made her famous meatball sandwiches, which are her one culinary claim to fame, but they are to die for. We eat them with our Iron Horse brut champagne and watch *Nosferatu* on video.

"Forget Bela Lugosi and Frank Langella," she says as the tape rewinds. "Max Schreck is truly the best vampire ever."

I shiver. "That scene where he comes out of his coffin in the hold of the ship . . ."

She puts on a pot of decaf while I slice the pumpkin bread and put it on a plate with the brownies. "What's the poppet doing tonight?"

"I'm trying not to think about it. She went to a Halloween party with Felice. At least they don't hang out with DeeDee anymore."

"Was she the one with the slimy boyfriend?"

"Yes. I've been afraid to even mention it to Tyler—her mental state's so precarious these days—but I can't help wondering if Creepo's the one who got Barton the heroin."

"So she really thinks he did it on purpose?"

"That's what she said. She said Barton never did the hard stuff. But who knows?"

CM sighs. "Well, he did once. And that was enough."

· · ·

The weather holds for one more week and then the monsoon cometh.

"At least you don't have to worry about watering," Tyler says quietly. We're standing at the front window, watching the rain pelt the herbs. It's the first complete sentence in a civil tone of voice that's come out of her mouth since Josh and I staked out the garden. I'm almost afraid to make a sound.

"Now the real work begins," I say cautiously.

"What's that?"

"Slug patrol."

"Hmm." Her nose wrinkles with distaste.


At the bakery we're running a little late on preparations for Thanksgiving. Ellen is trying different pumpkin pie recipes, experimenting with pumpkin-pecan bread, and she's even come up with a pumpkin filling for the Mazurka bars, which is rapidly becoming a hot seller. We've got a huge pile of orders for Tyler's Indian Maiden Bread, for *pain de compagne,* and for dinner rolls.

The Tuesday before Thanksgiving a bitter-cold wind pours down from the north and low, fat clouds promise a deluge.

At seven-fifteen A.M. Cathy, our new *barista,* is on the job. She's a refugee from the Starbucks at Pike Market, and she's amazing to watch. She works the espresso machine as if she's performing a concerto that only she can hear—fast, inspired, precise—and she never confuses somebody's nonfat, decaf, no-whip mocha with their friend's double, skinny, extra-hot vanilla latte. Women in power suits and guys in jeans and work boots wait patiently beside grandmas in their warm-ups trying to get in their morning racewalk before the rain. Misha's running the till, and the racks behind her are full of bread. Jen's in back pulling muffins and scones out of the oven and wheeling the cooling racks out front. Ellen and I are sitting happily in the corner with coffee and pumpkin-millet muffins, putting together our orders for next week, and we can't resist looking around every few minutes, smiling at customers and then at each other.

It's one of those mornings when the bakery pulls me to stay, and if we had a cot out back by the ovens, the way a lot of French village bakeries do, I probably wouldn't go home at all.

Big, round drops are just beginning to splat on the sidewalk when a black Mercedes sedan stops out front and sits there in the no-parking zone with the engine running. The windows are all tinted, so you can't see inside, and Ellen and I watch idly, sipping our coffee, waiting to see who gets out. The car sits there for so long that I'm beginning to lose interest.

"Do you think I should go out and tell them they can't park there?" Ellen says.

Before I can answer, the passenger door opens and Maggie gets out, leans back in to say something, then shuts the door and dashes inside. Everybody in the place has been waiting to see who was in the mystery car, so when she walks in, they all turn to look.

Her upper lip is cut, pasted over with a small bandage, and a blue shadow lines the left side of her nose. Customers look away from her reflexively, then some look back, but she doesn't meet anyone's eyes. She just smiles a small, unfocused smile and heads for the work area.

Ellen and I exchange frowns.

"You know, I think I could do it," she says. "I could kill someone like that. I wouldn't think of him as a person, it would just be kind of like exterminating vermin. Sort of a public service."

"I don't understand why women put up with that shit." I finish my coffee and set down my cup.

She sighs. "Probably as many reasons as there are women."

We get up and carry our dishes back to the sink.

Maggie's in the storeroom. The apron hangs limp around her neck, strings untied. She's standing under one of the lights, dabbing something on her face with a small makeup sponge. She looks up and smiles when we come in.

"Aren't I a mess?" she says cheerfully.

"Are you all right?" Ellen asks. "Do you need to call somebody? Is there someplace you can go if you need to?"

Maggie looks dumbfounded. "What do you mean?"

While I stand there, debating how to best say this without actually saying it, Ellen looks her directly in the eye.

"I'm talking about family or friends you can go to. Or the women's shelter."

Maggie's cheeks flame. "What on earth for?" She looks in the mirror as if noticing for the first time that she looks like she kissed a stone wall. "Oh, you mean this?" She laughs. "I had a bit too much wine last night at the restaurant, and I got up to use the ladies'—it's in kind of a dark hallway, you've been there, haven't you, Wyn? You know how it is. Anyway, this other woman was coming out just as I was going in and she pushed the door open too fast, and of course I wasn't truly on my game, so I didn't get out of the way in time." Another laugh. "What a klutz. Tony was so upset, he insisted on taking me to the urgent-care clinic—"

"Bullshit." The word is flat and cold, bearing no resemblance to Ellen's usual voice.

For a split second something flickers through the tiniest chink in Maggie's gaze, but then she's back in control. "I'm fine," she says. "As soon as I get through fixing my makeup, I'll get started on those Thanksgiving cakes."

"Maggie..." Finally I find some words. "You don't have to live like this. There are plenty of things—"

"You know the term 'anamorphosis'?" She looks up from the mirror, expressionless, except for two small vertical folds in the smooth skin between her brows.

"What?"

"Anamorphosis," she goes on coolly. "It's a trick of artistic perspective. It's when an image appears distorted unless it's viewed from a particular direction at the correct angle."

For a few seconds, I just look into that flat brick wall of her expression, and then I turn around and walk back out of the storeroom. Ellen stays.

On the Wednesday morning before the holiday, just as I'm about to leave, Ellen hands me an envelope with our landlord's return address. Tyler's waiting for me out front, hopping around to stay warm, stripping needles off a branch of prostrate rosemary that grows in a half wine barrel beside the door.

"What's this?"

"A letter from Nate. He's sold the building. It means our rent will probably be going up."

"It probably would anyway, right? I mean, Nate's a nice guy and everything, but rents are going vertical all over the hill. I'm sure he'd want to be on a par with all the other building owners up here."

"True. I just wish he would've told us a little bit more about the new owner. Maybe brought him around and introduced him."

I look out the window. "Can I take the letter with me? I'm afraid she's going to denude all the plants if I don't get going."

Ellen nods. "Sure. Just don't share it with her, okay? We'll talk Monday. You two have a happy turkey day."

I stuff the letter down in my pocket and head out the door to interrupt Tyler's deforestation project and steer her toward home.

*November 14, 1990*
*Dear Ellen and ~~Diane:~~ Wynn:*

*This letter is being sent to you as tenants of 6005 Queen Street to inform you that I have contracted to sell the building. The new owner, Dr. Harvey Mendina, assumes title on January 15, 1991.*

*This was a very difficult decision for us, especially in light of all the exciting growth Queen Anne Hill is experiencing, but for sev-*

*eral years now, Libby's health has been deteriorating, and we have decided to leave the Northwest and move to Scottsdale, Arizona, where I believe the warmer weather will make her more comfortable. I've certainly enjoyed working with all of you and being able to call you my friends as well as my tenants.*

*I understand that this change may cause you some anxiety, but Dr. Mendina has assured me that he is most interested in preserving and protecting the heritage of our building and he is looking forward to meeting and working with everyone there. I'm sure he will be in touch before the end of the year.*

*Thanks for being such great tenants and best wishes for a happy holiday and prosperous new year.*

*Sincerely,*

*Nathan and Elizabeth Walsenberg*

# part three

## · eighteen ·

Now in the morning when we get home, instead of watering, I'm out picking off slugs and snails, watching them fizz when I drop them into my little bucket of saltwater. Josh and Turbo come out to watch.

"Having escargots for dinner?" he asks. I laugh, thinking of my first dinner in Toulouse, *les gros gris,* as Jean-Marc called them. "Why don't you just get some of those pellets?"

"Because those are toxic to birds. And other animals." I look at Turbo.

"Really?" He looks alarmed. "I didn't know that."

"Besides, killing them this way gratifies some latent sadistic tendencies of mine. I pretend they're my slimy ex and his beach-blanket bimbo."

The house is quiet, so I assume Tyler's asleep, and since it looks like we might actually have a day without rain on our hands, I make a provisioning run to Thriftway, buying everything I can carry. The bus stop is three blocks from our house, and by the time I get home, the bags feel as if they're full of rocks.

As I come around the corner of Josh's house, the sight of Tyler on her hands and knees in the garden brings me up short. She's gingerly harvesting slugs, depositing them in my slug bucket.

"Tyler," I call out. *Don't make a big deal out of it.* She turns, looking sheepish. "Give me a hand with these groceries?"

She runs over and takes one of the bags but doesn't look at me directly. "I just thought I should bust some slugs. Since you weren't here. I didn't want 'em to—you know—eat everything before you got back."

I put the groceries away and take a cup of coffee out on the porch. She's still kneeling in the garden, nose and ears red from the cold, breath escaping from her mouth in little puffs. I look at my watch.

"Aren't you having coffee with Felice today?"

She yanks at some little blades of grass that have sprouted up in the wake of the rain, and squints up at me.

"She told me she wanted DeeDee to come with us, and I said I didn't. She said it would be more fun with the three of us. Like it used to be." A tear rolls down her cheek, and she breathes deeply. "I told her, in case you forgot, it's never gonna be like it used to be. And she just said there's nothing we can do about Bart—Barton. Life goes on. 'Oo blah di oo blah da.' So I said"—another big breath—"then why don't you just have lunch with DeeDee yourself."

We're both kneeling in the mud, yanking at the marauding horsetails, when it occurs to me that it's time to show her the plaque. She doesn't look up when I go in the house, but when I come back with the brown grocery bag, she says, "What's that?"

"Something Josh gave me. To give to you." She stands up, wiping sweat off her face with the sleeve of her sweatshirt. Her hair has grown out in dark, spiky bristles and she's stopped wearing the pale makeup and black eyeliner. She looks... cute—although it feels strange thinking of her that way—sort of elfin and vulnerable. "And I don't want to hear anything nasty about it," I warn.

She pulls off one glove, reaches into the bag and finds the plaque. Dead silence. Her eyes brim.

"I know it's hokey, but he was so proud of it . . ."

Then her head falls back and she erupts into a lunatic cackle.

"Shut up before he hears you."

"It's perfect!" she shrills.

"What?"

She howls with laughter again. "This is so Barton. He was totally into that cutesy bird and butterfly shit!" She hugs it to her chest. "Oh God, he would love this!"

One gloved finger smears mud across her cheek, and she turns quickly, jabbing the stake between two clumps of lamb's ears. Then she's back on her knees, furiously ripping weeds out of the damp black earth.

I'm still watching her in amazement when she looks up. "Are you gonna help with these frigging weeds or what?"

On the night of December fifteenth, CM picks me up to take me out to dinner at Chez Shea for my birthday. Tyler's sulking because she's not invited. We get all the way down to the Denny regrade and she says, "Oh shit. I forgot my purse. Did I have it when I came to pick you up?"

"I'm sure you did."

"Well, it must be at your place." She does a U-turn in the middle of First Avenue, while I watch anxiously for the flashing lights of a patrol car. When we get back to the house, I hand her my key and she disappears inside. In a few minutes she's back. "I can't find it. And Tyler's gone. You'd better come help me look for it. I don't want to be driving around without my license."

"Swear to God, Mayle. The house isn't that big. How many places could it be?" I get out of the car, slam the door, and stomp back up the path.

When we walk into the living room, the lights go on and a bunch of voices are shouting "Surprise!" and "Happy Birthday!" I stare at the assembly. Kenny and Roz. Josh and Turbo. Ellen and Lloyd, Jen and Misha and Maggie—even the Mazurka Mavens.

Before I'm through sputtering my astonishment, Kenny and Josh have popped a few bottles of champagne and Tyler's got a Bob Marley tape on the boom box.

There's food—not exactly Chez Shea fare, of course—a Crock-Pot of white-bean chili, focaccia, corn muffins, cheeses, chips and salsa, veggies. When I see the cake, I know Tyler made it. It's a chocolate, buttercream-frosted replica of a loaf of bread. I look at her, but she's looking somewhere else.

The coffee table is covered with packages. I pick up the biggest, heaviest one first. It's from CM. I shred the wrapping off a two-foot-tall terra-cotta pig, dressed like a baker. "You have to give him a name," she says.

I clutch the pig in a torrid embrace while Tyler takes a picture with my camera. "Jean-Marc, *bien sûr*." There's a baker's apron with my monogram on it, some lavender bubble bath and body lotion. Goat-skin gardening gloves from Josh. A little date book called *The Baker's Book of Days* from the Mazurka Mavens, a silver bread charm from Ellen.

Tyler's gift is last. She hands me a flat package. Under the gift wrap there's bubble wrap and uncountable layers of newspaper. When I finally peel everything away, I'm holding a watercolor in a simple wooden frame—a perfect rendering of the Queen Street Bakery. Two figures stand by the door, too tiny for a positive ID, but one is short with dark hair and the other tall with wild, frizzy brown hair.

Tyler graciously accepts my hug for about one second before shrugging me off. "Shit, don't go getting all misty on me."

Just then, CM changes the music to *Motown's Greatest Hits* and the furniture gets pushed back against the walls and Turbo points his nose to the ceiling and howls.

Now the weather turns unseasonably warm. Some days the sun shines in a sky so blue and cloudless that I feel like I'm back in southern California. With all the unpleasant memories attendant on that scenario.

My divorce, for example, which should have been a historical footnote by this time last year, is still, incomprehensibly, stumbling through the halls of the L.A. superior court. Actually, the divorce itself is a done deal. My mother told me that David and Kelley got married in September.

It's the financial settlement that's bogged down. Elizabeth has given me all the reasons: I dragged my heels for the first year. David changed lawyers in mid-proceedings. Then he and his new counsel embarked on a whole different game plan, patterned after the siege of Leningrad. Paperwork creeps back and forth between attorneys, between L.A. and Seattle. Documents that Elizabeth subpoenaed from the mortgage company got lost. We had a trial date set for August till Adele King decided she was unavailable. This woman must have a scrapbook containing pictures of judges in compromising positions with barnyard animals. She seems to get everything she wants. And I'm beginning to detect whiffs of disinterest on Elizabeth's part.

Well, who could blame her? I'm bored out of my gourd, too. She says that's what they're aiming for: boredom, impatience, desperation, capitulation. It pisses me off just enough to keep me hanging on. Mac didn't approve. He told me in one of his infrequent advice-offering moods that as long as I was entangled in the legal battle, I might as well still be married to David. At first I thought he just didn't get it; now I'm beginning to wonder.

Other days, a hazy, anemic light is filtered through a gray and seamless marine layer that hovers along the coast. Those days are the worst. Not exactly warm, not exactly cold. Just moist and dim. The lines between daylight and darkness blur. Trees and shrubs drip incessantly. Not surprisingly, the flu is rampant.

At first Ellen avoids it by dint of her Wonder Woman constitution and dosing herself with echinacea and vitamin C and zinc. But eventually even she succumbs. When she shows up Tuesday morning with her eyes dark and hollow, her cheeks flushed, and the rest of her skin a whiter shade of pale, I send her home, and she doesn't argue.

Thank God for Rose. She's like those angel women who moved serenely among the sick during the bubonic plague, smiling, just doing whatever needs to be done. Misha comes back from her bout of illness, but Jen goes out. Kristen of the Mavens comes in, but Susan's gone for the holidays and Barb is sick. We've got orders piling up in back, one of the Traulsens has a Freon leak, and the repair service says most of their techs are out sick, so Saturday morning at the earliest. We stack and cram as much as possible into the other refrigerator.

On Wednesday CM goes home to L.A. for the holidays and I miss her comforting presence. My mother and Richard have planned to spend Christmas in Marin with Gary and Erica. I haven't heard from Mac in months and I don't even know where he is. I've given up looking at the mail. It feels too pathetic, shuffling through Christmas sale fliers, garish catalogs and magazines, searching for the envelope with a Canadian stamp.

Friday morning Maggie comes in early to finish decorating sugar cookies and a Christmas wedding cake. I give Rose a pile of orders and put her to work calling people and asking them to please come pick up their cookies and *bûches de Noël* and pumpkin pies and loaves of challah.

We started out the morning with a huge coffee urn full of hot, spiced apple cider so people could help themselves while they waited in line, but that ran out before noon and we were all so busy, nobody even noticed, much less had time to refill it. Suddenly an acrid, burning smell finds my nose, and I look up to see black smoke rising from the coffee urn.

Maggie sees it at the same time and runs over to jerk the plug out of the wall.

"I'm glad that wasn't my order I smelled," says an old man standing in line. He's joking of course, but we all just stare blankly at him, and his grin fades.

"I'm going to put this out back," Maggie says.

"Better get an oven mitt—" I start to say, but it's too late. She grabs the handles and lets out a shriek.

"The fucking thing's melted!" She shakes her left hand and looks around sheepishly at the people in line. "Sorry."

"Put some butter on that hand," says a woman in a flannel jumpsuit and UGG boots.

"Do *not* put butter on that!" A woman in a nurse's uniform rushes over to take charge, marching her to the sink and running cool water on her fingers. Then a smartly dressed grandma and a guy in a hard hat start talking about Unguentine. Pretty soon half the people in line are having a medical consultation about Maggie's hand. The nurse wraps the burn in gauze from our first-aid kit while the hard hat guy borrows two oven mitts, picks up the smoking urn, and carries it out the front door and around to the alley.

"You should get that looked at today," the nurse admonishes as she heads out, balancing a bag of apple-cardamom muffins and a box containing a cranberry-apple tart.

"Oh, I'll be okay," Maggie says.

I watch her for a few minutes, clearing tables, restocking the counter, wincing every time she touches anything with her left hand.

"Why don't you go down to the urgent-care clinic," I say. "We can hold the fort till you get back."

She shoots me a grateful look. "Okay. I won't be long."


By one-thirty we're getting slammed again and Maggie hasn't returned. If she's decided to go have lunch or do some last-minute shopping before she comes back, I swear I'll stuff an apple in her mouth and roast her. Rose is back on the register, I'm boxing up cakes and pies, and Tyler's restocking the case when the back door opens and Maggie's standing there, hand bandaged, holding two large pizza boxes from Olympia.

"I've got one house special and one vegetarian!" she sings out. *"Mangia!"*

We pull a couple of tables together and sit down to eat, rest weary legs and aching backs. Everyone has that glazed look of fatigue, and Tyler's eyelids are at half-mast. She's even too tired to needle Maggie.

"Girlfriend, I think it's time for you to go home and get some sleep."

She lets herself be persuaded.

Misha and Kristen toss their paper plates in the trash and plod back to the work area. When I can make myself stand up again, I open the register and ask Maggie how much the pizza cost. She looks flustered. "No, I didn't mean for you—it's my treat."

"Maggie, you don't have to do that."

"I know," she says quickly. "I just wanted to."

I try to see behind the shadowed smile in her dark eyes, but it's impossible, so I just say, "Well, thanks. It was a really nice thing to do."

· · ·

We lock the doors at three P.M. sharp. I take the cash drawer and checkbook over to a corner table, while everyone else begins the long afternoon of checking orders for tomorrow and cleaning up the chaos of today.

Rose says, "Wyn, do you have my check ready?"

I look up. "Are you leaving?"

"Yeah, don't you remember? I've got to take my mom down to pick up her car from the shop."

"Oh, that's right. Sorry. I totally spaced." I quickly add up the hours on her time card, scribble a check, and put it in an envelope with her name on it. "See you in the morning."

I collect the rest of the time cards and write checks out for everyone else. I separate the twenties, tens, fives, ones, banding them together. Then I count out the quarters, dimes, nickels, and pennies, coating my fingers with black grime and that awful metallic smell. I have to sit for a minute, absently rubbing grime all over my forehead, picturing my mental list of what still needs to be done. I've now been awake for twenty-four hours, at work for sixteen of them, and I feel that little buzzy sensation I used to get when I pulled an all-nighter to study for a test.

I really need to get some sleep before Tyler and I have to come back at eleven tonight. I count out an extra-large till for tomorrow, since it's the Saturday before Christmas, fill out the bank-deposit slip, and put everything in the cash box.

"Wyn," Kristen hollers from the back. "I think we've got a problem with the bottom oven."

"Be right there." I drop the cash box off in the storeroom in its usual place behind the baking powder and go out to see Kristen. She has one hand in the lower oven.

I stick my hand in. Probably not even 300 degrees. "What's it set for?"

"I've been turning it up all afternoon. Right now it's . . ." She peers at the black knob. It's so old that the numbers are pretty well worn off, and today it's encrusted with dough and batter, so it's really hard to read. "It's set on four hundred."

"Shit. Well, it isn't anywhere close to that. What else have we got left to do?"

"Gingerbread cookies, shortbread, sesame cookies."

"Just do what you can before five. If you can just shape the rest and put them on cookie sheets in the fridge, I'll try to bake them off tonight between breads."

I pick up the inventory clipboard. "Maggie, can you start cleaning up in the café? I need to check the supplies for tomorrow."

She blots her nose and forehead with her sleeve. "Sure, Wyn."

"Or... actually, Maggie, why don't you inventory the storeroom, since you can't use your hand very well. Just put in this column what we have on hand, and in this column what we need for tomorrow, and then—"

She takes the clipboard out of my hands. "I know how it works. I did it at Booker's all the time." I stare at her as she disappears into the hallway. I want to like her. Really. I just can't.

I bus the tables in a daze, separating the recycle stuff from wet garbage, piling cups and saucers, glasses, forks, and spoons in a plastic tub. At some point I look up to see Tyler at the door. She's grinning broadly and holding something up, pressing it against the glass. I move closer. It's an envelope.

It has a Canadian stamp.

## · nineteen ·

*Dear Wyn,*

*I know this won't get there in time for your birthday, but I did re-member it—the fifteenth, right? I hope CM was there to help you celebrate.*

*Right now you're probably wondering what the hell I'm doing up here, still in Beaverton, four months after I said I'd be back. I'm wondering that, too. All I can tell you is, I wasn't ready to leave. If you're still speaking to me when I come back to Seattle, I'll try to explain everything. I know you've heard it before, and you probably didn't believe it then, but I'll tell you again anyway. All of this has nothing to do with you. Or how I feel about you. Or how I feel about us. This is starting to sound somewhat convo-luted, but that's what living in a very long, very cold night has done to my brain.*

*I thought I was psychologically ready for the winter up here, but nothing can prepare you for this. I read in a book of essays about Alaska that up north, winter inhabits you. It's as good an explana-tion as I've heard. In some ways, winter is incredibly beautiful; it's also terrifying and depressing and boring and exhilarating. Often all at once.*

*There are so many things I wish I could describe for you—the wind rushing in at night to fill the darkness, the soft, purring sound of snowfall, like a big cat. (Yes, there is a sound, but you can only hear it in absolute silence.) The snow we've had so far is so dry it's almost weightless. Beautiful. And the sounds of the ice on the river. I couldn't believe it the first time I went down there with Chris after it froze up.*

*He says there's a whole language of ice talk. The moaning of new ice when you walk on it; the natives say it's the spirits of drowned people trapped underneath. The crack of a sheet of ice, splitting after a sudden change of temperature, like a gunshot. The small ticking sounds like insects in the evening as the temperature drops. The thunder of an ice shelf breaking off in the spring. That's one I hope to hear soon.*

*Last night I saw the aurora borealis—well, I've actually seen it several times, but the display was spectacular last night, first yellow and green, then changing to huge, undulating bars of blue and red. Some people say you can hear them. I didn't, but to look at them, you would expect some kind of sound. I've read all the scientific explanations of charged particles and magnetic waves, but as usual, the natives have the more satisfying explanation. They say it's the light from torches carried by old souls showing the newly dead the way to heaven. Whatever else happens, I think this is what I'll remember of this place.*

*It won't surprise you to know that I'm not doing anything for Christmas. I am, however, going to Chris and Nora's for Boxing Day (the twenty-sixth). New Year's Eve—don't know. Probably nothing. Or else listening to Elvis tapes with Chris and Nora.*

*Below is your birthday present. Conveniently chosen to make exchanges for size or color unnecessary.*

# Warming Trend

South by southeast a different winter waits.
Twice as startling, half as difficult,
But just as mysterious as this ocean of snow.

White sky falling
White sky filling
The horizon—
Erasing all but the map
Of rivers of dark curls on white linen,
The crimson valley between the cinnamon slopes
The warm sandy plain tumbling down to the lush delta
With its sweet secret cove.

*Miss you*
*Mac*

It's dark when I get home. There are no lights on and the phone
is ringing. I grab it, hoping Tyler's still asleep.

It's Ellen, sounding reasonably normal. "I just wanted to tell you
I'm going to open in the morning."

"Ellen, we're okay—"

"Don't argue with me. I'm feeling just good enough to be
grouchy. You and Tyler need to get some rest—"

"Tyler and I aren't sick. You are."

"Not anymore."

"You will be if you come back too soon."

"I want you guys to rest up because I'm going to need you on
Sunday and Monday."

"Oh, the refrigerator guy's coming tomorrow morning. And..."

I'm sorry to report that the lower oven is dying. A slow and pro-tracted death."

She groans. "Perfect. Did you call Frank?"

"I left a message with his service to come as early tomorrow as he possibly can."

"Of course we're going to have to pay overtime for all these repairs."

I can't think of anything good to say. "Well, call me if you change your mind. Otherwise I'll see you in the morning."

On Sunday winter gets serious, with a downpour and plunging tem-peratures. I can't believe how relieved I am to see it. I switch on my bedside lamp in the early darkness and lie in bed listening to the rain and reading Mac's letter and the poem again. He actually re-membered my birthday.

Since Tyler stayed over and worked yesterday morning, I told her I'd go in today and she could be off. I stand in the kitchen for a minute, drinking orange juice and watching the runoff from the roof splatter on the top of the garbage can underneath the window. Then I go back in my room to slip into the jeans and T-shirt that I left under the cov-ers all night to be warmed by my own body heat. I step into my Eddie Bauer rain ducks, put on my squall jacket, twist my hair up under my Dodgers baseball cap, grab my umbrella, and head for Queen Street.

The bakery is still quiet, just a few early birds sipping lattes and reading their papers. Someone has replaced the bell over the bakery door with this obnoxious device that plays the first line of "We Wish You a Merry Christmas."

"That thing's not going to make it through the day," I tell Ellen.

"Does Ms. Scrooge need a triple this morning?" She looks im-probably perky.

"A quad sounds even better." I take off my dripping coat and hang it in back where Misha and a sleepy Kristen are moving half sheets from the ovens to the cooling racks. The spicy scent of apple-cinnamon muffins mingles with the nutty aroma of cappuccino-hazelnut scones. I grab an apron and wander back out front, slipping it over my head. "Did all the equipment get fixed?"

"Yep. The oven problem was the wiring in the temperature gauge. Frank said it's a wonder it didn't start a fire, it was so badly corroded."

"So we dodged the bullet again."

She bangs the brew basket to dislodge the used grounds and sets up two double espressos for me. I hunt up my favorite cup, give it a blast of steam from the frother, and set it under the spout. The rich, dark liquid from two doubles nearly fills the cup.

"Oh, by the way," she says without looking up from the special orders she's flipping through, "I couldn't find the deposit receipt from Friday. Where did you put it?"

I pick up my espresso, blow on it, and start to take a sip, but I pause with the rim of the cup at my lips, while scenes from Friday afternoon's chaos pass before my eyes and light up, one at a time, like a slide presentation. Maggie getting burned. The pizza. Counting the till. Paychecks. The oven. Busing the café—

"Wyn."

My heart stops while my mind races ahead. The last image. Tyler standing in the doorway, grinning. Holding up Mac's letter. The blood drains from my face.

Ellen looks at me questioningly.

I grip the edge of the counter, swallowing drily. I turn my back to the customers and lower my voice. "Ellen. Oh God. I forgot. Everything was going nuts and I just ... forgot."

"You forgot what?"

"To make the deposit."

We stare at each other. In the work area, Misha and Kristen are dancing around the table to "Jingle Bell Rock."

Ellen puts the back of her hand on her forehead as if to check for fever. "So ... where's the money?" she says quietly.

"In the cash box."

It still hasn't gotten through my thick head yet. I'm still fretting because I got so engrossed in Mac's letter that I forgot to go to the bank, like a goddamned lovesick teenager. Slowly I tune in to reality. She had to open the cash box yesterday. If the money had been there, she would have known I didn't make the deposit.

"No," she says, making every word separate and distinct, "it's not."

I move through the next two hours in a haze of anger and self-recrimination, punctuated with bracing shots of disbelief. When Rose comes in, Ellen and I retire to the storeroom. She shows me where she found the cash box, which is exactly where I put it. Exactly where we always put it.

"When I opened it up, there was only one envelope, and it had the cash for Saturday morning in it. It kills me to think that somebody who works for us, somebody we know and who . . ." Her voice dissipates like smoke. "Who was in here Friday?"

"Basically everybody. I did the money as soon as we closed the doors. We still had a million things to do."

She looks around. "But who was in here last?"

Suddenly it all comes together. "Maggie." I close my eyes, shaking my head in disbelief—whether of her colossal nerve or my colossal stupidity I can't say.

"I let her do inventory because she burned her hand. I stayed out front and cleaned up the café." I close my eyes. "Oh God, Ellen. I'm so, so sorry. I can't believe I'm so stupid."

Ellen's barely listening. "She has to know that we would have figured out by now that it was missing."

"But she doesn't know that we know it was her."

"Maybe."

"She strikes me as one of those people who's so arrogant, they think they couldn't possibly get caught."

"She strikes me as desperate," Ellen says thoughtfully.

"Desperate?"

"Yeah. I mean, they've most likely got plenty of money. Why would she steal our paltry little deposit?"

"I can't imagine."

"Look, she's not stupid. She knows we'll figure it out before Monday. So what does she do?"

I shrug.

"She runs away."

"Runs away?"

"Of course. Somewhere that Mr. Wonderful can't find her. Or won't bother. If he's like most abusers, he probably keeps a pretty tight grip on the purse strings, so where does she get enough to disappear? I bet you anything she's long gone."

Everything she's saying makes sense, of course. In hindsight, a lot of things make sense.

"So . . . how much was there?"

"Two . . ." My voice cracks. "Two thousand and some change."

We sigh almost in unison.

"Do you hate me? If I were you, I'd fire my ass."

She gives me a rueful little smile. "Are you kidding? Without you we'd have to close the doors tomorrow."

"Without my mother's money, you mean."

"Dumbhead. You're the one who makes the great bread. The one who managed to tame the wild blue-haired kid. Where would we be without you?"

"About two grand ahead. I think I'm going to throw up."

"Oh, stop it. This isn't a dark-night-of-the-soul kind of screwup. It's just a plain old everyday garden-variety screwup."

I shake my head. "I didn't even tell you the worst part."

"Okay, tell me the worst part and then we'll get back to work."

"The reason I forgot to make the deposit is . . ." I bite the inside of my cheek. "Tyler came over with the mail. There was a letter from Mac, and I was in such a hurry to get finished so I could read it that I just . . . forgot."

She laughs. "If it'd been me, I would've sat down and ripped into it right then and there."

"I don't guess we have insurance."

"Not for that."

"Ellen, I'll pay every cent of it back."

She shakes her head and puts her arm around my waist. "Let's worry about it later."

When we break for lunch, Ellen calls Maggie's house.

"Oh, hi. This is Ellen Liederman at the bakery. Is Maggie available?" I watch her face. "Oh. No, that's fine. I didn't know when she was planning to leave and I just had a question for her. No, it's not that important. It can wait till she's back. Thanks. Merry Christmas."

She sets the phone down. "Tony says she's gone to spend Christmas with her mother. She should be back next Saturday."

"You think she's actually coming back?"

"Not if she has any sense. I'd also be willing to bet she's not at her mother's. Or if she is, she's not staying long. I'd say she's putting as much distance as possible between her and Tony as fast as she can. At least," she adds, "I hope she is."

"Yeah, because if he doesn't kill her, I will."

She punches me in the arm. "Hush. I know it's awful, but we'll survive."

Christmas Day is anticlimactic for Tyler and me. We never did get around to decorating a tree, so there are no signs of the holiday except a few cards attached to the refrigerator door with magnets. The most visible indications of what the season means to us are the dust bunnies we haven't had time to sweep up, the basket full of dirty clothes that we haven't had time to wash, and an unnamed seasonally green flora growing in the corners of the shower.

We have scones and coffee for breakfast and exchange presents—I got her a fuzzy scarf and matching hat, in which she looks cuter than anyone has a right to. She got me a beautiful picture book of Toulouse. I haven't told her about Maggie yet. I know what her reaction will be, and I hate to admit that she was right, even if it was for all the wrong reasons.

At eleven A.M. she gets dressed and goes off to spend the day with her dad and stepmother, leaving me to deal with the dust bunnies, dirty laundry, and green stuff in the bathroom. My mother calls from Gary's to wish me a merry Christmas, and I try to act as if I'm having a cozy, quiet, and thoroughly enjoyable celebration, but I don't think I've fooled her. In the background I hear the cheer-leader princess shrieking with laughter, probably due to sugar shock, and a sound track of unrelenting percussion.

"Andrew got a drum set," she says through clenched teeth.

My quiet little house suddenly seems like a refuge.

When the house is clean and the last load of clothes is tumbling around in the drier, I feel the gnawings of hunger. A quick survey of the refrigerator confirms my suspicion that there's not much around to nibble on. I think the last trip to Thriftway was a week ago. We've been living on pizza and frozen leftovers for a while.

I decide to make *la fouace aux noix*. Hearth bread with walnuts. It's sort of festive without being too complicated, and I can take a loaf over to Josh and Turbo. I start rummaging through the pantry. White flour. Whole wheat. Yeast and salt. The remains of a bag of walnuts. In the fridge I find milk, but no butter. Damn. You can't make *fouace* without butter.

I shrug into my parka and dash out the front door, down the drive, and across the lawn in the stinging-cold rain. I barely get my hand to the door before I hear Turbo's early-warning guard-dog howl.

Josh opens the door with a glass in his hand. He's wearing baggy jeans and a WAZZU sweatshirt with a colorful array of stains and spots on it. "Hey, Wyn."

"Hi, you guys. Merry Christmas." When I lean forward to kiss his cheek, he smells like bourbon.

"Come on in. It's cold out there."

I follow him into the den, which I think used to be a bedroom. The place has been transformed since the last time I saw it. He's ripped off the fake wood paneling, given the plaster a new coat of white paint, replaced the original oak trim and doors, taken up the gross brown carpet and refinished the oak floors, installed bookcases and a leather couch and one of those coffee tables made from a slab of redwood burl. A fire flickers softly in the brick fireplace. "This is gorgeous. I can't believe it's the same room."

"Thanks." He picks up the remote and turns off the soccer game on the television.

"You don't have to turn off your game. Who's playing?"

"I have no idea. It's just something to focus my eyes on." I see in my peripheral vision the bottle of Jack Daniel's sitting on the end table, half full.

"Let me fix you a drink—"

"I'm not really into the hard stuff—"

"Actually, neither am I," he says quickly. "I have a really nice bottle of cabernet I've been meaning to try. I bet you're a red wine kind of girl."

"Um...actually I came over to borrow a stick of butter. I know it's sort of tacky to borrow ingredients from someone to make him a present, but...I was going to make some bread."

I can see him deflate.

"But, hey, it's Christmas. I could use a glass of wine."

"Great. Turb and me are about up to here with our own company. You have a seat and I'll be right back. Oh, here, give me your jacket."

The second my butt meets the couch, Turbo hops up next to me and lays his head on my thigh. "Are you supposed to be up here?" I whisper. He ignores the question, closing his eyes in contentment.

"Where's Tyler?" Josh calls from the kitchen.

"She went over to see her dad."

"Where's he live?"

"Phinney Ridge."

"I hope she gets back okay. They're saying this might turn to ice tonight."

"Well, I guess it won't kill her to spend the night over there. We don't have to work again till Thursday night."

He reappears with two crystal wineglasses and a bottle.

"Beautiful goblets."

"Yeah. They belonged to Fran's mother." He looks at Turbo and laughs. "All I have to do is turn my back and you co-opt the best-looking woman in the room."

"I didn't know if he was allowed up, but he seemed to know what he was doing."

Josh pours a glass of wine and hands it to me. "Theoretically he's supposed to be on a towel, but he keeps taking the towel and hiding it somewhere."

We touch our glasses together. "Merry Christmas. Again."

He takes a big swallow. "Well, it's Christmas, anyway. As for the merry part, I'm not convinced."

"Yeah. I'm not especially fond of Christmas either. At least not since my father died."

"When was that?"

"Oh, about seventeen years ago. When he was alive we used to go to Lake Tahoe for the holiday. Rented a cabin. Sometimes we had snow. It was so beautiful."

"Then what? After he died."

"After he died my mother and I never knew what to say to each other. We didn't have a lot to talk about the rest of the time either, but Christmas was even worse. We'd just kind of tiptoe around everything, ignoring the memories, pretending that we didn't care. Then when I was married, it was a whole different thing. Lots of parties, presents, food, wine. I think my mother was uncomfortable with that. She didn't come around much during the holidays."

"Is that why you didn't go home?" He finishes his wine and pours himself another glass.

"No, actually, it's better now. She got remarried last year. To a nice guy. She's happy, I think."

"What about you?"

"Since David and I split up, it's mostly a nonevent. I don't think Christmas will ever mean that much to me again."

He chuckles. "I mean, what about the rest of the year? Are you happy?"

"Oh." I shrug. "Sometimes. Things haven't worked out quite like I planned, but . . ." Then I laugh. "How did we get into this discussion?"

"I think what happens is, Turbo's not real talkative. So when I get a chance at conversation with someone, I'm all over it." He pours more wine in my glass, even though I've only drunk about a quarter of what I had.

"Easy. I'm supposed to be making bread."

"Much as I like your bread, I'd rather have the company today. It's a hard time. These holidays." His eyes cloud up behind the wire rims of his glasses, and for one awful minute, I think he's going to start crying.

"I know," I say. "I'm sorry."

He seems to reach somewhere inside himself and tighten the loosening grip on his emotions. "Why is it, do you suppose, that we fall in love with people and they fall in love with us, only to find out later that it's all wrong?"

"If I knew the answer to that, I'd be making big bucks on a radio call-in show."

"When Fran and I first got together, it was like . . . for the first time in my life, everything—even the bad stuff—had a meaning." He finishes the wine in his glass and pours some more. "I swear I think it's what I miss most—things making sense." He lays his head back on the couch. "It's the shits when they don't anymore."

Again I have that sense of his being right on the edge of tears. His pain is so fresh and sharp, and so on the surface, that listening to him is like being scraped raw. I can't help wondering what she was like. If she was worth breaking a good heart over. Then I remember what my mother said last Christmas sitting at the kitchen table: *Sometimes you want something so badly that whether it's worth it or not doesn't matter.*

"She used to say—she said, 'Joshua, life with you is never boring. If it ever gets boring, I'm out of here.' And we'd laugh." He takes another big gulp of wine. His words are getting a little soft, a little blurry around the edges, and it's making me uncomfortable. I really want to go home and make bread, but I can't just get up and leave. "So I guess I musta got boring. 'Cause she's definitely outta here."

I run my hand over Turbo's warm, soft head and he opens one eye to look at me. "I don't think it means you got boring," I say.

He turns a little bit on the couch. "Tell me what you think. I mean, you're a woman. What do you want? What did she want?"

"First of all, just because I'm a woman doesn't mean I understand her. Sometimes I don't even understand what it is that I want." I hold my glass up to the lamp to see the light through the wine. "People change, I guess."

"What about your hugband . . . um . . . husband?"

I wave my hand. "He's ancient history. I've given up thinking I'll ever figure that all out."

"I would've said you pretty much had it figured out. You seem like a pretty grounded lady to me."

I smile. "That's because you don't know me."

His misty blue eyes find mine. "Not as well as I'd like to."

I set the glass down. "Josh, I think you should stop drinking."

"Huh?"

"If you want to talk, I'd like to stay and talk. But if you just want to get obliterated, you don't need me to watch."

His face reddens. "So go, then." His abrupt change of mood is startling.

I scoot forward and stand up. Turbo gives me an annoyed look, then slithers off the couch, following me into the foyer. I put on my jacket and open the door. "I'll take him out for a minute and then let him back in."

"I'll do it. Don't worry, I'll do it." His voice is thick with anger and with pain and with booze. "You just get to your bread. You just go hide out there in your kitchen with your bread."

I have a sense of him getting up quickly from the couch, momentum propelling him forward, and then there's a yelp and a crash. I wheel around and Turbo's out the door like a shot.

"Oh, shit! Josh, are you all right?" I kneel beside him as he rubs his left shin.

"Yeah, I'm okay. Just embarrassed as hell." The wind whips the door, banging it against the wall. "Gotta get that silly pup inside. He's got about as much sense as his owner."

"I'll get him." I zip up my parka.

"Better take a cookie." He points to a dish of bone-shaped biscuits on a small table by the door.

In a few minutes, Turbo is getting toweled down in front of the fire while he licks the last cookie crumbs off the floor. I shift my weight from one foot to the other.

"I guess I better get going."

Josh concentrates on blotting the rain from the soaked ends of the dog's ears. "You still want some butter, help yourself. It's in the refrigerator door."

"Thanks. I'll be back with some bread later. Thanks for the wine, too."

He looks up at me, suddenly sober. "I'm sorry, Wyn. I didn't mean that. About you hiding in the kitchen."

I smile at him. "It's okay. I suppose it's true. In fact, I know it is. I do hide in the kitchen. In bread." I wrap my old scarf around my neck. "But that's not always a bad thing."

## · twenty ·

## *Mac*

Christmas night.

Eleven P.M. and it's been dark for eight hours. But his body clock still keeps to the rhythms of the last six years.

Eleven o'clock would be peak time at Bailey's. He'd be cueing up another tape, trading bad jokes with Kenny. He misses their easy conversation, the way they worked instinctively around each other.

If it was Saturday night, Wyn would be there, parked on her stool at the far end of the bar, reading, nursing one glass of wine. Quiet, awkward, she never seemed to grow more comfortable about being there while he worked. She didn't talk much, or even make eye contact. She always seemed somehow embarrassed to be hanging out there.

But at last call, it was like throwing a switch. She came alive. She'd put the book away and her eyes would follow him as he and Kenny cleaned up, counted the money, locked up the place. When their eyes met she would smile that almost shy, secret smile that made a tightness in his chest. Made him wish sometimes that they could skip going out with Kenny and Roz, CM, and whoever else ended up tagging along to Lofurno's or Wild Ginger or the noodle place.

But the waiting made it even better. Knowing that soon enough they would be in his bed and she would press herself against him and he'd be breathing the scent of her. Of the bread. He loved the strength of her arms, the coil of her legs around him. Loved all the noise she made, oddly exuberant. It didn't seem to fit with the rest of her personality, which was very controlled, and it captivated him. To know that he could make her let go, make her lose the control that she struggled so hard to maintain the rest of the time.

He rolls over on his side, face to the wall, feeling drowsiness spreading in his limbs, sleep taking hold. Finally. He closes his eyes, the effort of it pushing him into unconsciousness.

He sits up suddenly, wide awake, aware of another presence. The room is inky dark. "Who is it?"

The sound of a match scraping. Light flares as the lamp's wick catches and burns. He squints into the glare.

"Bernie? What the hell are you doing here?" He turns, placing both feet on the floor.

"Wow, that's rude. You must've been hanging around me too long."

She sets the glass globe over the flame and sits down next to him on the bed.

"I had a bad dream." Her breath is a haze of whiskey.

"You can't stay here. Let me get dressed and I'll walk you back to the house. Did you bring a flashlight?"

"Nope." She smiles. "I know the way by heart. I used to play out here when I was little. This was my playhouse." Her hand lights on his knee and travels north. He feels the chill of it right through his thermals. "You want to play house?"

He removes her hand to her own leg. "You need to get out of here. Right now."

"Oh, come on. You know you want to."

"I don't know any such thing. And even if I did, I wouldn't do it. Pearl trusts me—"

She laughs harshly. "And here I was thinking you were such a smart guy. You don't even get it. Why do you think she brought you here? So you could patch the roof? Tend bar? Duh... You're supposed to fall in love with me. Or at least knock me up and then marry me."

"Me?"

"Well, don't let it go to your head. The only requirements for the job are that you're white, don't drool at the table, and don't drink at work." She inches closer. "Don't you like me? Don't you think I'm pretty?"

He removes her hand from his leg again, trying to ignore the stiffening in his penis. "I do like you, but not like that. It wouldn't be good for either of us."

"Oh, for Chrissake. Who says it has to be good for anybody? Don't you sometimes just want to fuck your brains out?" She slides closer. "I do."

"Well, I don't. What I want is for you to get up off this bed and get your buns back to the house. Now." The last word floats in an icy breath. He's starting to shiver.

Suddenly her arms lock around his neck and her mouth is on his throat. He finds himself wondering how it happened with Chris. And where and when. It's not as if there were a lot of places to go in Beaverton for privacy. She interprets his hesitation as acquiescence and shrugs off her parka, letting it hang down from her shoulders, looking up at him.

He grasps her wrists firmly, removes her arms. "Bernie, stop it. This isn't going to happen."

Her bewilderment flares into indignation. "Goddamn you. Fucking asshole. Who the hell do you think you are? You just walk in here—"

"Sorry, but you walked in here. Now walk back out."

"You're just like all the rest of them. You come on like Mr. Sensitive—"

"I thought we could be friends—"

"*Friends?*" She spits out the word. "Men don't want to be friends.

They want to fuck. And then they want to leave." Her face puckers with fury, and little bubbles of spit collect in the corners of her mouth. She flails suddenly, nicking his face with a fingernail.

In a second he's up, pulling her to her feet, gripping her arms from behind, and propelling her toward the door. She bends at the knees, digging her heels into the floor and begins to shriek. "You bastard, you piece of shit!"

"Be quiet."

"I'll tell Pearl you tried to rape me—"

"In my room."

"You asked me to show you how to clean the stove—"

"In the middle of the night? Come on, Bernie. Listen to yourself. You've just had a little too much to drink, that's all. It happens. Come on, I'll walk you—"

She wrenches free suddenly and runs out the door, leaving him staring after her, half-convinced it was a weird dream. When he touches the nick on his face, the blood is already starting to congeal.

"Happy Boxing Day." He holds out a bottle of champagne to Chris. "Is that what you're supposed to say?"

Chris grins. "That works. How are you getting along over there?"

The thought of last night jolts him, just before he says, "Fine."

Nora appears, to take his jacket and kiss his cheek. "Happy Christmas, Mac. I'm so glad you could come."

He stuffs his gloves in the sleeves of the parka. "It was hard fitting another party into my schedule, but, considering that I'm wearing your husband's clothes, I thought I'd better put in an appearance."

She looks at the gouge on his face. "What did you do to yourself?"

"Cut myself shaving. I think I need a new blade."

"You made a good job of it, all right. But you can dull the pain with some of Chris's special French seventy-six punch. Go on into the parlor. The food's in there."

Pearl May sits on the edge of a Victorian velvet chair, spine as straight as a soldier, holding a cup of punch.

"Mac! How nice." She holds out a hand. "It seems so silly that I have to go to someone else's home to see you. How's your work progressing?"

"Very well, thanks," he lies and smiles. His glance takes in the whole room. "Where's Bernie?"

"She's resting this afternoon. She had a bad night last night."

He wonders if she has any idea how bad. "Sorry to hear it. How's Emmett?"

"Exhausted. Cranky from too much sugar. Half his toys are already broken." She laughs. "A typical Christmas."

Nora comes around with a plate of small biscuits filled with ham. "These are sourdough biscuits," she says. "Not traditional Boxing Day fare, but very traditional Yukon fare."

"What exactly is Boxing Day?" Mac takes a biscuit and a napkin from her.

"Boxing Day," Pearl May says, tilting her head to one side as if she were reciting a poem. "Boxing Day was first observed as a holiday in the mid-nineteenth century. Servants of various kinds received a Christmas box of contributions from their employers. Also, I believe poor people carried empty boxes from door to door, and the boxes were filled with food, Christmas sweets, and money."

"How like the Victorians," Nora says, laughing. "Every other day of the year, they'd just as soon run their carriages over the poor sods, but on Boxing Day they toss them a few table scraps."

"Spoken like the sweet Irish lass that you are." Chris gives her a kiss on the neck. "Mac, a glass of my famous French seventy-six punch."

"What happened to French seventy-five?"

"Mine has a secret ingredient."

A sudden growl turns them all toward the hallway.

"I know that growl," Mac says.

"Hi, y'all." Rhiannon comes in, slipping out of a long, black cape. "I was too cold to wait for somebody to open the door. Jester, down. That's a good boy. Stay."

The dog promptly lays his head on his paws and closes his eyes.

"I love this cape," Nora hugs her. "Let me take it and hang it up and you'll never see it again."

"My *French Lieutenant's Woman* cape. Now if I just had the Meryl Streep face and body to go with it. Hey, Pearl May. Howdy, stranger." She presses her cold face against Mac's.

Over the next few hours, people come and go. Dirk from the post office and his wife, Mimi. Olivia Myles, who owns the hardware store. Her cousin Henry and his wife, Charlotte.

Mac stands near the stove, warming his back. Drinking, eating, talking when necessary, but mostly watching and listening. It's been almost two months since he's been around other people for any length of time, and he vacillates between expansiveness and claustrophobia. In the end, he's reluctant to leave.

At some point, he settles on the couch, and Rhiannon suddenly appears beside him. "Have you been avoiding me?"

"No. Why would I avoid you?"

She tugs on a strand of gray hair. "I thought you might still be mad about your reading."

"I was never mad about it."

"Well, you were some kind of something." She gives him an appraising look. "Too close to the bone, huh?"

He tries to laugh.

"Don't deny it. I know what I saw. And you haven't been back to see me since."

"There's four feet of snow on the ground, Madame Blue. And I've been holed up working."

"How's it coming?"

He leans back against a tufted throw pillow. "What do the cards say?"

"They say you're spinnin' your wheels like a tractor pull."

He nods slowly. The punch is starting to take him down. He looks at the liquid in the bottom of the glass. "This stuff has the same basic formula as jet fuel."

"I'm telling you, Mac. Make peace with your brother."

"It's a bit late. He's been dead since 1974."

She blinks twice. "You can still deal with it. You're the damn writer. You figure it out."

He inhales deeply, suddenly exhausted. "I'll take it under advisement. And now, I think I'll go home while I can still walk."

"Well, stick to the roads. You have a flashlight?"

"Yes, I do."

The moon is so bright he doesn't really need the flashlight. He must be drunk because his brain keeps repeating the line from "'Twas the Night Before Christmas," about the moon on the crest of the new-fallen snow giving the luster of midday to objects below.

He doesn't know what time it is. He walks slowly, thinking of Bernie's mother, drunk, freezing to death in the snow. He kicks at the drifts edging the snowplowed street. He can see how it happens. It's so cold here, about twenty-two below tonight. And remote. No one would find you in time. It sounds oddly cozy.

The lights are off in Pearl May's house. When he starts through the trees, he turns on the flashlight. Which is probably why he doesn't notice at first that there's a light on in the bunkhouse. Even after he sees it, he doesn't really notice it. It doesn't register until he's about to step onto the porch and he realizes that the door is open a crack. He stops himself, nearly falling over to avoid clomping on the wooden step.

Suddenly he's sober. He pushes the door open just a hair wider and looks in. His stomach drops. Bernie's standing by the stove, ripping pages out of his notebook and feeding them, one at a time, into the fire. Her head jerks up when he steps into the room. Her eyes glitter like black ice.

For the longest time, it seems, they stare at each other.

"What the hell are you doing?" It feels as if he's shouting at her, but it comes out a whisper.

Her mouth turns down at the corners. "What does it look like I'm doing?"

"It looks like you're destroying something that doesn't belong to you."

"Wrong about that," she says. "It does belong to me. It's my goddamn life you've got in this thing. Mine and a lot of other peoples' in this town. Why the hell did you think any of us wanted to be in your stupid book?"

"Bernie, it's just a journal. I can write anything I want to in my journal. About anybody."

"Not about me," she says calmly, throwing in the page she's just ripped out. "You think you can just come in here and use people like lab rats. Watch us running around in our little holes and then you write about us. Who the hell do you think you are?" She rips out another few sheets and tosses them into the flames.

"Stop it. You don't know what you're doing."

She raises her chin. "Says you. Anyways, I'm almost done here. What are you gonna do, hit me?"

"No. Much as I'd like to."

"Have me arrested?"

The thought had crossed his mind, at first, but of course it's ridiculous.

"Tell Granny on me?" she taunts. She throws the last two pages into the fire, and holds the empty notebook up by one side. "So how does it feel to be so pissed off and there's not a goddamn thing you can do about it?"

"I'm not pissed off." Although the thought of slamming her against the wall does have a certain appeal.

"Yes you are."

"Okay. I am pissed off. But I'm sorry, too."

She looks vaguely unsettled. "For what?"

"For you. Because you really don't understand the whole thing."

"What whole thing?"

"That"—he gestures at the notebook cover—"had nothing to do with you. Nothing to do with anyone here."

Her eyes shift to the stove, then back to him. "You wrote stuff about all of us."

"Yeah, I know, but it wasn't really about you."

"What the fuck are you talking about? You're so full of crap. I'm out of here." But she doesn't move.

"It wasn't a book. It was a journal. It was really about me. How I saw things, what I thought about them, how I felt."

"Right." She snorts. "Who the hell wants to read that shit?"

"That's sort of my point. No one, Bernie. Just me."

She twists her hands together. "Why would anyone do something that stupid? Write to themselves. Yeah, boy."

"You should try it sometime," he says quietly.

A wild laugh bursts from her chest. "I'm not that crazy."

"Actually, you are." The stove's heat is beginning to penetrate the heavy parka. He takes off his gloves, unfastens it slowly.

"Screw you, McLeod. I'm outta here." But she stands still, running the zipper head up and down the track of her open coat.

"My family was kind of messed up, too. I started writing like this to help myself understand it. So I could live with it." He eases out of the jacket and hangs it on the back of the chair.

She peers at him through her thatch of hair. "Did it help?"

"Some." He shrugs. He finds her eyes. "But I'm not finished. I've got a long ways to go. You know what I mean, don't you?"

When she exhales, she seems to shrink, like a deflating balloon.

She tosses the empty notebook on the table and walks past him without saying anything, disappearing up the snowy path she knows so well.

At six A.M. he's standing on the packed snow of the porch. Daybreak is still four hours away. He looks up. Orion's gone down in the west. The dipper, big, bright, and low, has turned so that Arcturus seems to almost sit on top of Dawes Hill.

He stamps his boots and turns reluctantly back inside. He lights one kerosene lamp, then the other, turning the wick up slowly so as not to crack the chimney. The pale light hovers over the table, gradually spreading into the dark corners of the room. He holds the thermometer where he can read it. Seventeen below.

Opening the firebox door, he rakes up the coals, opens the vent, and lays on some kindling. When he closes the door, the fire snaps back to life. He goes to stand by the window. Nothing much to see except a small patch of yellow lamplight on white snow. Beyond that is only the dark, the cold. The cold he feels now has no temperature. It's more the absence of something, a blankness that seeps into his bones like the cold, and settles there.

The only thing left now is to begin. Again.

## twenty-one

A t Harrington High School in 1972, there must have been a rule that said girls had to wear miniskirts and boots or hip huggers and shoes that looked like they were borrowed from the football team's place kicker. And it was also decreed that every girl should have long, straight hair, parted in the middle.

Amanda Petrie was a girl who broke all the rules. She wore something called harem pants, loose and flowing and gathered at the ankle, and long sweaters. Or she wore knickers and knee sox and short, boxy pullovers. She had baby-fine blond hair, cut really short. She did it herself with cuticle scissors, she told me once, and it set off her face like a cameo. Fine and sharp. Her features were small, except for her big blue eyes, and pretty unremarkable. Until she smiled. The first time I saw her smile, it was like being punched in the stomach.

I was barely fifteen. Too tall. Unbearably clumsy except on the soccer field. I had a weird little stubble on my chin that I kept hoping would become a beard. It was completely demoralizing that it took several days to get to the point where Suzanne would even notice it and tell me to shave. Kevin, who was sixteen then, was already performing the manly ritual of shaving every day and sported bushy sideburns. I was taller than he was, but his football and baseball workouts had shaped him into a wedge of solid muscle.

He, of course, dated the prom queens, the cheerleaders, the baton twirlers, the class officers...and anyone else who caught his fancy. When he'd been through all the ones at Harrington, he started on neighboring districts. Girls were calling the house starting at about four in the afternoon. And since we usually weren't home till around five or six from football practice or whatever practice, Suzanne took the calls. She was always threatening to get an unlisted number, but she never did. I did think she rather enjoyed the spectacle.

I didn't date much. First of all, I couldn't drive. I didn't even have a learner's permit. There was no way Suzanne was going to play chauffeur. Even if she'd wanted to, Kevin usually had the car. She said I should go with Kevin and his girl du jour, something she quaintly called a "double date," but he didn't want me tagging along, and there weren't many girls I wanted to date badly enough to put up with him for an entire evening.

Once or twice was enough.

His behavior could range from charming to brutish, depending on the girl and the stage to which the relationship had progressed. At one time or another, I got to see the full spectrum. At the beginning he was always devoted, self-deprecating, funny, sincere. He got rowdier if he thought the girl would tolerate it, would exhibit jocklike tendencies toward practical jokes. But if she was intellectually inclined, he could be serious. Spend afternoons reading "real" books by Updike and Vidal and John Cheever. He could talk about the war, civil rights, ecology, if it was called for. I always knew when things were cooling off because he didn't mind being rude, having a laugh at the girl's expense, or flirting with someone else right in front of her. Eventually he would quit even pretending an interest. Quit calling. Refuse to take her calls. Pass her on the street without showing any signs of recognition. He had no qualms about humiliating anyone.

Amanda was in Kevin's class, a year ahead of me. She was study-ing art. She took all the painting and drawing and photography classes, but what she really loved was sculpture. She wanted to take metal shop to learn to use a welder's torch, but girls weren't allowed in that class.

So while she bided her time, waiting to graduate and get the hell out of Glen Bay, she did her own kind of sculptures with whatever materials came to hand. Rusty tools. Lint from the clothes driers at the laundry. Old silverware and dishes. Discarded clothing and shoes. Records. That's how I met her.

I was at one of my favorite record stores in the village of Glen Bay one afternoon, flipping through the used 45s when I looked up and saw this girl standing at the cash register, tapping her foot im-patiently. The geek who worked the register on Saturdays came out from behind the counter with two shopping bags full of records, handed them to her, and she pulled what looked like a ten-dollar bill out of her purse and gave it to him.

I was stunned. Even the used records cost more than that. This girl was either putting out, or she knew something I didn't know. I si-dled up to the counter and pretended to be looking at the album cover for some dorky Roberta Flack LP they were playing, all the while trying unsuccessfully to see what records were in the shopping bags.

The only one I could identify was Little Richard. I was kind of excited. I didn't know many girls in those days who were into Little Richard. Especially since he'd given up rock and gone back to singing gospel music, so his old stuff wasn't getting much airplay.

I was straining to read the back of the jacket, to see what songs were on the album, when I looked up into her eyes. There's a line in *The Maltese Falcon,* where Hammett describes Brigid O'Shaugh-nessy's eyes as "a cobalt prayer." Suddenly that line was making sense to me.

"If you're that interested, go ahead and have a look," she said. I couldn't tell if she was serious, pissed off, or amused.

"You like Little Richard?" I asked.

"Who?"

"Little Richard. You just bought his record."

She peered down into the bag. "So I did. I don't know. Never heard of him. He looks weird."

"If you never heard of him, why did you buy it?"

"I don't listen to them."

"What do you do with them?"

"Melt them."

My stomach lurched. "Melt them? Why?"

That's when she smiled and I surrendered. "To make sculptures."

I followed her out of the store, trying to explain that you didn't melt records, because they were like books. They told stories in music. She was unmoved.

"They're cultural symbols," she said. "I use them to make art."

"They're already art."

That was the first thing I said that she really heard. She turned suddenly to look at me.

"All right, then." She gave me an appraising once-over. "You come listen to them with me. Then I'll decide. I'm Amanda Petrie. What's your name?"

"Mac McLeod."


She lived in the neighborhood called South Shore. It was where all the doctors and dentists and attorneys and professors lived. The house was a contemporary, wood and glass, the front jutting out like the prow of a ship. Inside it was all angles and open spaces, soaring ceilings and weird hanging lights.

"What does your father do?" I asked.

"Not much. He's dead."

I felt the blood rise up into my face.

"What about your mother?"

"She's a doctor. A dermatologist. What about yours?"

"My father's dead, too. Suzanne works in a gallery."

"That's your mother?" I nodded. "Why do you call her Suzanne?"

"Because that's her name."

She liked that answer.

She got Cokes from the refrigerator and we went into a room she called the library and we started pulling LPs and 45s out of the shopping bags and putting them on her mother's turntable. It was an expensive one, the kind that didn't have a drop. You had to manually place the records on one at a time. She held them carefully at the edges, like she knew how. There were four huge speakers placed at appropriate angles in the corners of the room.

After about an hour she said, "What does Mac stand for?"

"McLeod."

She laughed. "What's your first name, really?"

"Matthew."

"Matthew's a good name. You should use it."

"I like Mac better."

"Well, I go by Amanda. Don't *ever* call me Mandy." She made a little face. "It's so dippy."

"I won't." I kept waiting for her to ask if I was Kevin McLeod's brother. Everybody did eventually. She didn't.

Suddenly it was dark outside. I looked at my watch. "I guess I better go."

"Okay." She seemed perfectly content to have me there, and just as content to see me off. There was an awkward silence while I tried to figure out how to ask if I could see her again.

She was busy dividing the records into piles: keep or melt. I watched her, shifting my weight from one foot to the other. She picked up a stack of 45s and took them over to the desk under the window. She pulled a piece of paper off a memo cube, scribbled something on it, and handed it to me.

"This what you're waiting for?"

I looked down at the phone number in my hand. "Yeah. That's it."

"Okay, then." She smiled at me again, and I walked all the way back to Grove Avenue without once feeling the ground under my feet.

I wanted to spend time with her—lots of it—and while I didn't think her enthusiasm was equal to mine, at least she didn't seem to have any objections. More important, she didn't appear to be interested in anyone else. She was the one girl I'd met who I could talk to about music. She didn't always get what I was saying, and she didn't always agree with my opinionated pronouncements, but she always listened, and she usually had something to say. We went to the teen dance clubs once or twice, but only if I knew the band. Even at that, we didn't dance much. Especially not the fast ones, because I was about as coordinated as a frog in a blender. We went to see James Brown at an old theater in Brooklyn. We took the train to Manhattan and spent whole days in the Metropolitan Museum of Art or just roaming around Central Park and the Village.

She liked to tell me about art, whichever artists intrigued her, whatever style or medium or school or period held her interest at the moment. She liked modern art and sidewalk art. She even liked graffiti.

It was weeks later the first time I kissed her. After school, under the bleachers. Early spring, and it was so cold, I could hardly feel her mouth under mine. But just the idea of kissing Amanda was nearly enough to stop my heart.

She put her arms around my waist and said against my chest so that it reverberated in my breastbone, "It's about time, McLeod. I was starting to think you were gay."

We progressed fairly quickly after that—her mother was hardly ever home—from exquisitely painful make-out sessions in the library, after which I'd limp home, only to be greeted by Kevin's smirk and his "Nice hard-on, Mattie," to the day we finally ended up in her bedroom on top of the coverlet, completely naked.

I'd never done it before, but I was horny to the point where technique was not my prime concern. And then she suddenly rolled away from me, breathing heavily. "We can't," she panted, and I thought I was going to die. "We can't mess up my bedspread," she finished.

I started to laugh, and then she started to laugh. We got up and turned down the covers and then she fished in her nightstand drawer for a condom. I'd seen them, but I'd never used one before, and I was suddenly terrified that I was going to make a mistake here, on the doorstep of the rest of my life.

I was pretty focused on my overwhelming need to do something about the ache between my legs and my simultaneous fear of looking like the virginal twerp that I was, so it didn't occur to me that a girl who kept condoms in her nightstand would probably know how to use them. She graciously spared me the embarrassment by putting it on for me.

That summer Amanda went to Italy on some kind of exchange program to study painting. I turned my attention to the serious business of getting my driver's license. I had my learner's permit, but I would be sixteen in November, and I planned to cut school and go to the DMV that morning.

So that summer Suzanne agreed to take me out every Saturday morning to practice. Kevin had his nose out of joint because he wouldn't have the car, but for once, Suzanne held firm.

"You can go wherever you need to go with one of your buddies, Kev. God knows you drive them all over creation. Or you can wait till after lunch when we get back. You're going to be gone next year, don't forget, and I can't be chauffeuring Mattie around."

He tried not to be too obnoxious about it, because he was working on her to buy him a car to take to school.

Those Saturday mornings in her old Dodge Charger—that was the only other time I recall having Suzanne all to myself, other than going to the city for my allergy shots when I was a kid. We never talked that much, just about things like right of way and using the high beams, but there was a certain level of comfort in it.

I allowed myself to think that maybe when Kevin left for college, things might be different. I invented elaborate scenarios of me coming in late after soccer practice, her fixing my dinner and then leaning on the pass-through, asking me about my day. Or sitting next to me, smoking a cigarette, carefully blowing the smoke away from me, wondering how Amanda was, if I'd decided what to do about college, if I planned to work this summer.

On a Saturday morning in August we'd gotten a later start than usual, and she really put me through my paces, even letting me drive on the expressway, out to Walton and back. We exited on Downey, near the high school, and when we were sitting at the light, she said, "Want an ice cream?"

"Sure."

As if that weren't enough of a departure from her normal behavior, she reached over and tousled my hair a little. I angled my head away from her hand, afraid somebody I knew would recognize the car and see us. I was embarrassed to be embarrassed, but she didn't seem to notice.

"You look so much like your dad, Mattie," she said, and her voice had a dreamy, liquid sound that I'd never heard before.

I also couldn't remember the last time she'd mentioned him. After he died it was like he'd never existed. I stared straight ahead and all I could say was, "Don't call me that. It's such a kid name."

She laughed. "What should I call you?"

The light changed and I started across the intersection. "Mac," I said. "Just call me Mac, okay?"

We ended up at Dairy Queen, because most of the kids I knew would be at Mahon's and I didn't want to be seen having ice cream with my mother on a Saturday afternoon. We sat out at one of the little old picnic tables and I had a butterscotch sundae while she smoked a cigarette and drank a Tab.

"So you've got a girlfriend now, I hear."

I scraped the last of the butterscotch from the bottom of the plastic dish. "Only for the last eight months, but who's counting?"

She was unruffled. "What's her name?"

"Amanda Petrie."

"Oh?" She raised an eyebrow. "Dr. Petrie's daughter?"

"Yeah."

"Why don't you bring her around sometime?"

"She's in Italy," I said.

Suzanne smiled this kind of amused half smile she had, blew out some smoke, threw her cigarette on the pavement and stepped on it. "Presumably she'll be back at some point."

"Before school starts, I guess."

"Maybe you'd like to bring her over for dinner."

"Maybe."

We got back in the car and I drove home. When we pulled into the driveway, I turned off the engine and handed her the keys.

"I think you're gonna ace this driving test." She looked directly at me, and for a second I thought she might cry. "You're a good kid, Mattie—sorry. I mean Mac." And she tousled my hair again.

When Amanda came back from Florence, she looked different. Older, more sophisticated. She wore eye makeup. She had a lot of new clothes, mostly very short skirts. She said *ciao* all the time and everything was *primo* and she kept mentioning some guy named To-nio. Now she liked red wine. And she shrugged a lot.

Still, she acted glad to see me, so I tried to ignore all the new stuff. Or look behind it for the Amanda I'd known last year. But she seemed to have pulled out into the passing lane, waving at me as she went by.

She and Kevin were now seniors. He was class president, star running back of Harrington's best football team in years. He'd been offered football and baseball scholarships by Yale and Dartmouth and Brown, and was trying to decide where he wanted to go. I was hoping he'd choose Brown—the farthest away.


Life is full of inconsequential bullshit stuff that starts out being a minor annoyance and snowballs, picking up speed and setting things into motion, like one of those Rube Goldberg contraptions. Things that can change a whole day or a whole life. Things like a flat tire on a bike.

Amanda's birthday had happened in August while she was in Italy, so in mid-September we decided to celebrate with dinner at an Italian restaurant. Then I was going to surprise her with tickets to see a band called Hard Time. They were local guys, and one of them was a buddy of mine. He'd given me backstage passes. Okay, she hadn't been that excited lately about the music I liked, but I wanted to see them with her. Or maybe I just wanted them to see her with me.

All these plans, and I still couldn't drive. She said no problem, she'd get her mother's car and pick me up at six-thirty. I had soccer practice till five-thirty, but I was only fifteen minutes away by bike, and I figured I had plenty of time to get home, shower, and change. I wanted to be ready when she got there so we didn't have to spend any time chitchatting with Suzanne while Kevin strutted around checking out Amanda.

I came out of soccer practice, skipped the showers, and went straight to my bike, headed for home. I had left the village behind and was pedaling furiously past Cahill's farm when my rear tire suddenly started wobbling. I knew it was a flat.

I used every curse word I knew. I thought about leaving my bike in the ditch and running home, but I knew it wouldn't be there when I got back, so I walked beside it, as fast as I could. Past the farm there was a gas station. I called her house, but there was no answer. Then I called our house. No answer there either. Kevin had taken to hanging out after Friday football practice with some of his friends, one of whom worked at the convenience store and could usually come up with a six-pack.

The guy at the gas station tried to fix my tire, but the inner tube was so old and patched and cracked that it wouldn't hold. He said I could leave the bike there and pick it up the next morning, so I took off running. I was in pretty good shape, but I'd just spent two hours running up and down the soccer field, and it didn't take me long to get winded. Finally, at ten till seven, I limped up our street. Amanda's car was in front of the house. Our car was in the drive.

When I walked into the kitchen, she was sitting at the table with a glass of wine in front of her, laughing at something. Kevin, showered and dressed and reeking of Jade East, was sitting on a stool drinking a beer. I was so pissed off and frustrated and exhausted that I just blurted out, "Where the hell is Suzanne?"

Kevin laughed. "She worked today, remember? I'm picking her up at the train in thirty minutes. And we're fine, too, thanks for asking."

Amanda laughed again, like that was the funniest thing she'd ever heard.

I felt all my blood taking the express elevator to my head. "I'm sorry." I looked only at her. "I had a flat. I tried to call you, but—"

"That's okay." She gave me one of her life-altering smiles. "I had to run an errand before I came. Go get dressed so we can go."

It was nearly seven-thirty by the time we left the house, and I knew there was no way we were going to have dinner and still make it to the show.

Amanda talked animatedly and laughed at everything, even things that weren't funny, while I sank lower and lower into gloom.

"What's the matter with you?" she asked at one point. "You can get your bike back tomorrow morning."

I just stared at her, and the chasm yawned almost visibly between us. She thought I was upset about the bike? I couldn't explain. I didn't even know where to start. She continued to chatter.

"Honestly, Mac, from the way you always talk about Kevin, I was expecting a two-headed monster. He's actually quite nice. And very funny. He said I should meet your mother. You never told me she was an artist—"

"I did, too."

"No you did not. You said she worked at a gallery. I thought she was, like, a receptionist or something. Kevin said she was accepted to study at the Sorbonne. I'd love to talk to her."

When I took out my wallet to pay for dinner, the tickets fell out, and she picked one up.

"But these are for tonight." She looked at me questioningly. "Why didn't you say something?"

I shrugged. "I didn't think we'd have time."

"We could have had dinner after the show."

"I didn't think you'd want to go."

She gave me a strange look. "Then why did you buy the tickets?"

"I don't know. Just in case. I don't know, okay?"

"Are you mad at me?"

I looked into her eyes then, and I was too tired and miserable to hide what I felt, so I just let it all rise to the surface and I held it there. Like an offering. "No. Not at you."

She pursed her mouth and shrugged. "I don't think I understand you anymore. Ever since I came back, you've been acting weird. You don't like my hair or my clothes or the way I talk. What is it you want from me?"

What did I want from her? Just everything. I wanted her to realize what was happening. Without my having to spell it out. I wanted her to say she would've liked to go to the show. I wanted her to say, "You were right about your brother. He really is a dork." And then laugh. Hell, what I really wanted was to rewind this day and play it back from the top, the way it should have gone.

"What, then?" There was no concern in her voice. Only curiosity.

I leaned back in my chair and let out a slow breath. "I don't know."

She picked up her purse. "I guess I better take you home," she said.

Two weeks later she and Kevin had their first date.

I didn't see her for a while. I knew the places she hung out at school and around the village and I scrupulously avoided them. But I did talk to her on the phone. When she called for Kevin.

He liked to pretend he was too busy to pick it up, so I'd have to answer it and then tell him Amanda was calling. I got to be like one of Pavlov's dogs. Every time the phone rang, I felt like throwing up.

What kept me from going completely into the void was the thought somewhere in the darkest recesses of my mind that it would be over soon. He'd dump her like he dumped everyone else, and I'd be there to pick up the pieces and magnanimously take her back. I spent quite a few nights imagining that conversation before I fell asleep.

The last football game of the year was November 1. By tradition, the last game of the season was a face-off with Palmer, our archrival, and everybody was psyched because we all knew we were going to wipe up the field with them this year. No way could we lose.

Amanda would be sitting in the bleachers—just above the place where I kissed her for the very first time, as a matter of fact—with all the other players' girlfriends. I took some comfort in thinking how much she'd hate that. Then after the game, there would be a dance, and after that, everyone would go on to private parties at people's houses. We'd be celebrating that victory for weeks.

My first inkling that things were not going according to plan was when I got to the game at seven and started looking for Jason Garfield and Buddy Love, the two guys from the soccer team I was supposed to meet. I was standing in front of the concession stand looking for them when a gang of about eight girls came out of the bathroom together, laughing hysterically. It didn't take more than a quick glance to see that Amanda was right there in the middle of it. All chummy with those girls she used to make fun of. The really creepy thing was that, except for her hair, she looked just like one of them.

When they walked past me, I stared at her so hard she must have felt it, because she looked up and our eyes met just for a second. She sort of hesitated, like she wanted to say something—or maybe that was wishful thinking on my part—but then I looked down at my watch and around like I was waiting for someone, and when I looked back, the girls had passed by and were going up the steps to the bleachers.

The second thing that went wrong was, at halftime, we were trailing, seven to six. Obviously our team wasn't the only one who'd gotten psyched up for tonight. Nobody paid any attention to the halftime show. We all just stood around in a stupor, muttering to each other.

I have no idea what went on in the locker room that night. What the coach said to those guys. I've never played football, but I've played a lot of sports, and I've known a lot of coaches. Everyone has a different approach to that kind of situation. Some rant and rave and try to shame you into winning. Some give the "Let's win one for the Gipper" kind of pep talk. Others act really calm, try to convince you with logic that you can go back out there and take over the momentum. I've even known a few who insisted on praying. As if God would give a shit if we beat Palmer.

Anyway, the team came out in the second half and did what they were supposed to do in the first half and we cleaned Palmer's clock twenty-one to seven. Two of our three touchdowns were scored by Kevin, of course. I was glad we won, but I knew he wouldn't be fit to live with for the next three weeks.

I don't know why I went to the dance. I knew exactly what would happen. And it did. I stood around with my hands in my pockets, trying to pretend I was excited about winning, having a great time, checking out the girls . . . and all the time, my eyes were scanning the dancers, looking for Kevin and Amanda. And finding them, far too often.

He was all over her, and I think she started to get embarrassed. Once I saw her step away from him, and she looked pissed. I wanted to go punch him in the face, but I kept telling myself that she'd made her choice and she could take care of herself.

At least twice I saw them go outside with some of the other players and their girlfriends. I knew they were going to the parking lot to drink or share a joint. Finally they left and didn't come back, so I figured they'd gone to a party. Buddy and Jason wanted to go to a party at one of the cheerleaders' houses, but I'd had enough.

I went to get my jacket where I'd left it on the back of a metal folding chair, and when I turned around, Amanda was standing there. She looked like she'd been crying. Her eye makeup was kind of smeary and her nose was red. My first thought was that it had happened sooner than I'd expected. Kevin had either dumped her or pissed her off so badly that she'd dumped him. I was trying to remember the noble, magnanimous speech that I'd worked out in my head for the occasion.

Then I started to listen to what she was saying. How even though we weren't together anymore, she really liked me and had always thought of me as someone she could turn to if she needed help. She kept going on and on, and I went from being elated to disappointed to crushed to resentful to really pissed off.

What I finally understood was that Kevin was totally blasted, and he was determined to drive and wouldn't give her the keys, and anyway, she was not feeling much pain either, and so would I take the keys away from Kevin and drive her home?

I stared at her. "Why don't you call a cab?"

Tears pooled in her eyes and started to run down her cheeks. "You really hate me, don't you?"

Part of me really did. But another part felt like a shit. And a third part wanted to put my arms around her and let her cry all over my Harrington High School soccer jersey.

She could see I was waffling, so she turned it all the way up. "Please, Mac, I'll never ask you for anything again. I'm just so scared to ride with him. He's totally wasted."

I eased into my jacket. I knew I should just walk over to the pay phone out by the gym and call her a taxi. I was still four days away from getting my license. But there was that fantasy I kept having about her falling into my arms at some point—yes, out of gratitude, first. But then, she'd gradually realize that she'd made a mistake, and tearfully beg me to take her back. How could she not feel the same way I did?

I sighed. I pulled on my gloves. I said, "Where is he?"

She took my arm and walked me out to the parking lot. Kevin was sitting in the driver's seat. Conscious, but just barely. He didn't put up much of a fight. The hardest part was getting him around to the other side of the car, but we managed and he promptly passed out. She climbed in back, and slumped against the door, exhausted.

I went out the back entrance onto Dunham Street, came around the corner, and pulled up at the red light.

"Thank you, Mac," she whispered.

The light turned green. I put my foot on the gas and pulled out into the intersection and the whole world ripped apart.

They said the guy in the van never even touched his brakes.

## · twenty·two ·

January 12, 1991
Ms. Ellen Liederman & Ms. Wynter Morrison
Queen Street Bakery
6005 Queen Street
Seattle, WA 98110

Dear Ms. Liederman and Ms. Morrison:

I am writing to introduce myself—Dr. Harvey Mendina, D.D.S. I am the new owner (as of January 15, 1991) of the Conant Wren Building, 6005 Queen Street, Seattle, WA 98110, of which your corporation, dba The Queen Street Bakery, is a tenant.

Even though I'm a resident of Bellevue, I very much appreciate the history and charm of the Conant Wren Building, and its place within the context of Upper Queen Anne. However, I would like to share with you my vision for the future of this architecturally signifi-cant building. As you are probably aware, there is a need for im-provements to the structure and an upgrade of its surroundings, e.g., landscaping, lighting, parking. In my opinion, this will bring the Co-nant Wren more into line with other businesses in the neighborhood, *and will contribute to the overall improvement of the neighborhood and the surrounding community. Of course, as we are all aware, these kinds of improvements require a substantial outlay of funds.*

*To that end I find it will be necessary to increase rents in the building by 20 percent, effective with your new lease (May 1, 1991). This will enable me to address complaints that have recently been directed to Mr. Walsenberg regarding plumbing, wiring, and general maintenance such as painting, the pressure washing of the brick, the replacement of doors and windows, as well as the restoration of some of the architectural details that have been lost or have fallen into disrepair.*

*Enclosed are two copies of your new lease reflecting this change, and I would appreciate your signing and returning them both to my office as soon as possible. I will then forward to you a fully executed copy for your records.*

*I look forward to working with you to ensure that the Queen Street Bakery and the Conant Wren Building live up to their full potential. In the meantime, should you have any questions or comments, please do not hesitate to contact me at (425) 433-0076.*

*Yours truly,*
*Harvey J. Mendina, D.D.S.*

I read the letter again, just to be sure I haven't missed some vital piece of information. Like the words "Just kidding!" buried somewhere in the text.

I set it down on the table, avoiding Ellen's eyes. "Did you know our building had a name?" I ask.

"Yep. It's up on this little stone medallion right in the middle of the roofline. It's just so dirty you can't see it anymore."

"Did you know it was 'architecturally significant'?"

She picks up the letter and stares at it. "No. I can't think why it would be. I've always thought it was fairly ugly."

"He can't do this."

She gives me a sad little smile. "Betcha he can. In fact, I'm not even surprised. The way things have been going in this neighborhood, it was only a matter of time."

"I wonder if anyone else has gotten a letter."

"Depends on when their leases are up, I guess. Maybe I'll mosey down the row and see what I can find out."

"We can get organized, you know. The people around here won't let it happen."

"Wyn, I wouldn't count on too much support. There are a lot of new people in the neighborhood. They probably moved here exactly because of things like this. It'll boost property values, pretty things up—"

"Making the streets safe for yuppies and franchises, I know. But he can't just come in here and kick us out. I think the first thing we have to do is call him and protest the increase. There must be some kind of law—"

She laughs, but not happily. "For somebody who's still trying to get a financial settlement out of her ex-husband, who's already remarried . . . you should know better."

"Well, if we can't fight it, there are other places that would love to have us. Ballard, Wallingford, Fremont. We have other options."

"Wyn, we're up to our ass in debt already. We can't just pick up and start over. We'd never see daylight again. I never should have let you sink your money into it, too. I should have seen the writing on the wall and just sold out to the Great Northwest Bread Company last year."

"There has to be something we can—"

"Wyn. You're not listening to me. I've been doing this for almost ten years. I'm tired of fighting. I'm tired of scratching out a living, worrying about when the ovens are going to go, what taxes are going to be next year if they pass that new assessment for small-business licenses. We can't even afford a new toilet. Life doesn't have to be that hard. There are other things I can do. And Lloyd's been bugging me about moving over to Whidbey.... He's tired of commuting."

I look out the front door. Across the street, where the vegetable market used to be, to the new, gleaming-white gallery with its huge windows.

"He can't do anything till our lease is up. Why don't we check with Gene and Myra. And those new guys, the ones who own the card store."

"Allen and Rob? They're probably not affected at all. They just moved in last summer, so their lease is probably safe for at least two years."

"Let's at least see what they know. And meanwhile, I'm going to call Mendina."

While I'm phoning the good doctor, Ellen goes next door to talk to Myra, then down to the end of the building to talk to Gene, whose photography studio is the largest rental space in the building.

"Any luck?" she asks me when she comes back.

"His receptionist sounds like that Lily Tomlin character, the telephone operator."

"Ernestine?"

"Right. 'The doctor is with a patient at the moment. May I tell him about what you are inquiring?' "

"About what you are inquiring?"

"I guess somebody told her never to use a preposition to end a sentence with. Anyway, I left a message for him to call here. I didn't say what it was about, but I'm sure he'll figure it out. What did Myra and Gene say?"

"Myra got a letter in December. Her lease is up in April. She hasn't decided what to do yet, she said she wanted to get together with us and talk about it. Gene's lease is up at the end of the year, but he said he'll probably just pay the increase. Business is good and he doesn't feel like moving."

"Must be nice."

When she folds her arms and slumps lower in the chair, I get the oppressive sense that it's already a done deal in her mind.

I give Mendina three days. When he hasn't returned my call by Friday morning, I call again. I get Ernestine again. Dr. Mendina is with a patient. Again. I leave a message again. I try calling on Saturday, thinking maybe he's there doing paperwork or something. All I get is voice mail.

By the following Tuesday I'm pissed. Ernestine answers and we go through the whole routine again, but this time, when she asks if she can take a message, I say, "How many do I have to leave before he calls me back?"

"I'm sorry, but Dr. Mendina is very busy—"

"I'm very busy, too. I'm also one of his tenants, and I need to speak to him. I'll hold."

"I'm sorry, but it isn't possible for you to hold. He's doing a root canal and he won't be available to take calls for at least an hour."

"Then tell me when he does take calls."

"Dr. Mendina does not take calls. I give him messages and then he returns calls."

"Well, he's not returning mine."

"I'm very sorry, but all I can do is give him the message."

At this point I'm wishing Dr. Mendina's hands were in my mouth right now so I could bite him, but I just say, "Then please give him the message that it's urgent that Wynter Morrison or Ellen Liederman speak with him as soon as possible."

I take the coffee cup Ellen's holding out to me. "I think Ernestine is a 'droid. She has certain programmed responses, and beyond those she does not venture."

"I think it's obvious that he doesn't have any desire to speak to us."

I sip my espresso and watch somebody's silky-haired golden retriever slurping up water from our dog bowl by the front door. He may not have any desire to, but he is, by god, going to.

· · ·

After closing on Sunday I meet Ellen at the bakery. It's one of those afternoons where the last thing you want to do is go out—dark, windy, cold, the rain coming in staccato bursts like machine-gun fire. When I get there Ellen has the space heater on and the teakettle boiling. While I'm hanging up my coat, she fixes a plate of cookies from the day-olds—oatmeal with walnuts and dried cherries, peanut butter with chocolate chips, snickerdoodles dusted with cinnamon.

When Myra taps on the door, I let her in and pull down all the shades in front. It still amazes me that people who've lived in this neighborhood for years, and know our hours as well as we do, can walk past at any time, day or night, and, if they see anyone inside, they'll try to come in. Or they'll stand there banging on the door till we come to open it and then say, "Oh, are you not open?"

"Thanks for coming," Ellen says.

"No problem. I was giving my Aunt Lou a root job anyway." She hangs up her dripping coat and rubs her hands together in front of the heater.

We pull out our chairs and sit down, and before anybody says anything, we all fix ourselves a cup of tea.

"Well...," says Ellen around a bite of oatmeal cookie. She looks at Myra. "Have you had any more thoughts about what you're going to do?"

Myra takes a tiny bite of snickerdoodle, edging a stray crumb from the corner of her mouth. She makes rapid little chewing motions and then swallows, all the while looking thoughtfully at the ceiling.

"You know, I think I'm just going to pack it in," she says finally. "I talked to my lawyer, and he says there's not much I can do. Bottom line is, Mendina owns the building. He said what I should've done was sign a new lease with Nate before he sold, and then it gets automatically assigned to the new owner . . . And he can't, you know, kick you out or raise your rent or anything."

"Well, that's good to know. Now that it's too late." I set down my tea. "I wonder why Nate didn't think of that."

Ellen rests her chin in her cupped palm. "Maybe he did. Maybe that was part of the deal with Mendina. Or maybe he was just so distracted . . . I mean, he said Libby was sick. He probably just wanted to sell off everything and get her out of here."

"I've been talking to my cousin about us buying a shop up in La Conner," Myra says. "I wouldn't make as much money, but it's cheaper to live up there, and probably cheaper to run a business, too." She breaks the rest of the cookie into small pieces. "What about you girls?"

Ellen sighs. "I feel like if we could just talk to him . . . maybe we could persuade him to go about this a little differently. I mean, he's starting off by creating a lot of bad feelings."

"I've read about things like this happening when neighborhoods change." I look at Myra. "Sometimes all it takes is the tenants standing together. And people in the neighborhood can make an impact, too, if they show a lot of support for existing businesses. Of course, it's easier not to fight. It takes time and effort away from all our shops. But if everyone just caves in to people like Harvey, then . . . well, there goes the neighborhood."

Her face gets mottled with red, which I assume means she's blushing.

"It never stops, either." Ellen takes the handoff. "They find out one person can be bulldozed, then nobody's safe. I think we should point that out to Gene. We all need to support each other—"

When she pauses for breath, Myra shakes her head sadly. "I just can't, you guys. I can't take the chance of being out of here with no place to go. I'm a single mom, and I don't get child support. And if I'm gonna move to La Conner before April, I gotta get on it—"

I pretend that I haven't heard her. "And the guys at the card shop don't care because it doesn't affect them. Yet. But what's going to happen to them when their lease is up? They get replaced by a Hallmark store, that's what. And the same thing can happen up in La Conner, Myra. Then where do you go?"

"Hopefully, by that time, I'll be dead." She tries to laugh.

"What about your kid?" Ellen says. "How's he going to like leaving all his friends and moving up there?"

"He's not. Obviously." She fidgets with the pieces of cookie, reducing them to little piles of crumbs. "But he'll get over it. We all have to do things we don't want to do." Abruptly she scoots back her chair and gets up. "I'm sorry, you guys. I gotta go pick up my kid." She reaches for her still-wet coat. "Thanks for the tea." Then she's out the door.

I give Ellen a disgusted look. "The tag-team strategy meeting falls flat."

Ellen laughs, laying her head down on her folded arms.

"What's so damn funny?"

"You." She sits up and gives my shoulder a squeeze. "You do a great guilt trip. I'm going to see about making you an honorary Jewish mother."

On Monday afternoon as soon as I wake up, I dress and tiptoe out of the house, leaving Tyler snoring like the Texas chainsaw massacre. It's amazing the sounds that come out of that delicate-looking little body. The wind is sharp and cold, cutting through my jeans, but at least it's not raining.

At the bakery the Mazurkoids are happily cutting and wrapping and labeling to the tunes of Van Morrison, and Ellen and I sit down with the telephone at a table in the empty café.

I take the first turn.

I try to make my voice as blandly pleasant as Ernestine's, but it's difficult. We go through the routine. She takes the message. I hand the phone to Ellen and she calls. After we've taken a couple of turns apiece, Ernestine says, "Miss Liederman—"

"It's Morrison," I tell her politely. "Ms. Liederman is my partner."

"Miss Morrison, I can't take any more messages from you."

"That's fine, we'll just keep calling back. In fact, maybe we'll get a few of our employees to call, too. Would that tie up your lines?"

"What is it you want?" It finally sounds as if there's a crack in Miss Ernestine's composure.

"The same thing we always wanted. To speak with Dr. Mendina."

"But I've explained that he's not available. I will give him your message, but he cannot come to the phone right now."

"That's fine," I say. "But since he never returns our calls, we'll just keep calling till he can come to the phone. 'Bye now—"

"Wait!" She's breathing heavily. "I'll see if I can get him. Please hold."

After an amazingly brief interlude, a male voice says, "Yes?" with just a trace of irritation.

"Dr. Mendina, I presume?" The humor is lost on him.

"Yes. What can I do for you?"

"This is Wyn Mor—"

"I know who you are, Ms. Morrison, and I have to say it's incredibly rude of you to interrupt my practice with these ceaseless, badgering calls, and I—"

"Excuse me, but I think it's incredibly rude of you not to return our calls. It's not as if we're selling magazine subscriptions. We want to discuss our lease."

"If you'd left a message, I would have called you back."

"When? I've left at least six messages, not counting today's."

"Really? That's odd. I don't recall seeing any of them."

"Well, then you might want to consider getting a new receptionist."

"I do apologize for the oversight. Now tell me what you'd like to discuss."

"We'd like to discuss the twenty percent rent increase."

"That isn't open for discussion."

"We would like you to understand that by raising the rent that much, you are, in effect, putting us out of business."

"I'm very sorry. However, the fact remains that increases are necessary in order to repair and restore the building."

"Don't you think twenty percent is a bit excessive?"

"I do not."

"It seems to me that it would be smarter for you to make a bit less money and keep long-term tenants in the place, rather than having a pretty building with a bunch of vacant spaces."

"I can assure you, Ms. Morrison, the spaces will not be vacant for long. If you choose to leave, that is."

"We don't choose to leave; you're kicking us out."

"I most certainly am not. Did I not send you a lease? All you have to do is sign it and you will be my valued tenants once more."

"Yes, well, the fact is, we can't afford it."

"Have you thought about increasing your prices? Rent is a cost of doing business, you know."

*Condescending bastard.* "Whatever your delusions—excuse me, I mean illusions—about this neighborhood, the people who live here are not going to pay three-fifty for a bran muffin."

"That's where I believe you're being very shortsighted. People—particularly the type of people who are moving to Queen Anne in droves—will pay whatever it costs. Particularly if you serve it up to them in beautiful surroundings. Now, I've seen the Queen Street Bakery, and frankly it could use some renovations. Get rid of those junky tables and chairs, get some Euro-style furniture, some French or Italian café tables, some nice, comfortable chairs. Upgrade your physical plant, go all stainless steel and glass, brighten the place up. Make it more sleek, contemporary—"

I laugh in spite of myself. "All that stuff costs money. Are you buying?"

"Ms. Morrison—"

"Besides that, the bakery is a fixture on the hill. People love it the way it is. They don't want some Euro-style coffeehouse. There are plenty of those around. The bakery has the character of the neighborhood—"

"And the character of the neighborhood is rapidly changing. I'm not changing it; it's been under way for some time. If I hadn't bought the building, somebody else would have, and you'd be facing exactly the same situation. So I'd appreciate it if you'd quit trying to cast me as the villain in this drama. The bottom line is, you can either sign the lease, change with the times, and become successful, or you can resist change, close your business, and find a job."

"You have no idea what you're really doing here—"

"Miss Morrison, you are really very much out of step with current trends. And I really need to get back to my patient. I'll wait to hear from you."

I hang up the phone and look at Ellen. She doesn't say a word, just looks right back at me. It's so quiet we can hear Myra's tape player next door. She must be alone, because most of her clients are middle-aged and older and they're not generally into Jimi Hendrix.

Finally Ellen slaps her palms on her thighs. "Well," she says, "I think I'll go home and have hazelnut pound cake with chocolate ganache for dinner."

## · twenty-three ·

It's six A.M. on March 1, and we're all waiting for Ellen, who's been in the bathroom for the last twenty minutes trying to stop crying. She came out a few minutes ago, then as soon as she saw all of us, she turned around without a word and went back in the bathroom. There's a deathly hush hanging over the place, and I find that I'm impatient. It's like those dreams about falling off a cliff, where you just keep falling and never get to the bottom.

The Queen Street Bakery doesn't have a lot of staff meetings. Ellen says the last one she can recall was when she and Diane bought the bakery from Patty Turnbull, who decided it would be less stressful to work as a paramedic.

So everyone knows something big is up, and most of them probably figure the news isn't good. Tyler, of course, already knows, so she's busy acting self-important and milking it for all the drama it's worth. She's sitting at a table with Misha and Jen. Rose is perched on the stool at the register and Susan, Barb, and Kristen are sipping lattes at another table. I'm leaning against the counter.

Finally Ellen appears, face splotched and puffy, eyes red. Her brave smile keeps twisting involuntarily. She walks over and stands next to me, resting her elbows on the counter. I notice that her hands are shaking.

"I want—" Her voice cracks and she clears her throat. "I want to thank you all for coming in so early this morning. I'm afraid the news I have to share with you is not good. I'll be brief. Our building has been sold. The new owner has decided to restore the place to its original glory, and in order to do this, he's planning to raise everyone's rent when their lease comes up for renewal. Ours is up May first."

She pauses for a moment, collecting herself. "The amount of the increase is so high, Wyn and I have concluded that we can't afford to keep the bakery open with our current operating budget..."

There's an audible, collective intake of breath. Everyone looks at everyone else.

"The only way to continue on here would be to raise our prices to what we both consider to be unconscionable levels, and we'd still probably have to cut staff. We believe that the result would be a decrease in our selection and quality at a price too high for a lot of people who've been coming here for years to afford. Besides, if you've worked here longer than about a week, you know that, as proud as we are of our baked goods, the Queen Street Bakery is not just about food. We have always been about the people who work here, and the people who buy from us, our customers. We're about the city of Seattle and we're about Queen Anne Hill. Our neighbor—hood."

Her voice breaks and she pushes a tear across her face with the back of her hand. "That neighborhood is now changing—for better or for worse, it's not my place to say. All I can tell you is that as of May First, the Queen Street Bakery will no longer be a part of it."

I keep expecting everyone to talk, to ask questions, but they don't. They just sit there, silent, staring at Ellen. Finally Jen wiggles her fingers tentatively.

"Have you thought about maybe...selling it to someone else?"

"We have. We listed with a small-business broker over a month ago. As of this moment, there haven't been any prospective buyers." She rubs her hands on her skirt in that nervous way she has. "I guess it's still a possibility, but it's not something I'm counting on.

"I want to say how lucky I feel to have worked with all of you. This place, all of you...have brought me great joy. There are so many things I know that I want to say to you—together and individually—and I will, before we—" She makes a funny little hiccupping sound, gives me a helpless look, and heads back to the bathroom.

For some reason I feel utterly calm. Maybe it's just the certainty that this is rock bottom. No matter what else happens, it has to be better than this.

I swallow the last of my espresso. "I've only been here about two and a half years—not nearly as long as some of you. But being part of the Queen Street Bakery is an experience that will stay with me for the rest of my life. Between now and May first, there's a lot to do. I've just discovered that it takes almost as much planning to get a place ready to close as it does to open. But right now we have two more months here as the Queen Street Bakery, and I would never want anyone on the hill to remember us as less than we've always been, which is simply the best. So"—I look at my watch—"I think it's time to get to work."

Everybody gets up and heads for the back, except Rose, who only came in for the meeting. She zips up her jacket, and pulls up the window shades. When she unlocks the front door and steps outside, there are already three customers waiting on the sidewalk.

Tyler and I walk across the street and head for home. By noon word will be out. By tomorrow people will be coming in wanting the details. Once again, I'm thankful I don't work days. If I had to repeat the story fifty times a day for the next eight weeks, I'd lie down in front of the monorail.

"So what now?" Tyler's voice startles me, and I look over at her, trudging beside me, head down.

"I guess we could go on the dole."

Her nose wrinkles. "The what?"

"The dole. Welfare. Unemployment."

"You wouldn't do that."

"Or, I could marry Josh. We could adopt you and consolidate the households. You could sleep with Turbo."

"Wyn..."

I smile feebly. "I'm joking."

"It's not funny." She gives me a disapproving frown.

"I was just sort of laughing to keep from crying."

No lights on at Josh's house. I haven't seen much of him since Christmas. I think he's embarrassed, which is silly. Who among us has not been made a fool by love? Maybe because he's a guy he thinks he shouldn't show it.

"What are we gonna do?" she asks again. This time we're sitting half asleep over bowls of oatmeal.

"I don't know. What would you like to do? What would you do if you could do anything you wanted?"

"Make bread."

I smile. "That's the right answer. All we have to do is decide where."

"You're not gonna, like, go back to L.A. or anything. Are you?"

The question makes me realize that I have thought about it, if only in passing. I don't know what I'd do there, but then, I don't know what I'd do here, either. I guess I could move to Ballard or Fremont or Wallingford. There are other neighborhoods with their own quirky personalities. There are other bakeries. Good ones. Artisan bakers I could learn from.

But to me, Seattle is Queen Anne Hill; Seattle is the Queen Street Bakery.

I rest my elbows on the table. "I suppose it's one possibility. We should consider everything."

" 'We'?" She throws me a cautious glance. "You mean, me, too?"

"Of course I mean you. Unless you don't want to live together anymore. It's your choice, too, you know."

Her face colors—a new phenomenon—but she doesn't say anything, just twirls the spoon in her cereal.



CM's been in Honolulu since the end of January, doing a guest-instructor gig for the winter quarter at the University of Hawaii. I picture her getting a tan and sipping piña coladas on the beach while I'm slogging through puddles and trying to decide what to do with my life. She has the bad taste to send me postcards of Diamond Head and a package containing swizzle sticks from the Tiki Lounge, a pink plastic lei, a Don Ho tape, and a poster of Jack Lord, from *Hawaii Five-O*, which Tyler appropriates to put up in her room.

I don't know what's up with Tyler these days. It's three weeks since the staff meeting and she hasn't mentioned the subject of our next job again. She seems content to make bread at night, watch daytime television with Turbo, listen to her Walkman in front of the fire, and read. Sometimes she reads the *Tassajara Bread Book* that I gave her for her birthday, but lately she's gotten into mystery novels, working her way through the alphabet with Sue Grafton's detective Kinsey Milhone. Maybe this means she's thinking about southern California. She makes occasional phone calls, but I can't tell who she's talking to or what it's about. At odd intervals she'll announce that she's going out, and she does. There's no pattern to what day or time or how long she's gone.

I don't ask questions.



One afternoon when she's gone, I decide to start cleaning out my desk, in preparation for the inevitable move. There are a couple of cookbooks that I've been lugging around with me since my days as the happy hostess of Hancock Park—stuff I can't believe I once cooked, like nasturtiums stuffed with goat cheese and chutney, consommé with tiny floating custards, duck à l'orange, and white-chocolate mousse in almond tuille shells with bittersweet chocolate sauce and raspberry coulis. I'm not saying I wouldn't eat it, of course. I just don't see myself ever again spending three days in the kitchen for a dinner party.

There's a huge stack of *American Baker* magazines, ticket stubs from movies, programs from a play or two. I don't know why I keep these things to begin with. I should learn to empty my pockets and my purse as soon as I walk in the door. There are birthday cards and Christmas cards. Funny cards and postcards—mostly from CM, but one or two from my mother.

My second desk drawer holds letters. Mac's letters. The sight of his scrunched-up writing makes my heart skip. I stare at the stack of envelopes, and suddenly I know why I haven't come up with any concrete plans, any but the vaguest ideas of what to do, where to go after the bakery closes. I'm waiting for him. Waiting for him to either come back or tell me he's not coming back.

I told him not to expect me to sit around waiting for him to show up, but that's exactly what I've been doing. It makes me angry.

When the phone rings I grab it and snap, "Yes?"

Silence. Then, "Wyn?"

"CM! How are you? Where are you?"

"I'm good. I'm still in Honolulu. I thought I had the wrong number. Are you okay?"

"No, but that's a whole long story."

"Well, I've got a big, fat, iced chai, and I'm sitting on my comfy little balcony watching the waves roll in. So spill it, girlfriend."

I take a deep breath. "Well, for starters, the bakery's closing—"

"*What?* Why?"

"The lite version is the building's been sold, and the new owner's jacking the rent up by twenty percent—"

"Why?"

I laugh. "Because he's an asshole."

"Well, there's always one more of those around, isn't there? When is this happening?"

"May first. That's the expiration of our lease."

"What are you going to do?"

"I don't know. Right now Ellen and I are just putting one foot in front of the other, getting ready to move out, arranging to sell the equipment, tying up loose financial ends. It's so weird."

"I'm really sorry. What does Ellen say? Does she want to open up somewhere else?"

"We can't afford it. It's going to take us both a while to pay off our current debt. And then, I think she's just worn out. She's been depressed, and she says she just wants to move over to Whidbey and bake Mazurka bars wholesale and read and sleep."

"I guess you can't fight that. She's been there a long time, hasn't she?"

"Ten years."

There's a silence. "Well, you blew my puny little newsflash right out of the water."

"No, tell me."

"I've got a new gig."

"That's great! I mean, is it great? Are you excited? What is it?"

"Associate director of the Los Angeles Dramatic Dance Theater."

"CM, that's fabulous. I'm so proud of you—Los Angeles? I guess that means you have to live there, huh?"

"That's what it means." The excitement in her voice ratchets up a few notches. "It's a fantastic opportunity. I applied months ago, but I couldn't even let myself think about it. I didn't think I had a chance. But I'm going to miss you so much. And the poppet, too. She sort of grows on you, doesn't she?"

"You just never know, we might end up being your neighbors."

"Really? I didn't think you'd ever go back. I thought you loved Seattle."

"I do. But I'm not sure I can stay here now. I was actually sort of toying with the idea of moving somewhere else, but I hadn't thought about where."

Static crackles along the phone line. "What about Mac?"

"What about him? I can't sit around waiting for him to make up his mind what he's going to do. He writes me all these letters, but he never says a damn word about when he's coming back. Or *if* he's coming back." She doesn't say anything to that. "So anyway, when do you have to be in L.A.?"

"As soon as I finish up here. End of the month."

"That quick?"

"They wanted me to come now, but I told them I couldn't just bail on my commitment here."

"Where are you going to live?"

"I haven't even thought about it. The theater's in West L.A., but I don't know if I want to live there. I'll probably stay with my mom till I scope things out."

"I'm so happy for you."

"Thanks, baby. I'm a little nervous—"

"About what?"

"It's a big job."

"Hey, no job's too big for an Amazon."

When Tyler comes home, I'm putting Mac's letters into an old three-ring binder. I'm not sure why. Maybe arranging them in chronological order, snapping the rings closed (so they can't escape), gives me at least the illusion of control.

She sits there watching me for a few minutes.

"Where have you been?" I hope it sounds conversational rather than inquisitional.

"Hanging out with a friend."

"Did you have fun?"

"Yep. What are you doing?"

"Just trying to get organized. For when we move."

She gets up. "You want a glass of wine?"

"Sure. Thanks."

"You mind if I have some?"

"Help yourself."

She pours two glasses of cabernet and sets them on the table. She sits down, tilting her head slightly and looking into my face. "So . . . where are we moving?"

"Well . . . how do you feel about going to L.A.?"

"Why there?"

"I just thought it might be fun for a while. CM just got a new job there."

She waits. Watches me for a few more minutes. "What about Mac?"

"He's doing whatever it is he needs to be doing right now. I can't waste a lot of time worrying about it."

" 'Zat why you're saving all his letters in that binder?"

I give her a dirty look. "Do you not want to leave Seattle?"

"I don't care."

I put my palms flat on the table. "Do you want to stay with me?"

"I guess."

"Don't overwhelm me with your devotion."

She grins slyly. "If I stay with you, will I end up talking like that?"


Monday morning, April 1. Dawn is a rosy haze. Ellen and I have an espresso and go over the bills after Tyler leaves. I give her my grocery list. I remind her to reorder T-shirts, especially the bread ones.

"Why?" she says.

I smile. "I think people are going to want them as souvenirs. I predict that we sell out by the end of the month."

"Yeah, I guess. The end of an era or something. And..." She half laughs. "If we don't sell them, we can donate them to a girls' soccer team."

"It's not too late to change your mind..."

She pats my hand. "Yes, it is. It is for me. I'm resigned to it. And I promised Lloyd that we'd move to Whidbey by the end of the summer." She smiles forlornly. "It wouldn't be the same anyway. The Queen Street Bakery doesn't belong in Ballard."

I happen to disagree. I think the Queen Street Bakery belongs wherever we decide to put it, but there's no point in going down that road. We don't have the funds, anyway.

Ellen says she'd like the small Hobart. The auction house will take the floor mixer, the refrigerators, the stove, espresso machine, all the fixtures. She and I will divide up the Cuisinarts, pans and bowls, utensils, and any dishes and display items we want.

"What about the ovens?"

She looks around forlornly. "Scrap. They're too old. Nobody would want them. You can have all the recipes," she offers.

I raise my eyebrows.

"Except for the Mazurka Bars, of course."

I laugh. "I knew it was too good to be true."

"I'd like to keep the rights to the Queen Street name. I thought, for the Mazurkas—"

"Of course, that's fine." I put my arm around her shoulders.

"Oh, don't do that or I'll start bawling."

## · twenty-four ·

It's after eight o'clock when I step out the front door, bell jangling merrily, and my eyes go instantly across the street, as if there's a big neon arrow pointing to the mud-encrusted white El Camino parked in front of the yoga studio. My knees almost fold.

Mac leans against the door of the truck, arms crossed, his breath making small white puffs in the cool morning air. His hair is long, pulled straight back, and his tentative smile stops my heart.

There's a huge disconnect that happens when you see somebody where you don't expect to see them. In my mind he's still in the Yukon, in that funky little town with the odd cast of characters. In reality he's probably been on the road for at least a week, but the sight of him here, alive and real, on Queen Street, feels like an illusion. A magician's trick.

He walks across the street to where my feet have sent down roots into the sidewalk.

"Wyn..." There's the smallest crack in his voice, and I slip into his arms, like a hand into a well-worn glove. He rests his chin on the top of my head for a long, silent minute. Then he says, "Sorry I'm late. Traffic was a bitch."

We hold on to each other, laughing, and the release is like knots falling out of a rope.

"When did you get back?"

"This morning. Just now."

I'm not sure if he's letting go of me or if I'm pulling away. We walk across the street, and I notice the mud caked in the truck's rims, the pitted paint under the grime.

"Elky looks like you just finished the Baja 500."

"I only wished I was somewhere that warm. I had to stop twice and wait out the weather," he says. "I've been on the road almost three weeks."

We get in and sit there, both of us looking straight ahead. Besides the unreality, an uneasiness has crept into the cab between us, insinuating itself among the smells of a long road trip—stale crackers, orange peel, coffee.

He slides his hands around the steering wheel. "I went by the apartment and your name was gone from the directory. What's going on?"

"It's kind of a long story. The short version is, I'm living with Tyler now. Over on Cedar Street."

"I was wondering . . ." He hesitates, but I know what he's going to ask.

"I can't, Mac. Our place is too small and . . . anyway, I just can't. I'm sorry."

He shrugs. "I can probably stay with Kenny for a couple of days."

"They have a child now. It's a whole different thing. You can't just walk in and expect to be sleeping on their couch."

"I'll figure something out." He turns to look at me directly for the first time since we got in the truck. "Looks like I stayed away too long."

"You stayed as long as you needed to. I think we both had some issues to work out."

He smiles ever so slightly. "That's my California girl."

He turns the key on, but doesn't start the engine. On the radio Bruce Springsteen is singing "Brilliant Disguise." He flicks it off. "I missed you."

I turn to him, leaning my back against the passenger door. "I missed you, too. But I told you when you left not to look for me standing on the porch waving my hankie."

"Veranda. I believe your exact words were 'Don't expect to come back and find me standing on the veranda waving my lace hankie.'" He makes a minute adjustment in the side mirror. "But I guess that's pretty much what I did expect. My mistake."

"Oh, stop it. You act like I'm punishing you. That's not how I feel."

"How do you feel?"

I can't help it. I burst out laughing. "This is totally amazing. You show up after a year in Siberia, no warning, no explanation, and suddenly you want to talk about feelings?"

"I thought that's what you always wanted me to do. Have you changed your mind?"

"It's been a hard year. I've changed my mind about a lot of things."

He leans his head back, and I notice the dark smudges under his eyes, the stubble of his beard. He probably drove most of the night.

"You need to get some sleep. We can talk this afternoon."

Without opening his eyes, he says, "Is it too late?"

"For what?" Yes I have a sadistic streak. I want to hear him say it.

"For us." He manages to invest it with such vulnerability that I want to cradle him like a child. However, I'm not going there. Not yet, anyway.

"We have a lot to talk about." I get out of the truck, walk around to his side, open the door. "Move over."

"What?"

"I said, move over. I'm driving. You're practically comatose." He slides over to make room for me and I climb in. "My landlord's a really good guy. He'll probably let you crash on the floor at his place, at least for the day." The Elky starts up without a protest, and I make a U-turn at the stop sign.

By the time I pull up in front of the house, Mac's snoring.


He knocks on the back door at four o'clock. He's showered and shaved, but his eyes still look tired.

"What are you making?" he asks.

"Struan. It's a Scottish harvest bread."

He smiles. "Don't you get enough bread baking at work?"

I look up from the jar of wheat bran. "Do you get enough music playing at work?"

"Touché." He pulls a chair out and sits down.

"Do you want something to drink?"

"Have you got any coffee?"

"Not made, but you can make some if you want. The pot's on the stove. Coffee's in that canister next to the sink."

He dumps this morning's grounds in the garbage, rinses the pot, and fills the bottom with water, the basket with ground espresso.

"Cups are hanging on that rack by the fridge." I measure out the coarsely ground cornmeal and the rolled oats, dump them in the bowl with the flour and bran.

"What's in here?" He picks up a small pan on the stove.

"Brown rice. For the Struan."

"It looks like it's got everything in it but the kitchen sink."

"That's because it does. It has all the harvest grains—corn, oats, wheat, millet, and rice. It was made in western Scotland on the eve of the feast of St. Michael the archangel. He was the guardian of the harvest. The oldest daughter of each house would bake the breads—small ones for the family and huge loaves for the community. On the feast day, they would take the bread to early Mass and it would be blessed in remembrance of absent friends."

The espresso pot begins to hiss and sputter. He pulls it off the stove, pours some in his cup and sits down at the table again. For a few minutes he just watches me add the brown rice, honey, and buttermilk to the grains in the bowl and stir it with a big wooden spoon.

"You're angry."

I stop stirring and let my eyes meet his. "I suppose on some level I am."

He drinks the rest of his espresso in one swallow and sets the cup down. "I feel like there's some kind of invisible wall around you. There are so many things I want to tell you and ask you. And all you want to do is tell me about the history of Scottish harvest bread."

I give the dough a last stir, and dump it out on the floured counter.

"Hard, isn't it?" I begin to knead the stiff, crumbly dough. "When you want to talk to someone, you need to know how they feel, what they think. And they just want to talk about how viruses mutate and how ospreys return to the same nest every year and that there are frogs in the Arctic that freeze solid in winter and—"

"Okay."

I keep kneading the bread. Struan takes longer than most breads because it has so many whole grains, but gradually it begins to change under my hands. The shaggy mass becomes lighter, more elastic. The grains even out, and what emerges is a beautiful golden, moist round of dough. When you press the heel of your hand into it, it gives way a little before springing back. I wash and oil the bowl, set the dough in, and cover it with a damp towel.

He watches me silently while I wash all the utensils and put them in the drainer, wash my hands and rub hand cream into them. I sit down across from him and we look at each other.

He clears his throat. "Josh seems like a good guy."

"The best. Did you meet Turbo?"

"Meet him? I slept with him." He smiles. "Of course, I think I was on his couch." He pauses. "Do you . . . Are you involved with—?"

"Turbo? Yeah. He's about the most reliable male I've ever met. All you have to do is give him toast and he's your love slave."

He waits for me to answer the real question.

I lean back and prop one foot up on the chair next to me. "No, I'm not involved with Josh. It would be way too convenient. His wife left him. You left me—"

"I didn't leave you. I just had to leave for a while."

"You weren't here. You weren't with me. That's all I know. Josh and I would probably get along really well, but he's still in love with Fran, and I'm . . ."

"You're what?"

"In limbo. I seem to have gotten used to your being gone."

His thumb explores a gouge in the battered tabletop. "Don't you think you could get used to me being back?"

"I suppose I could. The question is, do I want to?"

"That's definitely the question. What's the answer?"

"I don't know."

He takes my hand in both of his, turning it palm up, as if he's going to read my fortune. It feels good, just sitting here in the kitchen with him holding my hand.

"I want to tell you something." He traces the lines in my palm with his index finger, then looks up into my eyes. "I didn't leave because of you. But at first, I thought if I stayed away long enough, I'd find out that it didn't matter if I came back. If I saw you again. But what happened was, the longer I stayed, the more it mattered. Until finally it got to matter more than anything else. More than writing, more than going to Alaska, more than—anything. When you came out of the bakery this morning, the way you looked . . . I thought you were glad to see me."

"Oh, Mac." I let out a deep sigh. "Of course I was glad to see you. I am glad you came back. It's just—everything's changing so fast."

"Like what?"

"Just in the last six months—Tyler's best friend died, CM's gone back to L.A. We've lost our lease—"

"On the bakery?"

I nod.

"What are you guys going to do?"

"Close the doors. We're in debt up to our eyeballs, and Ellen's tired of swimming upstream. She wants to move over to Whidbey with Lloyd and just make Mazurkas wholesale. And I can't blame her."

"How did you lose your lease?"

"Nate, our landlord, sold the building to some dentist from Bellevue who's got delusions of grandeur. Our lease is up May first and he's raised the rent by twenty percent to finance his renovation plans for our 'architecturally significant' building. Nobody can afford to stay except Gene, the photographer."

From the corner of my eye, I see Tyler strolling out of the bathroom in her underwear. "Man on the hall," I holler, and she does a one-eighty into her bedroom. "So..." I look back at him. "I don't know what I'm going to do. I don't even know if I'm going to stay in Seattle."

"What about the divorce?"

"That's about all that's settled. I'm officially single. And we have a court date in June to divide the assets. I'm just trying to hang on."

"Well, I have some news." He leans back, balancing the chair on two legs. "I finished the rewrite."

I sit straight up. "Really?"

"Really." He smiles. "I worked on it all winter. I sent it back to Steve Devine three weeks ago, and he's now my agent."

"Oh my god, Mac, that's wonderful. You must feel so proud."

"What I feel is lucky. Incredulous."

"Hi, Mac." Tyler enters, now sartorially impeccable in her black jeans and black T-shirt. She looks at me. "How come everybody you know talks like that?"

"He's got an agent!"

"Awesome." She goes to the refrigerator and pulls out the orange juice. "Just like a real writer dude." She wanders into the living room, and I hear her talking on the phone.

I get up for a glass of water, and when I squeeze past him, he takes my arm. Part of me wants to sink back into the luxury of him. To wake up with him next to me. Then that other part of me—the small but vocal minority—is saying no. He hears it loud and clear. He drops my arm.

"You have to give me some time," I say.

"I guess that's fair."

· twenty-five ·

The familiar brown boxes have sprung up in our living room like mushrooms after a good rain. Since I left L.A. over two years ago, my personal belongings have probably spent fifty percent of the time in these boxes, either in storage, in transit, waiting to be in transit, or waiting to be unpacked.

It feels a lot like living inside a kaleidoscope. No sooner do I get situated in one pattern, then everything changes again and moves on, leaving me clinging by my fingernails to some little fragment of colored glass that used to be part of my life.

I plop down on the couch and put my feet up on the closest box. It's almost eight o'clock at night, and sun still beams in through the window, flashing into rainbows when it hits Tyler's lead crystal rotating slowly by its fishing twine. I have no idea where she is. She's been gone a lot lately, disappearing with her enormous tote bag thrown over her shoulder, coming back at all hours. I'm reluctant to ask her what she's up to; after all, I'm not her mother, and she is—technically—an adult, but I worry.

I think about calling CM. Then I think about having a glass of wine. Next I think about ordering a pizza or nuking some spaghetti sauce. I don't do any of those things, though. I just sit there. As if

I'm waiting for something. When the Elky pulls up across the street, I understand that I was.

It's been a strange three weeks. Knowing he was back but not really believing it. There hasn't been any communication aside from a few brief, awkward phone calls, that always seem to end with me saying *I'm not ready yet.*

Seeing him now, I realize that I am. Ready. Whether I want to be or not.

The first thing I notice when he gets out of the truck is that his hair is short. Practically a buzz cut. He gets it cut like that once every year. Every year? Both years that I've known him. For all the rest of the years, I have nothing to go on except his word. He looks left, then right, then jogs across the street, up on the porch. His hand is already raised to knock when he looks through the screen door and sees me on the couch.

"Hi," he says.

"You didn't call."

"I didn't feel like hearing you say you weren't ready. Can I come in?"

His old blue T-shirt is faded and threadbare around the neck, his jeans are worn smooth over his thighs. If you didn't look too closely, he could be twenty years old. Even from here to the door I can smell him. Soap and water, an after-work shower.

"You look like a man who needs a beer."

His grin comes straight to me, like a match on a trail of gunpowder. "I'll get it. Sit still." He heads for the kitchen. "What do you want?"

Excellent question.

"I think there's an open bottle of sauvignon blanc in there. If not, I'll have a beer."

He locates everything in the kitchen without much effort. I hear the clink of a glass on the counter, the hiss of carbon dioxide escaping as he pops the bottle cap on the beer. He hands me my wine and sits down on the sofa, close to me, but not too close. Now I can see the faint line on his forehead where the baseball cap rests. I want to reach up and put my fingertips on that little place at his hairline where the hair grows back instead of forward. But I swear I'll chew my hand off first.

I take a sip of the cold wine, focus on his fingerprints in the condensation. "I hear you're working for Josh."

He nods. "He's got a lot of rentals—"

"I know. I've lived in two of them."

He ignores my snappishness. "Some of them he's rehabbing. Some just need routine maintenance. I've been doing a little of both."

"Where are you living?"

"Charleston Arms. Furnished rooms to let. Hourly, daily, and weekly rates available."

"It's a flophouse."

The corners of his eyes crinkle. "Correct. I am flopping there. The Alexis was booked up." He takes a long drink of beer and sets the bottle on the floor.

"Don't kick it over. I can't afford to pay for having the carpet cleaned."

"If I kick it over, I'll pay to have the carpet cleaned."

I look at him sideways. "Why are you in such an obnoxiously good mood?"

"I'm in an obnoxiously good mood because I'm here, sitting next to you on your couch, drinking a beer after a hard day's work. You're in a bad mood because I'm here sitting next to you on your couch, and you want to be in a good mood, but you won't let yourself."

I glare at him. "How about I'm in a bad mood because I've lost my bakery and I'm broke and I have to go back to L.A. and go to court with my ex-husband and his new wife and fight about money and I don't know what I'm going to do after that."

He turns sideways to face me, his arm resting on the back of the couch, suspiciously close to my shoulder. "Those are all legitimate and weighty concerns. Nevertheless, I'm sticking with my original theory. You're in a bad mood because you won't let yourself be in a good mood. Because I'm here."

When I look over at him, he's wearing that sweetly serious expression I remember so well. I hate it when he's right.

"Can we just sort of . . . talk?" His slightly embarrassed look tells me that the irony of the situation isn't lost on him.

I lace my fingers together, resting my hands on my stomach. "Mac, this is so hard for me. I feel . . . I don't even know how to explain how I feel. It's a tightness, like I've got a grip on myself and I can't loosen it even a little, because if I do, everything goes."

"I probably know more about that feeling than you think." A pause. "How about this: I'll talk. You listen."

"That would make for an interesting change."

He breathes in, very slowly. "I'm not consciously trying to keep things from you, you know. It's just that talking about myself, my feelings— I think it goes against my most basic nature, and second, I never really had any experience of it growing up. You were close to your father, right? And you had your mother, too. I know your relationship with her wasn't always easy, but at least she was there. And for most of your life, you've had CM. My dad was gone even before he died—"

"What was his name?"

"Dennis. After he died, Suzanne was never all there, either. And then Kevin . . ."

"But you had friends, didn't you? From school or—"

"Sure, but you know how guys are. They don't have the kind of friendships women do. Especially at that age. We played sports, drank beer. A meaningful conversation for us would have been about cars or the possibility of getting a copy of the history test or lying about how far we got with some girl."

The breeze filtering through the screen door is getting cooler as the sun disappears. It feels good on my bare legs.

"I guess the closest friends I've had were Nick Hatcher and those guys I climbed with. And even then, it wasn't a talking thing. It was based on our shared love of rocks, and it stuck because of what we went through together. I know you don't think I ever tell you anything, but, believe me, I've talked more to you than I have to anyone in . . . a long time."

"You mean since Gillian?"

He shakes his head. "There wasn't a whole lot of talking going on there, either."

"Whose choice was that?"

"It wasn't a choice. It just was what it was. I liked her as a person, and I think she liked me, but the relationship was physical. She really wasn't into conversation."

"Well, I am." I lean my head back and close my eyes.

"I can't promise that I'll always blurt out what I'm thinking and how I feel. But I can promise that I'll try." He waits a few seconds. "I want to try."

I want to look at him, but I can't. My eyelids refuse to open, the same way they do when you try to look directly at the sun. But I sense him there, the heat of him, the displacement of air when he moves, the cool current of his breath.

My oma told me once that on the day of the vernal equinox, at the moment when the sun crosses the equator, an egg will stand on its end. That's what this moment feels like—eerily fragile. Standing on end, ready to tip either way.

He rubs a piece of my hair between his fingers. "I miss you," he says. "I miss your smell. And the way your hair curls so . . . emphatically. The way you always look surprised when you laugh. The way you stretch like a cat when you first wake up. And the way you castigate me for putting ketchup on my hash browns and—"

I smile, but a couple of tears leak out from under my eyelids and slide down to my ears. He brushes one away with his thumb and then, without intention, almost without awareness on my part, I'm holding his face in my hands, finding his mouth with mine, calculating how long it's been since I kissed him, trying to remember exactly why.

I expect it to be awkward after all this time, but it's almost frightening how easy it is, how comfortable. He seems less a stranger to me than I am to myself, taking me on a leisurely tour of my own body, reintroducing me to all those secret places that remain vaguely unfamiliar to me, although they clearly remember him. When his fingertips trace funny, looping circles on my skin, I imagine that they're not random, but a sort of spell written in runes. Or some kind of agreement, like selling your soul, that I've signed and that's now irrevocable and binding.

Sleep comes with the instantaneous release of shutting off a light.


I wake up in the dark and for a split second I'm startled by the sound of someone else breathing. Then I remember. I ease myself out from under his arm and tiptoe out to the bathroom. The light is still on in Tyler's room, and the cold breeze nipping at my bare butt tells me the front door's still open. I pull my nightshirt off the hook on the bathroom door and slip it over my head, and look around her door. The bed's unmade from this morning.

When I go into the living room to close the front door, I see lights on at Josh's house. He's probably sitting over there watching TV alone, Turbo splayed across his lap, ears spread out like ceiling-fan blades. In the kitchen I'm surprised to see that it's only 12:40 A.M. It seems like a different night that Mac wandered up on my porch instead of only four hours ago.

Didn't take me long to cave in. He was gone a year. I couldn't even hold out for a month. I pick his bottle up off the floor and pour the flat beer down the drain. I take a sip of the pleasantly cool wine and realize that the reason I woke up is that my stomach is growling. I'm hungry.

I fill a pot with water and put it on the stove, open the pantry door, and survey the possibilities. Dried *conchiglie*. Sun-dried tomatoes. Moroccan olives. Marinated artichoke hearts. Pine nuts. Olive oil.

"What are you doing?" Mac's voice startles me. He's standing in the doorway wearing only his boxers. I have to bite my tongue to keep from laughing at the M. C. Escher pattern of fish changing into birds.

"I was hungry." I hand him the food and examine the contents of the refrigerator, pulling out feta cheese and Parmigiano-Reggiano and half a lemon. "Want some pasta? You better put a shirt on. It's cold in here."

He laughs. "This isn't cold. Cold is twenty below zero."

I run water into the large saucepan and set it on the stove. "Thanks, Sergeant Preston, for the meteorology lesson."

He goes off down the hall and comes back with a sweatshirt.

"You would have loved the Yukon," he says.

"Probably. But then, I wasn't invited. And don't get too comfortable. I need you to chop some things."

"Even if you'd been invited, you wouldn't have gone."

"You don't know that. You don't know everything there is to know about me."

"I won't argue with that."

I hand him a knife and cutting board. "Sliver those sundried tomatoes and pit the olives and chop them in half."

"Yes, ma'm. Right away."

"Please," I amend.

We work in companionable silence for a minute, him chopping, me grating Parmigiano and crumbling feta cheese. Then he says, "Wyn."

I look up.

"I love you."

For a second I forget to breathe. "Excuse me?"

"I said, I love you." He tosses a handful of olives into the bowl on the counter.

I just stand there for a few more seconds. This isn't how I thought it would happen. Him, standing in my kitchen barefoot, in boxer shorts at one A.M. with olive oil all over his hands.

"It's an easy thing to say, McLeod."

"Not for me." He pops an olive in his mouth. "In fact, I've never said it before." He chews thoughtfully for a second, then deposits the pit in the garbage. "Unless you count last night, practicing in the mirror."

I scrape feta cheese off my hands. "I guess you'd better kiss me then."

When he does, I put my arms around him, being careful not to get feta on his neck, and he slips his hands up under my nightshirt.

"I said kiss me, McLeod. No freebies. You're getting olive oil all over me."

"I don't suppose you'd want me to lick it off," he offers helpfully.

"Not right this moment. I have to put the pasta in."

"So this is how it's going to be. Always runner-up to some kind of carbohydrate."

"Pretty much . . ." When he moves against me, I can feel his erection. His mouth brushing the notch of my collarbone makes my whole body simultaneously contract and expand. "Well, maybe there's a tad too much water there. Maybe we should let it boil down a bit."

"Good idea." But instead of heading for the bedroom, he backs me up against the wall. "We've never done it standing up," he says in my ear.

"Mac, this may not be the time to—I mean, what if—" Then I'm talking into his mouth, so he can't hear me. Okay, I know the olive oil is messy, but it makes his fingers glide over my breasts like—well, there really is nothing to compare it to. Nothing I've ever felt, anyway. I'm making a lot of noise, pressing against him, and then, he stops.

I open my eyes and look right into his.

"You didn't say it."

"What?" I gasp.

"When I said I love you, you didn't say it."

My head falls back against the wall. "Are we following a script?"

"Say it."

"You know I do."

"Say it, or I turn back into a frog."

I smile. "I love you, Mac McLeod."

He's just taking up where he left off when I hear, "Holy gua-camole!" My eyes fly open like window shades pulled down too fast. Tyler's standing in the doorway.

"Whoa, hide the salami in the kitchen," she hoots. Mac is laughing, sputtering, trying to tuck Elvis Jr. back inside his shorts.

I jerk the nightshirt down over my olive-oiled body. I grab my hair and pull it back, never mind that my hands are full of feta cheese. I wipe them on the nightshirt and I look at the two of them bent double with laughter, practically on the floor. And I say, with all the dignity I can muster, "So. How many want pasta?"


At first light, I open one eye, absolutely certain it's all been a dream. Then I see the warm bulk of him buried in my comforter, and I close my eye. But I can't go back to sleep. I just drift, dozing on his arm, waking periodically to watch him breathe, the tiny pulse beating in his throat.

I want to get up and clean up the kitchen. We left it looking like the sack of Troy. But it's cold out there, and it feels so good in here. Although a double espresso sounds very tempting.

He smiles without opening his eyes. "Stop it."

"Stop what?"

"I know you're lying there thinking about cleaning up the kitchen."

I stifle an embarrassed snicker. "I'm not either. I wouldn't—"

Now he rolls on his side, propping himself on one elbow, grinning broadly. "Don't even try to weasel out of it. I can hear the wheels turning."

"Maybe you should forget bartending and develop a nightclub act—mind reading by McLeod the Mysterious."

He pulls me against him, kisses me deeply and sweetly.

"I'm not so mysterious."

"Yes, you are."

His thumb strokes my bare shoulder. "How so?"

"Those letters. What was that all about? Why couldn't you just say those things to me?"

His eyes close. "I don't know."

I poke him in the ribs. "Look at me, McLeod. No more evasive tactics."

His eyes open again and there's a sadness in them. He rolls onto his back, one arm around me, the other behind his head.

"When I first got the manuscript back from Steve, I couldn't write anything. Not even in my journal. I'd think about things I wanted to write, but I'd get about two sentences out and that would be it. The thing that saved me was that first letter to you. After that, when I wanted to write, I'd start with a letter, and then just keep going. Finally all the rest of it just came out." He turns his face to me. "Sounds weird, doesn't it?"

Instead of answering, I get out of bed. In the bookcase I find the blue notebook.

"What's that?"

I walk over to the bed, holding the notebook like a fig leaf. "Your next book."

He takes the notebook from me and opens the cover. "My letters?" He flips through the pages. "In chronological order?" He sets the notebook on the floor and tugs me down next to him, laughing. "Ms. Morrison, you are so . . ."

"If you say anal, you're toast."

"Actually, I was going to say . . . awesome. Amazing. Astonishing. And . . ."

"And what?"

"A great muse." He laughs again.

"What's so funny?"

"I love that image of you. Stark naked. Hair curling over your shoulders. Blue notebook strategically placed. I think I need a picture of that to keep on my desk. To inspire me when I'm working."

I narrow my eyes at him. "I thought you didn't believe in photography."

"I've changed my mind." He pulls me over on top of him. "I now believe in photography. And all manner of things that I never believed in before."


On the last Friday of April, we have an all-day open house at the bakery. We bake off everything we can, trying to empty the storeroom and refrigerators. Starting early in the morning, we put out trays of food, the muffins—blueberry, pumpkin millet, apple cinnamon—our famous refrigerator bran muffins. Cappuccino-hazelnut scones, Jen's short scones; Scottish cream scones; apple-cardamom coffee cake, Ellen's cinnamon rolls; carrot cake and lemon tart; peanut-butter cookies, Garibaldis, Mazurka bars; Ellen's special gingerbread, hot with fresh ginger, sweet with honey and smoothed out with chunks of milk chocolate; our killer brownies with chocolate-covered raisins; big thermal carafes of coffee and tea. And of course the breads—white sandwich, whole wheat walnut, Tyler's Indian Maiden Bread, banana-cinnamon swirl, olive rosemary, pumpernickel raisin. With tubs of whipped butter and cream cheese. Everything is free except the T-shirts, baseball caps, and coffee mugs sporting Tyler's beautiful woodblock prints. They sell out by noon.

The place is mobbed all day long, with people coming in, eating and talking, laughing, crying, telling stories about the bakery. One woman tells us her husband proposed here over nonfat mochas. "At that table right there," she says, pointing to the corner by the window.

"That's so romantic," Ellen says, dabbing at her eyes. "Tell him to come in later and say good-bye."

The woman blushes furiously. "Actually, we got divorced last year and he moved to Minneapolis."

The mailman elbows his way in and hands me a couple of en velopes and a direct-marketing piece about leasing postage ma-chines.

"Sure am going to miss you guys." He helps himself to a scone. "It just doesn't seem right."

"Yeah, well..." I'm running out of gracious replies.

He elbows his way back out, and I look at the two envelopes. One, bearing the return address of a Capitol Hill law firm, is ad-dressed to Ellen. I reach over Jen's shoulder to hand it to her and glance at the other one, addressed to me. It's a long, odd-size enve-lope, one of those pale blue, tissue-papery ones. Then I notice the "*Par Avion*" sticker and French stamp. There's no return address.

Ellen's standing beside me. "What's that?"

"I have no idea." I slip my index finger under the flap and sepa-rate it carefully from the envelope. When I extract the triple-folded sheet of white paper, something falls out on the floor and Ellen bends to retrieve it. She straightens up, staring at the photograph in her hand, an odd smile coming slowly to her mouth. She doesn't say anything, just hands it to me and pulls the letter out of my grasp.

It's a picture of a startlingly blond woman wearing a bright teal-colored dress, hands on her hips, smiling broadly. Beside her is a huge painting, all red, purple, and orange. A sign underneath it says "*Oeuvres d'une Vie Ancienne, par* Dailie Valentin." It takes a full ten seconds of staring before I recognize the painting as a garish birthday cake and the artist as . . . Maggie.

*Holy shit.* I turn quickly to Ellen. "What's the letter say?"

"Nothing—"

"Don't tell me that!" I grab the paper away from her. It's blank. But stapled to one corner is an American Express money order for two thousand, one hundred and thirteen dollars and twenty-four cents. The exact amount of our bank deposit that never was.

I look into Ellen's dark eyes. "Dailie Valentin. Bless her heart," she says.

I rip the money order off the piece of paper. "Oh, rat's patootie!" I wad up the paper. "No explanation, no apology. Like it was just some . . . spontaneously self-approved, unplanned, interest-free loan. No, not even that. It's like she's doing us a favor paying us back. After all that shit—after she rips us off—"

My rant stops when I realize Ellen's laughing, silently, so hard she can't catch her breath, holding her sides while tears slide down her face. "Oh God, Wyn. You're a piece of work." She wipes her eyes and we study the photo, both of us temporarily removed from the commotion in the bakery. "Interesting painting."

"Not my cup of java, but then I'm sort of a representational kind of girl."

She thwacks the money order. "Well, somebody obviously likes them."

"True. But then the French love Jerry Lewis, too."

Tyler shows up about two-thirty with Mac, Josh, and Turbo trailing behind. Mac looks around the room.

"Looks like a wake," he shouts over the noise.

"That's because it is," I shout back.

"Except no whiskey," Josh says. He takes a wedge of shortbread and breaks off a piece for Turbo.

· · ·

By four-thirty nearly everyone has said good-bye, sworn that they'll never patronize any business that takes over our space, wished us good luck, and departed. Tyler announces that she's going out to dinner. Josh and Turbo are off for a run in the park.

Mac helps us clean up, which is mostly throw away, since we used paper plates and cups. He puts all the recyclables in our crate in the alley, empties everything else into the big metal Dumpster. Ellen and I hand out checks and hugs and the staff of the bakery goes home for the last time.

"You don't have to come in tomorrow," she says.

"Don't be daft. I'll see you whenever I wake up."

Mac says, "Would you like to come to dinner with us?"

She smiles and pats his arm. "That's really nice, Mac, but Lloyd's actually coming home tonight, so I've got his favorite pot roast in the Crock-Pot, and barring any unforeseen power failures, we're planning a nice meal at home. Thanks for helping out. See you tomorrow, Wyn."

I stand by the ovens. We never shut them off at night because they take so long to heat up, but this morning, after we finished baking, Ellen quietly turned the thermostats all the way down. They're made of steel and concrete, and because of the sheer mass, they hold the heat for hours. They're still warm now, but by tomorrow night, they'll be cold.

"Is the auction house taking the ovens?" Mac asks, as if he's reading my mind.

"No." I lay my hand against the warm, black side. "They're too old. Nobody would buy them. They'll just get—when they renovate—" I seem to be having trouble keeping my voice steady.

He comes behind me, wrapping his arms around my shoulders, resting his chin on the top of my head.

"I'm sorry," he says. "I don't think I knew what this place was to you."

My eyes brim. "That's okay. I don't think I did, either."

In a few minutes, the stone in my chest lightens a bit. "So, should we get pizza?"

"Actually I made a reservation at the Queen City Grill. I can cancel it, if you don't feel like going out."

I tilt my head back and smile at him. "No, that sounds nice. All I have to do is find something to wear."

I manage to unearth one outfit left over from my days and nights as an advertising executive's wife, a copper-colored sand-washed silk tunic and bronze panne-velvet leggings. The only reason they didn't get sold at a garage sale was because I always loved the earthy, metallic colors. I take out my one piece of good jewelry that isn't in my mother's safety-deposit box, a handmade silver necklace with a luminous moonstone that CM gave me for my thirtieth birthday.

I don't know why Mac picked the Grill, but now that we're here, it feels somehow appropriate to this day. It's in an old building on First Avenue, near the Market, one of those places where the mottled ochre walls and original brick are sufficient decor. The room is long and narrow, with a mahogany bar running down the right side to the open kitchen. The left side is all high-backed wooden booths; a few tables dot the minimal open space on the worn, wooden-plank floor. With candles reflecting in all the glass, and the softly glowing sconces, the effect when you walk in is like being inside a magic lantern.

The place smells like a grill should—like steak—and is full of men in blue jeans and Italian jackets and women in little black dresses.

The host shows us to a booth toward the back, and we settle in. "This okay?" he asks me.

"It's perfect. I just don't think I'm going to be much fun tonight."

"Don't worry," he says. "I'll supply the entertainment."

When the waiter brings menus, Mac orders a bottle of champagne without even looking at the list.

"Are we celebrating?"

He nods, his expression serious. "The end of chapter one. The beginning of chapter two."

I find myself smiling. "McLeod the Mysterious."

The champagne arrives and he assigns the tasting to me. It's a beautiful, wheaten-dry Château St.-Jean. After the waiter takes our order, I hold up my glass.

"Chapter one."

"Chapter two," he says, touching his glass to mine. He sets down his champagne and takes my hand across the table. "I'm sorry. About the bakery. I know it doesn't help much—"

"Actually, it does." I twirl my glass in a little circle of moisture. "It's funny. I tried to get Ellen to move to a different location, but she didn't even want to discuss it, and now I think she was probably right. It's time to move on."

"To . . . ?"

"I'm not sure. I still haven't gotten used to the bakery going away and you coming back. Tyler and I talked about moving to L.A. But I don't know. She's pretty opaque these days." I look in his eyes. "What are you thinking of doing?"

"Well . . . the options just got better."

"What do you mean?"

He looks down at the table, then back up at me. Then he says quietly, "Steve sold my book."

For a stunned minute I just sit there, and then, to my abject embarrassment, I burst into tears. He hands me his blue bandanna. "Don't worry, I'm not going to take this personally."

I try to smile, to talk, to laugh, and I just keep crying. The waiter brings our salads, and gives me an odd look. "Is everything . . . ?"

Mac says, "Good champagne always moves her to tears."

"I'm so happy for you," I sob.

He laughs. Picks up my hand and kisses it.

The tears abate and I blot my swollen eyes. "That's what I get for wearing mascara. Do I look like a raccoon?"

He nods. "But a very cute raccoon."

I get up from the table.

"Sit down. I'm kidding."

I sit back down. "You're sure?"

"Your mascara is impeccable."

"I mean, you're sure he sold it?"

He laughs. "Can you believe it?"

"Almost. Tell me everything." I pick up my fork and attack the salad.

"He's been sending me the rejections. I've gotten five. Then yesterday he called and said that Ames Sullivan at Drummond had made an offer—"

"How much?"

"Fifty."

I bite down on the tines of my fork. "Fifty dollars?"

"Fifty thousand."

"*Mac.*" My eyes snap open, wide. "Oh God. I think I'm going to cry again. What did you say?"

"I told him I'd get back to him."

I laugh so hard I almost spray him with champagne. "You liar."

"Okay. I said, not just yes, but hell yes."

"Ohhhhhh." I lean my head back so far it clunks against the booth. "This is so incredible. But he called yesterday morning? Why didn't you tell me before now?"

"It didn't seem like the thing to do. Not with the bakery and everything."

The waiter brings our entrées—salmon for me, New York strip steak for him—and clears the salads.

"Now the next part of the entertainment—"

I look up quickly. "There's more?"

"There is indeed. They want me to come to New York. Meet my editor and ... I don't know ... whatever famous authors do in New York."

"That's wonderful. You'll have such a great time."

"We. We'll have such a great time."

"We will?"

"I want you to come with me. We can't stay at the Plaza or anything. This trip. But we'll find someplace fun, and I can take you to all—what's wrong?" He sets down his knife.

"I can't afford to go to New York. I wish I could, but I'm stretched to my limit right now."

"Wyn, I'm inviting you. I'm buying."

"You can't do that."

"I can't?"

"I don't want you spending your advance on unnecessary—"

"How about you let me decide what I spend my advance on?"

"I just don't think it's a good idea to—"

"I think it's a great idea. We'll only be gone a couple of days. Come on, say yes."

I look at him very directly. "On one condition."

"What?"

"You take me to meet your mother."

His expression freezes into that awful blankness I hate. The whole mood of the evening is altered beyond recognition.

"You don't know what you're asking," he says.

"I'm asking to meet your mother, McLeod. Or was all that stuff a joke?"

He looks wary. "What stuff?"

"The stuff about trying to be open with me, letting me into your world. That's all I want. Since we're going to be there, it won't kill you to have dinner with her."

"She won't want to see me."

"Fine. If she doesn't, we don't go. But you have to call her and ask."

"I don't know why you think—"

"Because she's your mother, that's why. She's where you come from."

He stares at the bar as if one of the men in Italian jackets might come rescue him. Then he looks out the front windows. Finally his eyes shift back to mine. He sighs. Lifts his shoulders.

"Okay." His voice is quiet. "If that's what you want."

"It is."

I put my hand in his and he shifts slightly in the booth, as if shaking something off. He gives me a very small smile. "I think you're the most relentlessly honest woman I've ever met."

"Is that so bad?"

"I don't know. I'm not sure how I'll look under your microscope."

When we get back to the house, he walks me up to the door. I fumble in my purse for the key. "So when do I get to read it?"

Under the yellow porch light he looks momentarily lost, as if he's forgotten that books are for other people to read. "I don't know. After the edits, I guess." He moves, and his face is lost in the shadows. "I'll call you tomorrow afternoon."

"You're not staying?"

"No, I've got to get up early and drive to Lake City to work on one of Josh's apartment buildings."

I hesitate. "Are you angry with me?"

"No." He holds me for a minute. "I'm just—it's not going to be easy."

"What isn't? Meeting your mother?"

"None of it," he says. He tips my chin up to kiss me and then he turns and walks back to the Elky.

## · twenty-six ·

In the morning I lie in bed, wondering if Mac slept any better than I did. I rolled around like a top, getting entangled in the covers, then kicking them off. I got up at some point and fixed myself some hot cocoa and drank it at the kitchen table, trying to decide if I was pushing too hard too soon. Then I went back to bed to twirl some more.

At seven-thirty, I get up, pull on my sweats, and make a pot of espresso, since there won't be anything to eat or drink at the bakery today. The thought is abrupt and staggering. It's also totally unreal. Won't I just walk over there, and everything will be humming along, just like always?

Panic rings in my head like a bell. What am I going to do?

At the sight of the bakery, shades drawn, silent, I feel cold and sick. From a block away, I see a woman walk up, try to open the door. She steps back, obviously surprised, looks around, eventually focusing on something tacked up on the window.

She shakes her head, turns to walk away, then turns back, makes a half hearted gesture, as if she's talking to someone. She seems disoriented, frustrated, disbelieving. Like a kid whose bike's been ripped off. *But it was right here last time I looked!* Finally she hurries away. I let her get across the street before I approach the door.

Taped at eye level is a piece of paper—one edge ragged, like it was ripped out of a notebook—with what appears to be a poem neatly typed and centered on the page. I move closer and read...

## The Queen Street Gentrification Blues

To the tune of *The Midnight Special,*
apologies to Huddie Ledbetter

*Well, you wake up in the mornin', boy*
*The clock radio sings*
*You look upon the table,*
*You see the same darn thing*
*Got no doughnut on your plate, boy,*
*Croissants or scones you gotta choose*
*You want a latte or a chai tea, boy?*
*You got the Queen Street Blues.*

*Another Starbucks on the corner, boy*
*Hardware store done gone away*
*Just a sushi bar and Art Space*
*Lookin' like they're here to stay*
*They're redevelopin' the Thriftway, boy*
*See, you gotta pay your dues*
*Then you can get yourself a loft, boy*
*You got the Queen Street Blues.*
*You got the mean ol' Queen Street Gentrification Blues.*

I unlock the door and go quickly inside, smiling in spite of myself. Ellen's sitting at one of the tables, drinking coffee out of a thermos. The paper is open in front of her, but she's not reading.

"Where'd the song come from?"

She returns a wistful smile. "I don't know. It would be funnier if it wasn't so true." Her face is pale, and from her eyes I can tell she had the same kind of night I did.

"What time are they coming?"

"Sometime between nine and noon is all they said. Want some coffee?"

"No thanks. I had some at home." I sit down across from her.

"Want part of the paper?"

"No thanks."

"There's a couple of scones in that bag." She nods at the counter. "I . . . um . . . called him, Mendina. About the sign." She's been eyeing it for weeks. Our lovely little hand-painted wooden shingle that hangs out above the doorway like a proper French baker's sign.

"You decided to take it?"

She makes a little "humphf" noise. "I asked him if he would mind if I took it. Just as a keepsake."

"That was your first mistake." I lean back, propping my foot up on a chair.

"You know what he had the nerve to say? He says he's going to use it. Repaint it and use it for whoever—" She swallows. "Whoever comes in here."

"Bastard. Did you tell him to use part of the twenty percent increase to buy a new one?"

Tears brim in her eyes. "The worst part is, you know he won't. He'll just trash it. He's just being mean."

I have to laugh a little. "*Mean?* I'd say he's being a mother-effing, scum-sucking, dirtbag asshole dickhead. Did I leave anything out?"

Her chuckle opens up into full-throttle laughter. "No, I think that about covers it."

Then I laugh, too, and we sit laughing and wiping tears away until there's a sharp rap on the door.

"Davies Auction," a man calls.

For the next thirty minutes, we stand mutely watching three guys load equipment onto rollers and dollies and wheel it past us and out to the truck. But when one of them comes in with a pry bar, jams it between the display case and the wall, and gives a push, the ripping, splintering sound makes my scalp prickle. From the corner of my eye, Ellen's face looks as if they've just ripped off her arm.

She turns to me. "I don't think I can stay."

"It's okay. I'll lock up."

She hugs me, hard. "It's been good, Wyn. I'm so glad you were—" The rest of it gets lost in my shoulder. I let her go. "We're going to Whidbey for a few days," she says. "I'll call you when I get home and we can have lunch and sign papers. Okay?"

I nod. "Take care." It's all I can manage.

She walks quickly out the door and down the street and doesn't look back.

In an amazingly short time, the space is a cave, empty except for the big, black ovens. I go over to lay my hand against the side, like some old dog you have to put down. It's still warm.

"Does this go?" One of the men points at the chair I was sitting on. "Yes."

"Well, that's it, then. If you'll just sign this..."

When the truck is gone, I lock the front door, take a last look around.

Keeping a bakery clean is very nearly impossible. No matter how often you scrub and sweep, mop and wipe, there are spills and smudges and crumbs. Laid over everything is the fine dust of flour. It gets in your hair and your nose and under your fingernails. Every morning when I get ready for bed, there are traces of white on the floor where I stand to undress.

Even now—even with everything gone—this morning's footprints make trails through the fine dust of flour that still patches the floor.

I let myself out into the alley, and as I'm locking the back door, I hear someone banging on the front. No way. I'm not going back in there. I walk down to the far end of the building, out to the street, and peer around the corner.

Linda LaGardia is standing there, one hand on either side of her face, trying to see around the brown paper taped over the glass.

I take off running, toward home.


When I walk into the house, I hear noises in the kitchen. Noises that sound like a bunch of little mice scurrying over paper. "Tyler?"

I stick my head in the kitchen and she turns quickly, both hands behind her, like a little kid caught in the act. The kitchen table is covered with sheets of paper, pages from an artist's sketchbook. Watercolors, a few pastels, some charcoal sketches.

"What's all this?"

"Just some stuff."

I try to see around her. "So this is what you've been up to." I smile. "I thought maybe you had a secret lover."

She snorts, sounding remarkably like Linda. "As if."

She doesn't move away from the table. "Can I see?"

She shrugs. "They're not very good."

I pick up a watercolor of sailboats on a lake. There are two of the skyline viewed from West Seattle. Then I pick up a page from the bottom of the pile. It's a pastel portrait. Linda. Wiry gray hair standing up like she's been electrocuted, cigarette drooping out of the corner of her mouth. She's wearing her shapeless black pants, a long white apron, and her usual pissed-off expression. She's standing next to the ovens with the big wooden peel in her hand.

"This is perfect."

Tyler looks pleased.

"How did you get her to pose?"

"It wasn't easy. And then I had to let her smoke."

She's giving me a look I can't decipher. I sit down at the table.

"Why all the secrecy?"

She shrugs again.

"Your shoulders are going to get stuck to your ears one of these days."

She doesn't smile.

"Do you want to go back to school?"

"I don't know." She sits down. "I gave a portfolio to the art institute. They said they'd let me back in."

"That's good. If it's what you want."

"I don't know," she says again. She fidgets, weaving a thin black paintbrush in and out between her fingers.

"You're very lucky, you know. To be able to do both things. Lots of people have only one talent. You've got two."

The corners of her mouth droop. "Don't talk like a frigging guidance counselor."

"Okay. How about this: There are art schools in L.A., too. Quite a few, actually."

Again the wariness. "You want me to go? Even if I'm not making bread?"

"Tyler . . . ? Of course I do. You're my friend, not my indentured servant."

She moves the pictures aimlessly around on the table. "What about Mac?"

"You mean, is he going, too? I don't know. We haven't gotten around to discussing it."

"But you guys are sort of a thing, now."

"That's true, but I don't know what's going to happen."

She smirks. "Well, whatever it is, I hope it doesn't happen in the kitchen."

A hot blush rises in my face. "That was an aberration."

She laughs out loud. "No shit. It was a whopper."

"And don't change the subject. Whether he goes or not shouldn't have any bearing on your decision."

"But I still don't know."

"Okay, here's the deal." I put my hand on her arm, forgetting that she doesn't like it. She inches away. "Mac's agent sold his book."

She blinks. "Cool."

I laugh. "Try to contain your enthusiasm."

"It's good, it's great," she sputters. "That okay?"

"I think we're going to New York for a couple of days. Why don't you let me know when we get back?"

"Okay." She gets up and starts stacking her artwork, slipping it into a large brown portfolio.


Mac shows up on our porch just as the sun's going down and a hot-red glow backlights a few clouds. He takes off his baseball cap and kisses me and hands me a legal-size envelope. Inside are two tickets from Sea-Tac to JFK airport for next Tuesday afternoon, returning on Friday night.

"Can you hold on to those?" he says.

I put them in the mail dish on the coffee table and give him an inquiring look.

"An early dinner Friday night, and then she'll take us to the airport," he says.

I want to ask him what she said, how she sounded, but I just say, "Thank you for doing this." I slip my arms around his waist and lay my face against his chest. "You want a glass of wine?"

"I'd rather have a beer, if you've got any."

We sit at the kitchen table and watch the tail of Tyler's Felix the Cat clock swing back and forth.

"How did it go this morning?" he asks.

"Hard. Really hard. Especially for Ellen. That rat bastard told her she couldn't have the sign. I wish she'd just taken it."

"What the hell is he planning to do with it?"

"He says he's going to repaint it for whoever takes the space, but you know he won't. Anybody paying that kind of rent's going to want a new sign. He'll just put it out with the garbage." I look over at him. "By the way, you wouldn't happen to know anything about a song called 'The Queen Street Gentrification Blues,' would you?"

"The what?"

"Taped on the bakery window?"

His smile is innocent. "Never heard of it."

"Hmm. The phantom lyricist of Queen Anne Hill." I take a sip of my wine. "How was your day?"

"Long. I'm rebuilding storage units for one of Josh's apartment buildings." He gets up and swivels the chair around so he can straddle it, resting his arms on the back. "Have you given any more thought to what you want to do when we get back? Have you talked to Tyler?"

"Yes to both. I have to go back to L.A. next month anyway. My court date is June twenty-fourth. So I'll see how it feels, whether I think I can live there again."

"What are you going to do with all your stuff?"

"Put it in storage."

He drums his fingers lightly on the tabletop. "You want to go it alone? Or could you use some company?"

I look up at him. "Company would be good."

"We could drive," he says. "Go down the coast. Do a little camping."

I cringe. "Camping? Like cold showers and outhouses?"

He laughs. "Afraid you'll get your Ralph Lauren sweatpants dirty?"

I punch his arm. "Someday you're going to have to get some original material and stop stealing from Linda."

"What about Tyler?"

"She's undecided at the moment. She's been approved to get back into the art institute, based on the work she's been sneaking around doing. I swear I thought she was plotting the overthrow of the government."

"What do you think made her want to go back?"

"My guess is," I say, stroking the back of his hand, "that it was her backup plan if I rode off into the sunset without her. At least at first. And then, as she got into it, she probably started to remember how much she loved it."

"So what do you think she'll do?"

"I don't know. I told her she needs to let me know when we get back from New York." I smile suddenly. "We're going to New York! I haven't been there since nineteen... it was the summer of seventy-nine when I went there to visit CM. Oh God, we had so much fun."

"I haven't been back since seventy-seven. When I bailed from NYU and took off for Colorado."

"Just you and the Elky."

He shakes his head. "Nope. I didn't have the Elky then. I had no car and hardly any money. I hitchhiked."

I put my hands on my hips. "See, there's another thing I didn't know. Boy, you've got some catching up to do. Let's go to Olympia and get a pizza."

He stands up. "I need to just run over to see Josh for a second."

In a few minutes he walks out of Josh's house carrying a pair of big, nasty plier-looking things with a beak like a snapping turtle. "What's that?"

"It's one of those cutters you use to cut padlocks off storage units when the tenant's rent gets too far behind." He stashes it behind the driver's seat.


Later, after a mushroom, pepperoni, and garlic pizza, we cruise down Queen Anne Avenue and he turns left on Queen Street.

"Why are you going this way?"

He looks straight ahead. "I just thought you'd like to see the alma mater one more time."

I fold my arms. "Not really."

He pulls into the dark alley behind the bakery and kills the engine. "What are you doing?"

He grins. "How about a little post-dinner demonstration of my rock-climbing prowess. You know, it's one of those things you don't know about me."

"What?"

He gets out of the truck and grabs the cutter, hanging it in a belt loop. I jump out, running behind him. "Mac, you can't do this."

"Watch carefully and you'll see that I can."

"We're going to get arrested."

"If anyone gets arrested, it'll be me. Then you'll have to bake me a loaf of bread with a file in it."

At the corner of the building, he hops gracefully up on the lid of the Dumpster, the cutter dangling precariously from his belt.

"Jesus, Mac, be careful with that thing."

"Yeah, that could put a crimp in our sex life, couldn't it? Like that old limerick."

"What limerick?"

"I was hoping you'd ask." He clears his throat. " 'There once was a sailor named Bates—' "

"Shhh!"

His voice drops to a stage whisper. " 'Who danced the fandango on skates.' "

"Mac, for God's sake—" He grabs the drainpipe and tests it with his weight, then suddenly he's scampering up the corner of the building where the bricks meet at offset intervals, creating handy toeholds.

" 'Till a fall on his cutlass,

" 'Rendered him nutless . . .' "

He swings up onto the roof and stands looking down at me. " 'And practically useless on dates.' "

I start to giggle uncontrollably.

"You don't handle tension very well," he says. "You'd make a lousy spy."

He moves in a semicrouch along the front of the building until he's directly above the doorway of the bakery. "Hmm. Lots of pigeon shit up here. Okay, little Ms. Baker, move your buns down here under the sign."

I look around, reassuring myself that the lights are off in all the surrounding shops. The street is dark and quiet. "We're going to jail. Mendina probably has security patrols—"

"Hush. I'm going to cut this thing—don't stand under it till I tell you—and then I'll lower it down to you." He leans over the edge.

"Please don't fall."

"I've got my heels hooked under a conveniently located vent. On belay!"

"What?"

"Rock climbing lingo, my dear. I'll explain some night when we're hanging from the towel bar."

"Mac, hurry."

He braces the cutter against the wall and there's a metallic snap. One side of the sign sags, and he reaches over to anchor it under his elbow. "Look out below." There's another snap, and he grapples with the sign for a heart-stopping few seconds.

"Okay, reach. And be careful, it's heavier than it looks."

I stand on tiptoe, stretching as high as I can, while he lowers the sign, but I still can't reach it.

"It's just a couple of inches shy," he says. "If I let one corner go, you should be able to get a hand on it. Can you do that?"

"Of course, just—"

At that moment a car drives by, headlights illuminating the sign burglars. The driver slows and his head comes out the window.

*Shit.* My mind races to come up with some sort of explanation. We were just walking by and the sign was falling down, and, not wanting it to fall on an unsuspecting passerby, we decided to take it down...

"Hi," Mac calls to the guy. "Can you give me a hand with this?"

"Oh God, oh God."

The car pulls over, and a middle-aged man gets out.

"He's going to get a hernia, and then he's going to sue us," I hiss.

"What seems to be the problem?" He sticks his thumbs in the waistband of his pants. "I'm not exactly dressed for construction work."

I can't even look at the guy.

"She's not quite tall enough," Mac says. "If you can just reach up and take the bottom of the sign—you can rest it against the building if it's too heavy—and I'll be right down."

The guy pushes his sleeves up. "Of course it's not too heavy." He reaches for the sign and Mac lets go, and he eases it gently to the ground. "Whoo. This baby is heavier than she looks."

While I'm stammering thank-yous and giving him a Kleenex to wipe his hands, Mac clambers down and suddenly appears beside me.

"Appreciate the help." He holds out his hand. "David Franklin."

I don't dare look at him.

"Sam Turner." They shake. "Nice sign. What're you doing with it?"

"It needs some touch-up work." Mac grins easily. "Thought we might as well get it done while the remodeling's going on."

*Right. So we decided to take it down with chain cutters in the middle of the night.*

Sam Turner looks at the papered windows. "Oh. Yeah. Good idea. Well, you folks have a good evening."

We haul the sign around to the alley and put it in the Elky. Mac covers it with a tarp and lays the cutter on top. We climb in the truck and I sit there hyperventilating while he wipes his hands on a rag.

"I can't believe we stole it." My voice vibrates with a strange exhilaration.

"Hey, you started on a life of crime a long time ago. Remember that lipstick you and CM shoplifted."

He turns the key, but before he can put the truck in gear, I kneel on the seat next to him, take his face in my hands, and kiss the socks off him.

The thirteenth day of May is cool and breezy. We spend the morning packing, and after lunch the three of us squeeze into the Elky's cab for the ride to the airport. Mac has granted Tyler the use of the truck while we're gone and she's trying hard not to act thrilled.

When we get out at passenger drop-off, he lifts our bags out of the back and hands her the keys. "I'll take good care of it," she says. "Don't worry."

"I'm not worried," Mac says. "This truck's seen it all."

At the ticket counter we discover that the flight has been delayed.

"Air-traffic control is waiting for the fog to lift," the agent says. She types into the computer and the printer spits out our boarding passes.

Mac and I both turn automatically to look out the banks of windows.

"Not here. In New York." She hands us our tickets and smiles. "Can't take off till we're clear where we're landing."

We go through security and meander out to the gatehouse where I sit reading *B Is for Burglar*, which I borrowed from Tyler, and Mac paces, drinking Starbucks.

"It's going to be two A.M. when we get to the hotel," he mutters.

"Any more coffee and you'll be taking off without a plane."

"I'm switching to decaf," he says, heading back to the kiosk for a topper.

He disappears up the concourse and I look around the gatehouse. It's crowded now, not one empty seat. Everyone's heading for

New York on business. Or for fun. To connect to another plane going somewhere else. Or to go home. But right now we're all just waiting. Waiting to start.

Finally they make the boarding announcement and open the jetway. The plane taxis out behind about a dozen others. Another long wait, poised on the tarmac, then the jets rumble and we lift off, swinging in a wide arc to the west and south. By now clouds have moved in, obliterating every trace of what would have been a fabulous view of the city and Puget Sound and Mount Rainier; still we keep climbing, until suddenly we break out of the clouds into a cobalt blue sky.

When the flight attendant comes by, we order a split of champagne and drink it holding hands. Somewhere over the Midwest, Mac leans his head back against the seat and falls asleep.

I sit and stare out the window of the plane while the sun sets behind us, dissolving into a pool of red, then purple, and finally black. For a few minutes my eyes wander aimlessly in the dark; then twenty-seven thousand feet below us, tiny points of silver appear and begin to open up the night.

# acknowledgments

I always think I'm alone when I'm writing...until I get to this part of the book and I realize (again!) how much I've depended upon the kindness of strangers. And friends. And family. This time I'd like to thank:

Jerry and Karol Ryan, for sharing their memories and photos of the Yukon.

Grace Marcus, for giving me her beautiful poem, "Warming Trend," and for being a trusted reader and true friend.

Jo-Ann Mapson, for sage literary advice and abiding friendship.

Kathryn Brown, for letting me pester her with legal questions.

Kit Williams, baker without peer, for generous portions of advice and laughter.

My agent, Deborah Schneider, for never failing to understand where I'm going, even when I don't.

My editor, Claire Wachtel, for seeing the forest while I'm busy staring at the trees.

All the singers, songwriters, and musicians who live(d) their blues.

And of course, Geoff, for being my own personal North Star.

Last but not least, a hug for Leslie Mackie, owner of Macrina Bakery(ies), for bringing the old McGraw Street Bakery back to life and glory as Macrina Bakery at McGraw, the perfect neighborhood bakery.